Arcadia's Chil
The Fyfield Plantation

A sequel to Arcadia's Children 1:
Samantha's Revenge

Andrew R. Williams

Reviews

Sherin rated it ***** (five stars)

The much-awaited sequel to Samantha's Revenge, Arcadia's Children 2: The Fyfield Plantation is finally here. Of course, I picked it up right away : I wanted to know what happened : It's one of Andrew's inherent abilities to pull you into the story and make it realistic like you're living in the Arcadia's World! And yes, finally, the havoc wreaked by Samantha has come to an end, or has it really?
I thoroughly enjoyed the sequel and loved every bit of screen time Tarmy got. Besides Tarmy, I also loved Wren in this book. I loved every minute of their journey and the author made the plot interesting without a lot of technical jargons that's difficult to understand ... so anyone can read and enjoy this book

Piaras Cionnaoith rated it ***** (five stars)

Another well-crafted sci-fi fantasy sequel...
Author Andrew R. Williams weaves another fantastic sci-fi fantasy with intriguing twists and turns that will easily captivate the reader's attention from the opening page.

The author paints an exciting and adventurous story of aliens, robots and clones in a very vivid and convincing way. In addition, the characters are drawn with great credibility and integrity.

The story had every element a good story should have. An exciting plot, attention to detail, but best of all fleshed out, well-written and well-rounded character development. There's an abundance of well-illustrated scenes that make you feel like you are right there in the story, and that's something I really look for in a good book.

Huge Yakman rated it an amazing***** (five stars)

I haven't read the first instalment of 'Arcadia's Children', but that did not detract from my enjoyment of reading 'The Fyfield Plantation' at all. This is a really decent sci-fi story. What I liked most, was the way in which William's makes everything seem perfectly plausible and believable. If you read sci-fi, you want the world that opens up around you to be a place for great escapism, and that's exactly what happens on Arcadia. The attention to detail in describing the make-up of the planet, teleportation, and the technical information for systems used enhances the experience of the world the author has created. Even the storyline following corruptive 'Great Ones' who are growing a dangerous street drug, is relatable to current affairs, and makes the situation on Arcadia more conceivable. I thoroughly enjoyed this book and will be looking out for more in the series.

Dedication:

To Tom, Beryl, Bert, Peggy and Colin: gone but not forgotten.

The Author

By day mild mannered Andrew R. Williams is a chartered surveyor.... but after twilight falls, he snatches up his pen and lets the writing take control. The Arcadia's Children series are sci-fi thrillers which pour out of Andrew on only the coldest and darkest of nights. When he isn't writing, or chartered surveying, Andrew spends time with his wife Geraldine, staring up at the stars, and plotting eventual world domination. Don't let that calm demeanour and easy smile fool you, oh no.

Other books by Andrew R Williams:

Science Fiction
Arcadia's Children (Samantha's Revenge)
ISBN 978-1- 61309-710-6 (also in ebook)

Arcadia's Children 3: Pushley's Escape
ISBN-13 : 979-8655135970 (also in ebook)

Novel (Action Thriller)
Jim's Revenge: ISBN ISBN-10: 1916312411
ISBN-13: 978-1916312418

Technical Books
Technical Domestic Building Surveys
ISBN 0 419 178000 7 (also in ebook)

Spons Practical Guide to Alterations and Extension
ISBN 10: 0-415-43426-2 (also in ebook)

Web Links:
https://www.amazon.co.uk/Andrew-R.-Williams/e/
B001HPK7KK

https://www.arcadiaschildren.com/

http://www.authorsden.com/andrewrwilliams

Extract from Arcadian Archaeology

Arcadia

Arcadia is the third planet in the Salus System. As it is in a Goldilocks zone, Arcadia is an Earth-type.

Arden

Arden is Arcadia's main moon, largely-owned by the Minton Mining Company.

First Empire colonisation of Arcadia / Rediscovery

Although the actual facts will probably never be known, it is generally accepted that Arcadia was colonised partway through the First Empire Period. However, the colonisation was far from planned. As The Wreck is still in orbit around Arcadia and has been the subject of intense scientific investigation, it is generally thought that the colonisation of Arcadia was accidental and that the passengers and crew of the Empress of Incognita were marooned.

Since its rediscovery, Arcadia has been declared a POSSI (Planet of Special Scientific Interest) and colonisation has been restricted. The reason for this is that Arcadia is an Earth-type planet and has developed life forms of its own. To prevent transfer of potentially dangerous pathogens from Arcadia to the other colonies in the Salus System, the native population (the Ab - the descendants of the star ship survivors) are not allowed to leave Arcadia. As another precaution, access to the planet is largely restricted to archaeological teams and palaeontologists who are quarantined (usually on Arden) on their return from Arcadia.

The Wreck

Although badly damaged, The Wreck is still being subjected to close scrutiny. It has also become a significant tourist attraction. Since teleportation systems were installed, over two million tourists per annum visit The Wreck.

Character details from Arcadia's Children: Samantha's Revenge

Mick Tarmy - an ex-Ardenese police officer blackmailed into going to Arcadia by Samantha and becoming Mick Tarleton, a notorious war criminal.

Amanda Tarmy - Mick Tarmy's daughter

Hen Jameson – Arden's chief of civil police

Ord Morley, Vlad Pen and Ben Lieges; - police officers who used to work with Mick Tarmy

Claire Hyndman/Zia Warmers - Sent to Arcadia as Mick Tarmy's backup.

Alex - a TK5 - an ex-military patrol/attack droid and Claire Hyndman's invisible friend.

Nonie Tomio, Lascaux Kurgan and Chou Lan - archaeologists working at Cittavecchia currently trying to escape from the Great Ones and their spettri forces.

Alton Mygael (Oddface) - Director of Minton Mining Company Security.

Samantha - an Ingermann-Verex R9054 humanoid and Deputy Director of Minton Mining Company Security.
Mih Valanson - scientific technician working for Samantha - allowed Alex to escape.

Allus Wren - Senior Group Leader working for Samantha.

Henry - a spettro prisoner who is forced into working for Samantha

Hal Warmers - Zia Warmers' partner, a terrorist.

The Great Ones - a hostile Arcadian organisation dedicated to the conquest of humanity.

Irrelevant - a spettro commander working for the Great Ones.

Longjaw - a type of spettra, a mutant human, used by the Great Ones for general and military duties.

Ed Pushley - a senior archaeologist and also an agent for the Midwain Intelligence Service.

The Great Ones' Army comprises:

Spettri (Plural), Spettro (Male), Spettra (Female) - Mutant humanoids.
Arcadian wolves
Arcadian millipedes
Arcadian plesiosaurs

Klaien Mygael glanced at the SSIAT building and took a deep breath. Even though she knew there was a protection droid ready to come to her aid if anything went wrong, she still felt very exposed. Having lived a sheltered middle-class life, being asked to break the law didn't come easy.

Psyching herself up, she slipped on the distortion collar that Alton had given her and began walking towards the tall building. Crossing a pedestrianised area, she glanced at the reflection of herself in a nearby window and was pleased to note that the collar had altered her appearance completely; it had also made her look twenty years younger.

Reaching the main entrance of the SSIAT building, she saw one of the outer shutters was raised, and a lift door was visible. Activating her percom, she locked onto the building's external comms port and waited. A few seconds later, a power bubble formed, and the image of a droid appeared, an Alpha 300.

Without prompting the machine said, "It's after hours, the facility is closed."

Klaien hadn't been anticipating an automated response, and a mild wave of panic ran through her; something had gone wrong. She was seriously considering abandoning her mission when the bubble content suddenly changed, and Unnan Vardis' image appeared. "Sorry about that, the automated system cut in." He added, "Have you got the money?"

Klaien held up a large, brightly coloured paper bag, "It's in here."

The contents of the bag moved slightly. She realised that Rover was getting restless from being cooped up and hoped Vardis hadn't noticed. "Are you going to let me in?"

"Okay," Vardis replied. "Come up."

There was a slight whirring noise, and an outer lift door opened. Once inside, Klaien was whisked up to one of the upper floors. When the doors opened, she found herself in a lobby. A woman waiting there said, "Come this way. Unnan's through here."

ANDREW R WILLIAMS

As she pushed her way through a set of fire doors, the woman glanced back and added, "I'm Marci by the way - I'm Unnan's partner."

The comment surprised Klaien, during previous conversations, Vardis had implied he lived alone. After another five metres, Marci walked through an open door and led the way into a spacious living area. Klaien caught a glimpse of a charging unit through the slightly open door of an adjacent room and immediately worked out the truth. Although Marci looked human, simple logic implied she was a humanoid.

Noting the expression on Klaien's face, Marci glanced towards the open door and said, "Ha! I see my little secret is out; I hope you're not offended."

"Why should I be?"

A male voice said, "Some people are."

Glancing around, Klaien saw Vardis standing in a doorway, "Well I'm not. I was just surprised because you said you were single."

"In the eyes of the law I am," Vardis replied. "Marci and I are partners, but it's not recognised."

Getting straight to the point, he added, "So, let's see the money."

Klaien nodded and pulled out two large denomination money cards but kept a firm hold onto the bag. Vardis gave her a sharp look, "That's only half of what we agreed."

"You'll get the other half once the job's complete," she said, and passed over a sheet of plasti-metal paper. "Those are the teleport coordinates."

She glanced at her watch, "As agreed, in a few hours from now, two separate groups of people will come here. The first group want to teleport to Salus Transporter Nine and the second group wants to go to Awis Oasis."

"I want the rest of the money first," Vardis growled.

"Very well," she said "It's in the bag."

As Vardis was about to reach into the bag, it rustled, and a small rugby-ball shaped droid emerged.

"What's this?" He sounded startled.

"My insurance policy," Klaien replied. "This is Rover. He has the other cards in his internal safe and has orders to pay you the balance once we're all safety teleported."

Vardis gave her a hostile look. "Don't you trust me?"

"I once heard of a teleport operator who cheated a group of people," Klaien replied. "He promised to teleport them if they gave him a large sum of money. He took their money, but instead of teleporting them, he put them into stasis. He called the police and denied receiving any payments."

Vardis clicked his fingers and gestured towards Marci, "And she's my insurance policy."

Glancing around, Klaien saw that Marci was holding a stun gun and it was levelled at her. Vardis said, "Now get your droid to hand over the other money cards."

Klaien gave Vardis a sharp look which made him smirk. "You were right. I have no intention of getting your people out of here. Illegal teleporting is a criminal offence."

CHAPTER ONE

Cittavecchia, Arcadia

Irrelevant threatens the hostages

Pushley gave Mick Tarmy a lop-sided smile, "How's it going, Tarleton?"

One glance at Ed Pushley's face was enough to convince Tarmy that the other man wasn't in control of his faculties. Pushley's expression reminded him of how Claire Hyndman had looked a few hours previously when, for reasons best known to her, she'd suddenly slashed one of her hands with a commando knife and told him to taste her blood.

"What's the matter Tarleton—cat got your tongue?"

Instead of responding, Mick Tarmy stared at Pushley's power bubble image for a second or two and vaguely wondered what was creating it. Was it one of their percoms or was Claire Hyndman's invisible friend creating the bubble?

As it was of little importance which device was hosting the bubble, Tarmy's mind switched to more critical matters. Pushley's pupils were like pinpricks, which confirmed he was totally under the control of the spettro commander, the one he called Irrelevant.

Tarmy's thoughts were confirmed when the power bubble suddenly expanded, and he could see Irrelevant standing behind Pushley: the puppet master working his dummy. Irrelevant also had a restraining arm around one of the female archaeologists and a gun pointing at her temple. Fear was etched onto the woman's face, and it was obvious she believed she was going to die.

Speaking to Irrelevant, Tarmy said, "What do you want?"

"The shuttle's coming back," Irrelevant replied. "You will clear the landing pad."

"You can't be serious," Tarmy challenged. "After being aborted, the authorities aren't going to sanction another downshuttle without an enquiry."

Giving Tarmy a smug look, Irrelevant said, "Oh, but they are Mr Tarleton, if that really is your name."

When Tarmy didn't respond, Irrelevant added, "I'd love to know how you fooled me. There are very few humans who can shield their thoughts from me—so how do you manage it?"

Mick Tarmy just shrugged, "I've no idea—maybe it's the way I hold my mouth."

"Is that supposed to be amusing, Mr Tarleton?" Irrelevant snapped, "Because it hasn't amused me."

When Tarmy did not attempt to reply, Irrelevant said, "Before you start thinking about a surprise attack, don't forget you have no idea where I am hiding, and I can read the thoughts of your colleagues very easily. If you try to track me down or break your word, their thoughts will betray you, and I'll start killing the prisoners. So, you know what you have to do, start clearing the landing pad."

"So, the shuttle can land," Ed Pushley added.

Irrelevant smiled benevolently at Pushley, "By the way, Ed should take the credit for the shuttle reinstatement. He was very persuasive, y'know. He twisted his people around his little finger."

Taking his cue, Pushley became boastful, "When you've got friends in high places like I have, Tarleton, you can pull a few strings. Believe me; the shuttle *will* land in three hours, so everything had better be ready."

Irrelevant repeated his threat, "If you prevent the shuttle from landing or you attempt to stop us entering the shuttle, I'll kill a hostage immediately."

When Tarmy remained silent, Irrelevant said, "Come on Tarleton. I'm waiting for your confirmation that you intend to co-operate."

To reinforce the comment, Irrelevant twisted the arm of the woman he was holding, making her squeal out loudly. "Well, Tarleton?"

"Okay. I'll co-operate."

"I'm glad to hear it, but I warn you if you renege, we *will* start killing hostages." The woman let out another squeal of pain as the power bubble began to fade.

Mick Tarmy swore. "That's all we need, a hostage situation."

He glanced at the small convoy of dive boats loaded with refugees that were slowly making their escape down river and wondered why Irrelevant had done nothing to stop them leaving. He had a force of Arcadian plesiosaurs in the river, so he could have sent them after the cavalcade. Tarmy concluded that Irrelevant wasn't interested in anything but the shuttle landing. Maybe he was keeping the plesiosaurs close by to protect himself.

Tarmy's mind leapt into overdrive. The most logical place for Irrelevant to hide was on one of the numerous river islands in the meandering Fyfield River. Glancing upriver, he ran his eyes over the likely candidates. Eventually, they locked on to an island around six hundred metres away. It was the largest, and the closest island, and it was the most logical place for Irrelevant to hide.

Ignoring Irrelevant's comments about reading his associates' minds, Tarmy turned his attention to the assembled group, looking in turn at Claire Hyndman, Nonie Tomio, Lascaux Kurgan and Chou Lan; he said, "So, anyone got any good ideas?"

In response, Tarmy heard a distinct tut of disapproval. The tut seemed so loud he was surprised no one else reacted. He guessed that Claire Hyndman's invisible friend was communicating with him via a whisper probe.

As confirmation, a whisper said, "I suggest you get the others to clear the landing pad like Irreverent asked. That way he'll think you have decided to co-operate."

As Tarmy couldn't think of any better idea, and none of the others had suggested anything, he passed the message on. Although he could see their reluctance; Nonie, Lascaux and Chou accepted his request and began mooching back to the landing pad.

Claire Hyndman hung back, "What's going on? Surely you're not going to give in to Irrelevant's demands. He's bluffing."

The invisible droid whispered to Tarmy again, "I have a plan, but I need to discuss it with you privately. Get rid of my mistress. Make an excuse and walk away."

"Come on. What's going on?"

"Right now, I need to make an urgent call of nature," Tarmy replied. "I'll tell you when I get back."

Acting on the excuse, Tarmy walked for the best part of thirty metres, glanced back to make sure that Claire wasn't following, dived behind a large tree and looked skywards, "You said you had a plan."

A faint shadow moved in over him, "I do have a plan Corporal Tarmy."

Tarmy frowned. Claire's invisible friend had used both his real name and his rank; something it had only done once before.

"What plan?"

"I will explain shortly, but there are other matters to discuss first," the droid replied.

"He's holding people hostage," Tarmy snapped involuntarily; tugging at his hair in annoyance, "Can't we discuss *these other matters* later?"

"If you are not prepared to talk," the droid warned, "I may leave you to deal with Irrelevant on your own. On the other hand, if we deal with outstanding issues, and you follow my plan, the hostages can be rescued in a matter of minutes, Corporal Tarmy. They can also be rescued safely."

"How do you know my real name?"

"You gave me access to the RTTC, the one you are using as a diary," the quiet voice reminded him.

"You snatched it off me, more like," Tarmy snapped back.

Instead of debating the issue, the machine said, "I have been analysing the data from your RTTC. You held the military rank of Corporal First Class, not quite a Sergeant but not far off it. You were allowed to retain your rank when you joined the Ardenese civil police," the droid continued. "Although you have assumed the false identity of Mick Tarleton, your real name is Michael Tarmy. It would also appear that my mistress is unaware that you have deliberately taken the identity of a known war criminal."

When Tarmy didn't respond, the voice said, "As you are the most senior rank in this group, you are in charge."

Surprised by the machine's analysis, Tarmy said, "Funny that, from where I'm standing, you appear to be giving all the orders."

"I don't give orders," the droid replied. "I make suggestions after careful analysis."

After a slight pause, Tarmy pointed out an obvious flaw. "If you are what I think you are, a TK5, you were designed and built on Midway. During the last war, the Midwains were our enemies. I was Corporal in the Ardenese Defence Force, and during the last war we were on opposing sides."

"This is true," the voice agreed. "But you still are the most senior rank in this group, so you are in charge."

"Is that right?"

"Yes, Corporal Tarmy."

Realising he was allowing himself to be side-tracked, Tarmy said, "So what's your plan?"

"I need to discuss the other matters immediately," the droid insisted. "It won't take long."

Realising he wouldn't win unless he agreed, Tarmy gave his hair another tugging and said, "Okay, but if you are going to call me Corporal Tarmy, it's about time we were formally introduced. I'm guessing you're a TK5; what type of droid are you, and what do I call you?"

"You are nearly right, I am an enhanced TK5, and my name is

Alex."

"Enhanced?"

"I am equipped with cloaking and interRoC."

What's InterRoC?"

"Inter-robotic connectivity," Alex replied.

Tarmy was about to ask for further clarification, but Alex distracted him by saying, "I also have oracle and improved power systems which allow me to planet hop."

Tarmy latched on to the last claim, "You mean you could reach Arden under your own power?"

"Of course," Alex assured him, "with ease."

With a sense of rising excitement, Tarmy realised he'd found a solution to his biggest problem. "If I need you to go to Arden, will you?"

"Of course, Corporal Tarmy," Alex replied.

Momentarily forgetting about the hostages, Tarmy produced a handwritten letter and the RTTC out of his pockets and thrust them at the cloud hanging over him. There was a brief pause as Alex read the letter and then both the missive and RTTC disappeared from view.

Tarmy said, "If anything happens to me I want you to find Ord Morley and give him the letter and the RTTC. He's the only one who can save my daughter. Do you understand?"

Noting the worry in Tarmy's tone, the small machine said, "Might I comment on your proposals?"

"As long as you make it quick," Tarmy replied.

"Your letter implies you are hoping Ord Morley will rescue your daughter and organise an escape. But what if Ord Morley doesn't do as you wish him to do?"

"Why shouldn't he?"

"Because rather than do as you ask of him, he may decide to do a deal to save his own skin." The invisible droid said.

"Ord wouldn't do that," Tarmy replied. "I've known him for years."

"Are you sure?"

For the first time, Tarmy had doubts. If Morley let him

down, his daughter and his friends were doomed. While he was still thinking, Alex said, "There are ways of persuading him."

"What ways?"

"I think I should also pass your information to his boss, Hen Jameson."

Jameson was Arden's Chief of Police.

"Why?"

"Because Jameson will want to save his people if he can and lend his assistance," Alex replied. "More importantly, Morley is less likely to betray you if Jameson knows the details. I also have levers if you'll let me use them."

"Levers? What levers?"

In response, Alex created a power bubble that had an image of an arrest warrant inside it. As the bubble began scrolling, Ord Morley's name appeared Alex said, "The warrant is unsigned at present, but it will be shortly."

"How did you get that?"

"I told you I had oracle systems installed," Alex replied. "I can hack into most major computer systems."

Before Tarmy could ask any questions, the image in the power bubble suddenly became only too familiar. It was the same sequence that Samantha had shown him when she began blackmailing him: the unlawful shooting of a known criminal and Ord Morley's attempt to hush it up by placing a knife in the dead villain's hand.

Alex said, "If I showed Ord Morley these items as well, I think he'd be more co-operative. So, can I show them?"

Reluctantly, Tarmy nodded. "Okay, Alex, let's move on. What's your plan?"

Alex stalled again. "There are a few other issues. I need your permission to modify your RTTC diary record as I deem necessary before I hand it over to Ord Morley."

"You want to doctor it? Why?"

"Because if your plan fails and the RTTC falls into Samantha's hands," Alex reasoned, "she will know where you are and will send people to kill you and Claire. If you allow me to change a few facts, she won't be able to do that."

"What facts?"

"For starters, where you are planning to go if you escape," the machine replied.

Tarmy shrugged, "To be honest, I don't have a plan."

"I propose changing the RTTC to indicate you are headed towards the southern coast of New Australia," Alex said. "But if you have any sense you will go Awis Oasis until you make a final decision."

"Why?"

"Because Awis Oasis is corporate-owned, asks very few questions from visitors, and you will be relatively safe there."

Leaving Tarmy to think, Alex moved on, "There is another important issue to discuss. Your thought records indicate you believe Zia Warmers and Claire Hyndman may be the same person but in disguise."

"It had crossed my mind."

"You are wrong."

When Tarmy remained silent, Alex added, "For the avoidance of doubt, I was repaired and enhanced by Yan Farman, Claire's late partner. He instructed me to look after Claire if he died. I am following his orders. Naturally, as you are the senior rank here, I will also look to you for guidance."

Tarmy was stunned into temporary silence, and he went into re-think mode. If Alex was telling the truth, his theories had been very wide of the mark. He'd been badly wrong! Then again, it wasn't surprising he'd formed his original hunch.

Claire Hyndman and Zia Warmers were of a similar build, and both had a TK5 as a minder. With Claire Hyndman having the ability to face change at will, anything was possible.

Eventually, Tarmy responded, "Okay, as we're putting our cards on the table, is Claire Hyndman human? This face-changing of hers isn't normal. So, is she human?"

"Of course," Alex responded. "She cut her hand open so you could see her blood. Droids don't have haemoglobin in their systems. What else could she be?"

"She could be a spettra," Tarmy replied. "Something created by the Great Ones."

"She's not an alien in disguise."

"How did you know she'd cut her hand?"

"Because I sterilised and repaired the wound while you were otherwise engaged," Alex replied. "She explained what had happened. You refused to believe that she was human, so she cut herself to prove it."

Tarmy went silent, deep in thought. Military droids had very flexible programs and didn't comply with the normal laws of robotics; Alex might have just spun him a pack of lies. If Claire Hyndman had instructed the machine to give her a cover story, Alex could be lying.

"Supposing I believe everything you've just told me, what happened to Zia Warmers?"

Without hesitation, Alex said, "Zia Warmers died at a hyper-rail station on Arden."

"Died?"

"Zia Warmers perished in a firefight; her TK5 was destroyed too," Alex replied. "It was damaged beyond repair."

"How do you know this?"

"Ardenese news channels widely reported the shooting," Alex said.

"The Ardenese authorities don't publicise terrorist incidents," Tarmy quibbled.

"They do when they take out a terrorist cell," Alex replied. "A major counter-terrorism success is always reported—it boosts morale."

While his mind was still churning, Tarmy was tempted to ask Alex if his orders would now override Yan Farman's regarding Claire's safety but decided against it. His military experience had taught him that creating a conflict for a droid's programming to resolve could lead to unexpected consequences.

Keen to move on, Tarmy said, "Okay Alex, are we done? Can

we now discuss your plan?"

"Do you wish to release the captives?"

"Of course. We also have to prevent the shuttle returning."

"The shuttle will not be returning," Alex said. "I managed to contact shuttle control via Arcresten and told them it was unsafe to send the shuttle back."

"Arcresten?" Tarmy said. "What's Arcresten?"

"A Midwain military base on the Compass Islands."

"A Midwain military base?"

"Yes. You'd be unwise to go to the Compass Islands. Once you leave the Fyfield Reservation and enter Midwain occupied territory, you will run the risk of being arrested. Your best place to go would be Awis Oasis."

"Thanks for the tip," Tarmy replied. "I'll bear it in mind." He paused. "You're sure the shuttle is definitely not coming back?"

"The shuttle is not coming back," Alex confirmed. "I asked Arcresten to play along with the hostage-takers to give us time. Although the spettro you call Irrelevant has been told the shuttle will return, it will not. All downshuttles to Cittavecchia are cancelled."

Tarmy let out another sigh of relief. As he'd been talking to Alex far longer than he'd intended, he glanced back around the tree. Claire had joined the others, so he let out another sigh of relief. Alex had just confirmed what he'd been hoping. The shuttle return had been a subterfuge.

"Well done, Alex. That's one thing less to worry about, so where are the captives?"

"The one you call Irrelevant is holding them prisoner on one of the river islands."

"Ah, so I was right about that," Tarmy murmured, more to himself than Alex

"You said you had a plan. What is it?"

"Your biggest problem is that you are dealing with telepaths. Your hat is partially shielding your mind, but the others are unshielded. If the enemy senses your intentions, they will prepare a trap for you or kill the hostages."

"They didn't detect our approach when we started the attack on Cittavecchia," Tarmy pointed out. "We took them totally by surprise."

"You were lucky," Alex responded. "They were distracted by the desertions and explosions. They also had prisoners to monitor. Simple logic dictates that a person with telepathic powers can't monitor large numbers of people at once. As they were not expecting to be attacked, they let their guard down. But things are different now. The senior spettro, the one you call Irrelevant, will be expecting you to try something. As the others have unshielded minds, they are likely to unintentionally inform him of any plans you make."

Tarmy suddenly realised why Alex was speaking to him and not to Claire Hyndman. It wasn't just a case of deferring to his rank, junior though it was. The invisible machine had good reasons for avoiding Claire. Now that her implants had been removed, Alex believed her mind could be read.

Alex confirmed his thoughts by saying, "The others' minds are unshielded at the moment. But that problem is easily solved."

"How?"

CHAPTER TWO

Cittavecchia, Arcadia
Mick Tarmy attacks the river island

"**S**amantha gave you spare hats in case you lost the one you are wearing," Alex reminded him.

The mention of Samantha's name made Tarmy shiver. His mind conjured up the image of a tall, truncated cone-shaped humanoid with a strange wrap-round view panel enshrouding the top part of her body shell. A mental image of Samantha's forbidding human face flashed up in his mind.

He considered why he hated Samantha so much. Not only had she blackmailed him into doing her bidding, forcing him to come to Arcadia but, she still had his daughter illegally imprisoned. He thought about the deal he'd struck with her. He'd co-operate and take on Tarleton's identity as long as she didn't harm his daughter or police colleagues. But that would change!

Now she thought him dead; she'd renege on their deal without a shadow of a doubt; it wouldn't be long before she started arresting his police colleagues and his daughter would disappear for good.

Noting Tarmy's vacant expression, Alex cut through his thoughts, "We haven't much time to release the prisoners, Corporal Tarmy. You must issue the others with the spare hats before you discuss any plans."

"How did you know about the spare hats?"

"I found the information in your diary, your RTTC," Alex replied.

"There's just one problem with your plan," Tarmy said. "My case, the one with the spare hats was in the other air-car, the one that was destroyed when the bomb went off. So, I'm sure my case has also been destroyed."

"Your assumption is incorrect," Alex responded. "I transferred your baggage to the new air-car before I flew out with the bomb. The hats are available. With respect, Corporal, we must act quickly. We are losing valuable time."

"Okay. What's your plan?"

Alex immediately created a power bubble and displayed Irrelevant's refuge. Although the lozenge-shaped island was small, only two hundred metres in length by eighty metres wide, it was far from featureless. On the south and west sides, the river banks were plates of solid rock with the river cascading down a series of mini-waterfalls. On the north and east sides, the river waters were calm, gently lapping onto pebble-strewn beaches. Behind the north beach, there was a small stone hut and a low wall with three long-jaws huddled behind it. As he could also see their guns, Tarmy knew things could go badly wrong if he wasn't careful.

He saw an air-car partially hidden by a small tree. There were two people sitting inside. He guessed he was looking down on Irrelevant and Ed Pushley.

After doing his best to memorise what he'd just seen, Tarmy transferred his attention to the general landscape. Directly behind the hut and the air-car was a steep escarpment capped with Arcadian bluegrass.

While he was studying the bubble, Alex pointed out the obvious. "The island has a ridge down the centre. If you approach from the south, you should be able to land on the flat rocks, climb up and then attack from the ridge. If you are lucky, you'll catch them by surprise before they have a chance to kill any prisoners."

"Won't they hear the air-car approaching?" Tarmy queried.

"Not if you do as I say and approach from the south," Alex said and highlighted the foaming water. "The water noise should disguise your approach."

Tarmy thought about the plan for a few seconds. "Will you guide us in and help us?"

"Of course," Alex replied. "But it is best if you engage them with your stun guns. If I use my phaser, I could cause a great deal of damage. I might even kill some of the prisoners."

Exercising his newly acquired authority, Tarmy said, "Right! I want to move off in five minutes. I'll follow you."

Returning, Tarmy walked over to the air-car and looked inside the boot. His cases were there, hidden under a large tarpaulin. After finding the right case, he pulled out the hats, slammed the boot shut and walked back. As the others had cleared the landing pad, they were just lounging around. Tarmy began handing out hats.

Lascaux Kurgan immediately raised an objection. "You don't seriously expect me to wear this, do you? It doesn't even fit properly."

Tarmy responded by taking the hat back and adjusting the lining. He was about to hand it back when Nonie Tomio let out a yelp, and Tarmy realised that something had hit her. He was about to grab for his gun when Ollie, Nonie's pet Arcadian pterodactyl let out a loud chirp, fluttered down and presented her with a wallet. Nonie examined it. "It's Ed Pushley's."

She handed it to Tarmy. Briefly inspecting it, Tarmy said, "He must have dropped it when Irrelevant took him prisoner."

He pushed the wallet into his top pocket and went back to adjusting Kurgan's hatband. "The hats are compulsory, I'm afraid."

He waited until they'd all pulled on the hats before explaining the rescue plan. "Irrelevant, the spettro commander, is holed up on one of the river islands along with the remnants of his forces. He's also taken hostages. As you know, he's threatened to kill them. We need to get them out before he has a chance."

He pointed at his hat. "It's vital that we keep these on. In case you've forgotten, the spettri are telepaths. If they realise we are on our way, we could be in trouble. Although the hats are far from perfect, they should prevent them from reading our thoughts."

He inspected the weapons Kurgan and Lan were holding. As he suspected, they needed charging, so he hooked them into the air-car's power supply.

While he was still preparing the air-car take off, Claire moved over to him and became accusative.

"You've been talking to my invisible friend, without me, haven't you?"

He was tempted to ask how she knew but guessed at the answer. Although Alex was equipped with cloaks, he wasn't totally invisible. Someone like Claire who'd been used to Alex being around would have visually detected local distortions and worked out where he was. Pointing to the hat she was wearing, Tarmy said, "Alex was concerned that Irrelevant could read your mind now that he's removed the implants."

"On first name terms now, eh! Alex has told you his name," she sniped. Then, "That's nonsense, I've always been able to mind-shield. That is one of the reasons Samantha chose me."

Tarmy held his hands up. "Don't shoot the messenger."

He nodded towards the other side of the car, "Are you coming with me or not?"

Despite her display of bad temper, Claire nodded and called out to Nonie Tomio, Kurgan and Lan to climb in too.

The doors had barely slammed shut before Alex flashed his tail lights, signalling it was time to leave. Tarmy followed them and, as anticipated, Alex led them in a wide loop, ending on the far side of the river not far from the waterfalls. The tail lights dropped low, and Tarmy copied the example.

Once they reached the island, Tarmy landed on a large flat rock, passed out the rifles then signalled for the others to follow as he moved towards the ridge. After taking a few paces, he gestured for them to drop onto their bellies and began working his way toward the edge of the escarpment, worming his way through the tall bluegrass at the top.

He was pleased to discover the bubble image Alex had shown him had been accurate. Not only was the other air-car exactly where the power bubble image had shown it, the three long-jaws were still in place behind the stone wall.

Before Tarmy had time to think, Alex joined him in the bluegrass and extended the whisper probe, "You must act quickly. Use your stun guns before they detect your presence."

Gesturing for Claire to join him, Tarmy waited until she was alongside and then told her to concentrate on the three long-jaws. He began pumping stun blasts at the air-car before eventually, calling a halt to the firing.

Alex whispered, "Stay there. I will check if it is safe to advance."

The comment took Tarmy back to his army days when human troops regularly sent in their droid auxiliaries prior to the main advance. Once Alex had returned and confirmed that all the spettri were unconscious, Tarmy backtracked with Claire, Nonie, Kurgan and Lan following behind. As they passed their air-car, Tarmy noted that the boot was open and told the others to carry on to the beach and he'd catch them up.

He walked towards the air-car and glanced into the boot; he found a large bag stuffed with pay cards. Sensing Alex hovering over him, he asked, "Where did that come from?"

"I have read your diary; you need finance," the machine replied. "If you want to free your daughter from prison and allow your friends on Arden to escape, you will need it."

Although he knew Alex was right, Tarmy's police instincts cut in. "Where did it come from?"

"It was in the other air-car. It was with the spettro, the one you call Irrelevant," Alex replied. "Spoils of war, Corporal."

Tarmy jibbed, "I don't know if I can keep this."

"What you do with the money is your decision, Corporal Tarmy," Alex replied. "But I'd think about it carefully. If you really want to help your daughter escape from prison and prevent your friends from being arrested, you will need this money. As you can't return to Arden, you will also need finances to find somewhere safe to live. Without money, Samantha will find you again."

The mention of Samantha's name made Tarmy shiver again. Being forced to work for her again was out of the question. But despite logic, Tarmy conscience turned dichotomous.

"I'll have to think about it; it might be stolen. How much is in there?"

"Around thirty million Eron dollars," Alex replied.

Tarmy did a swift mental sum. For as long as he could remember, there had been around three Eron dollars to an ACU which meant the real value was only ten million ACU - but it was still a life-altering sum.

Before he could make any further comment, Alex extended a flexible arm from below his invisibility cloak and closed the boot. A moment later, the faint shadow hovering overhead moved away.

When he joined the others, Claire asked, "What's going on?"

Noting that Lascaux Kurgan, a woman with a self-confessed record of larceny, was listening in, Tarmy avoided the question. Telling Kurgan, there was a bag containing millions stashed in the air-car would be giving her an open invitation to steal it.

So, he said, "Nothing important - I'll tell you later."

Leading the way around the ridge to the stone hut, Tarmy checked that the three long-jaws really were stunned. He took their guns and handed them to Kurgan before pulling away the log blocking the entrance to the makeshift prison. But, not wanting the prisoners to see his face, he did not attempt to open the door. Instead, he told Nonie Tomio to release the hostages and moved over to the other air-car.

Opening one of the doors, Tarmy glanced at Irrelevant and was pleased to see that the spettro was out cold. He checked out Ed Pushley and was surprised when Pushley's eyes suddenly flickered open. As his pupils were still like pin-pricks, Tarmy guessed the other man was still under Irrelevant's control. Pushley opened his mouth to say something but the stun effect retook control and he fell back into unconsciousness.

After checking Ed Pushley's pulse, Tarmy glanced back at Irrelevant and then checked the spettro's pulse to determine if he was also alive. Satisfied that both were still in the land of the living, he was about to step back out of the air-car when Irrelevant suddenly grabbed his arm and pushed a gun into his ribcage. Giving Tarmy a lopsided smile, the spettro said, "Well, well, if it isn't Mr Tarleton. Once again, you have tried to outwit me, but you haven't succeeded."

When Tarmy remained silent, Irrelevant said, "What's the matter, Tarleton? Surprised I'm not unconscious? Alpha spettri are more resistant to stun guns than humans. It's part of our genetic design."

When Tarmy did not attempt to speak, Irrelevant said, "You're going to fly me out of here. I need to get off this godforsaken planet."

Tarmy said, "What about the Great Ones?"

"I'm not exactly in their good books," the spettro admitted.

Tarmy guessed at the reason, "As things haven't gone as planned they need a fall guy."

"You have it in a nutshell, Tarleton," Irrelevant replied. "I've also realised that I don't need the Great Ones. With my mental powers, if I went to live on a more civilised planet, I could be a multi-billionaire within a matter of years."

Tarmy suddenly picked up mental images of Irrelevant lounging by a swimming pool with four good looking women surrounding him. He then caught a mental glimpse of two other women with young children and realised if Irrelevant did escape from Arcadia, he'd do exactly what the Great Ones wanted. He'd use his mental powers to get whatever he wanted. With women aplenty, he'd also spread his genome throughout the System. With Irrelevant on the loose, humankind would be changed forever. Within a matter of years, Irrelevant would be back in favour, do a deal with the Great Ones and an invasion would start. Then they'd work their way through the Salus System, taking over, colony by colony.

As Irrelevant continued talking, Tarmy began thinking about the bag of money cards now in the boot of his air-car. If Irrelevant noticed it was missing, he'd be in real trouble.

But instead of noticing, Irrelevant kept on bragging. "As very few of you humans can resist my mental powers, why should I be a slave when I can be a king in my own right?"

He jabbed Tarmy again. "Come on, when the shuttle lands, you can help me set up the mobile teleport. I've been told it only takes a few minutes to assemble."

He waved the gun towards the driver's seat. Although Tarmy was tempted to take his chances and dive for cover, Irrelevant's gun hand seemed remarkably steady for a man who'd been stunned, so he decided not to tempt fate. Instead, he slid behind the seat and attempted to start the engine.

On the third try, the spettro issued a code word to the air-car, and the engine started up. Another poke in the ribs, "Okay, let's go, Tarleton."

As he made the air-car lift off and move across the wide shingle beach, Tarmy caught a glimpse of Claire, Nonie and the other women staring open-mouthed in his direction. A moment later the air-car left the beach, but before it could pick up speed and move out over the river, a large Arcadian plesiosaur reared up and blocked the way. Then, a second plesiosaur rose out of the water. Although Tarmy avoided a collision, it did no good because a third huge form appeared.

While Tarmy was instinctively jinking the air-car to avoid the obstacles, a light appeared and danced around the air-car. The light then turned into a huge head with a baleful expression on its face. Without needing to be told, Tarmy realised that the Great Ones were back in control of Cittavecchia. To confirm the point, Tarmy's mind began filling up with images of millipede troops slithering out of the jungles and retaking the whole area. The face sent out mental images that could only be interpreted one way: as he'd failed, Irrelevant had been branded a traitor.

As more and more condemnation was heaped upon Irrelevant's shoulders, Tarmy picked up on more reasons for the reason for the seething anger emanating from the head. The last bomb had done its deadly work; three of the Great Ones were dead, and another badly injured.

Although the surviving Great Ones had declared a state of mourning, Irrelevant had been condemned to an immediate death.

Losing his nerve, Irrelevant jabbed the gun into Tarmy again. "Turn around. Take me back to the island."

Tarmy swung the steering wheel and attempted to make the air-car swerve and climb, but two of the plesiosaurs arched their long necks around the roof of the air-car to block the escape. The third thrust its head through the roof door and grabbed Irrelevant by the upper torso, pulling him bodily out of the air-car.

The baleful head sent Tarmy a mental message indicating Irrelevant was to be punished for his arrogance and disloyalty to the Great Ones. Sensing that he might suffer a similar fate if he stayed, Tarmy triggered the roof door into closing and attempted to gain height again. This time the plesiosaurs did not try to block him, and he headed back toward the island, sweat working its way down his back.

As he closed the distance with the beach, Tarmy made his decision; he was going to take the money and run. The time had come to dispense with his police conscience; taking the money was the only sane and sensible option. With both Samantha and the Great One's on his case, he needed an escape route; the sort of escape route that only money could buy.

After landing, he deliberately left the air-car engine running, knowing it wouldn't restart without Irrelevant's code word. Climbing out, he expected Claire and Nonie to come rushing over to see how he was, but no one came near him. He looked back at the river and realised why.

Although the plesiosaurs had gone, the huge head was still hovering over the river, a malevolent expression still showing on its face.

As Tarmy watched, its mouth opened to display row upon row of razor-sharp teeth. It advanced, its mouth widening as it moved. Before Tarmy could react, he heard Kurgan give the order to fire, and volley after volley began hitting the head, but the pulse fire had little effect. Although parts of the face were getting damaged, the head was still advancing. Then there was then a blinding flash, and Tarmy guessed that Alex had opened fire. The first flash was followed by another, and the head began pulsing menacingly.

Fearing the worst, Tarmy shouted a warning and began to run. A moment later, the head exploded, and a cloud of gas began spreading outwards. Within seconds it began sweeping up the beach enveloping Tarmy who started to choke.

He felt something grab hold of him and lift him off the ground and guessed that Alex was trying to rescue him. A few seconds later, he smelt bluegrass all around him and guessed that Alex, had dumped him on the ridge.

As he felt himself sliding into unconsciousness, his daughter, Amanda seemed to lean over him. "I need your help, Dad."

Tarmy instinctively glanced up at the faint shadow floating over him. and called out, "Alex, I need you to go to Arden, as we agreed."

"You are not well," Alex complained "You could die."

A moment later, Tarmy felt a stabbing pain in his thigh. "What are you doing?"

"Trying to save your life," Alex replied.

"Go now! Now!" Tarmy ordered. "My daughter and my friends are in danger. Their lives are more important than mine. Take some of that money with you. Go! Now! You must stay with them and make sure they're all safe."

Without further argument, Alex moved away. After watching the TK5's faint shadow disappearing from view, Tarmy collapsed.

CHAPTER THREE

Minton Isolation Facility 1 Anubis Crater, Arden.
Viewing The Fyfield Plantation

"**S**o, where exactly are these transmissions coming from?"

As it was evident that Samantha was getting tetchy, the technician began looking for excuses, "Our satellites aren't the best ma'am."

"Nonsense," she snapped even though she knew the spy satellite in question was part of creaking surveyance system that had been placed into orbit around Arcadia over thirty years before. Not only was the system well past its best, but the Minton Mining Company Board had also consistently refused to bankroll the Ardenese Republic; despite the huge profits it made from Ardenese ore extraction, they wouldn't help fund any repairs or replacements

Still ducking and diving, the technician said, "If the fog clears we may get better images, ma'am."

Samantha let out a simulated snort to let the technician know she was far from pleased with his performance.

She was just about to follow up with a sarcastic comment when the technician said, "I have something now ma'am. The transmissions appear to be coming from a small area in the Fyfield River. The images suggest it's a very small river island. There appear to be a number of separate transmissions.

Samantha immediately thought about the hats she'd given to Tarmy because they had transmission devices built-in.

"A river island?

"Yes, ma'am."

"Why should we be getting signals from Tarmy's hats on a river island?"

"If Tarmy's air-car exploded like we think it did," the technician hazarded, "my guess is the hats weren't destroyed, they flew through the air, landed in the river and then floated downstream and beached on the island like flotsam. If they all landed close together, the same current would have carried them into a small area."

Although Samantha generally had little time for humans or human reasoning, she analysed the comments and decided they had merit. If Mick Tarmy's air-car had exploded when the bomb went off, it was possible that the hats she'd given to him had been blown away and landed in a tributary of the Fyfield River. From there, they could have been swept downstream.

But the theory had one flaw, "Why did they start transmitting?"

The technician shrugged, "Why they all started transmitting is anyone's guess; something hostile in the environment might cause a response."

Samantha snapped, "Something hostile? What makes you say that?"

"I'm picking up traces of an unknown substance hanging in the air around the island," the technician said. "I'm trying to analyse it, but I'm not having much success."

"This island. Have you noted any signs of movement?"

The technician re-used his previous excuse, "Most of the Fyfield Valley is classified as rain forest ma'am, the whole area is shrouded in fog."

This time Samantha gave him short shrift, "Our satellites may be old, but I know they are largely unaffected by most weather conditions."

Realising he couldn't win, the technician said, "I can just make out a structure, some sort of stone shed. There are also two air-cars. There also appear to be bodies lying around."

"Bodies? Any movement?" Samantha demanded, "Any signs

of life?"

"Nothing obvious, ma'am," The technician replied.

"Give me a better resolution."

After zooming in on the bodies, the technician waited. Eventually, Samantha said, "As you said, there are no signs of life. Maybe the gas killed them."

"It looks that way, ma'am."

Satisfied that Mick Tarmy was dead, Samantha let out a silent cheer. Now, Alton Mygael, the Minton Mining Director of Security would not be able to thwart the will of the Board any more.

She was just about to leave when the technician said, "There is no activity on the island, but I am picking up a great deal of movement near to Cittavecchia and in the surrounding areas."

"Show me."

As the satellite continued probing, Samantha realised the technician was right. There were obvious signs of movement near to Cittavecchia. Zooming in closer, she began seeing lines of scurrying creatures, "What are they?"

"They appear to be giant Arcadian millipedes, ma'am. Thousands of them."

After staring at the images for several seconds, Samantha concluded the rushing and scurrying was the result of the two recent explosions. A slight smile formed on her electronic face; without a doubt, she'd stirred up a proverbial hornet's nest.

As the satellite continued tracking, Samantha realised there was a large structure, an industrialised building, tucked away in a neighbouring valley. "What's that?"

The technician hazarded another guess, "Judging by the vapour it's emitting, it looks like a factory or some sort of processing plant, ma'am."

"A processing plant? What's that doing in the middle of a jungle?"

As he didn't know any more than she did, the technician remained silent and began making adjustments. Zooming to maximum, he focussed on images of neatly planted rows of bulbous plants growing in terraced paddy fields.

"Looks like a Zuka Plantation ma'am."

"Zuka?" she snapped. "Why do you say that?"

The technician shrugged, "I've read articles on it, ma'am. That's how drug producers grow Zuka. On its native planet, Zuka is a bog plant. It likes plenty of water. So, illegal drug producers grow Zuka in paddy fields."

"You seem to know a great deal about Zuka cultivation," Samantha challenged.

"My grandfather had a few Zuka plants once," the technician replied. "He grew them for the flowers; they have nice flowers when they're small. He was growing them long before anyone realised Zuka plants suddenly changed form as they mature. As you probably know, in their adult form they produce a highly narcotic excretion; Zuka milk, ma'am."

After begrudgingly thanking the technician, Samantha moved away. Whirring down a few corridors, she arrived at Alton Mygael's office. Simulating a discreet cough, she entered. As Mygael was wearing his usual electronic face mask and the corrupted image of his real face was virtually devoid of non-verbal communication, most of his human colleagues found it disturbing. But the anomaly didn't worry Samantha. Being an Ingermann-Verex R9054 humanoid, the Deputy Director of Minton Mining Company Security had little interest in such matters.

Glancing up, Mygael's face mask wrinkled slightly, hinting at a forced smile, "Yes, Samantha."

"As you know," she replied. "We have picked up transmissions from the Fyfield Valley, but they appear to be a false alarm. There is no evidence to suggest that Mick Tarmy or Claire Hyndman are still alive."

The forced smile on Mygael's mask evaporated and formed into a vague look of disappointment. There was, of course, a good reason for his reaction. Although Samantha had already told him that Mick Tarmy and Claire Hyndman had probably died in a bomb blast on Arcadia, he'd still cherished the hope that she was wrong. More importantly, although she'd delivered her message in matter of fact terms, he knew she was secretly exultant that Mick Tarmy was no longer in the land of the living. With Tarmy out of the way, she'd be able to renew her efforts to move against the civil police.

With the tact of a rhinoceros in a china shop, she confirmed his thoughts by saying, "Naturally, I am sad that Mick Tarmy and Claire Hyndman are dead, but at least it extinguishes the promises we were forced to give to Tarmy."

"Does it?"

"We *have* discussed this issue before, sir."

"I presume you are referring to the police."

"Yes, sir," Samantha replied. "If I could remind you, I am referring to the incident concerning the unlawful killing of a suspect. The police hushed it up. And as I just said, now that we are confident that Mick Tarmy is dead, there is no obligation for us to honour our agreements with him. Now, nothing prevents us from arresting Mick Tarmy's police associates."

Samantha placed a small tablet computer on his desk and requested his signature. Despite the risks he knew he was taking Mygael shook his head. "I don't like breaking my word. Although you seem to think that Mick Tarmy's death releases you from all obligations to him, I don't agree."

"The Board won't like your refusal on this matter," Samantha warned.

Taking the threat seriously, Mygael took the tablet from her, but instead of signing, he flicked through the document. He gave her a sharp look, "There are more people on this list than I ever envisioned. Most of these people are senior police officers."

"The incident in question took place several years ago, sir, most of the officers concerned have been promoted during that time. There is also the issue of collusion. The officers shown in the clip may just be the tip of the iceberg."

Still wanting to delay, Mygael said, "If you leave the tablet with me, I will consider the issue."

"I wouldn't consider it for too long, sir," Samantha warned. "The Board is pushing for results. If the local police are disgraced; we could amalgamate them with us. The Board would then be able to control this colony properly."

Mygael went very quiet. Although he'd always suspected ulterior motives behind Samantha's demands for action, she'd just confirmed his worst fears; the Board members were working towards extinguishing any remaining semblance of democracy on Arden. They didn't want local politicians sticking their noses into Minton business dealings; they wanted to be able to maximise their profits,

While his mind was still churning, Samantha said, "I also have another matter for you to think about. During our satellite surveillance, we detected what looks like a large Zuka Plantation adjacent to the Fyfield Valley."

Mygael let out a slight whistle, "I'd always suspected the Great Ones were behind the sudden influx of Zuka milk, no wonder they have the funds to wage an undeclared war against us."

Although his mask disguised his true features, there was no doubting his angry expression. "Pity you decided to kill Tarmy and Hyndman - we might have been able to use them on a second operation, but we won't be able to now will we?"

"I did not kill Tarmy or Hyndman, sir," Samantha snapped back. "They were just unfortunate casualties of war."

As Samantha began whirring her way out of his office, Mygael thought about the number of people who'd *unfortunately* died, working for Samantha. He then thought about the secret file he kept, the one that listed Samantha's *unfortunates.*

Was he going to be next?

Eventually, he came to a decision. After searching in his desk drawer, he located an unused disposable percom. After checking the charge, he tapped in a security code and sent Hen Jameson a message. Twenty minutes later, he received a response.

~*~

The Wreck Bar was situated adjacent to a large square in the centre of Arden City. In keeping with the name, it was liberally decorated with shots of the Empress of Incognita, the wrecked starship still in orbit around Arcadia.

As he began glancing around the individual photographs, Alton Mygael was reminded of a short holiday he'd taken with his partner Klaien to Bull Crater. While they were there, she'd insisted that they visit Pearl Crater and teleport up to The Wreck.

He grimaced at the thought. As he'd been gripped by severe post-teleport sickness during his guided tour around The Wreck, he'd spent most of his holiday in bed recovering. But the bad experience had taught him a great deal. And so had Vardis Unnan.

Crashing bore though he was, Vardis had given him great insights into the capabilities of the teleport in Pearl Crater. As Vardis had insisted on visiting him several times during his convalescence, Mygael knew that the teleport didn't just link with The Wreck. It regularly linked with passing transporters, to New Victoria, Constantine, and Awis Oasis.

Running his eyes around the crowded bar for a second or two and not seeing anyone he recognised, Mygael began wondering if he'd made a bad mistake.

Maybe going to the Wreck Bar had not the most sensible of moves. What if someone saw through his disguise and decided to report his visit to Samantha? If she found out about his meeting with Hen Jameson, Arden Republic's chief of civil police, she'd demand an explanation. Worse, it might be the trigger that gave her the excuse to terminate his career.

As he glanced around, Mygael's worries began to grow. What if Hen Jameson didn't show? Looking around one more time, Mygael headed back towards the entrance door. He'd barely covered two paces before a voice he recognised said, "I do hope you're not planning to run out on me."

Turning, Mygael glanced at the man standing behind him and realised that Hen Jameson was also wearing a distortion collar.

Jameson smiled, "So what's your poison?"

Wanting to keep a clear head, Mygael said, "A small beer, please."

After getting two beers from an automatic dispenser, Jameson led the way towards a private booth in a corner. Once they were seated, Mygael said, "Thanks for coming."

"I nearly didn't," Jameson admitted. "After my last run-in with Samantha, I was severely tempted not to. But we've always got on in the past."

"Is it safe to talk here?"

"Sure," Jameson replied. "There are three of my guys outside. He held up a bug-detector, "One of my men swept this area a few minutes before you walked in. No one will be listening in."

He ran the bug-detector over his own body. "And you have my assurance that I'm not wired."

Jameson then aimed the device at Mygael. When it remained silent, the director smiled, "You also have my assurance that I'm not wired."

Jameson came straight to the point, "So why did you want to see me?"

"I would have thought that would have been obvious," Mygael replied. "Over the last few weeks, I've warned you that some of your people are likely to be arrested."

"But you haven't given me names."

"For good reason," Mygael said. "Although I warned you, I couldn't supply the names of all the people because Samantha was keeping them secret."

"Keeping them secret? I thought she was supposed to be your Deputy."

Mygael gave him a wry smile. "Samantha was foisted on me by the Board. I didn't want her from the very start."

"A spy in the camp, eh?" Jameson replied.

Although Mygael silently agreed with the sentiment he didn't comment; instead, he pulled out the computer that Samantha had left with him. Suppressing power bubble mode, he slid it in front of Jameson. Like most of the Ardenese population, Jameson's reading skills were limited, so he fished out a verbaliser and ran it over the screen, but before it could turn the written document into the spoken word Mygael snatched the computer back. He then snapped, "This is a confidential document. I don't want the whole bar listening. I'll read it to you."

After dropping his voice to a whisper, Mygael read out most of the important sections but deliberately omitted the names of the people listed.

Despite his lack of reading skills, Jameson noted the omission. "You still haven't told me who's in Samantha's firing line."

Mygael smiled. "I'd be rather foolish to tell you everything without securing an understanding first."

"What understanding?"

Mygael opened his hands, "Simple. If I help your people escape, you assist me to escape as well."

Jameson look surprised, "Why do you want out?"

"The grapevine suggests that I'll be replaced in the near future," Mygael said. "I'd rather go than wait to be pushed."

"And why do you need my help?"

"Because I trust your people more than my own," Mygael admitted. "If your people are dealing with this, it's less likely to get back to Samantha."

"What makes you so sure you're due for the chop?"

"The whispers are coming from a trusted source," Mygael replied, "I have been giving the issue a great deal of thought over the last few weeks. As far as most of the Board is concerned, I have served my purpose. At best, I was only ever a figurehead."

Jameson smiled, "Why are you worried? If you get the

heave-ho, at least you'll leave with a big pension."

Mygael shook his head, "Figuratively speaking; I know where too many bodies are buried. I may get a pension, but I doubt if I will enjoy it."

"Why?"

"Because I have no doubt that Samantha will mind wash me within minutes of the announcement of my dismissal. Left to Samantha's tender mercies, I'll end up like a cabbage, a gibbering idiot."

"You're serious, aren't you?"

"Too right!"

"So, what's the deal?"

"Leaving Arden isn't that easy," Mygael said. "As you know, all the spaceports and most of the teleport systems are Minton controlled. But I've worked out a viable escape route. If I help your people escape, you help me escape."

"So, you're planning to go with my people?"

Mygael shook his head, "I will be using the same escape route, but I won't be going with your people."

Jameson was immediately suspicious, "Why not?"

"There's an old saying, never put all your eggs in one basket," Mygael replied. "If my plan works, your people will teleport to Salus Transporter Nine. If they don't get as far away from Arden as they can, Samantha will work out a way of arresting them. I will be going to the Awis Oasis on Arcadia."

Having a limited knowledge of Arcadian geography, Jameson said, "Where's that?"

"It's in the middle of the Great Rock Desert," Mygael replied.

"But why there?"

"I don't have a choice," Mygael replied. "If we use the teleport I'm thinking of using, it will only link with passing starships, New Victoria, Constantine and Awis. As Minton Mining have offshoots near to New Victoria and Constantine, they are hardly suitable destinations."

"You could also visit the Wreck," Jameson replied.

Realising that Jameson had worked out which teleport system he intended to use, Mygael said, "As you know, the teleport at Pearl Crater is run by SSIAT, the Salus System Interplanetary Archaeological Trust. As they don't like Minton, full stop, they are prepared to help us."

"Are you sure?"

"I spoke to a guy called Unnan Vardis," Mygael revealed. "If I pay, he'll operate the teleport and let us escape."

"The illegal use of a teleport is a criminal offence," Jameson replied. "If you're not careful, he could just take the money and then put everyone in stasis."

"What's that?"

"Everyone just disappears into a storage system. If there is no actual teleport, it's unlikely he'd be found out. A clever programmer could keep a victim or victims in stasis for years. Do you trust him?"

Although doubts were forming in Mygael's mind, he nodded, "I know him, he's sound."

After a long silence, Jameson said, "But why are you proposing to go to Awis Oasis? It sounds like it's in the middle of nowhere."

"Awis has distinct advantages," Mygael said. "Like most of Arcadia, it has a no-droid policy. More importantly, it's also surrounded by a modern Mannheim Shield, one that can prevent unauthorised droid access. Unless she orders her Black-Clads to come after me, it's unlikely that Samantha will be able to touch me there."

Jameson immediately picked up on the tongue slip, "I notice you said, her Black-Clads."

Ignoring the snipe, Mygael added, "Besides, I also have friends there—and some unfinished business."

Jameson said, "Like what?"

"I'd rather not say."

"The unfinished business wouldn't be Mick Tarmy, would it?" Jameson asked.

"What makes you say that?"

"It's just that Ord Morley and I had a visitation last night."

"What sort of visitation?"

"A droid," Jameson replied. "We think it's an ex-military machine, possibly a TK5 because it had invisibility cloaks. Mick Tarmy sent it with a message and some money cards."

"So, he *is* alive! Samantha is convinced he's dead."

"There is no doubt that Tarmy sent the machine back," Jameson reasoned. "So, he must be."

"More reason for me to go to Awis then," Mygael said, "So, do we have a deal?"

"On one condition," Jameson replied.

"What's that?"

"Once I've seen my side of the bargain through, I go with you to Awis. I'm too long in the tooth to wind up on an interplanetary transporter. But, like yourself, I have no desire to end up having Samantha mind-washing me any more than you do."

"No problem," the director agreed. "That's totally understandable. So, that's four of us going to Awis."

CHAPTER FOUR

Minton Isolation Facility 1, Anubis Crater, Arden
Getting Cold Feet

T hey were all drunk. After consuming a litre of Alcool, a locally distilled Ardenese whisky liberally spiked with Zuka milk, they were also totally fearless. If someone had told them they could fly, they would have all thrown themselves out of the nearest window.

After presenting his visitors with special protection helmets, Charles Limpum waved his access pass over a control port, staggered forwards and gestured for the others to follow. Once inside, Limpum slumped behind a control console and activated it. The other three men clustered around in morbid anticipation.

In a mad moment, Limpum had offered them an insight into what actually happened in the lower reaches of the Minton Isolation Facility 1, and they didn't want to miss anything.

Limpum instructed the voice-activated console to link him with Henry's cell. A screen immediately displayed a solitary human figure lying on a bunk facing towards the camera. As Henry was obviously asleep, Limpum did not attempt to wake him.

Instead, he glanced around at the others and said, "Henry's an interesting spettro."

"Spettro?"

"That's what we call them. They may look human, but they're not. The plural is spettri by the way: Some people call them Arcadia's Children."

"What's so interesting about him?"

"We had to isolate Henry from the other spettri because they tried to kill him," Limpum replied. "They tried to hang him. Luckily one of the droid guards saved him, and he's been a great boon to us since."

Philips said, "In what way?"

"Ever since we rescued him," Limpum replied, "he's sung like a bird. All I have to do is threaten him with the cull, and he tells me everything I want to know."

"Cull?" Philips said. "What's that?"

"The facility is getting overcrowded with spettri," Limpum replied. "Since we introduced the new facial recognition systems in major towns on Arden we've unearthed a load of 'em. There are around eighty of them down there now so sooner or later we'll either have to find more room for them elsewhere or start a cull."

"What's a cull?" Philips persisted.

"It means they're going to kill some of 'em," one of the other men said.

"Kill?" Philips objected. "You can't just kill people."

"Like I told you before," Limpum growled. "They're not human."

"That guy looks human."

"Well, he's not."

"So, when does the cull start?"

Limpum shrugged, "Dunno. When Alton Mygael's gonads drop, I suppose. He hasn't signed the cull order yet."

"So, who's going to kill 'em?" Philips demanded.

Limpum gave Philips a crooked smile. "Who d'you think? You and your Black-Clad buddies. Why d'you think Samantha's brought a contingent of you here? Like I said, as soon as Alton Mygael develops some balls, the killing will start."

Philips objected, "What if we don't want to kill 'em?"

"Not a lot of people know this, but Samantha has a room on the Minus Four level that contains mind-washing equipment," Limpum replied, "After a few blasts on the mind-washer, you'll be killing with the best of 'em."

Still quibbling, Philips said, "Why us?"

"Because," Limpum said, "at the moment the prison droids can't kill the prisoners. That's because our tech guys haven't worked out how to override the manufacturer's program yet. Besides, Samantha is going to use the killings as a test of loyalty—once you've killed; you will be bound to her by blood."

Philips thought about the gang tattoo on his neck, the one that proclaimed he'd killed four rival gang members. His life had changed when the prison authorities had offered him early release if he accepted a level two mind wash. Since then, he'd never wanted to kill again. When he'd first joined the Black-Clads, his senior, Allus Wren, had told him not to admit to being mind-washed.

If he couldn't kill the spettri, Samantha would reverse the previous mind wash, and he'd revert to the mindless animal he'd once been.

While Philips was thinking about his future, Limpum spoke to his console again, and the CCTV cameras sent views of the lower prison. Flicking between camera stations, Limpum finally located a group of spettri prisoners. Although not identical, most of them looked strikingly similar.

Philips stared at the small crowd of prisoners.

Limpum said, "You were demanding proof. Well, here they are boys! The spettri—Arcadia's Children."

As if hearing his comment, the prisoners in the basement all turned and stared at the camera in unison, the expressions on their faces showing hostility.

But despite the fear their hostile faces created, Philips had no desire to kill them.

~*~

When Senior Group Leader Wren arrived at his office, Lance Corporal Tam Philips was standing in the corridor outside. Philips half smiled, then, mindful of Wren's recent promotion, he came to attention and saluted.

Although Wren recognised Philips, he just said, "At ease Lance Corporal."

Once Philips had resumed his normal slouch, Wren eyed him thoughtfully. "You were with me when we were jumped at the warehouse by Alan Hyndman's gang, weren't you?"

"Yes, sir."

"Are you waiting to see me?"

"Yes, sir."

"What about?"

Philips moved closer and whispered, "I'd appreciate it if it wasn't out here, sir. Somewhere private if you don't mind."

As it was common knowledge that most offices and surrounding corridors were bugged, Allus Wren took the hint, let them both into his office, locked the door behind them and then opened a large walk-in store cupboard and nodded for Philips to follow.

Once they were both inside, Wren closed the doors, activated a link to a local music station and turned the volume up. Satisfied that the music would drown their conversation, he gave Philips a stern look, "So, what's your problem, Lance?"

Philips said, "Permission to adjust my uniform, sir."

"Is it absolutely necessary Lance Corporal?"

Philips made a slight gesture, one that was in common use in the Zadernaster Boys and then said, "Yes, sir."

"Okay, adjust."

Philips loosened his high neck collar and pulled it down to expose his neck tattoo. As the tattoo was virtually identical to his own, Wren said, "That's the Zadernaster tattoo."

"Yes, sir," Philips agreed, "Same as yours."

Tempting though it was to deny his past, Wren said, "As you say, the same as mine."

Alluding to the incident in the warehouse when Alan Hyndman's gang had jumped them, Philips added, "I saw your tattoo when they removed your body armour, Sir."

Suspecting Philips wanted to invoke the old pals' act, Wren

snapped, "Okay, let's cut to the chase—what do you want Lance Corporal?"

"I came to see you because I knew I could trust you, sir. You may outrank me, but we are still brothers beneath the skin."

Still suspicious, Wren said, "Presumably you've done something wrong, and you want me to bail you out."

"No, sir—nothing like that." Then, blurting it out, "There's going to be a cull. They're going to start killing the prisoners as soon as the director signs the order. And I don't want any part of it."

He pointed to another tattoo below the gangland tattoo, "I got remission because I agreed to have a level two mind wash. I don't want to go back to my old ways. I don't want to be involved in a cull."

Wren gave Philips a slightly disbelieving look, "Sounds like someone has been pulling your leg, Lance."

"No, no—they're going to kill the aliens in the basement prison!"

Wren burst out laughing, "Aliens in the basement prison; what *are* you talking about?"

Annoyed by Wren's reaction, Philips told him about Henry and the spettri imprisoned down below. "I think the name of this place gives a good clue as to its use. It's an isolation facility."

"It's is just a normal prison," Wren countered. "The only difference is, it's computerised and has droid guards."

As he had no desire to drag Charles Limpum's name into the conversation, Philips said. "I've heard whispers. The things they've got imprisoned down there are called spettri. They are from Arcadia, and they're aliens. They're imprisoned because they have special powers."

"And where did you hear this?"

Philips clammed up. "I just heard."

"You shouldn't go listening to gossip."

"It wasn't gossip," Philips snapped. "I saw them."

"You saw them? Who showed you?"

"I'd rather not say."

"I'm sure you wouldn't," Wren replied. "But you are going to tell me, aren't you?"

When Philips remained silent, Wren unbuttoned his own collar and exposed his matching tattoo.

"Okay Philips, as you just said, I may outrank you, but we are still brothers beneath the skin. If you want me to help you, I want the whole story, not just parts of it."

~*~

"Mind if I join you?"

Charles Limpum glanced around the canteen. As every other table in the room was empty, Allus Wren half expected him to quibble. Instead Limpum gave him a cautious nod and then said, "I've not seen you in here before, sir."

"That's because I've never been in here before," Wren replied before making a skirmishing attack on his dinner. "I came in to see you actually."

"Why, sir?"

"You were highly inebriated the other night and did things that, how can I put this delicately? Were somewhat indiscreet."

Running his eyes over Wren's black uniform and soaking in the significance, Limpum played for time, "Indiscreet?"

He locked eyes with Wren challengingly, and the size of his irises gave a clear indication that he was still under the influence of the Zuka milk he'd taken just before he'd given Philips and the others a guided tour of the interrogation centre.

"Yes," Wren replied. "Taking unauthorised personnel into a restricted area was not a good move on your part."

"I've no idea what you're talking about."

Wren extracted his percom, and as the canteen was empty except for them, he allowed the bubble mode to kick in, even enlarging slightly.

Limpum caught a glimpse of himself sitting at his console with three other men gathered around. One of them was Philips. Although the image only gave a limited view, Limpum realised there could be little doubt of what he'd been looking at.

"How did you get this?"

Wren said, "You didn't turn all of the CCTV cameras off."

Limpum paled, "What are you going to do?"

In response, Wren turned his percom off and took a bite out of a vegetarian sausage. He contemplated the question whilst chewing.

Eventually, he said, "That depends on you."

"What does that mean?"

Wren tapped the double oak leaves on his high collar, "I'm a Senior Group Leader. I should report you. But, as I just said, that depends on you."

"What d'you you want?"

"Why don't we start with you coming to my office so that we can have a quiet chat?"

Swiftly demolishing the rest of his dinner, Wren added, "I'll leave you to finish your dinner. But I expect you to meet me in my office in an hour. Understood?"

When Limpum just nodded, Wren snapped, "You'd better be there, or I'll come looking for you, and if I do, you'll be for the high jump. Do you understand that?"

~*~

Limpum arrived at Wren's office early. As he still had a wide-eyed look about him, Wren knew the drugs he'd taken were still in his system, but as he knew that they would make Limpum more co-operative, he had no qualms about it. Telling Limpum to step into his cupboard, Wren turned the music on again.

Once it was blaring loudly, he turned to face the other man.

Some of Limpum's fighting spirit had returned. "What have you brought me in here for?" he demanded.

"So, the bugs can't listen in to our conversation," Wren replied. "D'you want Samantha to find out what you've been doing?"

Limpum's bravado immediately evaporated at the mention of Samantha's name, and he shook his head, "No, sir."

Wren said, "Then let's play this my way, eh?"

Limpum nodded.

"So, let's start at the beginning. It would appear you invited three unauthorised personnel into your control room. Correct?"

Limpum nodded again.

"You do realise you'd be in serious trouble if I report this."

"Yes, sir. Please don't—it'll never happen again."

"You've placed me in a very awkward position, Limpum. I'll have to think about it. If you co-operate and I'm forced to make a report, I will ask for your cooperation to be taken into account."

When Limpum remained silent, Wren said, "Tell me what you know about these spettri, the Arcadian Children you've got banged up down below."

Limpum gave him a sharp look, "How d'you know what they're called?"

"The camera that caught you also recorded what you said," Wren replied. He added, "One other important point, Limpum - I ask the questions, you answer. So, I repeat, what you know about these spettri, the Arcadian Children you've got banged up down below?"

Limpum shrugged, "All I know is that they're some sort of mutant."

"How many of them are there?"

"Around eighty?"

"Where did they come from?"

"Originally from Arcadia," Limpum said. "They were sent by the Great Ones."

"Who are the Great Ones?"

Limpum shrugged, "Don't know."

When Wren gave him a stern look, Limpum bleated, "Honest, I don't know who they are. I just know about them, sir."

"Okay. Why are the Great Ones sending these spettri, er things, to Arden?"

"To invade us," Limpum replied. "We believe that they got to Arden as foetuses."

Wren frowned, "As foetuses?"

"Some female scientists returned to Arden after spending time on Arcadia," Limpum explained. "The women concerned didn't know they were pregnant, and nothing showed up during the quarantine period. It didn't show up because a spettri foetus can delay its birth up to twenty-four months instead of the normal nine. There's some flashy name for the way it works, but I can't remember what it is,"

He paused, then added, "As the spettri are programmed to kill their siblings and their parents as soon as they are strong enough, no one knows much about them."

Wren gave Limpum a hard look then activated his percom again in bubble mode. As Henry's sleeping form came into view, Wren said, "Who's this?"

"If you have the sound recording," Limpum challenged, "You'd know."

"The sound tailed off in places," Wren replied. "So, who is he?"

"He's called Henry, Sir."

"Tell me about Henry."

Once Limpum had finished, Wren said, "I'd like to speak to Henry."

A look of alarm flashed across Limpum's face, "I couldn't let you in. You're not authorised."

"The others weren't authorised, but I am." Wren then touched the two oak leaves on his collar again. "These say I am authorised. Don't worry Limpum. If there's any trouble, I'll take the blame."

Limpum gave him a sharp look, "If Samantha finds out I'll say you ordered me to do this."

Wren smiled. "I'll take that risk, but we are going to make sure all the cameras are turned off this time, aren't we?"

~*~

"Henry, you have a visitor."

Rolling off his bunk, Henry pushed a small step stool under the camera to make himself look taller and began mind probing. He immediately realised his interrogator was telling the truth; there was a newcomer in the control room.

He let out a grunt of annoyance. Although his mental powers still allowed low-level probing, both his interrogator and the newcomer were wearing shielded helmets so that he couldn't probe their inner minds.

Henry became petulant, "The visitor isn't very friendly; he's wearing a helmet."

There was a short pause then Limpum said, "Your visitor has agreed to take his helmet off as long as you agree not to take advantage of the situation. No funny business."

After contemplating, Henry said, "Okay—no funny business."

~*~

Wren pulled the helmet off. A fraction of a second later he felt what seemed like a huge slug entering his mind; it felt like it was slip-sliding over his brain, searching for information.

Eventually, Henry's voice said, "You were once a Zadernaster."

He corrected himself, "I said that wrong, you were a Zadernaster. You were in a gang. The Zadernaster Boys, one of the largest and most powerful gangs on Rasham."

Henry let out a slight cry of surprise, "While you were with the Zadernaster Boys, you killed six people."

When Wren remained silent, Henry added, "You used to live on Rasham, but after you became a Black-Clad, you were eventually transferred to Arden."

Then Henry became more personal, "You had a partner, but she was using you. She just wanted to escape from Rasham. You brought her to Arden, but within a matter of weeks, she left you."

Henry then stuck the knife in. "She's also engaged a flashy lawyer. She says she's going to sue you for every ACU you've ..."

Realising that Henry was deliberately playing with him, Wren cut the exchange short by putting the helmet back on his head. Limpum looked alarmed, cut the link with Henry, and then said, "What are you doing, Sir?"

"Henry is just messing about," Wren complained. "You told him not to."

"It wouldn't be wise to upset him," Limpum said. "He could tell Samantha that you've been here."

"Not if you tell him my rank and explain that I'm an official assessor," Wren replied. "One appointed by Samantha to assess him because she's become displeased with him and wants a second opinion. You can also tell him that he has offended me, and if he doesn't apologise, he will go on the next cull list."

"You know about the proposed cull?"

Wren nodded and pointed at the link with Henry's cell, "Tell him what I just said."

Once Limpum had relayed the message, Henry began running around his cell wailing.

Wren frowned, "What's up with him?"

"He's scared you really will include him in the cull; what did you expect, sir?"

After watching Henry's histrionics for some time, Wren said, "Tell him if he behaves himself and proves he's going to co-operate by giving me some information, I will give him a good report."

After Limpum had quietened Henry down, Wren said, "Tell me about the Great Ones Henry."

"I keep on telling you people about the Great Ones," Henry complained. "They control the Fyfield Valley and the Altos Plateaux. They are the real masters of Arcadia and one day they will reclaim what is rightfully theirs. Then they will take over the Salus System because you outworlders have no right to be here."

"Is that all?"

Henry thought about the question for a second or two and then said, "I've already told Samantha that three of the Great Ones died and one was injured when the bomb went off."

"What bomb?"

"The bomb that Mick Tarmy and Claire Hyndman dropped," Henry replied.

Limpum suddenly cut the link to Henry's cell.

Wren gave him a hard look, "What did you do that for?"

"Because the bomb attack on the Great Ones is highly secret," Limpum replied. "If you go spouting it about, we'll both be in trouble."

"What happened to Tarmy and Hyndman?"

"They're dead," Limpum replied. "Why are you so interested?"

"Because Claire Hyndman saved my life: where I come from if someone saves your life, you owe them," Wren replied. "If it hadn't been for her intervention, I'd be dead."

"If she's dead, she's dead," Limpum replied. "Shit happens."

Annoyed by the callous response, Wren grabbed hold of Limpum's scrawny neck, "How did she die?"

Fearing that Wren might get really violent, Limpum gasped, "I don't know for sure."

Wren's grip on Limpum's neck increased, "Tell me what you do know."

"I only know what Henry's told me," Limpum screeched struggling to loosen Wren's grip.

Wren finally removed his hands and said, "So, what did Henry tell you?"

Rubbing his neck, Limpum said, "Samantha came here with Alton Mygael, the director, a few days ago and asked Henry questions. I think Henry somehow managed to read some of the director's thoughts."

"How could he do that if the director was wearing a helmet?"

"I'm not sure, but Henry has let things slip," Limpum replied. "I think Henry has found a way of getting into the director's mind despite him wearing a helmet."

"So, what did Henry tell you?"

"Henry thinks the director believes that Samantha always intended that Mick Tarmy and Claire Hyndman would die during the bomb attack."

"Why?"

"Because once they'd done what she'd wanted, they were surplus to requirements, a dead man, or woman, can't talk." He became slightly philosophical, "Everyone in this place is on borrowed time, Sir. Look at Mih Valanson."

"Who's he?"

"He *was* one our best backroom boys," Limpum replied. "Unfortunately, there was an explosion in his workshop. Like I said, shit happens, especially around here. He's now in a cell, and I've no doubt Samantha will have him sent to penal colony shortly."

Limpum shot Wren a sharp look, "Be warned, sooner or later she'll turn on you. A bit of free advice, you obviously know about the proposed cull, sir, and you and the other Black-Clads will be expected to do the dirty work. The killing, I mean. I wouldn't refuse to get involved."

"Why not?"

"Samantha is currently setting all senior staff various tasks," Limpum replied. "Those who prove themselves worthy will be promoted and will help Samantha build a new model army."

"A what?"

"An army that's totally loyal to Minton and can be used against Minton's enemies," Limpum said.

"What happens to those who fail the test?"

"Samantha has a room on floor minus four that contains mind-washing equipment," Limpum replied. "In the event of a brainwash not providing the desired effect, I've no doubt the failures will be sent to a penal colony along with the likes of Valanson."

Wren changed tack, "So going back to Alton Mygael, the director. What else did Henry find out from reading his mind?"

"Henry also told me that Alton Mygael believes Tarmy and Hyndman are still alive, Sir."

"Why?"

"I don't know any more than Henry told me, sir."

~*~

Three hours after his meeting with Limpum, Wren's percom sounded, and a curt voice said, "Where are you?"

Although Samantha hadn't introduced herself, there was no mistaking her clipped tones.

Wren said, "I'm currently investigating a major theft from one of our depots, Ma'am."

"Leave what you're doing and get back here. I will see you in your office."

After cutting the call, Wren swore under his breath and latched onto the worst-case scenario: Limpum had covered his backside by telling tales.

CHAPTER FIVE

Minton Isolation Facility 1, Anubis Crater, Arden
Samantha reneges on her deal with Mick Tarmy

T he doors to Wren's office sprang back, and Samantha swept into view with an escort of three similar sized droids following her. Sandwiched between them was Lance Corporal Tam Philips.

As Philip's face was drawn and pale, Wren's heart sank to his boots. It would appear that Charles Limpum had decided to turn them both in. But just as Wren was preparing for a severe dressing down, Philips made a slight gesture, a Zadernaster Boys warning to say nothing.

Samantha's interaction screen became transparent and revealed a haughty female face inside. Guided by Philips' gesture, Wren did not attempt to speak; he just came to attention and saluted.

Samantha's CGI face gave Wren a slight smile of appreciation; although she didn't possess any fundamental orifices, she still liked having human arse-lickers pandering to her vanity.

Moving into Wren's Office, Samantha instructed Philips to follow and then shed her minders.

She came straight to the point, "I asked Lance Corporal Philips to attend this meeting because you've worked well together in the past. You have also proven loyal and trustworthy."

Wrens mind went into overdrive. Although Samantha's comments were suggesting that dragging Philips with her was just a coincidence, Wren distrusted coincidences.

Samantha said, "I have another important job for you to do."

Although tempted to grimace, Wren remained stone-faced. However, the poker-face didn't prevent his mind from taking him back to his near-death experience during Samantha's last operation. Samantha had sent both of them to a warehouse full of gangsters without any back-up.

She'd deliberately used them as live bait.

More importantly, if it hadn't been for Claire Hyndman's intervention, one of her father's thugs would have shot him in cold blood.

"I have something important to show you," Samantha said and created a power bubble with images moving around inside it.

After watching the jerky images for a few seconds, Wren realised he was witnessing a real-life incident, recorded by a body camera. Catching sight of a police badge, he guessed he was watching a group of local police officers chasing a crim. Then shots were fired. As the group moved towards the downed man, someone swore, "Shit, he's dead, and he wasn't carrying?"

A moment later, a worried face came into view and repeated, "He wasn't carrying, boss."

Another officer moved forward, slipped a large commando knife into the dead man's hand and said, "He is now. So quit worrying."

Once the sequence finished, Wren immediately had doubts. Although the images were jerking and looked authentic, the mere fact that the recording was so short indicated some editing had to have taken place. The worst-case scenario would be the whole sequence was a well-made reconstruction.

Wren said, "So why have you shown us this, Ma'am?"

Samantha let out a simulated tut, "This is evidence of police malpractice. It's a cover-up."

Still suspicious, Wren said, "Can I ask how you obtained the recording?"

"The perpetrators attempted to delete the recording, but we recovered it from police archives," Samantha replied. "I have been assured the recording can be verified and will be accepted as evidence when we press charges. There are two sets of charges to answer: one of illegal killing and the other of perverting the course of justice, in other words, a police cover-up."

Getting no reaction, Samantha handed Wren a small computer and said, "The whole sequence is recorded on there. I want you to ask to see the director and report it officially. You will then get him to formally authorise action against the guilty parties; you will find the form on the computer too. All he has to do is sign it; once he has signed the warrant, you are to assemble enough Black-Clad forces to round up all the names listed on the warrant."

"Look at the form and make sure you understand."

When Wren activated the form, he read the important parts and was about to skip to the end when he noted a reference to a complaint lodged by Alain Pen which accused his father and other police officers of treason. He skipped to the end. As the list seemed never-ending, he said, "I will need a large contingent to arrest this lot, Ma'am."

"You will be in total control of the arrest operation while I'm away," she replied, "Don't fail me SGL wren."

"Why do *I* have to get the director's signature, ma'am? Why aren't *you* reporting it to the director and getting authorisation?"

"Don't challenge my reasoning, SGL Wren," Samantha snapped. "Don't forget I am Ingermann-Verex R9054 humanoid, the most intelligent droid ever constructed. Not only am I your mental superior, I don't make mistakes—I want you involved because the director is already aware of the incident but has so far declined to act."

When Wren gave her a puzzled look, Samantha added, "If you were to present him with that information and imply that the facts are now common knowledge, he wouldn't be able to sweep it under the carpet. He wouldn't wish to be politically embarrassed if this came out and it shows that he deliberately ignored it."

Limpum's comments came back to him. Undoubtedly, this was a test. Looking for an escape route, Wren countered with, "If I go straight to him, won't it look as if I am going over your head? I normally report to you."

Samantha permitted herself a half smile, "You apparently missed what I just said. I will be away for the next few days. I will be visiting Arden City. I am expecting to be invited to join the Board to replace a member who will shortly be vacating his post. I will also have to attend several meetings with senior management. As I will not be available for some time, you will be reporting to the director anyway. You will therefore have an excuse and opportunity to ask for arrest warrants to be issued against all the police officers involved—understood?"

"What if the director refuses to sign?" Wren asked,

"Refuse!" She snapped back, and then her whole body shimmied with annoyance. "I am relying on you to make sure he doesn't refuse. You will make sure he agrees and signs. I want these people arrested."

"And how exactly do I make him sign?"

"Both you and Philips were Zadernaster Boys," Samantha replied. "As you both have violent pasts, I am sure you'll think of a way of securing his co-operation. Do I have to be more specific?"

"No, Ma'am."

After shimmying again, Samantha turned on her axis and moved towards the door.

Once she had left with her guards, Philips frowned, "I don't like that wobbling thing she does. Is it normal for a droid to do that?"

Wren placed a finger against his lips and nodded towards the storeroom again. After going through the usual procedure, he said, "So what d'you make of that?"

"This place is a madhouse," Philips replied. "What, with her shaking and her more or less instructing us to beat the crap out of the director until he signs; just what's going on?"

Ignoring the issue of Samantha's weird shaking Wren said, "It's a trap. Limpum must have told her everything. She's told us to attack the director, but if we do, she'll have us arrested."

Philips shook his head, "I know Limpum - He won't have said anything. He wouldn't do that. It's like she said, she trusts us because, unfortunately, we did too good a job last time."

"She used us as live-bait last time," Wren reminded him. "She's also setting us up again. If she can't get the director to sign the arrest warrants, what chance have we got?"

"She's made it quite clear; she wants us to strong-arm him," Philips replied. "The droids at this base are programmed not to harm humans unless they are defending someone from attack. But we can beat the director to a pulp if he refuses to co-operate."

"It makes sense, "Wren admitted. "It's also a test of loyalty. Who do we side with? The director or her."

Wren let his mind take him back to the gangland turf wars of his youth. In those days, most gang leaders were trying to climb the greasy pole to the top. Being one of the largest gangs, the Zadernaster Boys were always trying to absorb or gain control over rival gangs. Territorial disputes were also common.

Using his knowledge of the past, Wren applied it to the present. "I'm guessing; I think Samantha wants an excuse to make a move against the Ardenese police force. Using that recording gives her the excuse as long as the director signs. Once the senior police officers are arrested, I have no doubt company officials will take their place. Once that happens, there will be a push to assimilate the police into the Black-Clads. Minton Mining Company will then have acquired most of the levers of power on Arden and will be able to do whatever they want."

"So, what are we going to do?"

"We're going to do what she says for now. But look for a way out."

CHAPTER SIX

Minton Isolation Facility 1, Anubis Crater, Arden
Exodus.

Alton Mygael made a scrambled call to Hen Jameson but mindful that the call might still be intercepted, he kept the conversation short, "Have they gone?"

"They're on their way," Jameson confirmed. "What about you?"

"I've got a last-minute hitch," Mygael admitted. "But as it's confidential I can't talk about it. If I don't call you within the next two hours, assume I won't be able to join you for drinks and canapés."

~*~

When Wren arrived, he found Alton Mygael's door open, and a voice boomed, "Come in, Wren."

As the other man's face mask made Wren feel distinctly ill at ease, he hesitated. The pause brought an immediate rebuke. "Come on, man! Do you want to speak to me or not?"

"Yes, sir."

"Then come in. I can assure you; I don't bite."

Mygael glanced towards the door and noticed Philips' presence. As both men were heavily built and looked intimidating; he guessed that the time had finally come; Samantha had decided to make her move. Her timing was impeccable; she had made sure she'd left Minton Isolation Facility 1. So, if strong-arm tactics were used, Wren would get the blame.

Instead of showing fear, Alton Mygael said, "Ah! I see you're not alone, Senior Group Leader." He beckoned for Philips to enter.

Once Philips had done as instructed, the doors swished shut. Waving them both towards nearby chairs, Mygael said, "So What's this about?"

When Philips hesitated, Mygael snapped, "Sit down, man. You're making the place look untidy."

Once Philips was seated, Mygael repeated, "So, what's this about?"

With Samantha's orders still ringing in his ears, Wren plunged into the storyline that he'd been given and hoped it would work, "Some disturbing news has just come to light, Sir."

"Really? Like what?"

"Can I show you, sir?"

When Mygael consented, Wren activated the small computer that Samantha had given him. The power bubble sequence started up and began replaying the images of the police chase, the shooting and the knife being placed into the dead man's hand.

After viewing the images, Mygael leaned back in his chair, eyed Wren and Philips thoughtfully and said, "So, you want me to authorise you to arrest these people?"

"Yes, sir."

"You do realise that arresting police officers will cause a lot of ripples," Mygael replied. "I have always tried to avoid any confrontation with the civil police."

Glancing at the computer, Wren quoted from the Ardenese Consolidation (Legal Amendments) Act and then said, "As director for security, you have been granted the same powers as a judge. You can sign the arrest warrants."

There was an overlong pause before Mygael said, "Samantha put you up to this, didn't she?"

Taken by surprise, Wren hesitated. Mygael's electronic face mask twisted into a distorted smile, "I thought so."

He produced the computer he'd shown to Hen Jameson,

"She gave me this not so long ago. And I said at the time, I'd think about it. And I'm still thinking."

Wren frowned, "When I spoke to her, she was most insistent the matter was concluded, sir."

"She's wanted me to take action against the civil police for some time, Senior Group Leader. But I have resisted. D'you know why?"

"As you just said, you like to avoid confrontation with the civil police," Wren replied.

"That is true, but the main reason, in this case, is that I like to keep my word," Mygael said. "Samantha and I promised Mick Tarmy we wouldn't arrest these people if he volunteered for a dangerous mission on Arcadia, which he did. There is a possibility he died on that mission."

"Samantha believes Tarmy's death absolves her of all promises. I, on the other hand, don't believe that Mick Tarmy is dead. Even if he was dead, in my book, a promise is a promise."

"Mick Tarmy? I've heard that name before." Wren said. He tried putting the name to a face. "Ah! Wasn't Tarmy the injured police officer? The one I brought here a few weeks ago?"

"Correct," Mygael replied. "You arrested him and brought him here."

Wren smiled slightly. Tarmy's apprehension had been more like a kidnap. They'd just grabbed Tarmy, thrown him into a wheelchair because he couldn't walk very well and then flown him to Minton Isolation Facility 1.

"Both Samantha and I made promises to Tarmy," Mygael continued. "But promises mean nothing to Samantha. She is determined to damage the civil police by starting a scandal."

When Wren remained silent, Mygael said, "And do you know why Samantha wants *me* to sign?"

Wren shook his head.

Mygael said, "As you said, the Ardenese Consolidation (Legal Amendments) Act was introduced as a package of measures when the Minton Mining Company took over Arden's mining resources. And yes, I do have the same powers as a judge. But why does Samantha want *my* signature? Why doesn't she just go to a judge?"

"I've no idea," Wren admitted.

"Because it's highly unlikely that any self-respecting judge would ever agree to sign this warrant," Mygael replied. "It must be obvious even to you that the recording you've just shown me is a fake."

Neither of the men said anything, and their silence felt much longer than the sixty seconds it actually was. Mygael looked at Wren, "I suppose you will get into trouble if I don't sign."

"Yes, Sir."

"And would I be right in thinking that if I don't sign, you'll use force to coerce a signature out of me?"

Wren nodded, "It would pain me greatly to have to use violence but regretfully, yes."

Mygael's face mask formed into a slight smile, and he clicked his fingers. "Then I'd better save us both pain and sign, hadn't I?"

Surprised by the sudden capitulation, Wren handed the small computer over for signature.

Mygael opened a desk drawer and removed a stylus. But instead of immediately signing, the director said, "So, will you be in charge of the arrest teams, Wren?"

"Yes, Sir," Wren replied. "As soon as you have signed, I will be able to give the necessary orders."

"Pity it has to end this way," Mygael said, putting his signature to the document.

Once Mygael had handed the small computer back, Wren and Philips saluted in unison and then turned to leave.

"Before you go, there's something you both need to see."

Mygael pointed to a small side office, "It's on the table."

"Sir?"

"Go on; you need to see it."

As Wren and Philips walked into the room, Mygael repeated, "It's on the table."

Once he was sure they were both well inside the office and had their backs turned to him, Mygael reached into his open desk drawer, pulled out a small stun gun and fired twice.

Rising from his desk, he walked into the side room, and after kicking both bodies to make sure Wren and Philips wouldn't recover for several hours, he locked them in.

Making a scramble call to Jameson, he said, "Everything is now under control. I have to collect my guest, the one who will be joining us for drinks and canapés. We will be with you shortly."

Walking back to his desk, Mygael picked up two distortion collars and left, locking the main door behind him.

~*~

Mih Valanson heard the faintest of rattles and his mind began inventing scenarios. Were they coming for him or someone else? Was he finally going to be punished for allowing Alex, the TK5, to escape? Was he going to be dragged off and executed or deported to a far-off penal colony where his life expectancy would be around two years?

A moment later he heard the sound of heavy boots approaching, and his heart began thumping in his chest, deafening him.

The door to his cell slid back, and Mygael entered, whispering, "Come on, we're leaving."

Valanson swallowed the acrid taste of bile at the back of his throat, suddenly aware that his hands were shaking, and he was drenched in a cold sweat. "Leaving—for where?"

"Somewhere were Samantha can't harm you."

~*~

Klaien Mygael glanced at the SSIAT building and took a deep breath. Even though she knew there was a protection droid not far behind ready to come to her aid if anything went wrong, she still felt very exposed. As she'd lived a sheltered middle-class life, being asked to break the law didn't come easily.

Psyching herself up, she slipped on the distortion collar that Alton had given her and began walking towards the tall building. Crossing a pedestrianised area, she glanced at the reflection of herself in a nearby window and was pleased to note that the collar had altered her appearance completely; it had also made her look twenty years younger.

Reaching the main entrance of the SSIAT building, she saw one of the outer shutters was raised, and a lift door was visible. Activating her percom, she locked onto the building's external comms port and waited. A few seconds later, a power bubble formed, and the image of a droid appeared, an Alpha 300.

Without prompting the machine said, "It's after hours. The facility is closed."

Klaien hadn't been anticipating an automated response, and a mild wave of panic ran through her system; something had gone wrong. She was seriously considering abandoning her mission when the bubble content suddenly changed, and Unnan Vardis's image appeared, "Sorry about that, the automated system cut in." He added, "Have you got the money?

Klaien held up a large, brightly coloured paper bag. "It's in here."

As she held the bag aloft, the contents moved slightly. She realised that Rover was getting restless from being cooped up inside and hoped Vardis hadn't noticed.

"Are you going to let me in?"

"Okay, come up."

There was a slight whirring noise, and an outer lift door opened. Once in Klaien was whisked up to one of the upper floors. When the doors opened, she found herself in a lobby.

A woman waiting there said, "Come this way. Unnan is through here."

As she pushed her way through a set of fire doors, the woman glanced back and added, "I'm Marci by the way; I'm

Unnan's partner."

The comment surprised Klaien, during previous conversations, Vardis had implied he lived alone. After another five metres, Marci walked through an open door and led the way into a spacious living area. Klaien caught a glimpse of a charging unit through the slightly open door of an adjacent room and immediately worked out the truth. Although Marci looked human, simple logic implied she was a humanoid. Noticing the expression on Klaien's face, Marci glanced towards the open door. "Ha! I see my little secret is out. I hope you're not offended."

"Why should I be?"

A male voice said, "Some people are."

Glancing around, Klaien saw Vardis standing there and said, "Well I'm not. I was just surprised because you said you were single."

"In the eyes of the law I am," Vardis replied, a touch of bitterness entering his tone. "Marci and I are partners, but it's not recognised." He paused.

"So, let's see the money."

Klaien nodded and pulled out two large denomination money cards but kept a firm hold onto the bag.

Vardis gave her a sharp look, "That's only half of what we agreed."

"You'll get the other half once the job's complete," she said, and passed over a sheet of plasti-metal paper. "Those are the teleport coordinates."

She glanced at her watch, "As agreed, in a few hours from now two separate groups of people will come here. The first group want to teleport to Salus Transporter Nine and the second group wants to go to Awis Oasis."

"I want the rest of the money first," Vardis growled.

"Very well," she agreed. "It's in the bag."

As Vardis was about to reach into the bag, it rustled, and a small rugby-ball shaped droid emerged.

"What's this?"

"My insurance policy," Klaien replied. "This is Rover. He has the other cards in his internal safe and has orders to pay you the balance once we're all safety teleported."

Vardis gave her a hostile look. "Don't you trust me?"

"I once heard of a teleport operator who cheated a group of people," Klaien said. "He promised to teleport them if they gave him a large sum of money. He took their money, but instead of teleporting them, he put them into stasis and called the police. He denied receiving any payments."

Vardis clicked his fingers and gestured towards Marci, "And she's my insurance policy."

Glancing around, Klaien noted that Marci was holding a stun gun and it was levelled at her. Vardis said, "Now get your droid to hand over the other money cards."

He smirked, "You are right. I have no intention of getting your people out of here. Illegal teleporting is a criminal offence. Why commit a crime when I can just take the money off suckers like you?"

Marci moved forwards brandishing the gun, "We want the money."

Although she knew she was taking a risk, Klaien snapped, "Rover, attack!"

Rover responded with amazing speed. Flying across the room, he rammed Marci's gun hand and knocked the gun flying. The small machine rolled and flicked the stun gun towards Klaien.

Unfortunately, she fumbled the catch and Marci leapt at her. But before the humanoid could make physical contact, Rover slammed into her side and sent her sprawling across the room. Taking advantage, Klaien scooped up the stun gun and fired at Marci. A surprised look formed on the humanoid's face and she went very still.

Vardis leapt to his feet, showing real emotion, "What have you done to my Marci?"

He began advancing on Klaien menacingly. She immediately realised she was in an awkward situation. Stunning

Vardis would be easy, but if he was stunned, he wouldn't be able to work the SSIAT teleport.

Dodging around the furniture to avoid body contact, Klaien repeated the command, "Rover attack!"

The small droid reacted immediately and rammed one of Unnan's legs. It then slammed into Vardis three more times in quick succession, hitting him like a skilled boxer.

Fearing for his life, Vardis retreated into a corner and went into a ball. "Call it off! Call it off!"

Cancelling her order, Klaien scooped up the money cards and then moved a little closer to the cowering man.

"Right Vardis it's time for you to get busy."

"You shot Marci."

"She'll recover," Klaien said unsympathetically. "Tie her up."

Once Vardis had found some suitable cabling, he did as instructed. Klaien said, "Right let's get the teleport programmed."

"And what if I won't?" Vardis snapped like a petulant teenager.

Klaien clicked the shun pistol from stun to kill and pointed it at Marci. "If you let me down Vardis, she gets it."

In response, Vardis said, "So this has become a hijack, has it?"

For the first time since entering Vardis' apartment, Klaien smiled, "Yes, I suppose it has, Unnan. But it wouldn't have done if you'd kept your promise."

CHAPTER SEVEN

Minton Isolation Facility 1, Anubis Crater, Arden
Wren in pursuit

"**C**ome on, wake up."

As Wren's eyes opened, he heard the sound of a wailing siren, "What's going on?"

"Mygael shot us," Philips replied. "He suckered us. He told us to come in here, and he shot us when our backs were turned and then locked us in his office."

"Why's the alarm going off?"

"Like I said, we're locked in, so I set the alarms off to attract attention."

"Good thinking."

While Wren was recovering and attempting to make sense of what had happened, Philips picked up the folder Alton Mygael had left on the table. Opening it, he glanced inside and found several photographs. Each one showed a head and shoulders image. Across each, there was a red corner flash with white writing inside.

Looking at the first photograph, Philips read, 'Disagreement with Samantha—disappeared.'

Flicking to the next, he found another face with a similar caption. The next was the same. Eventually, he came to the last two pages and let out a slight whistle. Although he'd never seen Alton Mygael without his electronic face mask, the notation left little doubt it was him. He caught a glimpse of a very familiar neck tattoo. He glanced at the hurried handwritten message that Alton Mygael had left for Wren.

Swiftly going through the whole file again, he glanced at Wren and attempted to hand it over, but the alarms suddenly stopped, and several droids forced their way into the director's office. After one of them had helped him to his feet, Wren snapped, "Where's the director?"

The machine said, "He left about eight hours ago sir."

"Eight hours ago!"

"Yes, sir. I understand he's booked a short vacation at Bull Crater."

"Get one of our groups out to Bull Crater, immediately," Wren snapped. "The director is to be arrested."

The droid resisted, "On what charge?"

"Let's start with assault," Wren replied. "He shot Lance Corporal Philips and me—and if you need evidence, just look at the state of us."

He staggered his way to the directors' washroom. Even in a stunned state, Wren's internal plumbing had still been working. Philips swiftly followed suit.

"Looks like he's done a runner," Philips observed. He then attempted to offer Wren Alton Mygael's file again.

But instead of taking it, Wren pushed his way out the washroom and grabbed the small computer that Samantha had given him. He turned to one of the droids and snapped, "I need an air-car—I also need two SWAT teams—I will link up with them in Arden City."

He nodded at Philips, "Come on," and staggered out into the corridor.

Flapping the file again, Philips said, "I've got something to show you."

"Later," Wren snapped. "I said, come on."

Philips shrugged and pushed the file into one of his pockets.

~*~

"Where are we going?" Philips said.

"We're going to drop in on Vlad Pen," Wren replied. He

added, "His son, Alain joined the junior Black-Clads last year -
He recently submitted a report suggesting his father was plotting against the state."

Despite his gangland background Philips was still shocked,
"You mean he reported his own father? He grassed up his own
Dad?"

Noting the disapproval in Philip's tone, Wren said, "He's a
keen company man—or should I say, boy, don't knock it, that's
who we work for now, snitching is now considered a virtue."

Philips glanced back at the two other air-cars that were following them. As they were carrying a SWAT team, the Lance
Corporal said, "Why are we going in mob-handed?"

"Like I just said, Alain suggested his father was plotting
against the state; we can't take chances."

A few seconds later, Wren's air-car joined the L14 before
turning off towards Loxley Grange with the SWAT team not
far behind. As the air-cars moved in fast, sirens wailing, Philips
glanced out. Loxley Grange was typical of most of the com-
pany-built housing estates on Arden; it had no architectural
merit. Although the area was protected from Arden's airless
desert surface by a powerful Mannheim shield, inside it was
a cramped utilitarian jungle designed to house the masses at
minimum land take and minimum cost.

As they began weaving though the estate, Philips noted
that curtains were closing; it was obvious the local populous
had heard the sirens. As rubbernecking was discouraged, the
whole estate had decided to opt-out.

Once the air-cars landed, the SWAT team rushed towards
Pen's house. Getting no reply, they smashed open the front and
back doors simultaneously and barged in, guns levelled. After
a few minutes elapsed one of the SWAT team walked out and
told Wren that the house was empty. He said, "I think there is
something you should see though."

Climbing out, Wren walked toward the house with Philips
close behind. The SWAT leader took Wren into a room with a
sign on the door which read, "Alain's Room. Keep Out. On pain

of death."

Once inside, the SWAT leader pointed at a glowing power bubble floating in one corner of the room. The message in the bubble was brutal, "My father is a traitor."

The SWAT leader then said, "We also found these notes lying on the desk."

After swiftly reading them, Wren swore, "It looks like they've had this planned, like the director, they've done a bunk."

He found a percom number. Although it was a long shot, he instructed his percom to connect. When nothing happened, Wren let out a sigh and went to cut the link, but at that instant, another power bubble formed with a grainy image inside. "This is Alain Pen, tell Jon Vass, my leader, that I've been kidnapped; forced to leave against my will."

Wren said, "Where are you?"

"I don't know," Alain Pen said. "They've got me locked up like a criminal."

"Then how come they didn't take away your percom?" Wren asked.

Alain Pen's blurred mouth twisted into smugness. "I was given an emergency percom in case my parents confiscated mine. It's very thin," Alain explained. "I managed to hide it in my sock, and they didn't find it."

"Who's they?"

"Ord Morley and my parents," Alain said. "But there are a lot of people with them."

"Give me their names," Wren snapped.

Alain immediately rattled off a list of names. As he did so, Wren began mentally ticking them off against his list and realised he was wasting his time; Morley had managed to evacuate them all. Alain said, "I'm sure the escape was organised by Mick Tarmy."

"Organised by Mick Tarmy? Are you sure?"

"I bugged my parent's bedroom," Alain replied. "I heard them talking. Tarmy sent Ord Morley money cards to finance the escape." He then added, a bitter tone entering his voice, "I passed all my information to Jon Vass, my leader but he ignored it; he said I was making it up; he didn't stop them escaping."

After making a mental note to interview Jon Vass, Wren said, "This Mick Tarmy. D'you you know him?"

"Yeah," Alain replied. "He was one of my Dad's friends."

"So, you're sure that Mick Tarmy was behind the escape?" Wren said.

"Yes," Alain confirmed. Then the image in the bubble evaporated.

While Wren was still trying to reconnect, his percom sounded again, and Samantha's face appeared. "What's going on Wren? I have been told Alton Mygael shot you."

"That is correct ma'am," Wren replied. As he had no desire to admit that the operation had already gone pear-shaped, he changed the subject. "We are attempting to make arrests, ma'am."

"Did he sign the arrest warrant?"

"Yes, ma'am," Wren replied. "As I said, we are in the process of making arrests."

Samantha immediately came back with, "Two bodies have been found at the Pearl Crater air-lock; it might be connected with your operation; I suggest you get out there fast."

~*~

A Black-Clad Private pulled a blanket back and let Wren look at the first body. While he was staring down, the Private said, "There's another body over here too, sir."

Instead of moving towards the second body, Wren pointed and said, "He's still wearing his helmet camera. We need to look at it."

Tam Philips pulled rank, "Head camera, Private."

The Black-Clad stooped, removed the helmet camera and passed it to Wren who turned it over in his hands, noticing that the camera had an additional transponder wrapped around it.

"Let me see the other guy's helmet camera."

Once it was retrieved, Wren found it also had an additional transponder fixed to it. The discovery confirmed his original assessment. The Black-Clad patrol should have comprised of four people, but two of them had been shirking, swinging the lead. Instead of going on duty, they had given their transponders to the two who had gone on patrol. To anyone in the control room, it would have looked as if there were four people on patrol, but in reality, there were only two.

Wren assessed the situation; although most Black-Clad units were generally well-led, there were some rogue units. The less conscientious elements thought nothing of dodging a shift or leaving their posts early if they thought they wouldn't be missed. It was evident that this group were in the habit of handing their transponders over to their colleagues and taking it in turns to dodge shifts. It also stood to reason that if certain groups were lax, no one was likely to investigate a missing person report in case they embarrassed someone who'd gone home early.

Glancing at the Black-Clad Private's headset, he noticed that he also had an additional transponder and Wren realised the scam was taking place on every shift. Tempting though it was to vent his anger on the Black-Clad Private, Wren made a mental note to report it later, and to concentrate on the first helmet camera.

Setting it to play mode, he looked at the images it had captured and swiftly realised that there had been several vehicles in the air-lock at the time of the killings.

Flipping to magnify, Wren stared hard at the images. Within seconds, he recognised two of the men inside one vehicle; one was Ord Morley, the other was Ben Lieges, two of the people that Samantha wanted to have arrested. After examining the camera again, a date and time display flashed up.

Wren let out a sigh of displeasure and glared at the Private.

"According to this recording, these guards must have died nine hours ago. Nine hours is a long time. When were the bodies discovered?"

"About an hour ago, sir," the Black-Clad admitted.

"So, eight hours elapsed between death and discovery," Wren said. "Who discovered the bodies?"

"We did, sir," the Black-clad replied, nodding towards a second man. "But we'd only just come on duty. When we were partway through our patrol, we came upon them, and we immediately notified HQ."

Wren was tempted to vent his spleen on the unfortunate man but changed his mind. In hindsight, it was obvious that Alton Mygael knew about the escape plan. As the director had sucker-shot Philips and him, who was he to criticise?

Instead, he said, "Did you notify the police?"

"No, sir."

Reaching for his percom, he added, "Do you want me to contact them?"

"No, no. You did the right thing," Wren replied. "The police may have medical examiners to advise them, but in this case, the cause of death is obvious. They were shot. So, we don't need their help. We will conduct our own investigations, understood?"

When the Black-Clad looked uncertain, Wren said, "In case you haven't realised, the civil police don't like us one iota. The way they see it, the company police are impinging on their territory. Given the opportunity, they'd have us disbanded. If we tell them about the killings, they will just laugh their heads off. So, we don't want the police involved. Understood?"

When the Black-Clad nodded, Wren went back to his original observation, "So, no one realised they were missing for eight hours."

The Black-Clad nodded, "Looks that way, sir."

Passing the head camera to Philips, Wren began examining the first corpse more closely, searching for information. As the man's uniform was badly burnt, it was obvious that standard pulse weapons hadn't killed him.

Going through the same procedure with the second corpse and finding similar burns, Wren concluded something powerful had attacked them; a military droid perhaps.

Transferring his gaze to the air-lock Wren tried to visualise what had preceded the murderous attack. Why had the two deceased Black-Clads tried to stop Ord Morley leaving? As he hadn't activated the director's warrant, how would they have known to stop Morley and the others?

His thoughts turned to Samantha, and he realised that she had pre-empted the warrant and ordered that all exits from Arden were to be closely monitored.

Going back to his observations, he noticed pulse marks on the air-lock vision tunnel. He concluded that the two dead men must have recognised Ord Morley and Ben Lieges and fired at the airlock in an attempt to prevent Morley's group escaping.

He thought about the group he'd sent to Bull Crater. Realising they were wasting their time, he sent them a message. A few seconds later, the image of a Black-Clad Leader appeared in a power bubble. "I was just about to contact you, sir. No sign of the director or the Morley party arriving at their hotels."

"They never went to Bull Crater. So, come back."

Hearing a sound behind him, Wren turned and saw that a human technician accompanied by two droids had appeared and had started to check the air-lock.

Wren snapped, "What are you doing?"

"We've had a report that an air-lock is damaged," the technician replied.

"Who reported the damage?"

Pointing at the air-lock, the technician said, "That thing is covered in sensors. We knew something was wrong because the sensors reported a fault."

"And how long ago was that?"

"About eight hours ago."

Although the statement confirmed what Wren had already

worked out, he was still horrified, "So, you haven't bothered to check out a damaged air-lock until now?"

"There's no danger," the technician said with a blasé tone in his voice. "The outer door is sealed, and the lock taken out of service. If anyone wants to go to Pearl Crater, there are other air-locks further down the Mannheim."

"Pearl Crater, what's at Pearl Crater?"

The technician half smiled, "You must be new around here. Every year we get hundreds of tourists going to Pearl to teleport up to The Wreck."

"Pearl Crater has its own teleport?"

"Sure, it's been there for a few years now. Like I said, hundreds of people teleport to The Wreck every year."

Wren had an epiphany; Ord Morley and the others had used the Pearl Crater teleport to escape from Arden. There was also a strong chance that Alton Mygael had gone with them. He thought about the weak signal and message he'd had from Alain Pen. The evidence all pointed one way: Ord Morley and his group were now somewhere in deep space.

After telling the Black-Clad to organise the removal of the bodies, Wren ordered the air-lock technician to wait until they'd gone. He gestured to Philips, and they went back to their air-car. Once inside, Wren went very quiet. Eventually, he said, "You do realise that Samantha will go ballistic when she finds out."

"Yeah," Philips agreed. He pulled Alton Mygael's file out of his pocket. He said, "Before you do anything you might regret, you might like to have a look at this."

As Wren began flicking through the pages, he gave Philips a sharp look, "Why didn't you show me this earlier."

"I tried, but you weren't interested. Can I also remind you that you promised to find us a way of getting out of this madhouse?"

"Yes, I did."

"Well, we've now got to find a way out," Philips replied. "If that file is anything to go by, we'll wind up dead if we don't leave here fast. Are we going to accept Alton Mygael's offer?"

Although Philips was usually unflappable, Wren detected a distinct note of panic in his tone and concluded the events of the last few hours were beginning to wear him down. "Maybe; all we can do is go to Pearl Crater and assess the situation."

With that, Wren spoke to the air-car's computer and instructed it to take them to Pearl Crater. The machine rose into the air and moved into position behind the damaged air-lock. Realising they had a problem, Philips buzzed down a window and called out to the air-lock technician who was just lounging about waiting for the bodies to be removed. "We need to get to Pearl Crater. Where's the next nearest working air-lock?"

The technician gave him the answer without even looking at his computer, and after giving the machine its new co-ordinates, the air-car set off towards the new destination. Once they'd joined the queue, Wren thought about Morley's escape. If his theory was correct, the Morley group had been discovered, but before the two Black-Clads could report the attempted escape, a military droid had killed them.

Eventually, the air-car moved into the air-lock and once again, Wren couldn't help but wonder how Ord Morley must have felt. He'd been trapped in the air-lock, and there could have been little doubt he would have been captured if the unknown droid hadn't intervened.

While he was still staring out, thinking about Morley's escape, a Black-Clad Sergeant appeared and stared in. Philip's face registered panic, but Wren glared at him and snapped, "We're in uniform, and I outrank him. Stop looking guilty. Keep calm, and everything will be okay."

Despite his admonishment, a sense of déjà vu swept over Wren and he mentally cursed. But, just as he thought that fate had conspired against him, the Sergeant caught a glimpse of Wren's double oak leaves, stepped back, and saluted. Once Wren had returned the salute, the other man retreated.

"That was close," Philips said between gritted teeth.

Wren gave him an icy look. "Get a grip; we're in uniform. As far as anyone is concerned, we are still on Samantha's payroll chasing felons, not planning to do a bunk if we get half a chance."

After what seemed like an eternity, the air-lock opened, and the air-car began moving out across Arden's crater pocked surface.

Thirty minutes later, a sign in what looked like the middle of nowhere loomed up; one that indicated that the area belonged to the Salus System Interplanetary Archaeological Trust. After another five minutes, the Pearl Crater Mannheim appeared on the horizon, but Wren remained silent wondering what was going to happen when they reached their destination.

Once through the next air-lock, the air-car asked for instructions. Wren told the machine to park close to the teleport centre, and it began weaved its way around the small settlement before descending into an underground parking area below a nondescript office block. Glancing around, Wren realised the air-car had parked in the teleport centre, and he saw direction signs.

"What now?"

"We'll just have to play it by ear."

As they were travelling light, Wren told Philips to grab his belongings and instructed the air-car to park up. Following the signs, they took a lift to the teleport. Wren placed himself in Morley's shoes again; would he have felt the same strange expectancy, hoping he would but fearing he wouldn't escape from Samantha's grasp?

Once they were at the top, an Alpha 300 appeared. "Are you the Wren group?"

Taken by surprise, Wren didn't answer, but Philips jumped in. "Yeah. That's us."

Alpha said, "IDs, please."

When Wren and Philips presented their documents, the machine said, "I have a message for you."

It created a power bubble, and Alton Mygael's masked face appeared. A small box at the bottom indicated it was a recording.

"Firstly, I would like to apologise to you both for shooting you. With luck, you will have read my file and will realise that throwing your lot in with Samantha would be rather foolish."

The image made a slight shrug, "On the other hand maybe your loyalties are not with me. If they are not, please leave."

As the power bubble collapsed the Alpha 300 moved in front of them and said, "Will you be joining the director?"

Without waiting for Wren's approval, Philips said, "I will."

The machine extended one of its flexible arms, "Then I must take your gun. We will return it once you arrive."

Philips glanced at Wren. In answer, Wren gave his gun to the machine and said, "We will both be joining the director."

The machine presented them with two separate documents which had Zadernaster runes in various locations. Without needing to be told, both men realised what was happening. They were being asked for a reaffirmation of old loyalties, ones that had existed before they even thought about joining the Black-Clads.

Once Wren had signed, Philips followed suit.

After collecting the oaths of loyalty, the Alpha 300 waved a flexible arm towards what looked like a stage and told them to walk onto it. Ten seconds later Wren and Philips disappeared.

~*~

When Wren arrived, he felt distinctly unwell, but instead of admitting his weakness, he kept a straight face and did his best not to sway. Alton Mygael immediately came out of the shadows and extended a hand. "I'm glad you boys could make it."

He waved towards a woman standing nearby, "This is Klaien, my partner."

Gesturing towards two men, "This is Mih Valanson and this

in Hen Jameson; they teleported down with me a few hours ago."

Wren glanced at Klaien, Jameson and Valanson. Obviously fashion-conscious, Klaien looked overdressed for the occasion. In contrast, Jameson was casual, but Wren guessed his clothing was designed to support his cover story, a holiday at Bull Crater. He then assessed Mih Valanson.

As the technician had muscles that looked like knotted cotton, he didn't consider him a threat. On the other hand, the small stun pistol that Alton Mygael was holding in his right hand most certainly was. In all probability, it was the same gun he'd used on them in his office.

Noting Wren's look of disapproval, Mygael said, "Can I take it that you two will be on your best behaviour? We need to chat. Once we have, if you decide you don't want to help me, I won't hold you to your oaths, and you can teleport back to Arden."

When Wren nodded, Mygael slipped the stun gun into one of his pockets and ushered both the newcomers into a side room. He pointed at the bench seating running around the room, "Teleporting affects people in different ways, feel free to lie down."

When Philips gave him a pleading look, Wren slumped down, and Philips swiftly followed suit. Although Wren still felt groggy, he said, "Why have you done this?"

"Done what? Brought you back here?"

"Yes"

"A little bird told me that you wanted out."

"Let me guess," Wren replied, "Charles Limpum?"

"No, it wasn't Limpum."

"So, who was it?"

"Henry told me," Mygael replied, "The spettro."

When Wren frowned, Mygael added, "I was surprised to discover that Limpum allowed Henry to read your mind. Henry can get very naughty when he mind-links with someone new."

"Limpum was as high as a kite on Zuka milk at the time,"

Wren replied. "I never mentioned wanting out, as you put it, to Henry. I wouldn't have done, certainly not with Limpum listening in."

"You didn't need to," Mygael said. "You let Henry into your mind, and he immediately started delving. His mind doesn't always process everything it finds immediately; I have no doubt he analysed some of your inner secrets long after you left. He picked up on your concerns about Samantha. I gather that you weren't enamoured that she used you as live bait?"

As the expression 'live bait' was one of his, Wren did not doubt that Mygael was telling the truth. Henry had delved deep in a very short space of time.

Mygael added, "Non-military Droids are supposed to value all life of all sorts, human, animal or plant. Samantha doesn't."

"That's obvious," Wren replied.

"She also shakes." Philips cut in, "I didn't think droids were supposed to get angry."

"They aren't," Mygael said. "Neither are they supposed to lust for power."

Bringing the conversation back on course, Wren said, "Why did Henry tell you about me?"

"Before I teleported down here, I used to visit Henry when Limpum wasn't around. Henry is very lonely in solitary confinement. I became his father-confessor. He's told me things that he wouldn't tell anyone else."

Wren's cynical side emerged, "So you were happy to let Limpum be bad cop to your good cop?"

"Not really; as I said, I felt sorry for Henry," Mygael replied. "Henry's scared he'll be culled. Limpum and Samantha threaten him with the cull anytime they think he's holding something back."

"You still haven't answered the question," Wren said. "Why have you brought us out?"

"Us Zadernaster Boys should stick together," Mygael said. "Besides, if Tarmy is alive, I think he'll come here, and if he does, we'll need to protect him."

"Where's here?"

"Awis Oasis."

"Why should he come to the Awis Oasis?"

"As remaining in the Fyfield Valley would hardly be sensible, he has four options," Mygael said. "He could go back to Fort Saunders, downriver towards the Compass Islands, head south towards New Victoria or come to Awis Oasis. As he has assumed the identity of a known terrorist, he'd be arrested if he went to any of the first three destinations. Simple logic says he'll head here if he can."

"And why is Tarmy so important?"

"Because of what he knows," Mygael said. "Although I talked to Tarmy initially, Samantha made a whole series of decisions that I knew nothing about. If we threaten to send his testimony to the Interplanetary Police, the hawks on the Minton Board would be arrested. But it won't happen, they'll be allowed to resign and most of them will. Before they go the hawks will be asked to also agree to get rid of Samantha."

"Hawks?"

"As in hawks and doves," Mygael replied. "There are several hawks on the board. It was their idea to saddle me with Samantha; she was their spy in my camp."

"So, Samantha goes, and the hawks go," Wren said. "Then what?"

"As part of the deal, we will all return to Arden," Mygael replied.

Wren glanced at Philips. "That sounds all very cosy for you. But you will haven't said why you invited us along?"

Mygael smiled, "I have. As I said, us Zadernaster boys must stick together."

CHAPTER EIGHT

Fyfield Valley, Arcadia

On the river island

"Are you awake?" It was Nonie Tomio's voice. When his eyes fluttered open, she said, "I've been worried about you. You've been unconscious for a long time."

Tarmy turned his head in the direction of her voice. He could barely see her face.

"Why's it so dark?"

"Night has fallen," she explained. "We're only using minimum lighting to save power. The solar panels don't charge the batteries at night."

A moment later, a small light came on, "Is that better?"

Tarmy nodded and ran an appraising eye over her, "Why are you wearing that hat?"

"Because you told us to," Nonie replied, picking up another hat and placing it on his head. "According to you, the hats stop the Great Ones from reading our minds."

When Tarmy frowned, Nonie added, "The Great Ones? Surely you haven't forgotten the Great Ones?"

Tarmy shook his head, "To be honest, my mind seems like a blank; I can't remember very much."

"But you know who I am?"

He nodded. "You're Nonie Tomio. How could I forget you? You looked after me when I was beaten up at Fort Saunders, and it's obvious you're looking after me now." He opened his mouth as if he was going to say something else, but nothing came out. Instead, he reached out and gave one of her hands a slight squeeze.

Ignoring the intimacy, Nonie said, "Do you remember the Great Ones killing the spettro, the one you called Irrelevant? He was killed by a plesiosaur. Then the ogre, the head thing attacked us."

When a slight glimmer of understanding appeared on his face, Nonie added, "The Great Ones used some sort of gas against us."

"Gas! I remember that. We were shooting at that ogre, the head thing. Then it exploded, and then there was all that gas."

He squeezed Nonie's hand again. "Are *you* okay?"

She smiled, "I was lucky; I was standing further up the beach than you. Lascaux Kurgan realised what was happening and told us to get into the air-car. We dived in and slammed the doors shut just before the cloud could get to us. If we hadn't dived for cover, I think most of the team would be dead. And because some of us weren't affected, we've been able to look after everybody else until we were relieved when the boats came back."

"You said that Lascaux told you to get into the air-car. Was there anyone else?"

"Chou Lan."

"What about Claire?"

"We found her with you up on the ridge."

He frowned, "What ridge?"

"There's a ridge running down the island," Nonie reminded him. "God knows how both of you ended up there."

"How is Claire?"

"She's still unconscious but recovering," Nonie replied. "Ed Pushley and a few others are in the same condition."

Memories returned. "I thought Ed Pushley was in the air-car."

"He was unlucky as usual," Nonie said. "He decided to climb out just before the ogre exploded. He was too far from the air-car to get back in quickly enough. The gas cloud took him down."

"Did it kill anyone?"

"No," Nonie said. "We were lucky. I think the gas was supposed to kill us, but the ogre exploded too far out, and the wind carried most of the toxins away."

"There's one mystery that we can't work out though. How you and Claire managed to scale that ridge when everyone else collapsed when the gas cloud swept in."

When Tarmy did not attempt to answer, she added, "You had one of these stuck in your thigh. Claire had one too."

Nonie held an object up, and Tarmy immediately recognised the device. It was a CANA, an auto-injector containing a nerve agent antidote. He then remembered the pain in his leg and guessed that Alex must have carried emergency serum and had given him an injection. "Claire had one in her too."

"Yeah," Nonie replied. "But she wasn't quite as lucky as you. Hers didn't fully discharge."

"She will be okay though?"

"I'm hoping she'll pull through."

"Can I see her?"

"Later," Nonie promised, "but not yet."

Thinking about what she'd told him for a few seconds, Tarmy began to dwell on the exploding ogre head, and he remembered it wasn't the first one he'd seen. The first one had been one in the survivor tower. It had disappeared when the bomb struck its target. Why hadn't that ogre exploded too? Had the Great Ones bred different types of ogres to suit their purposes?

He began re-assessing the strange thoughts that had flooded through his mind just before Irrelevant died. At the time, most of the mental imagery had not made much sense. But now, some of the images had had a chance to coalesce.

If he'd interpreted the ogre's thought messages correctly, the second bomb had done its evil work. Three Great Ones had died, and one badly injured.

Observing the long silence, Nonie misread his thoughts and

squeezed his hand. "Claire's going to be okay."

"I hope so. Where am I?"

"You're in a cabin on one of the dive boats."

As it was evident that Tarmy was still having difficulty recovering his memory, Nonie added, "The dive boats are moored up alongside the river island, the one that Irrelevant brought the hostages to."

"I remember the boats setting off downriver," Tarmy said. "Why did they come back?"

"The Great Ones have blockaded the river lower downstream," Nonie replied, "They also brought in hundreds of Arcadian millipedes to patrol the blockades, so breaking through wasn't possible. If they had attempted a breakout, the millipedes would have sprayed them with that deadly venom they have, so the boats had no choice but to turn back."

"Are we trapped?"

"Yes," Nonie replied, "They've also thrown another blockade upstream too. They have got us sandwiched in the middle."

Tarmy frowned, "You seem very calm about all this."

Nonie shook her head, "I'm not at all, but I don't see any point in worrying. The only thing I don't understand is why they haven't attacked us. Other than building the blockades, the Great Ones haven't done much since the ogre was destroyed."

More implanted memories resurfaced, and Tarmy said, "The Great Ones haven't attacked us because they're mourning. When one of the Great Ones dies, they have to carry out certain rituals; I'm not sure how long the mourning process will take, but once it's over, they will attack again."

"As they're hard-hearted bastards, I doubt if they will mourn for long."

Nonie looked surprised, "Mourning; what for?"

"When the bomb went off, it killed three of the Great Ones, and badly injured another."

"Did you say bomb? What bomb?"

Although Tarmy's recollections were still vague, he remembered the salient issues, "The bomb was Samantha's doing. It was a reprisal."

"Who's Samantha?"

Tarmy's mind latched onto old memories again, "Samantha is a droid, an Ingermann-Verex R9054 humanoid to be exact. She's also the deputy director of security at the Minton Mining Company."

Before Nonie could ask any more questions, Tarmy said, "So, the Great Ones are in mourning. At least it will give us time to recover. What about food and supplies?"

"We won't starve. We've got supplies, and there are plenty of fish in the river. One of the plesiosaurs sometimes tries to steal our fish or attack people on deck, but we just drive it off."

Glancing around again, Tarmy noticed he was hitched up to a drip. "Did you do this?"

Tomio nodded, "When you're an archaeologist working out in the back of nowhere, you are given basic medical training. There are emergency medical supplies on these boats. I've been feeding you and some of the others intravenously, I have also been giving you LEDs, life extension drugs, to speed your recovery."

The comment gave Tarmy's memory another kick; he'd been given LEDs before but by whom? A moment later, Samantha's image appeared in his mind, and he remembered how the scheming droid had blackmailed him into coming to Arcadia. He then remembered she'd ordered the bombing of the Great Ones.

As more and more memories came flooding back, he said, "How long have I been unconscious?"

"You've woken a few times but then gone back into a coma."

"How long overall?"

"A full Arcadian day."

"You're joking?"

Nonie shook her head, "As I said before, I have been very worried about you."

So you think you have a great driving instructor!

AN INSIGHT TO DRIVE

L P

How to pass your driving test and
learn to drive at the same time

KATHY HIGGINS

AN INSIGHT TO DRIVE

The MUST read for anyone involved in learning to drive, teaching driving or looking at how to improve. All the information you need at your fingertips to make an informed choice on how best to learn, who to learn with, how to pass your driving test and what happens next.

Find out the stuff driving instructors DON'T WANT YOU TO KNOW, or the simple mistakes some of them make, which can make your learning time longer and more expensive.

Explore a whole host of myths and legends about driving and the test, and of course, no book would be complete without some funny stories.

Driving instructors this is the book for you so that your learners know they are in good hands, or it might just show you what mistakes to avoid, that simply damage your business.

Written by a multi-award-winning Driving Consultant and Instructor of over 20 years.

Kathy Higgins.Dip DI, F Inst MTD

www.insight2drive.co.uk

Published byBook Bubble Press
www.bookbubblepress.com

Jacket image by
Maria Rossi Photography

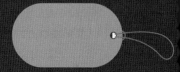

Tarmy's mind began to whirl. An Arcadian day was roughly three standard days in length. "So, nothing has happened while I've been out for the count?"

"No, since we destroyed the ogre, they have left us alone."

Despite her reassurances, Tarmy pushed the blankets back and attempted to swing his legs out. Nonie looked alarmed, "You can't get up. You're not well."

"If we just sit back and do nothing, the Great One will either kill us all or take us prisoner again," Tarmy replied. "This has given us breathing space. We have to take advantage of it, we've got to get ready."

Nonie replaced a restraining hand on one of his shoulders, "If you are determined to get up, I will need to disconnect your drip and catheter, and you must eat something first."

At the suggestion of food, Tarmy's stomach rumbled ominously, "Yeah, I guess I could do with something to eat."

After swiftly removing his encumbrances, Nonie pushed him back onto the bed then moved towards a cramped galley and began preparing food. While she was working, his brain started to whirr. If the Great Ones decided to attack again, what would be the best means of defence?

When Nonie returned with a bowl of soup, he began eating and thinking, "So, now I've recovered, how many of us are capable of fighting?"

Nonie did a mental headcount. "Fourteen. Some are archaeologists who came back with the boats, and you, me, Lascaux Kurgan and Chou Lan."

Pushing the bowl away, Tarmy said, "I'm going upstairs."

"Be careful. Take a gun with you. There are some on the rack and don't forget the plesiosaur; it might try to attack you."

After pulling a gun out of the rack, Tarmy hauled his unwilling body up the narrow stairs to the main deck and began glancing around.

With both Arden, Arcadia's natural moon and The Wreck high in the night sky, their combined light made it possible to see most of the sluggish Fyfield River. He could also make out the heavily forested banks. Then his eyes latched onto a pinpoint of light, which he guessed had to be coming from Cittavecchia.

While he was still staring at the light, he heard a slight swish. By instinct more than thought, he dropped to the deck just before a huge head swept over him. Then despite several days in bed, he rolled sideways out of reach of the plesiosaur.

While he was still scrabbling for his gun, someone else started shooting. Three shots later, the plesiosaur let out a squeal of pain and disappeared from view. Lascaux Kurgan and Chou Lan came loping down from the ridge and cut across a gangplank brandishing pulse rifles.

After ordering Lan to stand guard in case the plesiosaur renewed its attack, Lascaux came over and helped Tarmy to his feet. "You owe me twice now, Mick."

"Twice?"

"It was me who found you after the gas attack," she said. "And I've just saved you from being eaten by the plesiosaur."

"In that case, thank you," he said. "How are things?"

"Not good."

"What do you mean?"

Lascaux said, "Are you feeling fit enough to climb?"

When Tarmy nodded, she led the way back across the gangplank and climbed up the ridge before wriggling her way into the thick Arcadian bluegrass at the top. As Tarmy moved in alongside her, he remembered the attack on Irrelevant.

"Oh!" he said, realising that boats and the air-cars were on the far side of the island, hidden behind the central ridge.

Lascaux said, "I moved things around a bit because snipers kept on taking pot shots at us."

"Although we must be at least six hundred metres away, I thought we were only asking for trouble if we stayed where we were."

"Smart move," Tarmy replied.

"Not really," Lascaux replied. "Just common sense. After they'd shot at us a dozen times, I realised we were guaranteed to take some injuries if we stayed where we were."

"I see you've moved Irrelevant's air-car as well."

"It had a voice-activated ignition," Lascaux replied. "But I overrode it."

She handed him a set of night sights, "Want to have a look?"

As he took them from her and began scanning the surrounding forests, Lascaux said, "There's something I want to ask you. When the ogre, the head thing, was approaching, our guns were virtually useless against it. Then there was a blinding flash, two in fact and the ogre evaporated. Do you remember that?"

When Mick didn't respond, she added, "The strange thing was, and I still can't work it out, I found you and Claire on the top of this ridge. More or less where you are lying now, in fact."

"And why is that strange?"

"The side of the ridge near the beach is vertical and nearly five metres high. But you and Claire both managed to scale it after being engulfed in gas. Everyone else collapsed within seconds."

When Tarmy didn't comment, Lascaux added, "Both you and Claire had marks on your clothes that suggested something had grabbed hold of you and carried you up there."

Her final comment reminded Tarmy of his last conscious thoughts after the gas had hit him. He remembered being lifted off the beach by Alex and the strange dream he'd had of his daughter saying, "I need your help, Dad."

The last conversation he'd had with Alex jumped into his head, *"I need you to go to Arden as we agreed."*

"You are not well - You could die."

"Go now! Now! My daughter and my friends are in danger - You must make sure they're all safe."

As his memories came flooding back, Tarmy swore. Sending Alex away meant that defending the island would be even more difficult.

"What's up?"

As Lascaux was unaware that Alex existed, despite the fact

she'd been alluding to an unseen force, instead of admitting to what he'd done, Tarmy said, "Very shortly the Great Ones are going to attack. We have to work out how we can make sure we're not over-run."

"That might be more difficult than you think," Lascaux said and pointed upriver towards one of the other islands. After training the night sights on the island, Tarmy began to pick up images of Longjaws, the deformed humanoids that fought and laboured for the Great Ones. He could also make out millipedes hiding amongst the trees. He then saw a pontoon bridge connecting the island to both river banks.

While he was still assessing the pontoons, a large group of millipedes began moving across the pontoon bridge to reinforce the forces already on the island. Lascaux said, "They have taken the island and blockaded the river so we can't escape upstream."

She pointed to an island further down, and Tarmy realised the Great ones had constructed a similar blockade there too.

Lascaux said, "We're trapped."

She pointed at the bright light he'd noted when he'd first come on deck. "We also have another problem. Have a look what *they're* doing over there."

Adjusting the night sights again, he began picking up images of more Longjaws. They appeared to be building something with logs.

Lascaux said, "They're building rafts. When they have finished, they will invade this island. I guess that they'll probably wait until another thick fog covers the river, so we won't see them approaching. Fog or not, when they do come, we can either stand and fight or take to the boats. If we take to the boats, my guess is that they'll gradually box us in. It doesn't look good."

Staring at the rafts, Tarmy wondered why the Great Ones were adopting such a primitive approach. They had been using air-cars, so why had they suddenly abandoned them?"

He thought about Alex; their loyal TK5 had destroyed at

least ten of the Great One's air-cars, and they'd captured two air-cars. As the Great Ones were probably unaware that Alex had been sent to Arden, they assumed he was still a force to be reckoned with. As their air-power had failed, they were now going back to basics, and as they had an infinite supply of raw materials and a massive army to call upon, they could afford to lose personnel. More importantly, they were prepared to squander lives.

Conversely, Tarmy had very few on his side, and he didn't want to lose anyone if it could be avoided. He began mentally kicking himself again. If Alex had carried out his orders, the small machine might not return for days. Worse, if he became involved in a firefight, he might not return at all.

Lascaux mirrored his thoughts, "Let's hope your invisible droid comes back before it's too late."

"What invisible droid?"

"When we were escaping from Cittavecchia, something very powerful began blasting at the ugly bitches who invaded," Lascaux said. "Then, when we came out to this island, you were following something. Whatever it was also blasted the ogre, it then dumped you and Claire on top of the ridge."

"Do you want your detective badge now or later?" Tarmy grumbled.

"So where is your droid?"

"What makes you think it's missing."

"Because from time to time I've seen a strange shadow floating over your head," Lascaux replied. "And I can't see it now. Also, the way you've been acting. If you knew where the droid was, you wouldn't be worried about the Great Ones. You just get it to blast its way out of here, wouldn't you?"

Tarmy said, "Alex will be back shortly."

"I hope you're right.

~*~

"So, how is she?"

"Different," Nonie replied.

Tarmy frowned, "What's that meant to mean?"

"She's changed," Nonie replied. "It started about twenty minutes ago. If I hadn't seen it happening with my own eyes, I wouldn't have believed it."

She then turned on a small LED lamp and moved it close to Claire Hyndman. Although Tarmy knew that Claire could face change, he still let out a slight gasp. "Did you dye her hair?"

"I most certainly didn't," Nonie snapped. "I've got my hands full as it is. I haven't got time to do things like that. What's going on?"

Picking up the lamp, Tarmy moved it closer to Claire. Her hair had been blonde, but it was now copper. After moving the lamp closer, Tarmy realised that her skin was a lot paler than he remembered. As her eyes were also slightly open, he could also see that her irises were no longer blue; they were amber.

Eventually, he said, "One thing's for certain, it suits her."

"Stop being obtuse, Mick," Nonie snapped. "What's going on?"

Tarmy shrugged, "I don't know for certain. I know she can face change."

Nonie gave him a disbelieving look, "That's not possible."

Tarmy shrugged, "If you say so. All I know is I saw her when she'd changed herself into a Longjaw."

"What d'you mean? Have you seen her do this sort of thing before?"

"Yeah," Tarmy replied.

Nonie frowned, "You seem to be taking this all very casually."

"That's because I've already seen it happen and have asked the same questions as you have," Tarmy replied.

"But you're okay with it?"

"No, I'm not. It worries me, but I don't have any answers." He changed the subject. "How is she medically?"

"She's stable," Nonie replied. "But I don't expect her to come out of the coma just yet."

"It doesn't make much sense. I'm okay. Why hasn't she come around?"

"I told you," Nonie replied. "Her CANA didn't fully discharge."

Taking hold of one of Claire's hands and squeezing it, Tarmy moved back slightly and then glanced at Ed Pushley who was lying in a nearby bunk. Although he was tempted to challenge the other man's presence in the same room as Claire, he let it go. As bed space was at a premium, objecting to it wouldn't help matters. Instead, he said, "How's he?"

"Still in a coma," Nonie replied.

~*~

An hour after Tarmy left, Ed Pushley said, "Dove sono?"

Nonie Tomio's forehead wrinkled, and she glanced at Chou Lan, "Did that make any sense to you?"

Chou shrugged, "Dunno. I think he's speaking an Ab language."

"Cosa sta succedendo?"

"Why's he taking in Ab?".

"I've no idea," Chou replied. "Maybe the gas has affected his mind."

"Dove sono?"

"I don't understand Ed," Nonie said.

Pushley turned to face her, "Nonie!"

"Yes, Ed, it's Nonie."

"Dove sono, Nonie?"

Chou had a flash of brilliance, "I think he wants to know where he is."

"You're safe," Nonie assured him. "You're on one of the dive boats."

Pushley blinked a few times and spoke again, this time no longer in Ab. "Dive boats?"

Sensing he'd returned to normal, Nonie started to explain the situation.

Interrupting her, Pushley said, "Gas attack?"

"Yes," Nonie confirmed. "There was a gas attack, but you're safe here."

Blinking owlishly a few times more, Pushley levered himself up onto one elbow and looked around the cramped room. He noticed Claire Hyndman lying in the next bunk, "Who's that? I've not seen her before."

"Never you mind," Nonie replied.

As she hadn't sated his curiosity, Pushley grabbed at the bedside notes before Nonie could react. Swiftly reading them, he glanced back disbelievingly, "It says this is Claire Hyndman, but she looks nothing like Claire."

Nonie snatched her notes back. "The gas has had a bad effect on some people."

"I wouldn't have thought the gas would have caused her to change like that," Pushley replied disbelievingly. "But, thinking about it, I've seen something like this before."

"Care to share?"

"She could be a monarch," Pushley speculated.

Nonie's forehead wrinkled, "Doesn't that mean she's some sort of royalty?"

"No," Pushley said scathingly, the master speaking to his imbecile assistant, "Monarch is a military term, a code name. As Arcresten is only a few hundred kilometres from here, she probably came from there."

Annoyed by the tone of his voice, Nonie snapped, "What are you talking about Pushley?"

"I mean what I just said," Pushley replied. "She's probably not Claire Hyndman. More than likely she's an imposter."

"Nonsense! I've known Claire for years."

"And may I remind you," Pushley replied. "Claire disappeared for a long time. When she came back, you said she'd changed."

Although she knew that Pushley's memory of events wasn't too far off the mark, out of loyalty, Nonie said, "You're talking squit, Ed."

Nettled, Pushley attempted to pull rank, "Hey! I'm both your superior and your commune leader."

Pushley's pompous attitude reminded Nonie of why she disliked him so much. "I think the gas must have addled your mind, Ed."

"How dare you!"

"Well it must have done," Nonie challenged. "You've obviously forgotten that I left your commune years ago. And I've not regretted the decision. Another correction: you were my superior. Now you're just a refugee, like all the rest us."

"You'll regret taking that attitude with me," Pushley snapped, climbing out of bed. "Where are my clothes?"

"You're not well enough to get up yet."

Still, in a sulk, Pushley disconnected himself from the medical equipment surrounding him, he opened a small cabinet, found his clothes, and began pulling them on. Once he had dressed, he left without further comment and climbed up to deck level.

Once he'd stepped out, he discovered that the convoy was enshrouded in the thick, cloying fog that often covered the river. It was so thick he couldn't see further than ten metres. Working his way towards a temporary awning someone had erected as a shelter, Pushley slumped down and began brooding on Nonie Tomio's disregard for his authority, but before long he fell into a light sleep. As the dream-world claimed him, Pushley found himself back in James Minegold Pushley's neat office. Glancing up, he ran his eyes over the large, wall-mounted certificate proclaiming that James had been elected as a Midwain Senator a year and a half before.

"You wanted to see me, sir."

"I've had a word with a few contacts," Pushley Senior said. Without bothering to make eye contact, he added, "Unfortunately, it would be political suicide if I tried to help you dodge the draft. Not only that, if I lose face, it might also weaken my position in our commune. If I did as you requested, I could also face a leadership challenge in our commune."

"But Father, you can't do this to me."

"My hands are tied," his commune-father replied. With his eyes still firmly settled on the screen document he was reading, he then added, "It's time you learned to stand on your own feet, Edward. Do you want to be a loser all your life?"

When his son didn't answer, Pushley Senior said, "Believe me, Edward, a few years in the army will make a man out of you."

"Or turn me into a corpse, sir."

"Discussion over," Pushley Senior replied, waving a hand towards his office door.

A moment later, his father's image disappeared, and Pushley's dream state resurrected Irrelevant. Irrelevant's ghost said, "Don't panic Ed, I won't harm you."

When the fear on Pushley's face began to ease, Irrelevant continued, "You know, Ed, we have a lot in common, you and me."

"I that so?"

"Most certainly," Irrelevant said, "For starters, both of us started our lives in breeding pouches."

Pushley frowned, "I was created in an artificial womb if that is what you mean."

"As was I," Irrelevant replied. "The only difference is the Great Ones hatched me. Most of your people use advanced technology because modern women in your society, women with money, don't like natural childbirth. As a bonus, applied eugenics helps to eliminate genetic defects."

"The only real difference between us is I was born to be a slave—you were born with a silver spoon in your mouth." He paused.

"Can you stop scowling and listen? Unfortunately for you, when they took you out of the artificial womb and handed you over, your Senator father took an immediate dislike to you."

"I suppose that's one of the drawbacks to being created in an artificial womb. If your adoptive parents don't bond with their new charge, life can become very hard on all parties. It wasn't your fault; the honourable Senator didn't like what came out of the hatchery."

Irrelevant's ghost took up the Senator's theme, "Maybe he was right. Maybe you've always been a loser, Ed."

There was a silence as Irrelevant waited for Pushley to digest what he'd just said before he changed tack. "If you help me, Ed, you could be a rich man. Richer than your commune-father. I have a plan."

"What plan?"

"If you do as I tell you, my plan will make you very rich," Irrelevant's ghost whispered. Then more enticingly, "If you do as I tell you; you will be able to make your commune-father eat crow. You'd like that, Ed, wouldn't you?"

"Yes, I would like to make my father eat crow. What's your plan?"

After listening, Pushley smiled. He was going to make his father regret the day he was born. With a warm glow of anticipation sweeping over him, he slumped into a sleep, so deep he missed Lascaux's shouts.

CHAPTER NINE

Fyfield Valley, Arcadia
The Great Ones attack again

"**Y**ou'd better come up," Lascaux called out. "I think the attack has started."

Leaving the dive boats and scrambling back up the ridge, Tarmy slumped down in the bluegrass again. "What's up?"

Lascaux pointed towards Cittavecchia. At first, Tarmy couldn't make out what she was pointing at because although dawn had finally arrived, the whole valley was still cloaked in thick fog. Eventually, he realised what she'd seen. Between the drifting fog banks, he could just make out several heavy, log rafts. Although they all had crenulated dwarf walls, he could still see armed Longjaws and squirming millipedes lurking behind them; there could be little doubt that the Great One's time of mourning had expired, and the invasion force was on its way.

A moment later, a volley of pulse shots ripped through the bluegrass indicating that the would-be invaders had detected his presence. As more and more shots were fired, Lascaux pulled back slightly from the top of the rise, but Tarmy stayed where he was and flipped open the laser sights on his rifle.

Guessing that the flimsy wooden walls wouldn't offer much protection, he began pumping shots into the crowded lead raft. Cries of pain floated across the river.

His fire was immediately answered, and they began scything down more of the bluegrass around him. Realising his enemy had worked out his location, Tarmy rolled sideways, squirmed along the ridge, and began firing again. He rolled back toward Lascaux and thrust his rifle in her direction. "The battery's out. Give me your rifle and tell the others to get ready to cast off the boats; we won't be able to hold them for long."

As Lascaux went sliding down the slope, Tarmy heard her raising the alarm. He crawled back into position and went back to firing, but despite his efforts, the rafts continued to advance. Realising that he couldn't stop the invasion, Tarmy followed Lascaux down the slope and began barking orders. In less than a minute, the dive boats began pulling away, bouncing on the swell created by the waterfalls higher up. Calling to Lascaux, he pointed to the air-cars, "Come on there's not much time."

Lascaux ran to the air-car. Getting in, she immediately took off. Tarmy followed, instinctively moving in a running crouch to avoid any enemy fire. As he started his air-car and rose from the ground, he caught a glimpse of movement in the blue-grass ridge not far from where he'd just been. Gaining more height, he saw swarms of millipedes working their way down the ridge and realised that the Great Ones had launched a two-pronged attack. it was apparent the force coming from the direction of Cittavecchia had been designed as a diversion while the main force attacked from the island higher upriver.

As the movements in the bluegrass became more pronounced, millipedes cascaded down the slope like a tidal wave of writhing bodies. Once they had occupied the area where the air-cars had been parked, the millipedes began firing poison blobs at the retreating dive boats. As the blobs hit the water, fish began flipping around as the poison sent them into death throes.

Lascaux drew her air-car alongside and shouted out, "Let's hope your invisible droid comes back. Otherwise, we're stuffed."

Tarmy refused to be drawn. Instead, he shouted back, "We

need to save power, land your air-car next to the boats."

In the seconds before he followed her, Tarmy watched the invasion rafts manoeuvring to create another pontoon between islands. It was apparent Lascaux was right. The Great Ones intended to box them in.

Turning his air-car, he set off after Lascaux's machine, but instead of landing, he flew close to the other bank of the Fyfield River and ran his eyes over the Arcadian swamp oaks and water gum trees and vaguely wondered if the other bank offered an escape route. As he went closer still, the air-car passed under the overhanging canopy, and he heard something heavy hit the air-car roof followed by a heavier thud.

Knowing he'd acquired unwanted guests, probably millipedes, Tarmy pulled away from the trees and began jinking the air-car in the hope of throwing them off.

When that failed, he pulled out his stun pistol and began firing at the millipedes through the roof of the air-car, still jinking. One of the millipedes suddenly slipped off and fell into the water below. Knowing there had to be a second millipede still clinging on, Tarmy began firing again. The beast on the roof responded by partially sliding down the windscreen, glaring in at him. It sent Tarmy a mental message, one that left him in no doubt that the Great Ones knew that he was still alive and that he would be punished for causing the deaths of three of their group.

To reinforce the threat, his mind began conjuring up images of a cramped feeding chamber, and Tarmy could see himself cowering at one end. A moment later, a huge grub broke through the cell wall and began advancing, jaws slavering.

As he'd grown used to death threats he ignored the mental attack and began blasting at the millipede again. But instead of sliding off, the millipede raised its hood menacingly and started raking the windscreen with its teeth. Tarmy suddenly realised that the creature was a different colour and a lot larger than the other millipedes he'd seen before; this was a king millipede.

Having no other way of dislodging it, Tarmy fired his stun at it three more times but to no avail. Knowing that he had to get rid of the beast before returning to the convoy, Tarmy forced the air-car onto a steep dive, plunged into the river and then remained submerged for several minutes.

Not being able to breathe, the huge beast eventually let go and swam away. Once he was sure the king millipede had gone, Tarmy changed course and then re-emerged from the river.

Turning his air-car, he headed back to the dive-boats and noticing that while he'd been submerged, they'd been circled and lashed together. There were sinister shapes in the water which reminded Tarmy of his own near-death experience when one of the plesiosaurs had tried to drag him overboard.

Suddenly he realised why the refugees had taken up a defensive position; they had substantially reduced the exposed perimeter, which made another attack far less likely.

Tarmy focussed on the space in the centre of the circle that the refugees had left for him and landed his air-car next to Lascaux's. He opened the roof door carefully, and after checking there was no poison on the air-car's bodywork, he pulled himself out and climbed up on deck. Reaching the top, he was surprised to find Ed Pushley standing there, "How long have you been awake?"

"Not long," Pushley replied. He then glanced around, "We don't appear to be moving."

"That's because we aren't."

"I hope you're going to get us out of here."

"I'm doing my best."

The comment brought a look of fear to Pushley's face, "If they get hold of me, they'll kill me for sure."

"We're all in danger. Why *you* in particular?"

Pushley made a diplomatic retreat, "Yes, I suppose we all are."

"As I said," Tarmy replied. "I'm doing my best."

Remembering he still had Pushley's wallet, he fished in his top pocket. He pulled it out and then handed it over, "You dropped this."

Pushley's eyes lit up, "I wondered where that had got to. Thank you, Tarleton."

Tarmy was tempted to correct Pushley and tell him his real name was Mick Tarmy but decided against it; what did it matter? Instead, he said, "I would have handed it over earlier, but you were still in a coma." He paused.

"Pleased though I am you've recovered; I'm going to have to go. I've got things to do."

Moving away, he went looking for Lascaux.

Finding her, he said, "If you see any more rafts on the move, let me know, okay?"

"Okay."

"D'you know where Nonie is?"

Lascaux pointed.

"Thanks."

Once with her, he said, "I see Pushley's recovered."

"Yes, but he's acting a bit weird."

"Two weird people in one day, eh!" Tarmy replied, "First Claire and now Pushley."

"Pushley was particularly weird," Nonie said. "When he came out of his coma, he started speaking in a strange language."

"Did you recognise it?"

"No," Nonie replied. "Chiu Lan thought it was an Ab dialect."

"That is strange," Tarmy replied and then changed tack. "How's Claire?"

"Still unconscious, I'm afraid."

Tarmy shook his head, "How come Pushley's up and about, and Claire isn't."

"Pushley was still half-stunned when the gas attack happened," Nonie reasoned. "As his body was partially closed down, he probably didn't absorb as much gas."

While Tarmy was still thinking about the anomaly, Lascaux shouted down, "Mick, you're needed up here."

Running upstairs, Tarmy joined Lascaux at the side of the boat. The rafts were on the move again, but this time there were gaps between them, revealing that they were all linked with stout chains to make sure that the dive boats couldn't force their way through.

Lascaux returned to an old theme, "Pity your invisible friend isn't here."

Ignoring the comment, Tarmy pointed downriver towards the other blockade, "Time to move."

"Okay," Lascaux agreed. "But it won't buy us much time. If your invisible friend doesn't turn up soon, we're in real trouble. I hope you realise that."

As she moved away and began giving orders, a quiet voice whispered, "It's nice to be missed. Did you miss me, Corporal Tarmy?"

Glancing up, Tarmy saw a faint shadow overhead, "Alex! You're back. Yes, we've all missed you. Is my daughter okay? Did she escape?"

"Yes, Corporal Tarmy," Alex replied. "I made sure she was safe before coming back; she is now on Salus Transporter Nine."

"What about the others?"

"They escaped too," Alex replied. "And so did the second group."

"What second group?"

"I am not sure of the full details, but Ord Morley knew and agreed to it," Alex replied. "The remainder of the money is also safe."

"What money?"

"The money captured from the spettro you called Irrelevant," Alex replied.

Another jig-saw piece slipped back into his memory, "Ah! The money. Where is it now?"

"Somewhere safe," Alex assured him. "Would you like me to remove the blockade?"

"Yes, but I'll come with you," Tarmy said, moving towards

the air-cars. Watching him move, Lascaux called out, "Where are you going?"

"As promised, the cavalry has just arrived," Tarmy called back.

"You mean your invisible friend is back?"

"Exactly. We're going to see if we can destroy the pontoon bridge. If we do manage to make a gap, get the boats through it as fast as you can."

He was about to take off when he heard a clump on the roof, and Nonie swung herself down into the seat next to him, brandishing a pulse rifle, "I'm coming with you."

"What about Claire and the rest?"

"Aren't I entitled to a break?" she asked. "The others can look after the patients for a while."

Tarmy was tempted to ask who the others were but let it slide.

Nonie said, "I gather your invisible friend has returned."

"How do you know about ...?"

"Lascaux told me," Nonie cut in. "Mind you; I'd more or less worked out we had a military droid helping us out. What with enemy air-cars exploding right left and centre, it stood to reason that we had an invisible angel looking after us."

Taking off, Tarmy followed Alex's tail lights until they were both around a hundred metres from the blockade. Bringing his air-car to a hover, Tarmy began checking out the structure. Not only was it well built, the whole area was pulsing with activity. Knowing that a breakout attempt was about to be made, teams of Arcadian millipedes were attacking the surrounding trees, cutting through their branches with their sharp mandibles. Once the branches were on the ground, others were dragging them along the pontoon to strengthen the floating barrier.

While Tarmy was still hovering, he saw a solitary figure standing on the river bank. Although the spettro was some distance away, Tarmy could tell that his general build and colouration were the same as Irrelevant's. But there was a significant difference: the spettro standing on the river bank had four arms.

Not believing his eyes Tarmy moved in for a closer look. The spettro reacted by turning to face the air-car and gesturing with both sets of arms. Although he had no proof, Tarmy concluded that if the Great Ones ever managed to escape from Arcadia and colonise the Salus System, the spettro's body form would be the one that would be introduced to replace the existing two-arm human population. Four hands are better than two.

Suddenly, he was hit by a mental blast. Despite the fact his hat reduced the mind invasion to a minimum, there was no mistaking the spettro didn't like him hanging around.

Annoyed, Tarmy glanced at Nonie, "How about giving him a taste of his own medicine?"

Nonie dropped a side window and fired. Although the shots went wide, the spettro dived for cover.

Before they could celebrate their minor victory, Alex suddenly flashed out a warning with his lights. Taking heed, Tarmy swerved and avoided a barrage of pulse shots. A second later, two enemy air-cars flashed past. This was the first time he'd seen an enemy air-car since he'd come out of his coma; the sudden re-appearance surprised him.

The two air-cars swung around and moved in for a second attack. Moving in formation, they bracketed Tarmy's air-car with pulse bursts, but luckily there were no direct hits. Turning again, both machines moved in for another run, but before they could fire, there was a flash, and the lead enemy air-car burst into flame and began trailing smoke. Realising it was out-gunned; the second dived out of danger and took refuge in the surrounding forests.

Alex's shadow appeared alongside Tarmy's air-car, "Permission to attack the bridge?"

Tarmy nodded and watched the machine's faint shadow moving towards the blockade. A moment later, one of the log rafts erupted and debris scattered in all directions.

Alex set about the others, but this time, he concentrated on the chains linking the pontoons. Within seconds, sections of the pontoon bridge began breaking away and drifting in the current. From hiding, the four-armed spettro went back to bombarding Tarmy's mind with more dire threats, but Tarmy just grinned because he knew they were winning; with Alex returned to the fold, the spettro was as dangerous as a sparrow fart.

Alex turned his attention to the millipedes still clustered at the ends of the broken barrier. Despite their losses, the millipedes continued firing into the air in an attempt to hit their invisible foe. Within a matter of seconds, the river was covered in venom and dying fish.

As the battle continued, two log rafts exploded cascading hundreds of millipedes into the water. Most began to swim, but there were other inert bodies just floating with the current.

After two more rafts had exploded and more millipedes swam for their lives, the remaining millipede army began retreating, leaving the way free for the dive-boats to escape. Five minutes later, the dive boat formation began moving through the gap.

As Tarmy prepared return to the safe haven in the centre of the dive boat formation, Alex came alongside, "Corporal Tarmy, there people asking to be rescued."

Not wishing to abandon the convoy, Tarmy snapped, "Who?"

"There are two men in a large building in the next valley; they are to be rescued."

The small machine moved away. Although reluctant to follow in case they were attacked again, Tarmy tagged along behind.

Making his way, through the thick mists still enshrouding the forests, he began to catch glimpses of powerful lights. A moment later a huge industrial building came into view looking totally out of place in its forest setting.

Nonie pointed, "Look over there."

Following her finger, he saw that the whole building was surrounded by tiers of paddy fields running up the nearby hills, obviously not for the cultivation of rice. The huge bulbous shapes sitting in the shallow artificial lagoons could only be Zuka.

Interrupting his thoughts, Alex reminded him of the rescue plea and rose until he was hovering over the huge flat roof where he came to a halt. As Tarmy instructed his air-car to adopt hover mode, an access door suddenly burst open and two men began hobbling towards them.

Nonie became alarmed, "This could be a trap."

Tarmy ignored the warning; one look at their thin, emaciated bodies, the ragged clothes they were wearing, and the look of fear ingrained on their faces was enough to convince him these men needed help. He moved towards them, opened one of the doors, and the two men began painfully climbing in.

While the second man was still half in and half out, a siren began wailing, and three sinister multi-legged shapes suddenly emerged from the access door and scuttled towards the air-car. As Tarmy had seen several smaller Arcadian wolves during his interview with the Great Ones, he was only too well aware of how dangerous these animals could be.

Realising the second man was in a highly vulnerable position; Tarmy grabbed hold of him, dragged him into the air-car and then triggered the outer door. A fraction of a second later the first Arcadian wolf slammed into the air-car and began snapping at the bodywork with its powerful mandibles. Tarmy drew his stun gun and fired at it. As the first wolf staggered away, Tarmy instructed the air-car to climb with the other two wolves leaping into the air and clinging onto the bottom of the air-car. Tarmy slammed on the air-car's drive and moved off quickly again. After a few seconds, the wolves lost their grip and the air-car shot away.

Once clear of the plantation, they turned back towards the convoy, Tarmy placed the machine onto auto, turned to face his new passengers and extended a hand, "I'm Mick Tarmy. If you come with us, you may hear some people call me Mick Tarleton, but my real name is Tarmy."

"Why's that?"

"It's a long story," Tarmy replied. "When I've got time, I'll explain."

This," he said, indicating Nonie, "is Nonie Tomio."

Nonie swivelled to face the two men and then said, "And you are?"

The first man said, "I'm Red Moxstroma." He nodded at the second man, "This is Bryn Rosslyn."

"So, what's your story?" Tarmy asked.

Both men looked uneasy, "You connected with the police?"

Tarmy was tempted to reveal that he was an ex-Ardenese police officer, but as he was way out of his jurisdiction, he shook his head.

Satisfied, Moxstroma opened up, "We've been held prisoner here for two years."

"Why?"

The uneasy look returned, "Let's just say we made a bad mistake."

"What sort of mistake?"

"We trusted Hal Warmers," Rosslyn cut in. "We also trusted the Great Ones. We thought they'd keep their word, but they didn't."

Although Tarmy knew Hal Warmers from his army days, he kept a poker face, "So, this Hal Warmers character did the dirty on you, did he?"

Both men nodded. Moxstroma said, "We both met Hal Warmers during the last war. We were working in Army stores. At the time, he was dabbling in the black market." "Let me guess," Tarmy said. "From time to time you supplied Warmers with items that had accidentally fallen off the back of a lorry."

"Correct." Rosslyn agreed.

Moxstroma took over. Nodding towards Rosslyn, he said, "As the Arcadian Colonies were growing fast, a few years back

Bryn and I went into business together as nurserymen. People started buying stuff for their gardens."

"Things were going well. Then Hal Warmers turned up on our doorstep and started to blackmail us. He wanted money. He showed us copies of files and said they would end up with the authorities if we didn't fund him. After he'd been black-mailing us for a while, he turned up with some Zuka seeds wanting us to grow Zuka plants for him in our nursery. He said if we co-operated, he'd see us okay and we'd be quits."

"So, it was stick and carrot," Tarmy replied.

"Yep."

Tarmy played a hunch, "So, let me guess. You supplied Hal Warmers with the Zuka plants, and you came out here to help the Great Ones construct the Zuka plantation. But once you'd finished, they didn't let you go."

Moxstroma nodded, "That's about it."

While Tarmy weighed up the story, something very large emerged from the surrounding mists and bore down on them. The air-car's computer system took evasive action and narrowly avoided a mid-air collision. As the air-car pulled away from its adversary, Alex came alongside and said, "You must go. Quickly"

"What was that thing?"

"It was an FA49," Alex replied. "There are two of them."

"Oh! Shit!" Tarmy cursed. "Where the hell did the Great Ones acquire FA49s?"

"Never mind that now. Go now. Hide in the forest," Alex snapped. "If they find you they will shoot you down. I will deal with them."

"Hide in the forest!" Tarmy snapped back. "The forest is crawling with millipedes."

"Keep the windows closed," Alex replied unsympathetic-ally and moved away.

As Tarmy moved towards the forest again, Nonie said, "What's an FA49?"

"Flying armour. Basically, a flying tank," Tarmy replied. "An

FA49 is about twice the size of an air-car, heavily armoured and is usually equipped with a massive Gatling gun capable of firing thousands of rounds per minute."

"That sounds bad."

"It could be if we don't find somewhere to hide," Tarmy replied, flipping the air-car back into manual. He turned, flew for several metres, and nudged the air-car into the moss-covered middle canopy of an Arcadian bottlebrush tree. Realising the mid-branches would not support the air-car's weight; he kept the machine on hover but twisted it so that he had a clear view of the river. Almost immediately, the dive boats came into view. It was obvious the escaping archaeologists were in trouble because several of them were firing into the river as if trying to drive off some unseen predator.

Tarmy thought about the Arcadian plesiosaurs that had killed Irrelevant. Undoubtedly, the Great Ones had regained control over the plesiosaurs and had instructed them to shadow the convoy in the hope of attacking the escapees or picking off anyone unfortunate enough to fall overboard.

A few seconds after he'd hidden in the tree, a dark shadow moved over them. Bryn Rosslyn lost his nerve. "The FA49s found us. I told you this was a bad idea, Red. They won't let us escape."

Wanting to avoid panic, Tarmy intervened, "Keep quiet. We'll be okay as long as you don't do anything stupid."

The two men did as instructed, but they both continued staring up through the roof window as if expecting the hovering FA49 to come crashing down on them. After what seemed an eternity, the dark shadow moved away. Red Moxstroma glanced at Rosslyn and said, "See, it's gone."

"Gone where?"

"I've no idea," Tarmy admitted, "but if they can't find us, they'll probably go after the convoy."

"Shit! So, what do we do?"

"We stay hidden and allow Alex to take 'em on," Tarmy said. "By modern military standards, FA49s are obsolete. In the real world, they're museum pieces. They wouldn't last five minutes on a modern battlefield."

"And how does that help us," Nonie cut in.

"As Alex is relatively modern, a TK5, and has cloaks and Mannheim shielding, he should be able to knock them out. On the other hand, the Great Ones have numbers on their side. It will only take one lucky shot, and they've won."

Nonie said, "What can we do to help?"

"It might sound cowardly, but unless you *want* to commit suicide, we're best staying here."

"What about the convoy?"

"I'm afraid they're on their own for the time being," Tarmy replied. "If the Great Ones are determined to wipe them out there's little we can do about it."

One of the FA49s came into view, accompanied by three air-cars. A loud voice boomed out. "Drop your weapons and sail your boats towards the bank. If you don't comply, we will open fire."

"Can't we do something?" Nonie said. "Create a diversion or something."

"Did you hear what I said?" Tarmy snapped. "Unless you're desperate to commit suicide, there is not a lot we can do."

The voice boomed out again, "Drop your weapons and sail your boats towards the bank. If you don't comply, we will open fire."

Although resistance was pointless, one of the archaeologists raised her pulse rifle and fired at the FA49. Although the pulse fire bounced off the heavily armoured vehicle, the flying tank fired warning shots over her head. "Drop the gun and raise your hands—or you die."

Realising she was hopelessly outgunned; the archaeologist did as instructed. "Sail your boats towards the bank."

As the boats turned, giant Arcadian millipedes emerged from the forests and lined the riverbank, their cobra-like hoods expanded. There could be little doubt they'd kill at the slightest provocation.

"Why are *they* doing this?"

"Doing what?" Tarmy said.

"Taking the archaeologists prisoner again?"

"They've been trying to prevent us from escaping ever since Irrelevant fell from grace," Tarmy replied. "Now we've found their Zuka plantation they have even more reasons for wanting to stop us leaving the Fyfield Valley. They won't want us escaping and giving away the plantation's location."

"Even if the location was given away, the Fyfield Valley is a reservation," Nonie said. "An interplanetary agreement protects the valley; it couldn't be attacked."

The comment brought a wry smile to Tarmy's lips, "Interplanetary agreements didn't stop Samantha from bombing the Great Ones."

"They also want us," Moxstroma reminded them. "If they take the others prisoner, they could use them as hostages and blackmail us into surrendering."

Tarmy glanced at the dive boats again. As they were moving towards the bank, he sensed that it wouldn't be long before the archaeologists would fall into the Great Ones clutches again.

"Where's Alex? He's their only hope."

He'd barely asked the question before one of the enemy air-cars burst into flames and fell into the river. Realising they were under attack, the other two air-cars moved close to the FA49 for protection. They'd barely completed the manoeuvre before a second air-car burst into flames. Not wishing to join the others, the third air-car turned and fled.

Responding to the attack, the FA49 swiftly turned and fired into the surrounding forests. Tarmy guessed the murderous blast hadn't been made at random. No doubt the huge machine's antiquated computer system had worked out where Alex had been when he opened fire and was now firing its main armament in the hope of hitting its invisible opponent.

As the firing continued, the tops of several forest giants were scythed off and fell into the Fyfield River. After fifteen seconds, the FA49 fell silent and then began swivelling back towards the convoy of small boats. For a fraction of a second Tarmy thought the FA49 commander was going to blast the convoy as a reprisal. Instead, the voice repeated, "Sail your boats towards the bank immediately."

The order had barely been given before Alex fired a second shot.

In response, the huge machine began swivelling again and opened fire on another area of forest, but this time the burst of fire stopped within a matter of seconds. The inexperienced commander had run out of ammunition.

A moment later, Alex emerged from the forest like a faint shadow. Moving in close, he began pounding the FA49's weak spot. Three direct hits later, one of the hatches flew open, and a Longjaw climbed out in a cloud smoke and dived into the river, swiftly followed by two more. Within seconds, an Arcadian plesiosaur surfaced close to them and allowed them to climb onto its back.

Lacking a crew, the FA49 lost stability and began wobbling alarmingly. It began to drift towards the convoy as if it was determined to take revenge on the archaeologists. Just as it looked as if the convoy would be crushed by its massive bulk, it lurched towards the riverbank and crashed into the surrounding forest, bursting into flames. As black smoke billowed out of the jungle, the archaeologists reacted by pulling away from the banks again.

Realising their quarry was escaping, the millipedes began firing venom at the retreating vessels. Within seconds parts of river became a foaming mass of black poison. Luckily, the dive boats were too far from shore to be hit.

Once they were back in the main current, the archaeologists began waving and cheering wildly, celebrating the victory. But their joy was short-lived because the second FA49 suddenly appeared. Alex briefly opened fire, moved off fast and hid in the forest canopy.

Taking the bait, the second FA49 moved after Alex and

began firing. But unlike the first FA49, the bursts of fire were shorter. Clearly, the second FA49 commander had learned from the failure of the first FA49.

A few seconds later, another phaser flash hit the second FA49. Swivelling again, the flying tank began to machine gun the forest. As he watched, Tarmy sensed that Alex was playing smart. Although Alex had Mannheim force shields, he was taking no chances. Knowing that the FA49 could do severe damage if it got lucky, Alex was fighting a guerrilla campaign; hit and run. Instead if trading shots with such a powerful adversary, Alex was attempting to make the FA49 waste its ammunition in the same way that the first one had.

When another phaser bolt hit the FA49, the commander retaliated with a third burst of fire, but the blast swiftly terminated. Sensing that the FA49 was vulnerable, Alex came out of the forest again, moved in fast and went straight for the other machines poorly armoured zone. Four shots later, smoke began pouring from the second FA49. It plunged into the Fyfield River and began to sink. Tarmy watched as another Arcadian plesiosaur surfaced close to the sinking machine and rescued the crew.

Alex's faint shadow appeared alongside Tarmy's air-car again. The small machine made him and Nonie jump by hitting the side of the air-car hard. His muffled voice then said, "Don't open the window. You're in danger."

"You must keep your windows shut there is danger all around. the Great Ones have detected your presence."

As if to confirm Alex's comments, something heavy fell onto the roof of the air-car. Although the roof door was closed, the window blind was open, so it was possible to see their assailant. A giant Arcadian millipede immediately began dribbling venom onto the plasti-metal roof window and attacked the air-car's bodywork with its razor-sharp teeth.

Tarmy pulled out his stun gun and began blasting at it through the glazing. At the third shot, the creature went into a twitching fit, slid off the roof window and plunged into the forest below.

Without further discussion, Tarmy reversed the air-car out of the tree and headed back towards the convoy. He knew that the air-car had poison clinging to it, so instead of landing near the convoy, he dropped to river level and submerged. Within a matter of seconds, large blobs of poison began drifting away in the current.

A plesiosaur appeared from nowhere, and Tarmy braced himself for impact. At the last moment, the plesiosaur veered away, obviously fearful of coming into contact with the vicious poison still clinging to the sides of the air-car.

After remaining submerged for the best part of twenty minutes, Tarmy judged that the poison would have washed away, and surfaced alongside the other air-car.

As Tarmy opened the roof door and began checking there was no venom clinging to the bodywork, a group of archaeologists moved to a side rail and began to cheer. Then Lascaux appeared and began to clap.

"Well done, Mick. We thought we were all done for. Your invisible friend sorted them out good time."

As Tarmy helped Nonie, Moxstroma and Rosslyn out of the roof door, Ed Pushley suddenly appeared. Eying up Moxstroma and Rosslyn, he asked, "So, where did they come from Tarleton?"

Instead of supplying a full answer, Tarmy said, "These two gentlemen asked for our help. We couldn't refuse, now could we?"

Pushley smiled at the two newcomers. "Aren't you going to introduce us?"

Once Tarmy had done as requested, Pushley began ingratiating himself, "Why don't I take Red and Bryn to get some food? They look as if they could do with it."

Lascaux appeared and gave Red Moxstroma a nudge. "Yeah, you need looking after."

As Pushley and Lascaux moved off with the two men in tow, Pushley half-turned and glanced back at Tarmy, "Good work by the way Tarleton. When those FA49s turned up, I thought we were finished, but your TK5 certainly saw them off."

Tarmy cursed because it was evident that everyone now knew of Alex's existence. Following Nonie, he went below to see how Claire Hyndman was fairing but swiftly realised there was no change.

~*~

Shortly after arriving back, Nonie and Chou came to see Tarmy. Nonie said, "I hope you realise that Pushley's pumping Moxstroma and Rosslyn for information."

"What sort of information?"

"Information about the Zuka plantation," she replied.

"So?"

"When I was at Fort Saunders there was a rumour going around that Ed Pushley was some sort of auxiliary agent and was feeding back information to Midwain intelligence," Nonie replied.

Tarmy smiled. "I can't really picture Pushley in the role of a spy. What useful information could he pick up in a back of beyond place like Fort Saunders?"

"Then why is he pumping Red Moxstroma and Bryn Rosslyn for as much information as he can get about the Zuka Plantation?" Nonie asked.

When Tarmy shrugged, Chou cut in, "He's also been telling people you're a dangerous war criminal."

"You know that's not true," Tarmy returned.

"I'm just telling you for your own good," Chou replied. "You know how gossip and politics work. If something is repeated often enough, it becomes the truth, even if it is a lie. People just say there's no smoke without fire."

She added, "I don't trust him. I never have done. Believe me; he's up to something." Pausing briefly, she asked, "What do you know about Red Moxstroma?"

Tarmy shook his head, "Not a lot. Why?"

"No reason," she replied, but Tarmy detected a hint of jealousy in her tone.

"Come on. Give," Tarmy said.

After a few second, Chou said, "Lascaux seems to have taken a fancy to Red Moxstroma. I don't know what she sees in the skinny runt."

As Tarmy had no desire to get involved, he tracked back to the original conversation, "Thank you both for telling me about Pushley. I'll keep an eye on him."

CHAPTER TEN

Fyfield Valley, Arcadia

Ed Pushley turns traitor

Other than a faint glow and hum of electronic equipment coming from one of the dive boats cock-pits and the rotating radar antenna high above, everywhere seemed quiet and lifeless. Worse, with the external lighting deliberately turned off to conserve power and the thick fog still swirling in from the river, moving around the dive boats was difficult. Even the powerful handheld torch Ed Pushley was carrying didn't help much.

Once he'd carefully worked his way along one of the gangplanks connecting the boats, Pushley glanced around furtively. Satisfied that no one was watching, he let himself into a small store-room.

Squeezing in, he closed the door and ran his torch around the inside of the store. He suffered a brief heart-stopping moment when the torch picked out the fluorescent flashes on a safety jacket, "God! Who's that?"

Getting no response, Pushley reached out and realised it was an empty jacket, one that had been hung there; there was no one lurking in the storeroom.

Heart was still pounding, Pushley began talking to himself, "Get a grip man! You've got a job to do."

Recovering his composure, he made sure he remained undisturbed by jamming the door shut. Satisfied that no one was likely to surprise him, he placed the torch on a shelf, turned it slightly to give him the best light and pulled out his wallet. After struggling with one of the small compartments, he eventually retrieved what he'd been looking for; a slim card-shaped object tucked into the lining.

Turning it over in his hand to make sure it wasn't damaged, he muttered, "Excellent."

Pulling the lining again, he searched for a sheet containing access codes.

Finding it, he flattened it out and began muttering to himself again, "So far so good. Let's hope this works."

He tapped in a release code, and the emergency percom lit up. As the small device began linking with the outside world, a power bubble formed but it was empty except for a series of scrolling images advertising the wonders and benefits of deep space cruises around the Salus System.

As he attempted to link, Pushley experienced a slight pang of guilt. Tarleton had saved his life, wasn't reporting him a gross betrayal? Another prick of conscience; maybe he shouldn't.

But then, his heart hardened because he could feel Irrelevant's ghostly presence whispering to him, urging him on. Wasn't this all part of the master plan they'd discussed?

He had to do it. Tarleton was a war criminal, so he had to report Tarleton's presence with the convoy.

Pushley wasn't surprised by what the whispers kept telling him. Ever since he'd shrugged off the after-effects of the gas attack, his mind had become full of whispers. From the start, the whispers had been telling him that Tarleton, Hyndman and Tomio had to be punished because they had destroyed the master plan: Irrelevant's plan.

If it hadn't been for them, the invasion of Cittavecchia would have been successful. If it hadn't been for them, the shuttle would have landed, and the Great Ones would have acquired a portable teleport. If they'd acquired a teleport which would have meant they would have been one step closer to taking control of the Salus System. But that hadn't happened because Tarleton and his associates had blocked the landing pad with the heavy plant.

For second or two, Pushley resolved to carry out his allotted task but before he could, his conscience cut in again and his emotions began to roller coaster once more. Should he or shouldn't he?

He was on the point of doing a U-turn when Irrelevant's whispers came back and reminded Pushley that Tarleton was a man with blood on his hands; didn't that obviate any indebtedness he might have to the other man?

Irrelevant's whispers said, "Repeat after me—I owe Tarleton nothing—I owe Tarleton nothing—I owe Tarleton nothing."

As Pushley repeated the chant, all his guilt disappeared. With his mind back on even keel, he began thinking about the irony of the situation. If Tarleton hadn't returned his wallet, he wouldn't have access to the emergency percom, and he wouldn't have been able to contact the outside world.

After several seconds, Pushley became impatient and tapped in the release code again. On the second call, the power bubble ditched its advertising feature, and a gender-neutral face appeared; he was asked to identify himself, provide his identity code and with whom he wished to speak.

"Ed Pushley, agent Q449. I need to speak to Brigadier Wolff."

There was a brief pause before the CGI face said, "Brigadier Wolff's on Midway. I'd have to hyper-link."

"Then hyper-link, damn it. This is important."

"Hyper-link access is restricted."

"This call concerns the whereabouts of a known war criminal by the name of Mick Tarleton. I also have information concerning a major Zuka plantation. My information is very important. Put me through!"

Instead of a response, the face froze. Thinking he'd been cut off, Pushley said, "Hello, hello—are you still there?"

The face reactivated and adopted a more personal approach, "I'm tracking your location, Ed."

Although it was obvious something was happening, Pushley was still very conscious that time was ticking away; he suspected the emergency percom only had limited battery life and he wanted to deliver his message and conserve the battery for future use.

"Why d'you need my location?"

"It's essential for hyper-link, Ed."

Eventually, the face added, "You appear to be in the Fyfield Valley. Is that correct?"

"Yes. And I need to speak to Brigadier Wolff urgently."

"And I mean urgently."

The words had barely left his mouth when another face appeared in the bubble, "Hello Agent Q449. Why do you wish to speak to Brigadier Wolff?"

Guessing that he'd been connected to Wolff's Rottweiler, an assistant tasked with the job of filtering the Brigadier's calls and only accepting the most important, Pushley began name dropping, "I'm Senator Pushley's son, and I am also known to General Canaris."

When Rottweiler sniffed dismissively, Pushley went back to plain facts. "This call concerns the whereabouts of a known war criminal by the name of Mick Tarleton. I also have information concerning a major Zuka plantation. My information is very important. Put me through!"

After a slight pause, the bubble image blanked, and Pushley overheard Rottweiler speaking to someone. Then another face appeared.

"Wolff—what can I do for you?"

"This is Ed Pushley, sir. Agent Q449."

A new silence told Pushley that despite his previous reports Wolff had no idea who he was. But then the Brigadier took him by surprise, by saying, "Ah! Yes. You're the archaeologist chappy from Fort Saunders, aren't you?"

Noting the slightly condescending tone of Wolff's voice, one that suggested archaeology wasn't a real job, Pushley began name dropping again. "General Canaris recruited me personally and asked me to report back if I found anything of real interest concerning the Great Ones' finances."

"And have you?"

"I certainly have," Pushley replied. "They have a large Zuka plantation in the Fyfield Valley."

"What's Zuka?"

Realising that Wolff only concerned himself with military matters, Pushley said, "Zuka milk is the main ingredient of Flash, a powerful street drug—one that your predecessor was very concerned about. General Canaris was of the opinion that there was drug production on Arcadia. He specifically asked me to let him know if we discovered any evidence that Zuka was being grown there."

"Why would General Canaris be interested in illegal drug cultivation? Surely that's a police matter?"

For a second, Pushley was left speechless, he but then said, "Arcadia is largely an unpoliced planet, sir. More importantly, he was concerned that the drug money is being used to buy armaments, fund guerrilla activities and high-level assassinations all over the Salus System. Eventually, there comes the point where the police need assistance."

"How d'you know they're growing drugs?"

Not wishing to admit his information was hearsay, Pushley lied, "A few hours ago I flew over a plantation, sir. I recognised the Zuka plants." He then allowed himself some artistic licence. "The plantation was massive. I suspect there will be other plantations in the area too. My contacts suggest that once the plantation is in full production, it will provide the terrorists with funds of several billion every year."

Pushley heard another stage whisper and Wolff began to show interest, "Now you mention it, General Canaris did suggest there might be illegal drugs being produced on Arcadia."

Although he hadn't heard much of the whisper, Pushley presumed that Rottweiler had intervened and supplied Wolff with important information. Heartened that Rottweiler now appeared to be an ally, Pushley said, "If you destroy the plantations, it will cut off one of the Great Ones' major income streams."

"I'll look into it," Wolff replied.

Don't forget we also have a war criminal on board, sir," Pushley reminded him

"Name?"

"Mick Tarleton."

"Mick Tarleton!" Wolff replied. "I'd heard whispers he was in the Fyfield Valley. Are you sure it's him?"

"Positive. I also suspect his female companion is a monarch."

When silence returned, Pushley said, "You *do* know what a monarch is?"

Another stage whisper and then Wolff said, "Of course I know what a monarch is. If the monarch in question is attached to Tarleton, no doubt it's been instructed to track him."

"You might be right," Pushley conceded. "But I think it's on the loose."

"Thank you," Wolff replied. "I have noted your concerns and will notify the appropriate people. I have no doubt they will contact you."

Wolff then cut the link making Pushley swear out loud. With limited life in his emergency percom, the battery was likely to expire long before someone did come back.

While he was debating what he should do, the CGI face returned and said, "You have an incoming hyper-link, agent Q449."

"Is the call important?" Pushley queried. "My percom battery could run out."

"That's highly unlikely," the image replied. "Emergency percom batteries have a two-year life. Now, will you take the call?"

Relieved, Pushley nodded. A moment later the CGI image was replaced by a hawk-faced man. "My name's Oryx—Colonel Stert Oryx."

Pushley remembered the Brigadier's last comment; he was

going to notify the appropriate people. As if to confirm his thoughts, Oryx said, "You have just been in communication with Brigadier Wolff. I understand you know the whereabouts of Mick Tarleton."

"Yes."

Oryx responded with, "This conversation will remain confidential," and then recited an official caution reminding Pushley security protocols bound him. He left Pushley in little doubt that if he was indiscreet; he was likely to end up behind bars.

Oryx then held up an official-looking identity card, one that showed his face, his rank, and a circled acronym, InSP - WCD.

When Pushley frowned, indicating he had no idea who Oryx was or what the ID meant, the other man said, "I'm a Colonel with the military police. I've been after Mick Tarleton for years. With your help, I'll take him."

When Pushley remained silent, Oryx said, "Are you aware that Tarleton has a bounty on his head?"

When Pushley showed surprise, Oryx told Pushley just how valuable Tarleton's scalp was. The whispers at the back of Pushley's mind immediately told him to ask if he would get the reward.

Oryx gave him a beady-eyed look. "Are you prepared to help me?"

"Of course."

A slight smile formed on Oryx's thin lips. "If we get him based on your information, I will make sure you get the reward."

The whisperer let out a loud cheer and told Pushley that any plans Tarleton might have had for the future were going to be blown out of the water, totally destroyed.

Oryx said, "Where are you?"

Once Pushley had covered the same ground as he'd covered with Wolff, Oryx said, "Is Tarleton likely to leave the convoy?"

"I don't know what his plans are," Pushley admitted. "At the moment Tarleton appears to be staying with our boats. He has two air-cars at his disposal, but they are tied up and floating alongside the convoy.

The whisperer prompted Pushley into saying, "I need to warn you, Tarleton is not alone."

"How may associates?" Oryx demanded.

Pushley trotted out a list of names that included, Claire Hyndman and Nonie Tomio.

"Anything else I should know?"

"I believe one of Tarleton's associates may be a monarch."

Oryx said, "Are you sure?"

"Claire Hyndman can face change at will," Pushley said. "There's not much doubt in my mind she's a monarch."

"Anything else?"

"I suspect Tarleton has a TK5 minder."

"A TK5? Are you sure of that?"

"I served with the 145th Robotics Company during the last war," Pushley replied, a hint of pride entering his tone. "I'm sure Tarleton has a TK5 minding him, so don't say you weren't warned."

"I won't," Oryx replied. "I'll make sure I come suitably prepared."

"So, you're going to arrest him?"

"Like I said, I've been after Tarleton for years, "Oryx replied. "Of course, I'm going to *attempt* to arrest him."

Pushley immediately latched onto the stress in the last comment; the implication was obvious. Men like Oryx rarely took a fugitive alive. If they were alive, they could be dangerous; corpses never caused trouble. More importantly, as most war major criminals were classified as legitimate military targets and had been condemned to death in absentia, most justice departments preferred receiving a body; it was a lot less trouble that way.

"One other point," Pushley continued. "Will there be a reward for the monarch?"

"If there is a reward on the monarch," Oryx said, "I'll do my best to make sure you get that too. It won't be much though; monarchs are expendable. Don't forget in a war zone; monarchs only have a combat life expectancy of two weeks."

"When you arrest Tarleton," Pushley said, "Does that mean you will also rescue me?"

"Of course," Oryx replied. "One other point; if you could disable the air-cars, it would be helpful. We don't want Tarleton escaping before we get there."

Once Oryx had cut out, Pushley vaguely wondered if he should leave the small device turned on in case Wolff called back, but the whisperer told him to wipe and turn off. Now he was effectively part of Oryx's team, why did he need Wolff?

Once he was sure there was no evidence left of his calls to Wolff and Oryx, Pushley slipped the percom away and thought about the air-cars. As he had very few engineering skills, disabling them might prove a problem but decided that snipping a few wires might do the job. Searching the store, he found a set of heavy cutters and slipped them in his pocket.

Carefully emerging from his hiding place, Pushley closed the door and glanced around. As the damp cold air hit him again, his face began twitching. At first, it alarmed him because he'd never suffered from a tick before. It occurred to him that the sudden bout of twitching was probably the result of his multiple stunning and the gas attack; it was a forceful reminder he still hadn't fully recovered.

Attempting to control the twitches, Pushley thought about the air-cars. His whisperer began stoking Pushley's greed by reminding him of the bag containing the money cards. Could that be in the air-cars? Why not kill two birds with one stone? Find the money and disable the air-cars.

Checking to make sure he was alone, Pushley began making his way down a series of gangplanks. He lent over the side of the lead dive boat and began playing the torch into the void beyond.

Ensuring there were no lurking plesiosaurs in the vicinity,

he began searching for the air-cars. Locating one, he swiftly checked for plesiosaurs again, swung his legs over the side and quietly lowered himself down onto its roof. He walked towards the roof door.

As the door had expanded into ventilation mode, big enough to ventilate the inside of the vehicle without letting rain in, he pushed a button to make it contract and then dropped down inside the vehicle.

His backside had barely touched down on a seat before something let out a demonical screech and then flapped its way out through the roof door.

Pushley's face began to twitch violently, "What the hell was that!"

The flapping suddenly stopped, and something landed back on the roof. A small face glanced over the rim of the roof door, cautiously observing him.

Pushley let out a sigh of relief. Although it was dark, the internal lighting in the air-car was picking out a very distinct outline; it was Ollie, Nonie Tomio's pet Arcadian pterodactyl. The creature had obviously been able to squeeze through the ventilation gap in the roof door and had decided that the empty air-car made a good roost. Giving the animal a stern look, Pushley flapped his arms and hissed, "Piss off."

Fearing the pterodactyl might raise the alarm, Pushley remained where he was, listening, ready to abandon his plan if he was likely to get caught.

In the quiet time that followed, he glanced around the air-car's interior and was reminded of how Irrelevant, had died. One moment he had been in total control, the next, one of the Arcadian plesiosaurs had thrust its head through the roof door, grabbed Irrelevant by his upper torso and dragged him out.

Fearing the same might happen to him if there were any plesiosaurs in the area, Pushley closed the roof door. But even with the door closed, memories of what had happened to Irrelevant still came flooding back. He shivered slightly; although he'd been half stunned and lying in the back of the air-car when the plesiosaur attack had occurred, he'd felt the plesiosaur's teeth biting into Irrelevant's body. Pushley recalled the fear running through him when the huge creature began crushing the life out of Irrelevant.

There was no doubt he'd felt Irrelevant's pain; simple logic dictated he'd still been mind-linked with Irrelevant just before he'd died.

One thought led to another, and Pushley recalled the strange back-surge of energy that seemed to hit him as Irrelevant was finally crushed to death. It was as if Irrelevant's soul had begun searching for a new home and had decided to take up residence in his mind.

Thinking about the back-surge for a while longer, Pushley shuddered again; the whisperer in his mind; could it be Irrelevant's soul? Could Irrelevant's spirit have entered him and turned him into a dichotomous being? If it had, it would account for the way he felt.

From being comparatively disinterested in money-making, his mind had become obsessed with the power and security only money could bring in its wake. He began thinking about the irrational hatred he'd developed for Tarleton, Hyndman and Tomio.

Although none of them had caused him personal harm, they had destroyed Irrelevant's master plan. Now Pushley was feeling the urge to punish Tarleton, Hyndman and Tomio for what they'd done.

While he was dwelling on past events, the whisperer intervened and told him to forget his fears and turned Pushley's thoughts malevolent again. Involving Stert Oryx was a masterstroke. In a few days, Tarleton would probably be dead, Hyndman deactivated and Tomio facing a lengthy gaol sentence for aiding and abetting a war criminal.

Sitting quietly for a while longer, Pushley decided to continue with his plan and began searching the air-car. The bag with the money cards had to be hidden somewhere.

After checking the glove compartment and finding it virtually empty, he squirmed into the back, flapped down the rear seat and then shone the torch into the boot.

"Shit!"

The boot was empty; it had been unloaded. Swearing again, Pushley pulled out the heavy cutters he'd found in the store and thought about disabling the air-car he was in. He changed his mind. He had another air-car to search, and if he set off an alarm by mistake, it would wreck his whole plan.

Climbing off the first air-car, he checked there were no plesiosaurs in the area, re-set the roof window and moved towards the second air car. Dropping into it, he went through the same procedure, but swiftly realised he was wasting his time. The second air-car was empty too. Annoyed, Pushley slammed the seats back into position. Then, when his anger finally took over, he pulled out the heavy cutters.

~*~

Flying around the drifting dive boats for some time, Ollie finally picked up his mistress's body signature and homed in. Hearing his fluttering wings, Nonie Tomio glanced up.

Perching on her shoulder, Ollie sent Nonie a mental image. As the image hardened in her mind, she recognised Ed Pushley's face. Ollie sent her an image of an air-car, and she realised where Pushley was.

Ollie took to his wings again and began leading her towards the air-cars. Reaching them, she glanced down and noted a faint light inside one of them. She could hear Pushley cursing and slamming seats into their housings. Calling down, she said, "What are you doing, Ed?"

The cursing and slamming stopped.

"What are you doing, Ed?"

Although taken by surprise, Pushley recovered quickly and called out, "I lost something. But I've found it now."

As Pushley had obviously been in a bad mood when she'd arrived, his answer surprised her, "What did you find?"

Pushley emerged; face twitching and brandishing a medallion. "It's nothing important, but it had sentimental value. Must have dropped it."

Nonie knew he was lying because as far as she knew, Pushley had never been inside the air-car that Mick had been flying.

As he climbed back onto the deck of the dive boat, Nonie held out a hand. "Mind if I have a look, Ed?"

"It's personal," Pushley replied, but handed it over. The plasti-metal medallion was still warm as if it had been in close contact with his skin, Nonie's suspicions were confirmed. Pushley hadn't found the medallion; he'd taken it off and pretended he'd just found it. He'd been searching the air-car for something else. But what?

Although she was tempted to challenge him, Nonie just glanced at the medallion and asked, "So, what was this for?"

"Bravery," Pushley replied, puffing out his chest slightly.

Although she'd learned to read some of the local Ab language, she didn't understand the inscription. "I can't read it, what does it say?"

"It's in Latin, an ancient Earth Language," Pushley replied, "As I just said, it's for bravery." He grabbed the medallion back. "It was given to me by one of the Ab chiefs from the Compass Islands."

When Nonie gave him a sceptical look, Pushley said, "During my military service, my robotic company was based at Arcresten for a while."

"Arcresten? Where's that?"

"Arcresten is on East Island; it's in the Compass Islands. If these boats continue drifting downriver, that's where we'll be in a few days."

"Presumably, Arcresten is a military acronym?"

"Yes. It stands for Arcadian Research Station Ten."

"You said you were in charge of a robotic company. Excuse my ignorance, but what exactly is a robotic company?"

~*~

Pushley's mind immediately took him back to his former life. Despite his commune-father James Minegold Pushley being a wealthy man, he'd not been able to avoid the draft. Or, more precisely, his commune-father, being a dyed in the wool right-winger, had refused to pull strings to help his adopted son dodge his patriotic chore. Although most of Pushley's associates had commune fathers only too willing to save their offspring's hides, James Minegold Pushley had political and commune ambitions; better to lose a much-despised adopted son than lose face in the political and commune hierarchy.

As a consequence, instead of dodging the draft, Pushley junior had spent his young adult life dodging phaser fire and anti-gravity mortar shells.

Worse, having little aptitude for army life, Pushley junior had only managed to attain the rank of Lance Corporal, something his Senator father had found hard to swallow.

Of course, when Pushley reminisced, he implied he'd been in command of his company.

"Most of the time, my company comprised ten TK5s, and a small group of human controllers," Pushley told Nonie. "But the number of TK5s in my company could rise to twelve when the need arose."

Without bidding, vague memories of young faces surfaced from the back of Pushley's mind. However, he'd been very much the outsider; the rich kid who'd drawn the short straw, and most of their names had evaporated from his memory. The only names he remembered were the bullies, like Donann, Qist and Narton, and those who'd chosen to stay behind on Arcadia when the war was over. People like Yan Farman and Hal Warmers.

"So, your base was near here?"

Pushley nodded, "As I said, I was stationed on the Compass Islands, for nearly three years."

"Why?"

"Special operations," Pushley replied. "The Compass Islands were occupied by our forces because they are close to the Great Ones' heartland but are easily defensible. The Great Ones have always caused trouble. We suspected they were involved in spying and passing on classified information to the enemy. We were there to make sure they behaved themselves."

As always, he then brought the conversation around to himself, "It was listening to the Ab myths that triggered my interest in Arcadian archaeology and made me want to stay on Arcadia."

As Pushley turned to move away, Nonie worked up the courage to say, "Why were you really searching the air-car, Ed?"

"I've told you," Pushley replied. "I was looking for my medallion."

Nonie gave him a stern look, "I'm sorry, but I don't believe you."

Pushley bridled, "Excused me?"

"That you were looking for your lost medal," she said. "You were searching the wrong car. What were you really after?"

"How dare you suggest dishonesty," he snapped. "You need teaching a lesson."

Having endured Ed Pushley's pompous behaviour for most of her sojourn at Fort Saunders, Nonie unwisely provoked him further by taking up a martial arts stance. "You? Teach me a lesson? Come on then Ed! Medal for bravery! Let's see how good you are. "

Pushley's face turned beetroot red, and without warning, he hit her mind with a blast of energy. As she was still wearing the hat Tarmy had given her, it deflected most of the blast, but some of its power still got through. A fraction of a second later, she found herself in a strange chamber, a huge grub burst through one of the walls and slid towards her menacingly. But before it could attack her, the mental image evaporated and she found herself staring at Pushley, mouth open in disbelief.

He said, "If you cross me again, I'll teach you a lesson you'll never forget."

When she didn't respond, Pushley growled, "That nasty dream you've just had is going to become recurring. It's going to be a reminder that there's far worse to come if you cause me any trouble."

To prove his point, Pushley forced her back into the dream world again, and the huge grub moved towards her slavering for her flesh. But once again, just before it could strike, Pushley pulled her out of her dream world again and said, "So make sure you keep your nose out of my business in future."

As Pushley stalked off into the fog, Nonie remained transfixed to the spot, mind whirring. Had Pushley really forced her to have some sort of terrible nightmare? After remaining rooted to the spot for the best part of ten minutes, Nonie came out of her reverie and began thinking about telling Mick Tarleton what had just happened.

Before she could, her mind dragged her back into the dream world, and the grub monster returned. After suffering the same experience three times in quick succession, Nonie suddenly realised what Pushley had done. He *had* implanted the grub-monster in her mind to scare her into submission. She guessed that if she went to see Mick Tarleton, the bad dream would grow even worse.

Eventually, the dream sequence seemed to run its course, and she began to recover her confidence. She glanced down at the air-cars again and wondered if Pushley had damaged them. Knowing that she'd need to carry out tests, she went back to her cabin, she picked up the air-car fobs and went back.

After carefully lowering herself onto the air-car she'd caught Pushley searching she let herself in. Although the air-car interior was only dimly lit, her eyes immediately alighted upon a pair of heavy cutters. As they were close to the location where Pushley had supposedly found his medal, she concluded that they belonged to him.

She thought about the display of bad temper that Pushley had been showing and sabotage flashed into her mind. Had Pushley been disabling the air-cars?

Fearing the worst, she passed one of the fobs over the air-car's control unit and began running a system check. Eventually, the onboard computer confirmed that there were no faults.

As she'd been holding her breath without realising it, she let out a sigh of relief and moved to the next air-car to repeat the process. Once she was certain that Pushley hadn't sabotaged either of them, she climbed out and code locked both roof windows so he couldn't get back in. As a further precaution, instead of returning the fobs, she slipped them into one of her pockets.

Satisfied she'd done everything she could, she hauled herself back on deck. Feeling tired, and mentally drained, she decided to go back to the small cabin where she slept, but partway there Chou Lan suddenly loomed up out of the fog. She smiled, "Good news. Claire's come out of her coma."

Despite her recent bad experiences with Pushley, Nonie changed her plans and followed Chou back to the makeshift ward. Chou added, "You'll be pleased to know her face has returned to normal."

"Is she on her own?"

"No," Chou replied. "Mick's with her."

Nonie's mood immediately nose-dived again. Although she was pleased that Claire had recovered, she couldn't help feeling a twinge of jealousy.

CHAPTER ELEVEN

Fyfield Valley, Arcadia

Lascaux Kurgan is disturbed by Ed Pushley

Pushley frowned. Although he couldn't see anyone following him, he could sense at least one presence. Annoyed, he began issuing mental threats. A few seconds later, the presence moved away.

Once he was sure, his movements weren't being tracked; he opened a door that led to the below deck rooms and then began searching.

~*~

Lascaux Kurgan felt someone shake her; torchlight cut through the darkness. Waking with a start, she realised Ed Pushley was slumped down beside her, face twitching. His jerking features made all the more unnerving because parts of his body were obscured by darkness. As Lascaux barely knew Pushley, she feared the worst; the creep intended forcing himself on her. She immediately pulled out a large commando knife and thrust it in Pushley's direction.

Pushley threw himself sideways. "There's no need for that —put the knife away—please! I can't help my face twitching— it's the after-effect of multiple stunning."

Accepting his reasoning, Lascaux revised her judgement, lowered the knife but didn't re-sheath it. Instead, she moved slightly and nudged the person sleeping next to her. A moment later, Red Moxstroma rolled over, gave Pushley a bleary-eyed look, and smiled, "Hi mate, how're yuh doing?"

Pushley immediately smelt alcohol on his breath. As if to prove the point, Moxstroma pulled out a bottle of Arcadian absinthe and offered it to him. When Pushley declined, Moxstroma pulled the bottle back and turned over again.

Pushley glanced at Lascaux, accusatively, "Where did he get that?"

"We found a stash of it," she replied. "Now—what do you want?"

As Moxstroma had started to snore, Pushley ignored his presence and said, "I need to talk to you, Lascaux. It's important."

When Lascaux remained silent, Pushley repeated, "It's important."

"D'you know what time it is?" She complained, glancing at her watch.

"That's why I'm here now," Pushley replied. "It would appear that most people are sleeping. I don't want people listening in. How would you like to earn some money?"

Lascaux was immediately interested, "How much money?"

Her suspicions then returned. "And what do I have to do to earn it?"

In reply, Pushley pulled out his wallet and held up a money card. He then added, "This is real money—not your devalued local currency."

As anticipated, Lascaux made a grab for it, but Pushley was too quick for her and whisked it away.

"You still haven't told me what I have to do."

"I've lost a bag," Pushley replied. He gave Lascaux a detailed description. "It looks like canvas, but it's actually made from reinforced plasti-metal fibres and has a special locking mechanism along the top to secure it. It has runic symbols on it. "

"How did you lose it?"

"Someone must have stolen it," Pushley lied. "But that doesn't matter. I don't want to cause trouble. I just want the bag back. I need you to find it."

"Why have you come to me?"

"Because I've been told you know your way around," Pushley replied. "I hope I haven't been misinformed."

"What's in the bag?"

"The contents wouldn't be of a great deal of interest to you," Pushley said, "The bag contains local artefacts which I want to take back with me."

"What's an artefact?"

Pushley immediately quoted, "An artefact is an object made by a human being; one of cultural or historical interest."

"What are they worth—these artefacts?"

"Very little," Pushley replied. "But I have a strong personal attachment to them."

When Lascaux went quiet, Pushley added, "Do you want to earn some money or don't you?"

"How much?"

Pushley waved the card he was holding under her nose again. "Four hundred ACU, but you don't damage the bag, understood?"

When she nodded, Pushley waved the card he was holding under her nose again, "I'll give you this one hundred card as a gesture of goodwill, and if you bring me the bag, intact, I'll give you another three hundred ACU, understood?"

Sensing she could push for more, Lascaux said, "Five hundred, and you've got deal."

Pushley suddenly felt very angry, "You're a grasping so and so. D'you know that?"

Ignoring the temper tantrum, Lascaux raised her knife again and said, "D'you want the bag or don't you?"

"Of course, I want the bag."

"Then it's five hundred."

As Pushley's anger began moving towards flashpoint, he mentally debated whether he should force Lascaux into submission using his mental powers but changed his mind. Not only would it take time to successfully bend her to his will; he'd have the continuing mental effort of keeping her onside. Not wanting Lascaux to become a continuing drain on his energy, he went back to his original idea. Bribery was the best way of dealing with someone like Lascaux. "Okay—if you find the bag, I'll give you another four hundred."

When she didn't answer, Pushley said, "One last point. Once I've paid you, you don't mention the bag or our arrangement to anyone else, understood?"

Lascaux smiled, "So, what's really in the bag?"

Pushley sighed. "I've told you—artefacts—nothing special."

"I bet they're worth a small fortune," Lascaux surmised. "Come on, level with me and give me a proper deal."

"Five hundred, take it or leave it," Pushley replied. "If you don't want to help me, there will be others who will."

Realising Pushley was about to pull out, Lascaux started to backtrack, "Hang on, hang on, five hundred right?"

"Five hundred," Pushley agreed. "Now do we have a deal?"

"Yes."

"Good," Pushley replied. "Find the bag and bring it to me undamaged and the hundred ACU you are holding in your hot little hands becomes five hundred."

But instead of confirming the agreement, Lascaux said, "Tarleton had a bag like the one you're describing, I saw it. I can't imagine Tarleton collecting artefacts."

"You saw the bag?"

"Years of practice, I've got eyes in the back of my head. I caught a glimpse of it," Lascaux replied. "It was in the boot of one of the air-cars."

"Well, it's not there now because I've looked. And for your information, the bag is mine. Tarleton was just looking after it for me," Pushley replied, anger growing again.

"The bag was in Tarleton's boot before the plesiosaur killed the spettro commander and you were in the same air-car," Lascaux said. "You'd also been a prisoner for several days; you couldn't have given Tarleton the bag."

Pushley's temper finally erupted, and before he could stop himself, he said, "The bag is mine and even it if wasn't, it will be no use to Tarleton. Very shortly he'll be arrested."

"Arrested?"

"Your big buddy Tarleton is a war criminal."

"You're joking."

"I'm certainly not," Pushley snapped. "I wouldn't joke about something like that. Unfortunately, I didn't find out until we'd flown out of Fort Saunders. He left Cittavecchia at great haste."

"Tarleton save my life," Lascaux said.

"He saved mine too," Pushley replied. "But that's not the way the law works. You don't get good boy credits for helping little old ladies cross the road. You get a kick in the goolies if you do something wrong. The law punishes you if you break it; I've seen Tarleton's file; he's killed hundreds of people with the bombs and booby traps he's made over the years. Believe me, very shortly he'll be arrested."

Still angry, he growled, "And Claire Hyndman will be arrested too."

"Claire?" Lascaux asked, "Why?"

"Let's just say she's not what she seems."

Lascaux went into echo mode, "Not what she seems?"

"She's what is known as a monarch," Pushley amplified.

"And what exactly is a monarch?"

Pushley suddenly checked himself, "I've already said too much."

"What's a monarch?"

When Pushley remained silent, Lascaux said, "If you don't tell me, maybe I should ask Claire."

"You will do no such thing," Pushley snapped.

"Then tell me," Lascaux replied.

"This goes no further, understood?"

When Lascaux nodded, Pushley said, "Hyndman has been genetically modified. Particularly her bone structure. It enables monarchs to face change; Claire has been seen face changing by Nonie and Chou."

"You're joking!"

"I don't make jokes about things like that."

"Modifying someone must be illegal."

"Under normal circumstances, yes," Pushley agreed. "But the military has the right in times of extremes to acquire prisoners on death row and use them as monarchs. The logic is, why kill someone when they can partially atone for their heinous misdeeds by serving the state."

"So, Claire must have killed someone?"

"By implication, it would seem so," Pushley agreed. He added, "As far as the military are concerned, she has the same status as a droid, she's expendable."

Pushley then added, "All you need to know is she's also on a wanted list, I've only told you all this so that you knew what sort of people you are dealing with."

When Lascaux went very quiet, Pushley became worried. "I hope you won't go blabbing. It's confidential. If you blab, and Tarleton escapes, there's a strong chance you'll be arrested for aiding and abetting a known war criminal, understood?"

Lascaux nodded, "Understood; I'll keep my mouth shut."

She then stuffed the money card inside her bra, "If the bag is on the boats I'll find it - If you renege on the deal, the bag goes over the side, understood?"

"Understood," Pushley replied. "But keep your mouth shut about what I just said."

"As long as you pay me what I'm due, Ed, my lips are sealed."

CHAPTER TWELVE

Fyfield Valley, Arcadia
Nonie Tomio ignores Pushley's warning

"So, what do I do Ollie?" Nonie said.

Her pet Arcadian pterodactyl glanced in her direction but remained silent; it was no real surprise. Although the animal was highly intelligent, his vocabulary was limited. In any case, like most Arcadian creatures, he mainly *spoke* telepathically.

"Come on, Ollie," Nonie chivvied, "What should I do?"

Reading Nonie's thoughts, Ollie realised the question concerned Ed Pushley and began stepping, raising one foot and then the other. As she'd learned most of her pterodactyl's foibles, Nonie guessed at the truth. It was apparent Ollie was scared of Pushley. Without a doubt, her pet had been conscious of the bad energy flowing from Pushley long before she had.

Her thoughts about Pushley immediately triggered the bad dream again; her mind transported back to the feeding chamber. A moment later, the huge grub smashed its way through the paper-thin walls and began lurching towards her again.

Sensing her mental fears, Ollie let out a loud screech and brought her back to reality. It was at that point; Nonie made her decision. She had to do something. She couldn't just lie there, brooding. Even though it was evident that Pushley had somehow implanted the *bad dream* into her mind as a way of bullying her into silence, she couldn't just ignore what had happened. Turning to Ollie, she said, "I need you to follow Ed

Pushley."

Ollie replied by sending her Pushley's image followed by a bright red swirl, a point-blank refusal. He then confirmed it by squawking, "No."

"Go on!"

Despite her urgings, Ollie didn't move or say another word.

"Go on," Nonie wheedled, "I need you to keep an eye on Ed Pushley."

Instead of flying off, Ollie went back to stepping. Realising the pterodactyl would continue to refuse unless she changed tack, she said, "You don't have to go very close to him, you can scan him from afar. Okay?"

Although Ollie stopped stepping and seemed to be taking notice, Nonie still sensed reluctance. "Just keep track of him, use your infrared. Just let me know if he starts moving around. I also need to know where Claire and Mick are."

This time Ollie sent her three mental images: Ed Pushley, Mick Tarmy and Claire Hyndman. Ollie then sent her an image suggesting a little bribery might make him more co-operative.

Nonie said, "If I keep giving you snacks, you'll get fat."

Ignoring the caution, Ollie sent her another *feed me* image.

She decided to give in and offered him a small chunk of chocolate and a big smile. After grabbing the tit-bit before she changed her mind, Ollie briefly savoured it and then let out a slight squawk of acknowledgement before flying off. A few seconds later, his infrared vision cut through the fog and sent Nonie a mental image of Ed Pushley.

Unlike the sort of image normally seen in an infrared camera, Ollie's mind had somehow managed to convert Pushley's image to full colour. The clarity was such that Nonie could see that Pushley was in the prow of one of the dive boats with his face set like thunder.

As he just appeared to be staring moodily out over the misty waters, Nonie began wondering what he was doing. Could he be plotting something? She realised that he had something to his ear and was talking. Pushley was using a percom, and it was evident that he was in contact with the outside world!

As Ollie's imaging moved closer, Pushley suddenly turned as if he was conscious that he was under surveillance and swiftly pocketed the percom. Pushley gave her an accusative glare, one that seemed to bore into her very soul. He hit her with a mental blast.

While she was still fighting the blast, Pushley hit her with a second, and she found herself back in the strange chamber with the huge grub bearing down on her again. This time, Pushley's voice echoed in her mind, "I told you to keep your nose out of my business. Interfere again, and you'll disappear, permanently. I'll throw you overboard to the plesiosaurs, and that's not a threat it's an absolute promise."

As the grub continued to advance, she could smell its fetid breath. Then it raised its head exposing a row of sharp teeth. But before it could strike, the image of the grub began to shimmer and began to fade away. At first, Nonie couldn't work out what was happening, but then she sensed that Pushley's mental battery, the energy powering the nightmare had suddenly run out of power. Without a doubt, Pushley had hit a mental pain barrier and hadn't managed to break through it.

She'd barely let out a sigh of relief when Pushley's mental voice fleetingly returned, "Tarleton is mine. If you get in the way, I'll get rid of you. As I said, I'll throw you to the plesiosaurs and let them take you for a death roll."

She then felt a distinct click as Pushley's mental battery completely ran out of power.

Although her mind cleared, Nonie was still shocked by the mental assaults she'd suffered; she slumped back onto her makeshift bed and began thinking about what had just happened. From bitter experience, she knew some spettri had special mental powers, but Pushley had never demonstrated such skills before.

She then began thinking about the last thing that Pushley

had said, "Tarleton is mine."

The tone of the message indicated a deep hatred of Mick, even though Mick had saved Pushley's life. She thought of the worst-case scenario; was Pushley planning to kill Mick?"

But why should Pushley hate Mick enough to kill him? It didn't make sense. She began thinking about what she had to do. If she didn't warn Mick, Pushley might decide to ambush him. If she warned Mick, at least he'd be on his guard.

While she was still thinking, Ollie located Claire Hyndman and Chou Lan. As they were both still in the recovery ward, it was apparent that Claire had followed her advice and had remained under observation until they were sure she was fully recovered. Ollie then sent back Tarmy's image.

Mick was slumped beneath a temporary awning tinkering with something electronic. Nonie immediately made a swift mental calculation. As Pushley seemed to have temporarily exhausted his powers and Claire was still in the ward, now was the best chance of speaking to Mick without interruption.

Although she knew she was taking a serious risk, she set off in Mick's direction using her torch sparingly to pick her way through the drifting fog banks. Once she'd reached her destination, she coughed discretely to attract his attention and then slid down beside him.

Despite his welcoming smile, fear made her blurt out, "I hope I'm not going to regret coming here to talk to you. If Pushley finds out, he'll probably kill me."

Tarmy's brow furrowed, "Why should Pushley want to kill you?"

"He said he would kill me if I poked my nose into his business," Nonie replied. "And in the violent mood he's in, he probably would kill me."

Tarmy's expression changed from worry into anger, and he tried to stand up. Realising he was about to rush off and confront Pushley, Nonie grabbed hold of one of Tarmy's arms and restrained him, "Whoa Tiger. I didn't come here to start another war."

When Tarmy relaxed slightly, Nonie said, "Listen to what I've got to say before going off on one."

"Come on then, spit it out," Tarmy growled. "Why did he threaten you?"

Sensing he was still close to flashpoint, Nonie grabbed his arm with both hands and pleaded, "Listen! I need to tell you things."

"Okay. So, give me the whole story."

Nonie glanced around at the small groups of archaeologists who'd had chosen to huddle together for shared warmth on the upper deck rather than endure the airless conditions below deck, "Can we go somewhere more discrete?"

Tarmy said, "So, where d'you have in mind?"

Remembering she had the access fobs in her pocket, she produced them and then said, "We could use one of the air-cars."

Once they had made their way there, Nonie triggered the roof window of one of the air-cars, and they both climbed inside. She was just about to close the window when Ollie reappeared and fluttered through the opening. As usual, Ollie sent her a mental greeting. The pterodactyl sent her an image of Ed Pushley pacing around one of the upper decks like a caged tiger. Fluttering his wings again, Ollie landed on one of the back seats.

When Tarmy cocked an eyebrow, Nonie said, "Don't worry, he'd house trained. He won't do his business on the upholstery." She closed the roof window.

Once they were sealed in, Tarmy said, "So, what's going on?"

"I caught Ed Pushley searching the air-cars."

She then pulled out the heavy cutters. "After he'd gone, I checked the air-cars out and found these. He must have dropped them. I think he was intent on sabotage, but I interrupted him."

After taking the heavy cutters off her, Tarmy examined them closely. "They don't look as if they have been used to cut any wiring."

"Like I just said," Nonie cut in. "I think I interrupted him before he got a chance to do any damage."

After giving the cutters another once over, Tarmy said, "Why would Pushley want to sabotage the air-cars?"

"I've no idea," Nonie replied. "Unless it's connected with the conversation I saw him having on his percom."

"Percom?"

"Didn't you know he had a percom?"

"No."

"Well he has; as I said, I saw him using it."

"Who was he calling?"

"How should I know," Nonie replied. "But he said, 'Tarleton is mine.' I suspect all of this has something to do with you. So, what did he mean? What's going on, Mick?"

Dodging the question, Tarmy said, "Where is he now?"

"Look, I said I didn't want you to do anything rash," Nonie repeated and grabbed hold of his arm again. "At the moment, he's just mooching around, scowling. Ollie was watching him. I'll get him to go back on watch once we've finished here. Then I'll let you know if he does anything suspicious."

"Okay," Tarmy agreed. "You caught him in the air-cars. It's also obvious something else happened. So, what happened?"

"It's difficult to explain."

"Try," Tarmy said.

"It wasn't just what he claimed to be doing or what he said."

When Tarmy frowned, she realised she wasn't making much sense and added, "When I caught him in one of the air-car's he claimed he was looking for something."

Tarmy remembered the bag containing the money cards. Alex had said it was somewhere safe. Could he have put it back in one of the air-cars? Could Pushley have been looking for the bag?

He glanced at the cutters again. Had Pushley brought them with him to cut the bag open?

"Did he say what he was looking for?" Tarmy asked.

"He showed me a medal when he climbed out."

"A medal?"

"He said he'd dropped it, but he couldn't have because he's never been in that air-car. I suspected that finding the medal was a lie, and I challenged him. It was a bad move because he turned nasty. He told me to keep my nose out of his business."

She hesitated, then added, "There's something else; he did something to my mind."

"Did something to your mind?" Tarmy echoed.

"I suddenly felt as if I was in a waking dream; he somehow sent me to some sort of chamber. Then a huge grub appeared and tried to attack me, eat me alive," Nonie replied. "It scared me. It seemed so very real."

~*~

Her description immediately reminded Tarmy of the recent threats that the four-armed spettro had made and the dream-threats Irrelevant had used on him over the last few days. He then recalled how Irrelevant had died. As there could be little doubt Ed Pushley had been under Irrelevant's power at the time of his death, could it be that Pushley had somehow inherited some of Irrelevant's abilities when the spettro died?

After thinking for a few seconds, about the possibility of some sort of mental transference, Tarmy opted for a more logical explanation. As The Great Ones had lost at least a dozen air-cars and two FA49s and the blockade had failed, it was logical they'd look for another way to attack the convoy.

Could it be they'd fallen back on their mental powers? As Pushley had succumbed to mind control before, could it be the Great Ones had control of him again? If they had, Pushley could now be a fifth columnist intent on sabotage.

With this in mind, he began thinking about arresting Pushley, but Nonie cut across his thoughts. "I think Pushley's looking for something. Something of value."

Once again, Tarmy thought about the bag containing the money cards. As Pushley had been with Irrelevant for some time before he was rescued, maybe he'd seen the bag. Perhaps, he knew what it contained. If it were true, Pushley had no desire to help the Great Ones; he just wanted to feather his own nest.

While his mind was still churning, Nonie said, "Look, Mick, will you be straight with me?"

Tarmy frowned again, "Aren't I straight with you? I thought I was."

"I want to know where I stand," Nonie replied. "I've risked my life coming here to tell you what I've discovered. If Pushley finds out that I've talked to you, I have absolutely no doubt that he'll kill me."

"Look, I have always appreciated what you have done for me," Tarmy replied.

"Have you?" Nonie snapped. "You only seem interested in Claire."

"That's not true," Tarmy replied, and before she could answer, he reached out, took hold of one of her hands and pulled her towards him and kissed her. "I like you a lot."

"Only like?"

"Okay, love," Tarmy admitted. He said, "When I was in Cittavecchia you know as well as I do, I was badly beaten. I was attracted to you instantly, but as I was going on a dangerous mission, one that would probably kill me, getting involved didn't seem fair on you."

"Does it now?"

"Yes."

"If you leave, will you take me with you?"

"Of course," Tarmy promised.

"What about Claire?"

"Yes," Tarmy replied. "Claire comes too."

"What if I said I wouldn't come with you if she came along," Nonie challenged.

"I thought you were scared that Pushley would kill you?" Tarmy countered. He pulled out his stun gun, "If you did refuse, I wouldn't want to do it, but I'd probably incapacitate you and cart you off with me anyway."

When Nonie's expression changed into an *I'm-not-sure-if-you're-joking* look, Tarmy re-holstered his gun and said, "I hope you won't put me in that position?"

"What is it with you and Claire?"

"Look, it's complicated," he replied.

"In what way?"

"For starters, I owe Claire; she saved my life."

"I sense an *and* in there somewhere."

"Alex is Claire's minder, not mine. At the moment Alex appears to have accepted me as group leader, but I suspect he might change his allegiances if I upset Claire. As Alex is the only thing, other than good luck, that has kept us alive; I don't want to fall out with Claire."

"Alex?"

"Claire's invisible friend."

"So, let me get this straight. Having Alex to protect you is more important to you than Claire, which means you're just using her."

"That's your interpretation," Tarmy hit back, "I didn't say that. That's not how I see things. I like Claire a lot. Besides, like I just said, I owe her. She saved my life. If it hadn't been for her, I would probably have ended up in a feeding chamber similar to the one you saw in your dreams with wolf larvae ripping chunks of flesh out of my living body."

"Tell me how she rescued you," Nonie said.

After briefly telling her about the underground prison, he added, "I'll explain everything when we have more time." He then brought the conversation back on track. "You were telling me about the bad dream."

Realising that Tarmy wouldn't open up until he was ready, Nonie relented and changed tack with him, "The dreams *are* bad. Terrifying. And they are recurring, Pushley has definitely done something to me."

"Your hat should be protecting you," Tarmy said. He added, "Give me your hat."

Once she'd taken it off, he began inspecting the lining. Eventually, he found a slight break in a beaded link; shining his torch into the hat, "How long has it been like this?"

Nonie shrugged, "I think I snagged the beads yesterday."

After repairing it, he handed the hat back. Once she'd replaced it on her head, he said, "Well. How is it now?"

After a slight pause, she smiled. "I can't quite describe it, but my mind seems clearer now."

Tarmy pointed at the peaked cap he was wearing, "I've become an expert in hat production. I made this one myself, once I'd realised what the beads were, making a hat is easy-peasy."

He added, "With any luck, you won't get that bad dream again."

"Pushley said, 'Mick Tarleton is mine.' What did he mean, Mick?"

Tarmy sighed. "Looks like I'm in big trouble. I think I need to level with you. My real name is Mick Tarmy," he replied. "But I've been using the alias Tarleton."

"Why?"

After swiftly explaining about Samantha's blackmailing, and being forced to take on Tarleton's unwanted mantle, Tarmy said, "It's obvious that Ed Pushley has learned that Mick Tarleton is a wanted man and is planning to have me arrested. Maybe I ought to go and explain my position to him. Maybe I should have done it before."

"No," Nonie told him. "Pushley won't believe you, and there's a strong chance he might decide to kill you."

Tarmy went silent for a second or two and mentally ran through the armed confrontations he'd had during his career. If he wasn't careful, Pushley might suddenly pull a gun. "Okay you win; I'll avoid Pushley."

"You mentioned Samantha. Who's Samantha?"

"Samantha is a high-power droid running security and special operations on Arden," Tarmy explained, and added, "Samantha sent Claire and me on what she intended to be a suicide mission. Luckily, we were able to avoid being killed. Although the bomb destroyed its target, we didn't die in the detonation, which was what she'd planned. If she gets to know we're still alive, she'll probably send people to Arcadia to kill us."

"Why did you agree to take the mission?"

"I tried everything I could to avoid working for Samantha," Tarmy replied. "But she bullied me into it. I think she also brainwashed me."

"What makes you think that?"

"Things that happened," Tarmy replied. " She put implants, controllers, into my brain. She also put controllers into Claire's brain too. Luckily, we discovered them and managed to extract them, safely, with Alex's help."

When Nonie remained silent, Tarmy added, "Samantha also threatened my friends and family. My daughter was arrested without charge and imprisoned. As she's now safely aboard Salus Transporter 9, I can hopefully start to rebuild my life."

"Tell me more about the real Tarleton."

"Tarleton was a war criminal. The real Tarleton died some time ago, but they suppressed the news of his death. Because I look like him, Samantha forced me to take his identity. As I said, she blackmailed me into taking this mission."

"What exactly was the mission?"

"To find and destroy some of the Great Ones," Tarmy replied.

"And did you?"

"Yes," Tarmy admitted. "But, as I said, I think Samantha wanted it to be a suicide mission. At the moment, I'm sure Samantha thinks both Claire and me are dead. If we all escape before Pushley can turn me in, she may never find out we're still alive."

"What happens if she does find out you're still alive?"

"She will probably send someone to kill us to stop us talking," Tarmy revealed. He then let out a bitter laugh, "So I'm between a rock and a hard place. If I'm not careful, Pushley or his associates will try and kill me. If they don't, Samantha may."

"You said Samantha would kill you to stop you talking.

Talking about what?"

"About the secret prisons and about the deliberate contraventions of Section Thirty-two of the Consolidated Space Agreement," Tarmy replied.

"And what's that when it's at home?"

"Under Section Thirty-two of the Consolidated Space Agreement, the Ardenese Government should have placed Arden into quarantine from the moment the first Arcadian Child was discovered and identified as an alien being. The Ardenese Government should also have issued warnings to surrounding colonies."

"And they didn't."

"No, they didn't," Tarmy confirmed.

After the conversation turned into silence for some time, Tarmy leaned over and kissed her again. Nonie responded by moving closer, but before a real clinch could develop, they were surprised by a loud noise close at hand. They realised that they could hear footsteps on the roof of the air-car. Ollie immediately let out an alarmed squawk and then sent Nonie an image of Pushley's twitching face.

Tarmy pulled out his stun gun and was about to open the roof light when Nonie hissed, "No, don't; Pushley's back; he could be armed."

Tarmy instinctively extinguished the dash lights and glanced up. Two seconds later, he caught a glimpse of heavy boots moving over the roof window. He could hear a scrabbling noise as Pushley attempted to override the external locking mechanism. There was a scuffling sound, and Pushley crouched down low and brought his twitching face close to the window; he attempted to stare in.

They could both hear Pushley bellow in anger when he realised he'd been locked out. After letting out a few more choice oaths, Pushley climbed to his feet again and then went stomping back the way he came. They then felt the air-car bounce slightly as Pushley leapt off and scrambled onto the deck of the nearest dive boat.

As silence returned, Nonie said. "D'you think he saw us?"

"I doubt it," Tarmy returned. "These windows are slightly tinted, and I turned off all the internal lighting."

As Nonie let out a sigh of relief, Tarmy added, "One thing for certain, now I don't have any doubts about what you were telling me—Pushley is a very dangerous man."

"So, what are we going to do?"

"Get out of here."

"So, you mean to desert the convey?"

Tarmy corrected her, "I've always promised, we'd stay with the convoy for as long as we could."

"So, the answer is yes?"

"There's no choice," Tarmy said. "It's obvious it would be stupid to go to the Compass Islands because my guess is that Pushley has already reported my presence. If he has, I'll be arrested as soon as the convoy arrives. If I stay with the convoy, Pushley's people may even come upriver to get me. Going back to Fort Saunders is also another non-starter."

"As Fort Saunders and the Compass Islands are out of the question," Nonie replied. "The only other sensible place you could head for would be the Awis Oasis."

Although Alex had already suggested Awis Oasis, Tarmy was slightly scathing, "Some fly-ridden pool of water in the middle of nowhere?"

Realising that Tarmy didn't know anything about Awis Oasis, and was envisaging a cartoonist's oasis, one that had two palm trees growing alongside a puddle, Nonie said, "Although it is surrounded by desert, Awis Oasis is like a small island in the middle of a sea of rock and sand. The oasis is approximately eighty kilometres by twenty kilometres wide. It also has two large lakes inside it. Awis Oasis has a population of nearly fifty thousand people. There used to be a large Ab population there, but colonists have largely displaced them."

"Okay. If I go to Awis Oasis, what's the difference? How will that help me?"

"Awis Oasis is the sort of place where they don't ask too

many questions," Nonie replied. "The Awis Oasis makes a living exporting Arcadian dates and trading with people crossing the Great Rock Desert."

"By trade, you mean shady deals."

"Most of the trade is legal," Nonie replied very matter of factly. "On the other hand, having a few shady dealers might be useful. I've no doubt there will be people who can forge you and Claire new IDs."

"Okay," Tarmy agreed. "We have a plan."

He then became practical, "We will have to get some supplies onboard the air-cars."

He then thought about Pushley, "Maybe I ought to find Pushley and stun him to make sure he doesn't try to prevent us leaving."

"No," Nonie replied. "It could backfire, and he might kill you. Let's avoid him if possible."

CHAPTER THIRTEEN

Arcresten

Stert Oryx arrives

T here was a slight shimmer and then nine shadows appeared in the teleport; three were active, the other six in stasis.

As the three active images began to harden, human figures began to reassemble. Being a stickler for detail, Vert Zardus immediately raised a small device to one eye and then ran it over each reconstruct in turn. He then let out a sigh of relief when the device verified that Stert Oryx and his two companions were genuine; rejecting a teleport visitor was always a messy business.

As the reconstructs continued to develop, Zardus began thinking about the file information he'd read concerning the three men. If the records were correct, Stert Oryx had been part of a guerrilla army during the last war. Although he'd never been officially commissioned by a regular army group, he always styled himself, Colonel.

At the end of hostilities, Oryx had been warranted by the Interplanetary Criminal Court to track down and sanction war criminals and had formed his own action group. Although the records were vague, Zardus had calculated that Oryx and his deputies had successfully sanctioned at least twenty-three major war criminals.

As the reconstructs developed still further, Zardus noted that Oryx and his men were wearing casual civilian clothing. However, Zardus wasn't surprised; if the records were correct,

Oryx's team never advertised their presence. Like a pride of lions stalking their prey, Oryx's group believed in stealth, keeping a low profile. It was why Oryx always used safe military teleport stations when he could. That way, there was less likelihood of the media taking an interest and alerting criminals to their presence in an area.

Zardus transferred his attention to Oryx's companions. Slon and Lane Syn had been part of Oryx's guerrilla group and had joined his action group from the day it was founded.

While he was still staring upwards, the other six shadows started to take on real shapes, and it soon became obvious two were multi-seat air-cars; the other four shapes mystified him for a while. Although it was apparent they were some sort of armoured droid, as Zardus couldn't identify them, he was reasonably sure they weren't from a known military stable. Still, the mere fact that Oryx had brought them with him indicated he meant business.

After another thirty seconds, Oryx's body hardened, and he stepped out of the teleport. Slon and Lane Syn immediately followed his lead. After making formal introductions, Oryx moved forward. Two steps later, one of his legs buckled. Although he swiftly recovered, after taking two more steps, his legs gave way entirely, and he landed on his knees; it provided enough evidence to confirm he was suffering from post teleport sickness.

Zardus immediately waved at a waiting medi-droid and then instructed it to seat Oryx in a wheelchair. The other man gave him a sharp look, "I don't need mollycoddling Zardus. We need to get after Tarleton. We have had a sure-fire lead, and we need to get after him before he disappears again. He's a *real* slippery customer."

Zardus refused to be bullied, "Not until you've been fully checked out and have recovered."

Reluctantly, Oryx allowed himself to be wheeled away, but he glanced back at Slon and Lane Syn and called out, "Looks like you two will have to go after Tarleton on your own. Get the air-cars and the droids ready and move in fast. There's no time to waste."

The other two men turned to carry out their orders but had barely walked three steps before they also started staggering like drunks. Zardus nodded at the other medi-droids, "Get these two into recovery as well."

Slon and Syn immediately objected, "We're both fine; we need to leave."

In response, Zardus triggered three internal Mannheim force shields. Realising that they were boxed in, Slon turned sharply fully intending to rebuke Zardus again. Instead, the sudden movement sent him crashing to the floor.

"I think my case is proven," Zardus said, and then waved at the support droids again. "Neither of you is fit enough to leave just yet."

Frustrated, Slon Syn shouted, "You'll regret this," as he was wheeled away. He called out, "If Tarleton escapes because you've delayed us, the boss will cause mayhem."

Unflustered, Zardus said, "I would be failing in my duty if I didn't have you checked over."

"How long is all this going to take?" Slon Syn snapped.

"The usual recovery time for an extended teleport is two to three hours," Zardus replied and then gestured for the medi-droid to proceed. He then followed the machine into the recovery area. Stert Oryx immediately gave him a blinding look. "What the hell's going on. Why are my guys in here too?"

"For the same reason you are," Zardus growled. "As teleport manager on this facility, I can't pass any of you fit for operations until you've recovered."

"How long is all this going to take?"

"Slon asked the same question," Zardus said, "And I give you the same answer, the usual recovery time for long-teleports is two to three hours."

"If Tarleton escapes because you've delayed us ..."

"I know, you'll cause me grief," Zardus replied. He then added, "But you have to realise I can't let you leave here for at least two hours; you may as well relax while we sort out all the bumf."

"What bumf?"

"I told you before you teleported down that you'd require a Section 13A permit," Zardus replied.

When Oryx tutted, indicating he had a strong dislike for red tape, Zardus passed him the certificate that had been laminated in transparent plastimetal. "One 13A permit. Don't say I'm not co-operating."

Oryx glanced at the document suspiciously, "And I want this because?"

"Because the whole of Arcadia is a POSSI—a planet of special scientific interest, the use of droids is restricted—a Section 13A permit also gives you an extended exemption to operate them in native reservations like the Fyfield Valley. The exemption is valid for 28 standard days—if you can't corner Tarleton in 28 days, you're not trying."

When Oryx's suspicious look changed to one of surprise, Zardus added, "I hope you realise we had to call in a lot of favours to obtain the Section 13A."

"Where is this leading?"

"It's not leading anywhere," Zardus replied. "I was asked to help you capture Tarleton, and that's what I'm doing."

"I've heard whispers that Tarleton has a monarch with his group," Oryx said. "Do you want it back?"

"We haven't got a missing monarch," Zardus replied. "We mostly suspended the monarch program once the war was over."

Moving in like a well-trained lawyer, Oryx said, "Mostly suspended, not totally suspended?"

"I've never been involved with the monarch program," Zardus replied. "And to be honest, I'm glad I never was, it seems a grisly business converting a human into a monarch and then sending it out on covert operations and almost certain death."

"Monarchs are a lot cheaper to create than an advanced

droid system," Oryx replied. "They are also more intelligent than most droids."

"I'm sure they are," Zardus replied. "But as I just told you, I've never been involved with the monarch program."

"So, what do I do with the monarch?"

Zardus shrugged and said, "That's up to you. We don't want it back." He added, "Do you mind if I ask you about the four armoured droids you've brought with you? What are they?"

"They are Ingermann-Verex A10s," Oryx replied.

"Never heard of them," Zardus replied.

"They are favoured by most police forces to protect city-centre locations," Oryx revealed.

"Protect them from what?"

"From robberies, terrorist attacks and wonky droids," Oryx revealed. "I used them before they had stun and anti-droid weapons. They are just a precaution. We've been told that Tarleton has a TK5 minder."

Zardus' attitude changed. From being laidback, he became edgy, "We used to have a squadron of TK5's stationed here, but they were withdrawn a few years back. In those days we were allowed to overfly parts of the Fyfield."

He added, "We lost one."

"Could be your missing machine then," Oryx replied affably. "If we can, we'll bring it back."

Zardus said, "If it is our machine it's not a standard TK5, it's an enhanced TK5 equipped with cloaking and interRoC."

Oryx brushed the information to one side, "I have seen A10s in action. As we're four against one, a single TK5 won't stand a chance."

Realising that Oryx was not the sort of man to listen Zardus wondered if he was wasting his breath but still told the other man about the lurking dangers in the forests surrounding the Fyfield River. After explaining that the Arcadian millipedes were highly venomous, he began briefing Oryx about the vastness of the Altos Plateaux and the Fyfield Valley reservation. Partway through, Oryx yawned and said, "How much longer do we have wait?"

Zardus glanced at a wall clock, "Another two hours at least."

Realising Oryx wasn't listening, Zardus said, "One last thing..."

He opened up a power bubble, and a man's face appeared inside it. Oryx immediately went hyper. "That's Hal Warmers—I've been after him for years. Where was this taken?"

"Yesterday. One of our agents reported his presence in Awis Oasis," Zardus replied. "As you are on Arcadia, I thought you might want to bag him too."

CHAPTER FOURTEEN

The Fyfield Valley

Pushley's forced into action

Having spent hours surreptitiously searching the most obvious nooks and crannies on the boats, Lascaux Kurgan was beginning to wonder if Ed Pushley had sent her on a fruitless errand. Worse, with only her torch to light the way, she was also getting jumpy. Although she couldn't see anyone watching her, she felt as if unseen eyes were noting her every move.

As she worked her way across a gangplank between one dive boat and another, something moved in her peripheral vision. She glanced sideways, but all she saw was a heavy mist bank rolling towards her. Annoyed by her own jumpiness, she began moving around, looking for places where someone might hide Ed Pushley's bag.

Although she didn't realise it, she eventually came to the locker room Pushley had used when he'd initially contacted Oryx; she went inside. Like Pushley, she jumped when her torch illuminated the fluorescent flashes on the safety jacket, but once she'd recovered her composure, she began searching.

Fifteen minutes later, she opened a large box and found a bag that matched Pushley's description perfectly; it was made of some sort of tough canvas covered in strange runic symbols; it had a long locking mechanism to seal it shut. Disbelieving Pushley's claim that the bag only contained worthless artefacts, Lascaux unsheathed her knife and tried to force the lock with the sharp point, but it resisted. Trying a more brutal approach, she attempted to cut through one of the seams.

Failing to gain entry, she inspected the bag more closely; she eventually realised that Pushley had been telling the truth; the bag was made from woven plastimetal fibre; the sort of fabric used in anti-stab jackets. After trying to cut the bag open one more time, she gave up and left the storeroom to search for Pushley.

She found him sheltering under an awning. Keeping a firm grip on the bag, she waved it at him, "Is this what you've been looking for?"

When his eyes lit up, she held a hand out, "Time to honour your debt, my friend."

He was on the point of opening his wallet when he frowned, "Bring it closer."

Still keeping the bag out of reach, she moved a little closer and held it up.

Pushley found his torch and shone it on the bag. He suddenly frowned and shook his head, "Sorry, that bag is similar to the one I'm looking for, but it's not mine. Mine had mainly blue runes on it; that one's got mainly red."

Lascaux looked peeved. "You're joking. You didn't tell me what colour the runes were."

"You didn't ask."

"I didn't think I needed to," Lascaux snapped back. "So, I've wasted my time."

Pushley waved her away with one hand, "Yes. You've wasted your time. So, don't ask me for money. That's not my bag. Come back when you've found the right one."

The dismissive, patronising tone of Pushley's voice triggered deep-seated resentments in Lascaux's psyche, the sort that comes from being the underdog for too long. From being annoyed, she hit flash point and exploded, "You skinflint! You're trying to cheat me."

As expletives rang through the air, someone turned the deck lighting on. Realising Lascaux's swearing was attracting attention, Pushley hissed, "Keep your voice down."

He thrust a low denomination money card into Lascaux's hand. "It's the wrong bag, I tell you. But take that for your trouble and go away."

Although she grabbed the money, Lascaux's chin shot out pugnaciously, "That's not what we agreed."

"And that's not the right bag," Pushley snapped back. "Now, please stop shouting."

The comment made Lascaux do the exact opposite. Raising her voice, she called out, "This guy is a cheating bastard."

She moved towards the side of the boat and threatened to throw the bag overboard. The threat had barely been issued before someone raced forwards and snatched it out of her hand. "That's my bag you thieving bitch."

Lascaux turned fast, knife drawn, fully intending to use it on her opponent but before she could stab her intended victim, a voice rang out, "Drop the knife Lascaux."

Glancing sideways, she saw Claire Hyndman. Although she looked shaky, still not fully recovered from the gas attack, the stun gun she was holding was absolutely steady, levelled straight at her. Two other women stood next to her. One had a pulse rifle, and Chou Lan was brandishing a rocket pistol. For a fraction of a second, it looked as if Lascaux would ignore the challenge.

"Drop it, or I'll fire," Claire repeated.

Glaring at the three women for a full five seconds, Lascaux let her arm drop, but she kept hold of the knife.

"I said, drop it!"

The knife clattered to the deck.

As Claire gestured with her stun-gun and Lascaux moved away, Pushley shouted, "It was just a misunderstanding."

Lascaux half turned. "You're a cheating bastard, Pushley."

As she continued walking, the real owner of the bag began to follow, but Claire Hyndman held up a hand. "I'd back off if I was you. You've got your bag back. Now go."

Once the other woman had retreated, Claire took Lascaux to one side and said, "So, what was that all about?"

Instead of answering the question, Lascaux went on the offensive, "I thought you were in a bad way."

"I was, but I'm not now," Claire replied.

Annoyed with Pushley, Lascaux began operating her mouth without engaging her brain, "Is it true Mick Tarleton is a war criminal?"

"What!"

"Is he a war criminal?"

"It's news to me if he is," Claire countered. "Who said he was?"

Lascaux pointed at Pushley, "He did. He said a guy called Stert Oryx will be waiting at the Compass Islands and is going to arrest Mick when we arrive."

"Arrest Mick?

Enjoying Claire's worries, Lascaux revealed more information, "According to Pushley, Stert Oryx is going to arrest you too."

Claire looked shocked, "Why should anyone want to arrest me?"

"Pushley said you are genetically modified. Not a real person. According to him, you weren't born, you were hatched in a laboratory. They've even got a name for people like you. You're a thing called a monarch."

"A monarch," Claire echoed, "Genetically modified?"

"That's what he said," Lascaux replied. "He reckons you and Mick are wanted. What's the betting that Pushley is hoping to collect the reward money for shopping you to the bounty-hunters."

"I hope you realise that's a load of bullshit."

Lascaux shrugged. "If Mick is guilty, Oryx has good reasons for arresting you too."

"Like what?"

"Let's start with aiding and abetting a known war criminal," Lascaux replied.

"Well Pushley's wrong on all counts," Claire hit back. "Look, neither of us wanted to come here. We were forced to. There is no reason for this Stert Oryx guy to arrest us."

Lascaux nodded in Pushley's direction. "He seemed certain that both of you were going to be arrested." She smiled cunningly. "In my experience, the police arrest first and ask questions later. Despite what they say, you're assumed guilty and have to prove your innocence. Worse, some just shoot first and don't bother to ask questions. I don't know who Stert Oryx is, but Pushley is convinced he's after Mick."

Claire frowned, "How would Pushley know that Stert Oryx is waiting for Mick."

Seeing a way of blackening Pushley's character still further, Lascaux said, "My guess he's spoken to Stert Oryx. He's probably been using a percom you know nothing about."

Claire gave the other woman a hard look, "You stay there while I talk to Pushley."

Turning to the archaeologist with the pulse rifle, she said, "Make sure she doesn't move. And you," to Chou Lan, "Come with me."

Seeing them walking towards him, Pushley became defensive, "What's the lying bitch been saying? I didn't ask her to go around stealing other people's property."

Claire responded as if he hadn't spoken. "Have you got a percom you haven't declared?"

Realising he could be body searched, Pushley came clean, "I have an emergency percom, yes."

"But you never thought to use it when we were all trapped at Cittavecchia?"

"I've never used it because there was no point. It's exactly what it says it is—an emergency percom. It only has a very limited range. We're too far from civilisation for it to connect. In any case, I was under observation the whole time I was at Cittavecchia, so I couldn't use it."

Claire clicked her fingers, "Let me see it."

Reluctantly, Pushley pulled out his wallet, retrieved the wafer-thin percom and handed it over. After interrogating it and getting negative responses, Claire frowned. "It doesn't seem to have been used."

Although he knew he'd obliterated all traces of his call to Stert Oryx, Pushley still breathed a sigh of relief. Confident that nothing could be proven, he retrieved the percom and said, "I've just told you. It has a limited range. There was no point in even trying to contact anyone."

"So, you haven't been in touch with Stert Oryx then?"

"Never heard of him," Pushley replied. Then innocently, "Who is he?"

When Claire didn't answer, Pushley added, "Even if I did know someone called Stert Oryx, I haven't been in contact with him."

"So, why are you accusing Mick of being a war criminal."

Pushley looked surprised, "I'm not."

He glanced at Lascaux, "Is that what she told you?"

"Yes."

"Lascaux has a vicious tongue in her head," Pushley said. "She also has a very vivid imagination."

For a fraction of a second, Pushley thought his glib tongue had won the day, but Claire said, "I think we need to see Mick."

She gestured for Pushley to step onto the gangplank leading to another dive boat. In response, Pushley half turned as if intending to comply with her instructions but suddenly he swung back, lashed out and caught Claire squarely on the jaw. As she went down, he grabbed her stun gun, shot Chou Lan before she could threaten him with the rocket pistol she was holding and said, "I think you're right. We need to see Mick."

Situations reversed, he told Claire to stand up. Once she had, he moved in fast, swung her around and placed the gun against her head. He glanced at the strange eddies in the fog banks. Without a doubt, the TK5 was waiting for an opportunity to jump him. More to bolster his own courage than anything else, he said, "I know you have a TK5 protecting the convoy, but it's not going to come to your assistance."

Although Claire was tempted to bluff, she didn't because she knew that Pushley was right. If Alex used his phaser, he'd probably end up killing her and taking out the side of the dive boat.

While she was still thinking about Alex's ability to intervene, Pushley forced her across a gangplank. A figure suddenly loomed up out of the mist. Without asking questions, Pushley fired the stun gun and stepped over the fallen body. Annoyed by the indiscriminate use of weapons, Claire half turned and said, "What did you do that for?"

Pushley hissed, "Keep moving. And don't get clever. If you attempt to warn Tarleton, I'll shoot you too, and I'll throw you overboard. You won't be able to swim if you're stunned. You'll drown."

"If you kill me you'll miss out on the reward, won't you?"

"The reward for you is minimal," Pushley replied, "Hardly worth worrying about. On the other hand, Tarleton's bounty is well worth collecting. Now shut up and get moving."

After firing at several more refugees on the way, Pushley told her to stop. Claire wondered if he intended to carry out his threat of drowning her, but instead, Pushley moved close to the side of the dive boat and glanced over the side. Catching signs of movement in one of the air-cars, he chuckled, "I thought so."

"What's so funny?" Claire snapped.

Instead of answering, Pushley swung her around and pushed her towards an external tool rack and instructed, "Take down one of those long poles."

Once she'd done as instructed, "Okay, lower the pole over the side of the dive boat."

Eventually, the pole hit the roof of one of the air-cars. Hearing the thump, Pushley said, "Knock a few times."

"Why?"

Although she couldn't see his twitching face because he was still holding her from behind, she felt him smile. "Your lover boy is down there doing the business with Nonie. Tap on the roof again and tell them to get up here."

When he didn't get the reaction he'd been hoping for, Pushley growled, "I said to knock on the roof and then call down to them."

Shouting down, she knocked again. On the third knock, there was a slight whine as a roof door opened a fraction, wide enough for her to see Mick and Nonie.

Pushley said, "Tell Tarleton and Nonie to get up here."

After she'd called out, Pushley joined in, "Sorry to disturb your horizontal gymnastics Tarleton. Leave your gun in the air-car, and you and Nonie get up here now. If you refuse, I'll stun Claire and throw her over the side."

A few seconds later, Mick hauled himself on the deck, and Nonie followed.

Pushley smiled, moved close to one of Claire's ears and said, in a stage whisper, "I do hope this display of infidelity hasn't come as a shock to you, my dear."

Instead of being drawn, Claire remained silent.

Irritated by her lack of response, Pushley said, "Well we can't dwell on it, can we?"

Then, without explaining, Pushley fired twice. As Tarmy and Nonie hit the deck, Pushley whispered, "You're doing very well, Claire. You make an excellent shield. The time has come to make sure we're not interrupted."

He pushed her forward again, shooting at refugees as he found them.

~*~

Bryn Rosslyn dodged sideways, dropped down beside Red Moxstroma, and hissed, "Hide!"

"What the hell's going on?"

"Shush," Rosslyn whispered "Hide. Pushley has a gun, and he's shooting people."

Without further explanation, Rosslyn scrabbled across the floor on his hands and knees, opened a cupboard door and wormed his thin body between the stored items. Hearing shouts from outside, Moxstroma followed Rosslyn's example and found a hiding place. There was a chink he could stare through, and he saw Pushley appear in the doorway with Claire Hyndman squirming in his arms.

Claire began wriggling hard and said, "You've got it all wrong Pushley, Mick's not a war criminal."

Pushley laughed, "Maybe he is, and maybe he isn't, but there is still a reward on his head, and I intend to collect it."

As Pushley dragged her off and everything went quiet, Moxstroma said, "He's gone."

"I'm staying here for the time being," Rosslyn whispered.

"Did you hear what Ed Pushley said?"

"Yeah," Rosslyn whispered back. "I think we can discount everything he told us as a crock of shit."

"Right!"

~*~

When Mick Tarmy awoke, he felt strange; his arms and legs felt numb. It was as if parts of his body were missing. He realised he was no longer in the air-car with Nonie and more importantly, water was flowing past his face. He was sprawled across a float, and he realised he was hanging over the edge of an inflatable dinghy. As passing ripples splashed him, he heard someone close by whisper, "Ha! Good, you're awake, Mr Tarleton."

Although the voice sounded vaguely like Ed Pushley's, it had a clipped, precise edge to it which reminded Tarmy of how Irrelevant had talked.

While his mind was still whirring, the voice said, "In case you're wondering what's going on, Tarleton, I took the liberty of partially stunning you and rolling you into a dingy."

"Eh? Shot me? Why?"

"Civic duty. You're a wanted war criminal, Tarleton. You couldn't be allowed to escape."

"I'm not a war criminal. My real name is Michael Tarmy, and I'm a police officer."

"I'm sure you're a man with a thousand aliases, Tarleton," Pushley replied breezily. "Once I've handed you over to Stert Oryx, I'm sure he'll listen to what you have to say and then decide if you are telling the truth or lying."

"Who's Stert Oryx?"

"He hunts down war criminals," Pushley in Irrelevant's voice explained. "All being well he'll be coming upstream shortly, and I will get a reward for handing you in."

"You might as well kill me now then," Tarmy replied.

"Now, why should I do that?"

Mike Tarmy answered with a cynical laugh, "I've never met Oryx, but I bet he doesn't ask too many questions. I also doubt if he takes prisoners. I am a police officer, not a war criminal. If you hand me over to Oryx and he kills me because of your misinformation, you could find yourself facing a murder charge."

"I'm prepared to compromise."

"Is that right?"

Although he couldn't see the other man, Tarmy guessed at what was coming next.

"Of course, I might be minded to let you escape if you told me the whereabouts of a bag that was in the possession of the spettro."

"I've no idea what you're talking about."

"Yes, you have," Pushley cut in. "As I expected you to prove difficult, I've taken a few precautions."

"Really?"

"I know you have a TK5 watching your back," Pushley said. "This boat has a tarpaulin draped over it so it can't see me. As I used to command TK5s, I'm only too well aware of their shortcomings. For instance, I know they have no secondary armament; they can't snipe; which means if your TK5 attempts to blasts me with its phaser, it will probably destroy the dingy and everyone in it."

Although he remained silent, Tarmy concurred with the analysis. Alex's phaser was powerful enough to destroy robotic infantry and bring armoured vehicles to a grinding halt so any attack on Pushley would probably vaporise everything around him too.

When Tarmy remained silent, Pushley said, "Don't think anyone's going to rescue you, either. I worked my way around the entire convoy and stunned everyone I found. I also have Claire and Nonie with me. They're also partially stunned and hanging over the side of this dinghy, the same as you are. One push and they'll drown."

"Let them go," Tarmy said, "And I'll let you know where the bag is."

"No, no, no," Pushley replied. "They are my bargaining chips. As you three appear to be in the process of forming your own private commune, a good old ménage à trois, keeping them both close seems sensible. Now, where is the bag?"

Tarmy heard both Claire and Nonie cry out.

Pushley said, "Can I remind you, if you don't tell me what I want to know, I could push them overboard. As you are all semi-stunned and your arms and legs aren't working, you won't be able to swim."

He paused, and in his Pushley/Irrelevant voice added, "I've always thought that drowning must be a nasty way to die; your lungs filling with water and being unable to breathe. The fear and panic must be intense."

There were two more squeals of pain in swift succession, and Pushley/Irrelevant whispered, "I can tell that you're surprised that I can inflict pain mentally. Then again, I was also surprised to find myself in Pushley's body."

"You're Irrelevant!"

"No, no, Mr Tarleton. I'm now Ed Pushley, and I have all of Pushley's documents to prove it. Luckily, I also have my old powers. They are not quite as strong as they were, but they are strong enough. I do not doubt that once I've left this God-forsaken planet and returned to Midway, with my mental powers, I'll be a multi-millionaire within a matter of years. "

"What do you want Irrelevant?"

Claire and Nonie squealed again.

"My name is Pushley, Tarleton. Please remember that you or your girl-friends are going to get very badly burnt."

"Okay," Tarmy replied. "What do you want Pushley?"

"I've already told you; I want the bag."

There were two more squeals of pain. A moment later, Tarmy felt as if a red-hot poker had been pushed against his arm. After inflicting pain for a full five seconds, Pushley whispered, "I want the bag. Where is it?"

Before Tarmy could answer a quiet voice said, "I have the bag."

Pushley jumped with surprise. "Who's that?"

"I'm Alex."

"Who's Alex?"

"The TK5," Tarmy replied. "That's what we call him."

"Where's the bag?"

Alex said, "I have a secret compartment."

Jabbing Tarmy, Pushley said, "Tell Alex to uncloak and come to the rear of the dingy."

Once Tarmy had issued the command, Alex appeared, uncloaked.

"Right," Pushley instructed. "Tell Alex to place the bag in the boat and then back off."

Once Alex had done as instructed, Pushley waved the gun he was holding at Alex, darted forward, and grabbed the bag. He then darted back again, fearful that Alex might grab him with one of his flexible arms. Tarmy heard the bag being unzipped and Pushley let out a sigh of satisfaction. "Looks like you're a loser again, Tarleton."

He pulled Tarmy's hat off and began to examine it. Finding the beads inside, he let out a slight laugh, "So that's how you prevented me from mind linking properly."

Tarmy felt a fat slug entering his mind. But just before Pushley could breakthrough, the false memories that Samantha had implanted into Tarmy's mind came flooding out.

Pushley realised he'd seen these before and gave up probing. He jabbed Tarmy with the stun gun, "Okay, your mind is still closed to me, but it doesn't matter. I have the money cards, and shortly Stert Oryx will take you prisoner. I'll tell him Tomio has been aiding and abetting, that Hyndman is an escaped monarch, and they will be finished too."

Latching onto the last comment, Tarmy said, "What the hell is a monarch?"

Pushley chuckled, "Oh, sweet revenge. You really sound as if you don't know. Surely you must have realised that Claire isn't normal. Claire's body has been genetically altered. That's why she can face change."

"During the war, they used to manufacture monarchs at Arcresten. That's a military base in the Compass Islands. My robotics company dropped off at least twenty monarchs in the Fyfield Valley to spy on the Great Ones. Most were killed within a matter of hours, but it would appear that Claire Hyndman if that is her real name, managed to survive."

When Tarmy remained very quiet, Pushley stuck the knife in, "What's the matter, Tarleton? Don't you find Claire attractive anymore? Having a mutant for a girlfriend would certainly make me think twice. Ah! Yes, revenge is sweet."

He let out another sigh of satisfaction, "I've been thinking. Now that I have the money, I must make sure you don't try and escape, make sure you don't get a chance to pull any stunts."

Fearing that Pushley was about to use the stun gun on the 'kill' setting, Tarmy shouted out, "Okay, Pushley you've won! There's no need to kill us."

"Who said anything about killing? If I double stun your girlfriends and you, you won't wake up for at least twenty-four standard hours. By that time, you'll be in Stert Oryx's hands, and I'll be able to buy a slot on the teleport system at Arcresten to leave this God-forsaken planet for good.

Pushley moved away. A few seconds later, Tarmy heard the stun gun fire twice, and the inflatable boat pitched as Claire and Nonie's bodies lurched.

Moving back, Pushley placed the stun gun against Tarmy's head. But instead of firing, he said, "Maybe I should kill you. If it hadn't been for you, I wouldn't be in this situation."

Tarmy heard a series of distinct clicks as Pushley began ramping up the stun gun's power. He muttered, "Goodbye, Tarleton," but before he fired, a mechanical arm slashed through the thin tarpaulin covering the dinghy, caught hold of Pushley's jacket, and pulled him backwards.

Realising that his attacker had to be Alex, Pushley tried to turn the gun on the droid but became entangled in the tarpaulin. As Alex pulled, Pushley finally dropped the weapon and grabbed hold of a safety rope, keeping a firm grip on the bag he was holding. As the unequal tug of war continued, Pushley eventually felt his grip on the rope beginning to fail. The next moment, the flimsy tarpaulin split, and he was dragged through it. Realising he was about to plunge into the river, Pushley let go of the bag and made a grab for the dinghy's float but failed. A moment later, he belly-flopped into the river.

After flailing around in the dirty river water for a few seconds, Pushley began swimming, frantically looking around for the bag.

The bag! He had to save the bag!

As he thrashed in the water, Alex flew over him and propelled the dinghy towards the convoy. Swivelling around, Pushley finally located the bag, but it was already half-submerged. Striking out towards it, his hopes began fade. The bag was going to sink before he could get to it.

As it disappeared from view, Pushley dived below the surface but didn't find it. He dived again. Determined not to lose the wealth the bag contained, Pushley dived again and again. On the seventh dive, he finally came up clutching the bag in one hand.

He'd barely let out a whoop of delight before he felt something large moving under him. A second later, a plesiosaur partially emerged from the river water and swung its long neck in his direction.

Fearing he was going to suffer the same fate as Irrelevant, Pushley began screaming for help. In an attempt to discourage an attack, he shoved the bag into the plesiosaur's face. The huge creature momentarily swung away but came back and snatched the bag out of his hand. Swallowing it, the monster turned back towards its intended victim.

Realising he was still in danger, Pushley began swimming towards the convoy. He'd barely covered eight metres before the plesiosaur overtook him; its jaws closed on Pushley's jacket, and it began to roll, "Help! Help me!"

Alex's shadow appeared out of nowhere and slammed into the plesiosaur's head. The impact loosened the animal's grip, and Pushley began to swim again. Exhausted, he'd barely covered five metres before the plesiosaur recovered and renewed its attack.

The animal was within striking distance when Alex rammed its torso. The impact forced the plesiosaur to regurgitate, and the bag suddenly flew into the air. Alex deftly intercepted it and rammed the plesiosaur again.

As the huge beast turned and fled, Pushley began thrashing around trying to find the convoy in the dense fog. He picked out a dim shape and began swimming towards it.

Reaching the lead dive boat, he found a rope ladder and pulled himself onto the deck. He dashed across to the other side of the ship in case the plesiosaur snaked its head over the exposed side to make another grab for him. Once he was in a safe zone, Pushley slumped down. He'd barely done so before the bag landed at his feet.

Not believing his luck, he dived at it and swiftly ripped it open. He let out a howl of despair. Instead of finding it stuffed with money cards, it was empty. The thieving TK5 had emptied the bag and had stolen the money cards.

Furious, Pushley howled again and screamed out, "I'm going to kill you, Tarleton. I'm going to kill all of you."

He scrabbled around in the fog, searching the bodies of the stunned archaeologists for a suitable weapon until he found a pulse rifle lying on the desk. After testing in, he set it to maximum force.

Turning his face to the foggy sky, he shouted his threat again. "I'm going to kill you, Tarleton. I'm going to kill all of you."

CHAPTER FIFTEEN

The Fyfield Valley

Escape from the convoy

Pushley's voice carried clear despite the fog, "I'm going to kill you, Tarleton. I'm going to kill all of you."

"He's coming back," Bryn Rosslyn said and went straight back to his hiding place. It was only when the door had closed behind him he realised that he couldn't hear Red Moxstroma scrabbling to get inside his bolt hole. What Rosslyn did hear was heavy footsteps approaching, and then Pushley's voice repeated his threat, "I'm going to kill you, Tarleton. I'm going to kill all of you."

He heard a grunt and a pulse rifle discharge. Fearing that Pushley had just killed Red Moxstroma, Rosslyn slid a little deeper in the cupboard and then held his breath in case Pushley came looking for him.

He jumped out of his skin when there was a rap on the cupboard door, "Come on, we've got to go."

When there was no response, Moxstroma called out, "Come on; we've got to go," and pulled open the cupboard door.

Rosslyn looked up at him, disbelievingly, "Where's Pushley?"

"Come on," Moxstroma urged. "The air-cars are leaving."

After sliding out of the cupboard, Rosslyn noted that the other man was carrying a pulse rifle. Out on deck, Rosslyn glanced around fearfully, "Where's Pushley?"

"I hit him, but he ran off," Moxstroma replied,

Looking at Moxstroma's emaciated body, Rosslyn wondered how the other man would have the strength force Pushley into a retreat, "You punched him?"

Instead of answering Moxstroma urged, "Come on. I don't want to be around when that madman finds another gun and comes back."

As Rosslyn turned to follow, he nearly tripped on a long-hooked pole and realised that Moxstroma must have used it on Pushley.

~*~

The ripples on the river were getting worse; as the next wave hit Tarmy's face, he held his breath and gulped in air before the next wave washed over him. He caught a glimpse of the air-cars and realised what was happening. Alex must have been dragging the dinghy back towards the vehicles.

His thoughts were confirmed when the dinghy finally came to rest against the side of the lead air-car. Within a matter of seconds, his breathing eased as the waves died down. He heard a roof door slide open. Moments later, he heard Bryn Rosslyn and Red Moxstroma's raised voices.

He heard Alex telling someone to stand back, and heard Lascaux Kurgan shouting, "You've got to let us get on board. If you don't Pushley will kill us."

A moment later, there was a clumping sound. The first clumping sound was followed by several more. Tarmy guessed that Rosslyn, Moxstroma and Lascaux had refused to take no for an answer and had jumped into the air-cars before Alex could stop them. A moment later, the remnants of the tarpaulin were ripped from the dinghy, and a shadow moved in. He saw two slumped figures being transferred towards the air-car and guessed that Alex was hoisting Claire and Nonie into the vehicle.

Then Alex came for him. Grabbing his stout jerkin, Alex hauled him up and swiftly dumped him into the lead air-car.

Lascaux Kurgan immediately wormed her way towards him and said, "We've got to get out of here. I saw Pushley; he's armed, and he's after us."

Then the truth dawned; Tarmy was in no condition to fly the air-car. Fearing for her life, Lascaux began fighting her way towards the air-car's controls, but before she could get there, the roof door slid shut, and the air-car took off.

After they'd been flying for some time, Lascaux nudged him, "Any idea who's flying this air-car?"

Tarmy managed a slight smile, "I can only presume Alex, our invisible friend is flying us." He added, "Unless he's just programmed the air-cars."

There was a long pause, and Lascaux said, "Any idea where this invisible friend of yours is taking us?"

Tarmy shook his head, "Not a clue."

CHAPTER SIXTEEN

Arcresten
Oryx & Pushley in pursuit

Vert Zardus instructed one of his support droids to open the huge door giving access to the link tunnel. A waft of pungent air immediately swept in and began mingling with Arcresten's conditioned air.

Stert Oryx let out a mild curse, "It stinks."

"As we have a teleport, we don't use the tunnel very often," Zardus replied. "We only use it as an emergency escape or to allow heavy equipment in and out."

Staring into the tunnel, Oryx noted the walls and ceiling were glowing green. Sensing the unspoken question, Zardus said, "Luminescent fungi and Arcadian ferns populate most cave systems and man-made tunnels on Arcadia."

After directing Oryx's four A10s into the tunnel, Zardus waited until they had cleared and asked Oryx and his men to get into the air-cars. Once they had, he leaned into Oryx's air-car and said, "Good luck."

"I don't need luck," Oryx replied icily "Both Tarleton and Warmers are dead men walking."

~*~

After leaving the Compass Islands, Oryx's two air-cars headed upriver with the four A10s leading the way, but within fifteen minutes their forward progress slowed to a crawl. Anxious not to lose time, Oryx opened up communications with Slon and Lane Syn who were in the second air-car, "What's the problem?"

Being a man of few words, Lane Syn said, "Fog, sir."

"Fog!"

"Yeah," Lane returned. "That white stuff outside floating all around."

Oryx frowned, "Why wasn't I warned about this? Why should fog be a problem?"

"The A10s use Lidar, sir," Slon cut in. "It doesn't work that well in fog." As Stert Oryx usually shot the messenger, Slon added, "As the air-cars have Radar perhaps we should take point."

"If it saves time, so be it," Oryx snapped.

In response, Slon took his car to point, and within a matter of seconds, progress up the valley improved.

Sensing the progress, Oryx said, "How long before we make contact?"

"Just under three hours, sir."

~*~

"Contacts ahead," Slon said and then instructed the A10s to move in. As the A10s relayed images to them, Slon added, "I thought Tarleton had air-cars?"

"No air-cars?"

"No, sir," He added, "But I can see a lot of bodies lying on the decks."

"Shit!" Oryx snapped. "He's escaped!"

Although Slon and Lane Syn agreed, they both maintained a discrete silence because they knew their boss had a short fuse at the best of times. Eventually, Oryx broke the silence, "Put down near to the boats and find out what has been going on." He then added, "If you find Ed Pushley let me know. I want to question him."

~*~

"If you want to live, drop the gun."

Pushley let the pulse rifle slide from his hands. As the gun clattered onto the deck, Slon Syn said, "That was a very wise move." He shone a powerful torch in Pushley's face. Noting the heavy bruising on his detainee's face, Slon said, "So, what's your story?"

Guessing that Slon worked for Oryx, he responded with, "I'm Ed Pushley, the guy who called you in."

"Where's Tarleton?"

"He escaped," Tarleton replied.

Shining the torch on the bruising Slon said, "Did Tarleton give you that?"

Although Pushley hadn't seen his assailant, he played for the sympathy vote, "I tried to stop him leaving, but he hit me before I could react."

Keeping the torch on him, Slon said, "Looks like you did your bit."

He ran the torch over the stunned bodies, "Did Tarleton do this too?"

Pushley absolved himself from the mayhem he'd caused by nodding, "Tarleton just went berserk.

He's a madman."

Moving away from Pushley, Slon reported back, "I've got Pushley, but it looks as if Tarleton has escaped."

"I'm going to land," Oryx said. "Bring Pushley to me."

After Oryx had put down on the river, Slon frisked Pushley for hidden weapons, and ordered him into the air-car. Once he'd clambered down inside, Oryx gave him a frosty look. "You let him escape."

Pushley bridled, "I did no such thing."

"He escaped on your watch," Oryx snapped. "You were supposed to disable his air-cars."

As his injury had impressed Slon, Pushley pointed to it and said, "I did my bit."

"Your bit, as you put it, wasn't good enough," Oryx snapped. No doubt he would have continued with his dressing down, but Slon called down through the open roof window, "Sir, we've lost one of our A10s."

"What d'you mean. Lost?"

"One of the machines is not showing on our control panel," Slon revealed. He swore, "We've lost another…"

Swearing again, he added, "Now we've lost the lot."

Reading Oryx's mind, Pushley said, "I did warn you that Tarleton had a TK5 minder and its looks as if it's used its interRoC capabilities to seduce your machines."

"You didn't warn me *this* might happen," Oryx snapped. "What the hell is interRoC?"

Before Pushley could answer, two of the missing A10s emerged from the mist and turned to face Oryx's air-car. One of them announced, "You will load your air-cars with the stunned personnel and return to Arcresten."

Instead of responding, Oryx just stared at the two machines disbelievingly.

Getting no response, the A10 repeated itself, "You will load your air-cars with the stunned personnel and return to Arcresten." To reinforce the order, the machine activated a crowd dispersal Mannheim.

Oryx body was immediately filled with pain; it was as if someone had stuck a hundred pins into his skin.

"You will load your air-cars with the stunned personnel, and then leave," The A10 repeated.

Knowing it would use the Mannheim again if he didn't accept the order, Oryx snapped, "Do as it says."

Slon and Lane Syn immediately sprang into action and began dragging Pushley's victims over to the air-cars and loading them in. As the loading process proceeded, Pushley picked up on Oryx's simmering resentment; his plan had fallen at the first fence, and he was looking for a scapegoat, "Before you blame me. This is your fault. Because you were late, it gave Tarleton the chance to escape."

Annoyed by the accusation, Oryx reached for his pistol. Realising his life was in danger, Pushley shouted, "No."

Attracted by the noise, the lead A10 intervened by hitting

Oryx with another Mannheim blast. It

said, "You will *all* drop your weapons."

When Oryx and his men had complied, Pushley let out a sigh of relief and then repeated his previous statement, "This is your fault. You were late."

"We were unavoidably detained at Arcresten," Oryx snapped.

Pushley hit back with, "That's not my problem."

"It is," Oryx replied. "If we don't take Tarleton, there's no reward."

"Then we'll take him," Pushley replied. "He's headed for Awis Oasis."

"Awis Oasis?"

"Correct."

Hal Warmer's name resurfaced in Oryx's mind. If the reports were correct, Warmers was resident in Awis Oasis. Sensing he could still salvage the operation and claim another scalp as well, Oryx said, "You sound very confident. How d'you know?"

As Pushley knew that a man like Oryx would not believe him if he claimed to possess special mental abilities, he lied, "I overheard Tarleton discussing his future intentions."

"You overheard? Are you positive?"

"I'm absolutely positive," Pushley replied. "And more importantly, I know what I'd do if I were in your position."

"Oh! Really!?"

"Yes."

"Okay, clever dick," Oryx replied. "If you were in my position, what would you do?"

Pushley glanced at the nearest A10. He said, "You're going back to Arcresten whether you like it or not, once you are there, you can get yourself some proper equipment."

"Like what?"

"Even though Tarleton's TK5 was a superb droid in its day, it couldn't match a modern TK7."

When Oryx didn't reply, Pushley added, "When I was based

at Arcresten, it had a very powerful teleport facility. Teleporting down a couple of TK7s to deal with Tarleton's droid shouldn't be that difficult. You may have lost this battle, but if you play your cards right, you will win the war."

"It's an excellent plan," Oryx replied sarcasm very evident in his tone. "The main problem is, I tried to obtain access to TK7s, but they refused my request."

"Why?"

"TK7s are state of the art," Oryx replied. "The Midwain top brass made it quite clear that they are not prepared to release them to me."

"So, you are going to let Tarleton escape?"

"I didn't say that," Oryx replied.

"So, what are you going to do?" Pushley demanded.

"We're going back to basics," Oryx replied. "Awis Oasis has teleport facilities. It also has a droid free policy and has a protection Mannheim which works in our favour. If we teleport in, Tarleton's TK5 won't be able to protect him."

~*~

Glancing at the dash map, Oryx realised that Arcresten was only a few kilometres away. He immediately glared at Pushley, "I hope you realise that I'm going to look ..."

Reading Oryx's mind, Pushley cut him off, "This has just been a minor setback. You know where he is, all you have to do is go to Awis and round him up."

As the two air-cars and the four A10s broke free of the river fog, they entered the delta region; it was possible to see lights coming from the compass islands. Still feeling animosity seeping out of every pour of Oryx's body, Pushley began gently mind-probing again. Eventually, he found a scapegoat and decided to play the blame game.

"I hope you realise," Pushley said, "You're accusing the wrong man. If the people at Arcresten hadn't been so determined to work by the book when you teleported down, you would have jumped Tarleton before he had a chance to escape."

The comment had the desired effect.

"You're right," Oryx replied. "This is all Vert Zardus's fault."

Satisfied he was no longer in Oryx's firing line, Pushley began thinking about the future. If Oryx was given his head, he'd just take his prisoners and go. If that happened, the money retained in Tarleton's TK5 would be lost to him for good. His memory conjured up images of Claire Hyndman and Nonie Tomio's stunned bodies sprawled in the inflated boat. He remembered how enjoyable it had been torturing them.

If he could take them again before Oryx got to them, he'd be able to force Tarleton into handing over the money. Once he had that, Oryx could take them and good riddance.

~*~

Vert Zardus sensed trouble brewing long before Oryx re-entered Arcresten. The first sign of trouble was when the four A10s stopped escorting Stert Oryx's two air cars and went back upriver. The second clue was when the external cameras surrounding Arcresten began picking up images of bodies sprawled in the back of the two air cars.

As the air-cars finally arrived, Oryx glared at Zardus and then began ranting, "He escaped because you delayed us, he escaped."

As Zardus had been anticipating accusations, he called over one of the support droids and said, "Colonel Oryx wishes to make a formal complaint against me, would you please record it."

Oryx reacted as anticipated, "I haven't got time for this. We need to use your teleport again. Tarleton is going to Awis Oasis."

Zardus clucked his tongue, "I'm sorry, but regulations state that we can't teleport a subject within five days of another teleport."

Oryx pulled his gun, "This over-rides regulations. Now send us to Awis Oasis."

Zardus shook his head in disbelief, "I've seen some stunts, but this takes the biscuit."

Oryx fired his gun. Although the shot was deliberately wide, it left Zardus in no doubt that Oryx was determined to go after Tarleton. "Okay, let's see what happens."

Gun still in hand, Oryx nodded to Slon and Lane Syn and told them to step onto the teleport. After stepping on himself, he glanced at Pushley, "You're coming too."

"Me?"

"Yeah," Oryx replied. "I need you to positively identify Tarleton when we get there." Once Pushley had done as instructed, Oryx said, "Right do it."

With the gun still trained on him, Vert Zardus moved over to the main console. A few seconds later, an alarm went off, and a power bubble flashed up a sign. Teleport denied.

"What's going on?" Oryx demanded, waving his gun at Zardus.

"You can't teleport because the system knows you aren't stable enough for another teleport."

Oryx levelled his gun, "Override it."

"Okay," Zardus agreed. "It's your funeral." He began to flick buttons on the console in front of him. A split second later the gun that Oryx was holding disappeared out of his hand and went clattering across the main hall floor. When Slon and Lane Syn went for their guns, they realised that they had vanished too.

Smirking slightly, Zardus drew his own stun gun and gestured with it, "Get off the teleport."

Pushley was about to follow the other three off when Zardus said, "If you still want to go to, I can send you, but you will need funds. There is access deposit of one hundred thousand ACU per teleport."

"What's the point of Pushley going if we are not with him?" Oryx demanded.

Pushley saw the chance and seized it, "I have been to Awis Oasis. There are two major archaeological sites in the area, so I know the whole area well."

"You're an amateur," Oryx sniped.

Pushley hit back, "In case you have forgotten, I located Tarleton; you wouldn't be here if it wasn't for me."

"You're still an amateur," Oryx sniped. "If we can't use the teleport we'll use the air-cars and fly out there."

"And get shot down by Tarleton's TK5. Very sensible."

When Oryx shot him a blinding look, Pushley added, "And in case you've forgotten, I also have a vested interest in Tarleton and his associates. It is logical for me to go and locate him. Hopefully, when you arrive, I will have located them, and either taken them prisoner or will be able to assist."

"You're still a rank amateur," Oryx repeated.

Pushley was about to give him both barrels, but Zardus stepped in. "Gentlemen. If I can intervene, Mr Pushley's suggestion seems sensible."

He waved Oryx and his men off the teleport again. He then held out his hand.

Oryx snapped, "What do you want now?"

"An access deposit of one hundred thousand ACU for the use of the teleport and I'm sure Mr Pushley would like a few cards to line his pockets. He will have expenses, after all."

Realising he'd lost the debate Oryx pulled out his percom and transferred one hundred thousand ACU into the teleport account. He then begrudgingly transferred two thousand ACU onto a money card and handed it over.

Pushley sniffed, "That wouldn't pay my bar bill for two days in a place like Awis Oasis."

Oryx immediately snatched it back and placed another ten thousand ACU on the card. He passed it back, "Satisfied now?"

Pushley sniffed again, "I suppose it's better than a kick in the unmentionables."

Oryx gave him a sharp look, "You'd better find him, or you'll have me to answer to."

"I'll find him," Pushley said. "I just hope when I do you won't let him escape again."

Wanting to conclude the issue, Zardus cut in, "Are we done?"

When Pushley nodded, Zardus activated the teleport, and Pushley's body shimmered for several seconds. It then disappeared from view.

CHAPTER SEVENTEEN

Awis Oasis

Pushley goes to Awis Oasis

When Pushley arrived, a smartly dressed attendant moved in and helped him off the teleport. Without needing to be told, Pushley realised the attendant was a native Arcadian, an Ab.

Pushley took two steps, and his legs developed a will of their own. Knowing Pushley was suffering from mild teleport sickness, the attendant led him to a rest room. Once he'd been seated, the attendant produced a small computer; he proceeded, "Your travel mandate indicates you are here on business, Mr Pushley."

"Correct," Pushley replied. "I'm an archaeologist. We have a number of sites in the area, and I intend to inspect progress."

Satisfied with the answer, the attendant ticked a box. He added, "You are free to lie down if you wish, Mr Pushley." He waved a hand towards a nearby buffet table, "On the other hand, if you are hungry, please help yourself."

When Pushley showed surprise at the lavish spread, the attendant elaborated, "You may as well eat what you want. It's all included in the teleport service. Teleportation can make some people very hungry."

Sensing the other man was hovering, hoping for a tip, Pushley began gently mind probing. Within a matter of seconds, he'd extracted enough information to realise he was dealing with a person who could be easily coerced. The man's name was Yalt, and like most of the Ab, he didn't have a family surname. When such information was required, Yalt was forced to recite a long string of forbears; son of Wal; son of Coli; son of Frei and so on.

The mind-probing also told Pushley that Yalt's family had once lived in Awis Oasis but had been driven out when the outworlders invaded. Although Yalt had been born in the Fyfield Valley, the area that he'd been living in had been purged by the Great Ones, and he'd been forced to make the long return desert trek back to Awis. Luckily for him and his fellow refugees, as the outworlders weren't allowed droids to carry out their mundane tasks, they accepted the refugees back as pseudo-droids.

Pushley also discovered that Yalt had a zero hour's contract with the teleport company; as a consequence, he never knew what he would earn each week. Using the information that he'd gleaned, Pushley played Yalt like a fish on a hook, "So, is this your full-time job?"

The other man shook his head, "I do many things to earn a living. The teleport at Awis is not that well used, perhaps once or twice a week. I am only part-time; I only get work when the others are not here."

Although he already knew the truth, Pushley played dumb, "The others?"

"The teleport is mainly manned by outworlders," Yalt replied. "But the outworlders don't like working night shifts. They also want more money than I do. When the outworlders don't come in, I am asked to."

Pushley realised that he'd hit pay dirt, "D'you want to earn some money?"

When Yalt nodded enthusiastically, Pushley pulled a small denomination money card out of his pocket and said, "I'm only passing through, but while I'm here I would like to meet up with an old army buddy—his name is Hal Warmers. Do you know him?"

Yalt shook his head, "I do not know anyone by that name, but I will ask around."

Releasing the money card, Pushley said, "If you can locate Hal, I will reward you."

"I will do my best to locate your friend," Yalt promised. He turned to leave, but before he could Pushley said, "I also need a decent hotel to stay in, and I need to buy two percoms."

One of Yalt's eyebrows turned into a question mark, "Two percoms?"

Although he'd already known the answer, Pushley said, "Have you got a percom of your own?"

When Yalt shook his head, Pushley said, "As I will need to keep in touch with you; I will need two percoms. One for me and one for you. When I leave, I will let you keep your percom."

Realising that Pushley was going to be a much-needed source of income, Yalt said, "I would be pleased to help you." He waved at the food again, "Why don't you eat. I will be off shift shortly, and I could take you to the local market for the percoms and find you a suitable hotel."

Although he'd already extracted the information from the other man's mind, Pushley said, "How long before your shift finishes?"

As it was apparent that Pushley was going to accept his offer, Yalt said, "About an hour."

Helping himself to a large sandwich, Pushley took a bite. He then nodded, "That's fine, Yalt."

Yalt immediately froze, "How did you know my name?"

Fear then ingrained itself on Yalt's face. As he'd lived in the Fyfield Valley for most of his life, he knew about the powers of the Great Ones' servants, "You're a spettro, aren't you?"

Realising he'd made a major blunder, Pushley hit Yalt's brain with a mind slug and then attempted to undo his error. Eventually, he removed the mind slug and went back to his previous conversation as if nothing had happened, "So, you'll come back here in an hour then, Yalt."

There was a slight pause while Yalt's mind adjusted. He then said, "Yes, padrone. I will be back in an hour."

"Excellent," Pushley replied whilst taking more food from the buffet.

~*~

Yalt reappeared exactly an hour later. He was wearing the same clothes as earlier; except he was now wearing a peaked cap with a teleport badge on the front. After telling Pushley to leave his luggage and promising to arrange for its transportation to a hotel, Yalt led Pushley to a lift and activated it. A few seconds later, they emerged in the main entrance lobby of a small office building. Pushley immediately noticed a security camera slowly panning over the whole lobby.

Following his eyes, Yalt issued a caution, "In this town, there are many cameras. You have to be careful."

Once out in the street, Pushley began running his eyes over the sky. Although he knew that night must have fallen over Awis Oasis, it wasn't dark outside. Pushley realised that the protective Mannheim high above was sending down more than enough light for him to see clearly; there was no need for street lamps.

As Yalt began leading him down the street outside, Pushley saw several more cameras and realised that Yalt was right; there were watchers everywhere.

He began studying the strange architecture all around him. As most of the buildings were made from the pale, local sandstone, they had a welcoming ambience. Pushley guessed that the original Ab population had built them. A population now displaced by outworlder occupiers. It was also evident that the outworlders who'd stolen Awis Oasis must have placed a value assessment on the buildings and decided to keep them. Hostile conquerors tended to destroy everything in their wake and replaced existing buildings with their own. Instead, they had retained the buildings in Awis Oasis, and the whole area appeared to be a theme park for the rich.

As he continued following Yalt, he began glancing around

at the human population. On one side of the road, there were a small gang of workers, obviously of Ab extraction below ground repairing a drain. Further down, there were market stalls. Once again, the stalls appeared to be Ab run. In contrast, the people walking around the stalls were clad in contemporary outworlder clothing and wearing the superior air of the conquistador.

Although it was tempting to raise the issue with Yalt, Pushley let it slide; if Yalt was a member of the largely dispossessed Ab population, talking about such issues might inflame old wounds.

After walking for some time, Yalt brought him to a second open-air market and moved towards a stall selling percoms. After five minutes of haggling, Pushley left with two suitable machines. After ensuring that they were linked, Pushley gave one to Yalt. The effect on Yalt was immediate; he puffed himself up; he was now a man of substance; he now had an outworlder percom.

Slipping his own percom into his pocket, Pushley presented Yalt with another money card and said, "You were going to find me a hotel."

Yalt changed direction and two minutes later stopped outside a large building and pointed towards an impressive door. Assessing some of the markings on the walls, Pushley concluded that the building had once been a temple. While he was still evaluating the structure, Yalt said, "I am sure you will find this place to your liking."

Pushley asked, "So, what do I do now?"

"You will have to go in and book."

As Yalt was his guide, Pushley said, "Aren't you coming with me?"

"I am not allowed in hotels or bars; you will have to go in by yourself," Yalt replied. "If you ask them to collect your belongings from the teleport centre they will send someone around."

Realising there was some sort of no Ab policy in operation

in most public buildings, Pushley said, "Okay, but wait here until I come out. I have other things I need you to do. I won't be long."

With that, he walked across the road and booked into the hotel. Emerging again, he noticed that Yalt was talking to someone in his native tongue. As he crossed the road, he caught the name, Hal Warmers. Guessing that Yalt was trying to satisfy his final wish, Pushley said, "Any luck with finding Hal?"

"Perhaps," Yalt replied evasively.

"And what does that mean?"

"I may be able to arrange for you to see, Mr Warmers."

Sensing that Yalt's palms needed greasing again, Pushley pulled out another low denomination money card, but instead of handing it over, he said, "Arrange it."

Yalt walked over to the man he'd been talking to and began jabbering once more. Eventually, the other man demanded to use Yalt's percom. After a lapse of nearly five minutes, Yalt reclaimed his percom and came back. "It is done. He will see you," he reported and held out his hand.

Once Pushley had parted with another money card, Yalt said, "Come with me," and swiftly crossed the market square. He began striding up a steep hill. Unaccustomed to walking far, Pushley began perspiring badly. In the end, he shouted, "Slow down, Yalt, you're walking too fast."

Yalt took pity on him and paused. Once he'd caught up, Pushley said, "Where are we going?"

"You wanted to see Hal Warmers."

"Yes."

"I'm taking you to him."

~*~

Five minutes later, Yalt paused and pointed towards another impressive stone building that appeared to have been converted into a bar, "He is in there."

Pushley eyed the bar with suspicion, "Are you sure?"

Yalt nodded, "Yes, padrone. He owns the bar. I've been told he'll meet with you."

Pushley slipped him another money card and said, "Don't go away, Yalt, I shouldn't be too long." He walked away towards the bar.

As he entered, a barman appeared though a small arch in a back-fitting, "Yes, sir?"

Instead of ordering a drink, Pushley said, "I'm looking for Hal Warmers. Is he in?"

"Who's asking?"

"Ed Pushley."

The barman ducked back through the arch. A few second later Warmers emerged and said, "Well, well, well, if it isn't Ed Pushley. I heard that you were in town. Come on through."

Leading the way down a corridor into a small empty snug, Warmers ushered Pushley to a corner table and ordered drinks. Glancing around, Pushley said, "Not exactly overrun with clientele."

Warmers shrugged, "Wrong time of day. Most of the bars are quiet during working hours. Believe me; this place will be heaving later on."

Once Pushley was seated, Warmers asked, "Are you still based at Fort Saunders?"

"Yes," Pushley replied. "Officially, I'm still based there."

"You know," Warmers replied, a lecherous smile forming on his face, "on the odd occasion I visited you and Yan Farman I couldn't help but envy you both."

"Farman's well dead," Pushley replied icily. "He died a few years back."

"I know," Warmers replied, "It was all very unfortunate. A sad loss. Something venomous bit him, I understand."

"Yes."

Undeterred, Warmers continued, "It must be good, living in a commune."

As he suspected where the conversation was leading and

had no real desire go there, instead of providing Warmers with an affirmative, Pushley said, "It's what I'm used to."

Warmers echoed, "What you're used to?"

"Although some human colonies still retain the so-called normal family unit, one man and one woman, on Midway, commune living is the norm and has been for several generations," Pushley explained. "As living accommodation is expensive, most people have to band together to buy an apartment. For tax purposes and inter-personal reasons, they usually agree to form a commune. But it doesn't cause any real social issues. As overpopulation always has been a major human problem, most of the Midwain population aren't allowed to breed; they are either sterilised or on long term contraception if they are not deemed suitable for the breeding program. On Midway, most children are the result of strictly applied eugenics and are created in an artificial womb."

Warmer's mind immediately went into overdrive again, "So a guy could have several women in his commune and have sex with all of 'em."

"Communes come in all types," Pushley replied. "Some women prefer all female communes. There are gay communes. There are all sorts of combinations. As procreation is no longer a significant factor, it doesn't matter."

Warmers frowned, "You have communes at Fort Saunders. As some of the scientists working there aren't from Midway, what about them?"

"They have to accept our ways, or they are not invited to join our archaeological or scientific research groups," Pushley replied.

"So, everyone has to join a commune?"

"Yes; it's the norm."

Warmers' lecherous smile returned, "It must be good living in a commune, especially when there are more women than men."

As Pushley had had the same sort of discussion with non-commune people many times before, he let out a slight sigh,

"There was a time when archaeology was a male-dominated profession, but that was a long time ago. There are now far more women than men in the profession."

"Come on, level with me," Warmers challenged, "I've been told that the ratio of women to men is five to one at Fort Saunders. You must be rampant most nights."

Pushley finally smiled because he was slightly amused by the other man's descriptor of his sexual proclivities. At that point, Warmers' mind began discharging a series of images indicating he'd taken full advantage of the favourable statistics during *his* fleeting visits.

As Warmers' thought images began coalescing, Pushley recognised several of the women, four in particular. Instead of being impressed, Pushley became concerned and started to regret beating a path to Warmers' door. If Warmers knew some of the people involved in his plans, it might affect his judgement. More importantly, he was on Stert Oryx's list.

"Come on! What's it like being surrounded by so many women?"

Pushley smiled again, "Being on a commune does have its pleasures, I have to admit."

"I knew it," Warmers said, and his mind began discharging more sexually explicit images. Eventually, the deluge subsided, and Warmers said, "Anyway. Down to business. So, why are you here, Ed?"

Although Pushley had developed severe doubts about Hal Warmers' suitability, he responded with, "Until recently I was working at Cittavecchia, it's not far from here. So, I thought I'd pay you a visit."

"Did you say Cittavecchia?"

"Yes."

The affirmation immediately sent Warmers' mind back into overdrive and another deluge of images formed in Pushley's mind, and he realised Warmers was deeply involved in dealings with the Great Ones. More importantly, as it was apparent the Great Ones wanted Tarleton; Pushley now knew their interests might clash.

When Pushley went quiet, Warmers said, "Look, I presume this is not just a social visit, so what can I do for you, Ed?"

After thinking hard, Pushley decided to take a risk. "I'm looking for a man called Mick Tarleton. Do you know where I can find him?"

"Why do you want him?"

"He's acquired something of mine, and I want it back."

"What's he taken?"

"Just a bag," Pushley replied. He gave Warmers the same story he'd given Lascaux but embellished slightly, "It contains artefacts and my mini-computer containing all my site notes. They have no real intrinsic value, but it would be a personal embarrassment to me if they were lost. Years of painstaking research down the pan."

Warmers reacted in the same way Lascaux had, "What's really in the bag, Ed?"

"I've just told you," Pushley snapped and then stood up.

Realising Pushley had taken the hump and was about to stalk off, Warmers said, "Whoa, Ed, sit down. I'm sorry if I offended you."

Pushley turned and slowly sank back down into the seat. At the same time, he began to probe Warmer's mind gently. Within thirty seconds, he realised just how deeply Warmers was involved with the Great Ones. Not only was he fund-raising by distributing drugs; he was supplying them with arms and organising assassinations.

While he was still gently probing Warmers' mind, the other man said, "Do *you* know where Tarleton is?"

"No," Pushley replied. "If you recall, I asked you the same question a few seconds ago. But I believe he may come here."

"You're joking."

"Do I look as if I'm joking?" Pushley growled. "There's a reward on his head. If you help me take him, I might be prepared to make you deal."

After discussing the reward in more detail, Pushley added,

"Tarleton has two women with him, or should I say, one is a woman and a female monarch."

Warmers' eyes lit up, "A female monarch. Are you sure?"

"You know as well as I do, I worked at Arcresten during the last war," Pushley replied. "I've seen enough monarchs to recognise one."

"This monarch, is it reprogrammable?"

"Of course," Pushley replied. "They all are."

"Is it in good condition?"

"In good condition and fully functional," Pushley replied.

The comment immediately triggered Warmers' mind into supplying Pushley with another flood of information. Warmers had once owned a monarch he'd called Zia, but she'd died at a hyper-rail station on Arden during a shoot-out with the Black-clads. As Zia's talents had proven invaluable, it was obvious Warmers wanted a replacement.

The trickle of information became a flood, and Pushley realised why Warmers was so interested in the monarch. Not only had Warmers used Zia as bedfellow when it suited him; he'd also used her in a Mata Hari role, pillow talking Minton Mining Company executives into revealing confidential information. At a later stage, she'd assumed a terrorist role and had helped him co-ordinate assassinations of senior Minton Mining Company executives.

As more and more of Warmers' thoughts cascaded into his mind, Pushley began reconsidering Claire Hyndman's future. If he handed her over to Oryx, he would probably kill her out of hand and take her body back; on the other hand, if he allowed Warmers to acquire her, he stood a chance of making more money.

Pushley began to analyse Warmers' thoughts in greater detail; if he allowed Warmers to take Claire, no doubt he'd use and abuse her in the same way as he had done to Zia. He smiled; that would be much better revenge than allowing Oryx to kill her wantonly.

When another stray thought let Pushley know how much

the other man would be prepared to pay for a replacement monarch, he said, "If you help me catch Tarleton and the monarch. The monarch becomes yours to do with as you please. I get the reward for Tarleton and my bag back. Once I complete my business, I want to be teleported out of here to the first passing space transporter on its way to Midway."

There was a long pause as Warmers considered his proposal and Pushley half expected the other man to come back with a counter-offer. He sensed that Warmers wasn't a man of his word. He was the type who'd make a deal and then renege at the first opportunity.

The negative thoughts had barely surfaced in Pushley's mind before Warmers said, "That sounds like a good deal. But are you sure Tarleton is coming here?"

"He'll be here shortly," Pushley predicted. "I will let you know once he has entered Awis Oasis."

"I will have look-outs posted," Warmers replied. "I will know sooner than you will. So, are we good?"

Pushley remained silent for a couple of seconds and considered the treacherous thoughts he was still picking up. In the end, he said, "There is one other point. Something very important."

"What's that?"

Pushley immediately pushed the mind-slug deep inside Warmers' skull. He sent Warmers the same image sequence he'd implanted into Nonie Tomio's mind. As the huge grub broke through the cell wall and began advancing, Warmers began thrashing around in fear.

Pushley only stopped the grub from advancing when the barman called out, "Is everything okay in there?"

The man emerged into the back room. "Is everything okay?"

"It will be shortly," Pushley replied and shot him with his stun gun. He swung the weapon onto Warmers and immediately shot him in one of his arms.

"What did you do that for?" Warmers bleated.

"I thought we needed a little more privacy and to make sure

you didn't try nothing on, " Pushley replied and then acti-vated the mind slug again. When the huge grub broke through the cell wall again, Warmers started screaming out loud.

Cutting the sequence before the grub could strike home, Pushley asked, "Why is it I get the feeling you're going to do the dirty on me at the first opportunity?"

Instead of answering the question, Warmers gasped, "You're a spettro,"

He had second thoughts. "But you can't be a spettro, spettri can't leave the Fyfield Valley or the Alto Plateaux. Spettri die if they leave."

Pushley smiled, "Let's just say I've found a safe way out." He added, "If you try to double-cross me Warmers, I will know, and I will kill you."

Although Hal Warmers looked frightened, a slight smile formed on his face and his mind revealed the truth. As he'd worked with the Great Ones for years, Warmers had learned how to protect himself with shielding crystals. Unless Push-ley caused him serious damage while his defences were down, he'd soon be able to repel Pushley's mind-probe by merely wearing a protective hat.

Realising his control over Warmers would very shortly wane, Pushley took another tack, "As an act of good faith I want you to organise my teleport out of here straight away."

"Your teleport out of here," Warmers repeated.

"Yes. As I said before, as part of our deal I want you to or-ganise and pay for me to teleport up to the first passing trans-porter heading for Midway."

"What if there isn't one?"

"If that's not practical," Pushley continued. "I want to tele-port up to a space station so that I can board a suitable trans-porter when it passes. In the event of that occurring, you will also pay the additional teleport costs as well and the cost of my accommodation."

"That will cost a fortune," Warmers quibbled.

"I'm sure you can afford it," Pushley replied. "Don't worry, if you do your part and help me catch Tarleton and the monarch; you will be repaid in full."

Pushley then put his hand into one of Warmers' pockets, pulled out his percom and placed it in his un-stunned hand. Warmers glared at him, "What's that for?"

"Why not make some bookings now?"

When Warmers tried to resist, Pushley sent the slug back into his skull and activated the grub sequence again. As Warmers began screaming, Pushley added, "If I let the grub strike, you will probably suffer a major stroke and end up in a vegetative state. Do you want that?"

When Warmers shook his head, Pushley stopped the grub's progress and said, "Make the booking. I want the tickets in my hand before I leave. The teleport building is only just down the road; my man will go and pick them up.

As Warmers made his call, Pushley activated his percom. Speaking to Yalt, he said, "I have another job for you; there are tickets waiting for me at the teleport office, go and collect them for me. Give me a call when you're back outside."

Hanging up, he transferred his attention back to Warmers, "Now what shall we do while we're waiting?"

When Warmers gave him a hostile look, Pushley said, "I want to know the moment that Tarleton arrives. Understood?"

When Warmers' mind sent him a mental *up yours*, Pushley sent the mind slug back in, and at the appropriate moment, he halted the grub, "Now that you've paid for my teleport tickets you're definitely down on the deal. If you want your money back, you'd better do as I say. Understood?"

He added, "Then again, maybe I should kill you while I can and drop you from my plans." As he said the words, the grubs head suddenly rose ready to strike.

Warmers finally cracked, "No, no—I'll help you take Tarleton."

Pushley pulled a face, "I still don't think I can trust you."

"You can. You can."

Pushley considered the comment and said, "On Earth, before it was destroyed, there was a tribe called the Vikings. If someone broke their word to a Viking chief, a hostage ended up as a blood eagle. Just in case you don't know what a blood eagle was, they cut the living victim open with an axe and pulled their lungs out."

Pushley smiled, "Of course we live in a more civilised time now, but I still think I need a blood eagle guarantee of your loyalty."

After shooting Warmers in the other arm with his stun gun, he reached into another of Warmers' pockets and pulled out a wallet. After checking the contents, Pushley took a few photographs. Finding a programmable money card, Pushley shook his head, "Not enough on there; I think this needs topping up."

After sending the brain slug into action again, Pushley discovered the account that warmers had used to pay for the teleport tickets, and then used his percom to transfer the remaining funds onto the card.

Warmers gave him a daggers drawn look, "I'll make you pay for this."

"I agree with you," Pushley replied. "Given half a chance you probably will try to get your own back, but that's not going to happen."

A moment later Yalt called to say he'd picked up the tickets. Standing up, Pushley grabbed Warmers percom and put it into his top pocket. He said, "When Tarleton arrives, give me a call." He patted the percom he'd just stolen. "You can contact me on your own percom."

He levelled his stun gun and shot Warmers in both legs. "That's to make sure you don't follow me."

Outside, he joined Yalt and said, "I need you to find me some alternative accommodation."

"But you've only just booked into the hotel you're in," Yalt protested. "And it's a good one."

"It is," Pushley agreed. "But I don't want that man to find

me."

Yalt frowned. "There are not many good hotels in Awis."

"It doesn't have to be a hotel," Pushley replied, "Just somewhere safe."

Eventually, Yalt said, "I know of a house you can use, it's on the edge of town."

"Is it legal?"

Yalt turned his hands face up, and then moved them up and down like a balance, "Outworlders own it, but they don't come here that often. A cousin of mine looks after it for them."

"Are they likely to come back during the next week?"

"No, padrone."

"Good, that sounds fine," Pushley replied. "Show me to this house straight away and organise for my luggage to be transferred from the hotel."

"That might be difficult," Yalt said. "Ab are not allowed in hotels."

"I'm sure Ab cleaning staff are," Pushley said. "So, you should be able to get them to let you in."

Yalt rolled his eyes. Pushley passed him a small denomination money card. "Does that help?"

When Yalt grabbed it, Pushley said, "Remember, I don't want anyone knowing my new address. Got it?"

Yalt nodded and began to lead Pushley down a series of narrow passages. While he was walking, Pushley opened his wallet, extracted the emergency percom and called Stert Oryx.

Oryx was a blunt as ever, "What d'you want?"

Opening up his main percom, Pushley glanced at the photographs he'd taken of Warmers bank accounts. He said, "Do you have the authority to put bank accounts on ice?"

"On ice?"

"Frozen."

Oryx was evasive, "Whose bank accounts?"

"Do you want to take Tarleton, or don't you?"

"Of course."

"Then do as I ask," Pushley replied. "Lean on someone and

get the following accounts frozen until further notice." He read out the details.

Once he'd finished dictating, Oryx said, "Why d'you want them iced?"

"Leverage," Pushley replied

When Oryx just frowned, Pushley repeated, "You do want to take Tarleton, don't you?"

After getting Oryx to agree, Pushley returned the emergency percom to his wallet. He glanced ahead and noted that Yalt had stopped outside a two-storey stone-built cottage. Retrieving a key from beneath a mat, Yalt opened the front door and let Pushley in.

Being cautious, Pushley swiftly inspected the ground floor, went upstairs, and glanced out of the front bedroom window. As there was no sign of pursuit, he let out a sigh of relief and went downstairs.

Despite his observations, he gave Yalt a sharp look; he asked, "This place is safe, isn't it?"

"No one knows you are here, padrone," Yalt assured him.

"Keep it that way," Pushley told him. "And make sure my belongings are brought here without anyone knowing where you are bringing them."

~*~

Hal Warmer's confiscated percom suddenly warbled. When Pushley accepted the call, Warmers' face formed in a power bubble. The hostility radiated from it.

"That was a real dirty trick you pulled Pushley—if that is your name? You'll regret doing that to me. Any deals we had are off, and I want my money back."

"Sorry, a deal is a deal," Pushley replied. "And we have a deal."

Warmers let out a hysterical laugh, "You rob me blind, shoot me and leave me in a deserted bar. You've got to be out of your mind if you think I'd do business with you after you pulled that stunt."

"Before you paint yourself into a corner, I'd check your bank accounts," Pushley replied. "You'll find they're frozen."

Warmers snapped, "What d'you mean frozen?"

"As in, you can't draw any money out of them," Pushley replied.

When Warmers' eyes narrowed, Pushley added, "And they'll stay that way until you carry out your side of the deal."

"You can't do that!"

"I have done it," Pushley replied.

"What's your game, Pushley?

"For the avoidance of doubt, in a few days, a group of bounty hunters are going to arrive in Awis," Pushley revealed. "I have told them that I'll arrange for Tarleton to be detained and handed over when they arrive. That's where you come in. You grab Tarleton and his gang and leave them somewhere they can be picked up."

"And why should I help you?"

"Without money, you won't get very far," Pushley observed. "In addition, the leader of the bounty hunters is a man called Stert Oryx."

Warmers image in the bubble visibly paled.

"Ah! Good. I see you've heard of him," Pushley observed. "I'm sure you are on his list of wanted war criminals too. If you don't carry out my instructions to the letter, I'll make sure Oryx and his thugs come looking for you."

CHAPTER EIGHTEEN

The Tower

Checking out Awis Oasis

S haking him into wakefulness, Lascaux said, "We've stopped. The air-car has landed."

Tarmy attempted to sit up but realised he couldn't move because his arms and legs were still paralysed. The only parts of his body that seemed to work were his head and neck.

Eventually, he said, "Where are we?"

Lascaux shrugged, "I've looked out, but I can't see much."

"Didn't you open the doors?"

"They're locked," she replied. "The motor is also disabled, but there's a dash notice indicating your invisible friend will be back shortly. It looks like Alex wants us to stay here."

After thinking about the last comment, he said, "How come you're here?"

"It's nice to see you too," Lascaux replied.

"Let me rephrase the question," Tarmy said. "Why are you here?"

"Don't you remember, Pushley trying to kill us?" She added, "Mind you it wasn't easy getting into the air-car; Alex tried to stop us getting on board."

"Us? Who exactly is us?"

"Red and Bryn," Lascaux said.

"Red and Bryn?"

"The two guys you rescued from the jungle. They saw Pushley shooting people and didn't want to be left behind," Lascaux replied.

"What about Nonie and Claire?"

She pointed, "They're back there, but they are well out of it."

Tarmy said, "Anyone else?"

"Chou Lan. She's my buddy. I wasn't going to leave her behind, not with Pushley being like he is. He's gone nuts."

"Nuts?"

"A head-case, a nutter," Lascaux explained, "Around the bend."

She grinned, "Still. One good thing, the old gang is back together again."

"Yeah," Tarmy sighed. "The old gang's back together again."

As the air-car's internal lighting was providing a dim background glow, Tarmy began glancing around. "Are you sure Claire and Nonie are okay?"

"As far as I can tell," Lascaux replied. "But like I just said, they seem well out of it."

"I'm not surprised," Tarmy replied. "Pushley stunned them again; they could well be out for twenty or more standard hours."

"Why did he stun them again?"

"To make sure we couldn't escape."

Lascaux speculated, "Because he wanted to make sure he could hand you all in and demand the reward for your capture."

"Yeah," Tarmy agreed.

Realising Lascaux knew all about his supposed 'war-criminal' past, Tarmy nodded and explained, "For your information, I'm an undercover cop."

"Yeah, sure you are," Lascaux replied, sarcastically.

~*~

An hour later the roof doors suddenly opened and faint shadow floated into view. Alex said, "I need to speak to you Corporal Tarmy, in private."

"Corporal Tarmy," Lascaux echoed. Glancing at Mick, she added, "Why did he call you Corporal Tarmy?"

"I told you," Tarmy snapped. "I'm an undercover cop. My real name is Mick Tarmy."

"Okay," Lascaux said, this time in a believing tone.

Tarmy glanced up at Alex, "I can't move. Can you get me out of here?"

Alex immediately dropped three of his flexible arms into the air-car and pulled Tarmy out. Lascaux was about to follow, but Tarmy checked her, "You can get out to stretch your legs, but you are not to follow us. Understood?"

Lascaux responded by giving him a mock salute, "Yes sir, Corporal Tarmy."

After turning on his headlights, Alex began carrying Tarmy away from the air-car. Glancing around Tarmy saw the second air-car and expressed his surprise, "You brought both air-cars."

"If I had left one of the air-cars behind Pushley would have followed us." Alex reasoned.

Tarmy then caught a glimpse of the four A10s neatly lined up as if assembled for inspection, "Where did they come from?"

"Stert Oryx brought them with him," Alex replied. "I acquired them too."

"What are we going to do with them?" Tarmy said.

"They are spoils of war," Alex replied. "I have no doubt they will come in useful."

"But how did you manage to control four droids and two air cars?" Tarmy asked.

"I am an enhanced TK5," Alex reminded him and carried Tarmy towards an opening in a sturdy wall. Partway there, the four A10s broke rank and formed a cordon to prevent Lascaux following.

Once behind the mid-wall and well hidden, Alex came to a halt. Tarmy immediately asked, "Where are we?"

"I have bought you to a survivor tower which is approximately ten kilometres south of Awis Oasis," Alex replied.

The information triggered bad memories for Tarmy. "The last survivor tower you took us to was overrun by giant Arcadian millipedes within a matter of hours."

"There is no chance of a repetition," Alex promised. "This tower is surrounded by desert, and Arcadian millipedes are only found in the Fyfield Valley and Altos plateaux."

Alex added, "Besides, as it is sited adjacent to a deep wadi and difficult to reach in land cars, this tower is rarely visited. Local records indicate this particular tower hasn't been visited for over a year."

As Tarmy's legs were still not functioning, and he was only in a vertical position because Alex was holding him up, he asked, "Why have you brought me out of the air-car?"

"To speak to you privately, Corporal Tarmy," Alex replied. "I need your orders. Are you intent on going to Awis Oasis?"

"You told me that was the only place I could go," Tarmy replied. He then gave the droid a sickly smile, "But since we lost the money, it looks as if I'll have to think again."

"I don't understand," Alex said. "You have money."

"Pushley stole the bag with the money cards," Tarmy replied. "Without adequate finances, we're in trouble. I had hoped to get myself a new ID."

Alex suddenly dropped his cloaks and opened a metal safe suspended between his main struts. Tarmy's jaw dropped; the money cards were inside.

By way of explanation, Alex said, "Pushley said he wanted the bag. So, that is what I left him with."

Despite his partial paralysis, Tarmy laughed. Although he suspected Alex had deliberately deceived Pushley, the answer had all the hallmarks of droid logic; Pushley had demanded the bag, and that is what he'd been given. Alex had kept the contents.

"Do you still wish to go to Awis Oasis?"

Tarmy nodded, "The money changes everything. I still need a new ID. If I show Tarleton's documents in the wrong place, I could be arrested."

"Very few of the illegal colonies have yet to develop efficient border control points," Alex replied. "With money, you can enter Awis Oasis with ease."

"What do you mean by illegal colonies?"

"Most human colonies on Arcadia are illegal," Alex explained. "Before the war, all colonisation was forbidden, but the war brought disorder. Some rich people had been casting envious eyes over Arcadia for years; those who wanted a place in the sun acquired private teleport systems. Once they set them up and visited the planet, most of them decided they liked Arcadia. They then began building villas in the most beautiful locations."

"As most non-military teleports can't transport droids, the rich brought in human servants to deal with their needs. Populations swiftly grow."

"So how many illegal colonies are there?"

"Hundreds," Alex replied. "Mostly on the coast where there are good sands. Some colonies are very big, others tiny. A native Ab population originally inhabited Awis Oasis, and during the war, a droid excluding Mannheim was erected over Awis Oasis to prevent the area being used as a droid base by the enemy. The Mannheim is still active."

"After the war, the local population of Awis Oasis were attacked and driven from their homes by colonising outworlders."

"You're joking!"

"I am not," Alex replied. "Many outworlders consider the Ab, the native people, to be animals, far inferior to them and think nothing of killing them because they dress differently and seem so outlandish in their eyes."

When Tarmy just stared at Alex open-mouthed, the droid added, "Since the end of the war, Awis Oasis has become an area the rich use for part-time holiday homes. Although there is a small police force, most home security and property patrols are largely carried out by private security companies."

Alex then added, "Awis Oasis is also a tax haven, a place where dirty money is laundered. The private security guards are unlikely to ask many questions when you arrive. Instead, they'll just demand an access deposit of one hundred thousand ACU per air-car. In addition, you may have to offer them a bribe."

Noting the signs of worry on Tarmy's brow, Alex said, "The access deposit is usually refunded as long as a visitor doesn't carry out a crime or cause damage while in the Awis Oasis."

The TK5 then opened its safe again, "You have more than enough finances. I suggest you take what you need."

"I can't," Tarmy snapped, "My arms still don't work."

In response, Alex reached into his safe, removed several cards and then slipped them into Tarmy's top pocket.

Once he'd finished, Tarmy said, "All this stuff you've just told me; where did you obtain this information?"

"I am an enhanced TK5," Alex reminded him. "Collecting local information by hacking into computer systems is part of my duties."

After thinking hard, Tarmy then said, "If I can move around the illegal colonies fairly easily, are you telling me that I don't need a new ID?"

"Mick Tarleton has a price on his head," Alex reminded him. "Anyone who recognises you might attempt to kill you and claim the bounty. Acquiring new ID, one that suggests that you were a Midwain citizen would be a sensible precaution. In the event of you being stopped, you would be able to convince people that you are not Mick Tarleton."

"Okay," Tarmy said. "I'll go to Awis Oasis."

"There is a problem," Alex replied.

"What problem?

"As I explained, the whole of the Awis Oasis is protected by a droid excluding Mannheim," Alex replied, "Which means I cannot protect you if you go there."

When Tarmy showed signs of quibbling, Alex added, "If I went with you the Mannheim would swiftly degrade my systems. Irreparable system destruction would occur with less than two hour's exposure."

"Why did they keep the shield after the war was over?"

"It suited the newcomers. Also, for religious reasons," Alex replied.

"What religious reasons?" Tarmy queried.

"As I do not understand human religious beliefs, I can't tell you no more. All I know, there are no droids in Awis Oasis. It's a droid free zone."

"What about people like Stert Oryx? Am I likely to be in danger?"

In response, Alex formed a power bubble. A small tab in one corner indicated the recording had been made by one of the A10s. A moment later, the bubble was populated with images of Pushley and Stert Oryx.

"So, you are going to let Tarleton escape?"

"I didn't say that," Oryx replied.

"So, what are you going to do?" Pushley demanded.

"We're going back to basics," Oryx said. "Awis Oasis has teleport facilities. It also has a droid free policy and has a protection Mannheim which works in our favour. If we teleport in, Tarleton's TK5 won't be able to protect him."

Once the recording had finished, Alex said, "As it is almost certain Stert Oryx will come after you. I recommend you remain alert and leave Awis Oasis as soon as possible."

"Is there anything else I should know about Awis Oasis?"

"The only other thing you need to know is the outer gates to Awis Oasis are locked during the hours of darkness."

"So, it's an early morning start then." Tarmy replied. "Always assuming that my legs start working."

CHAPTER NINETEEN

Survivor Tower

Preparing to leave for Awis Oasis

oving to an opening in the tower wall, Tarmy began running his eyes over the surrounding landscape. With only Arden, Arcadia's main moon providing illumination the Great Rock desert looked sinister; a place of shadows, a zone where unknown monsters might lurk. However, as the area was lacking in fog or light pollution, the local constellations stood brighter than Tarmy had ever seen them before; Awis Oasis was a faint glow in the distance.

After running his eyes over the surrounding landscape one more time, Tarmy wondering what would happen once he reached the main gate leading into Awis Oasis. If Alex was right, personal documents wouldn't be required. Money was the key to gaining entrance. He thought about the most important issue. As a droid excluding Mannheim covered the whole oasis, once he passed through the Mannheim, he'd lack the protection he'd learned to appreciate.

While he was thinking, a quiet voice said, "The fungal growth doesn't suit you."

Glancing around at Nonie, Tarmy ran a hand over his unshaven face, "Growing a beard is the most logical disguise for any man."

"D'you really think so?"

With his disguise in question, Tarmy ran his hand over his face again and concluded it wasn't much of a disguise. Not only was his beard far from complete; it had reached the stage

where it felt as if it were an itching invader, an alien prolif-
eration spreading over his formerly well-shaven skin. Worse,
the fungal growth had patches of grey showing in places.

"So how long are we staying here?"

"Not long," Tarmy replied.

"And how long is not long?"

"Long enough for me to visit Awis Oasis and get out again.
Then I'll come back, and we will decide where we're going to
go."

"So, no exact time frame?"

Tarmy shook his head.

"So, what's your plan exactly?"

"I told you. To visit Awis Oasis and get out again as fast as
possible. Alex has recommended I go to Awis Oasis and find
someone who can forge me a new ID. I could get you a forged ID
too."

"That will cost money," Nonie predicted. "A forger is not
going to work for buttons."

"Don't worry. We have money," Tarmy assured her. He was
on the point of telling her about the money cards that Alex
had stashed in his safe when a quiet voice said, "That's very
nice for Nonie. What about me?"

Glancing around, Tarmy noted that Claire had quietly
moved in behind them. Tarmy said, "It goes without saying,
you need a new ID as much I do."

"Won't you need our photographs?"

Tarmy held up his percom, "I already have yours."

"I hope it wasn't taken when I was in metamorphosis,"
Claire replied. "We don't want anyone thinking I'm one of
these weird monarch things; a left-over mutant that no one
wants."

"She's been drinking," Nonie whispered.

Ignoring the comment, Tarmy said, "I don't think you're
weird."

Following Tarmy's lead, Nonie agreed, "And neither do I."

"I'm an inconvenience though," Claire replied. "If I weren't around, you two wouldn't have a third wheel cluttering up your life."

The tone of Claire's voice immediately reminded Tarmy of the time that Claire had slashed the palm of her hand so he could see her blood. She'd been trying to prove she was human. Now Pushley had revealed she was a monarch; her worst fears had been realised.

He sensed that she was having suicidal thoughts. Noting she was eying up one of the openings at the top of the high tower, Tarmy moved slightly, deliberately blocking any attempt she might make at throwing herself to her death.

After swiftly glancing at Nonie and noting the expression of concern on her face, Tarmy chanced his arm, "You are not a spare wheel, Claire. When we, when I leave, you are coming with me."

It was at that point that Tarmy was reminded of what Pushley had said when he'd taken Nonie and Claire prisoner. He'd stated he'd taken both women prisoner because it was obvious that he'd started a commune of his own.

While Tarmy's mind was still churning, Claire moved closer, and her face seemed more relaxed. "Okay. Always, we are assuming we can find a suitable forger in Awis Oasis, and we obtain false IDs. Then what?"

After telling them about the illegal colonies that had sprung up all over Arcadia, Tarmy said, "As people are likely to come for us if we stay in Awis Oasis because we can't go back to Arden, the logical thing for us to do would be to find a suitable colony and try to blend in."

Still, in a volatile mood, Claire said, "So, the best we can hope for is ending up in some illegal redneck colony, always looking over our shoulders in case someone comes looking for us."

There was a slight cough, and then someone standing in the shadows said, "Is this a private conversation, or can anyone join the party?"

Red Moxstroma then stepped out of the shadows closely

followed by Lascaux, Chou Lan, and Bryn Rosslyn.

"Well," Moxstroma said, "Can I join in?"

As the tension coming from Claire was still electric, Tarmy was relieved by the interruption. Glancing at Moxstroma, he said, "So, what do you want to say?"

"As I told you a while back, we have a nursery," Moxstroma replied. "Bryn and I will be going back there hopefully. You are all welcome to join us."

"That's very kind of you," Tarmy replied. "What sort of nursery?"

"I would have thought that was obvious. Trees and plants; native and imported."

"No Zuka?"

"No chance," Moxstroma replied, "Not anymore."

When Tarmy remained silent, Moxstroma added, "God knows what condition the place will be in at the moment, but we were making money. Even though New Victoria is classed as an illegal colony, since the mining started, the whole state has grown fast. Every year, hundreds of people teleport down to NV, looking for a better life; NV has a population of nearly four million and growing."

"At the present moment, New Melbourne and the surrounding towns have a population of nearly three million. People need homes and gardens. People with money buy plants."

Moxstroma glanced at Bryn Rosslyn and said, "If you guys hadn't rescued us, we'd still be prisoners, and the chances are the Great Ones would have probably worked us to death. What I'm trying to say is that we owe you big time. We believe in repaying our debts."

He handed Tarmy a scrap of plastimetal paper. "I heard what you were saying, but it will go no further." He added, "If you need IDs, this is the man who can help you."

The note had a name Targon Yatboon, and an address scrawled on it.

Tarmy said, "Is this person trustworthy?"

"He helped a friend of mine a few years back," Moxstroma

replied. He then added, "Having ID, is not essential in New Victoria but life's easer if you have it. So, I would go to him."

Claire cut in with, "Alex told me he couldn't go to Awis Oasis. Something about the Mannheim being able to damage his circuits."

"He can't go into Awis Oasis," Tarmy confirmed.

"I don't like the idea of leaving Alex behind," Claire said.

"Neither do I," Nonie joined in.

"Alex is staying here with you," Tarmy replied. "I'm going to Awis Oasis on my own."

"You can't go in on your own," Moxstroma objected. "You need someone to watch your back. In fact, I could take you to see Targon Yatboon. I'll go with you."

Running his eyes over Moxstroma's painfully thin malnourished frame, Tarmy knew that the other man wouldn't be much use if they did run into trouble. But instead of passing comment on Moxstroma's physical fitness, he just shook his head. "If I am unlucky and the authorities arrest me, I don't want any of you dragged down with me."

"I'm coming with you," Moxstroma insisted.

"And so am I," Claire cut in.

"And so am I," Nonie joined in.

"No," Tarmy returned. "This is not open for debate. Once we've got all the provisions out, I will take one of the air-cars. You lot will stay here until I get back."

"I'm coming with you," Red Moxstroma insisted, "End of."

"If he's going then I'm going too," Claire insisted.

"And me," Nonie said.

Ollie, Nonie's pet pterodactyl immediately sensed he was going to be left behind and let out a squawk.

Tarmy put his foot down, "We can't take Ollie."

Understanding Tarmy's thoughts, Ollie squawked again, but Tarmy shook his head.

Nonie gave in, "Okay, Ollie stays behind."

Picking up on her thoughts, Ollie let out another squawk of disapproval.

Once Ollie had quietened down, Nonie added, "But I'm coming to Awis with you."

"And me," Lascaux said

When Chou Lan and Bryn Rosslyn, remained silent, Lascaux added, "So that's settled then, these two stay behind to mind the fort and feed Ollie and we go to Awis Oasis."

She nudged Red Moxstroma and nodded towards Bryn Rosslyn and Chou Lan, "I hope we can trust you two while we're away."

~*~

"Knock, knock."

Instead of giving the expected response, 'Who's there', Nonie growled, "What d'you want?"

When Claire didn't answer, Nonie glanced sideways and noted the other woman had changed her appearance; she was back to having copper hair and amber eyes. Deliberately ignoring the face changing, Nonie said, "I asked you what you wanted?"

"To apologise," Claire replied. "I was a bit full-on, wasn't I?"

"You were blind drunk," Nonie corrected. "Where did you get the booze?"

"I found it," Claire replied

"Found it?"

"Do you want some?"

"No. Where did you find it?"

"I found a couple of bottles of Arcadian Absinthe stashed away in a locker," Claire replied, "someone must have hidden them onboard."

"No wonder you were drunk." Nonie scolded. "Arcadian Absinthe can be as high as seventy per cent proof. But why did you get smashed?"

"I thought we were friends," Claire replied.

"We are," Nonie replied. "Or I thought we were. Aren't we?"

Instead of answering, Claire began metamorphosing. Partway through the process, she started talking again, "Pushley said I was freak, one of those monarch things."

"And both me and Mick have told you we don't think you are freak," Nonie cooed.

"But you think it."

"Okay," Nonie agreed. "Seeing you change is a bit disturbing, but now we're used to it."

She gave the other woman a sharp look as she realised that Claire was morphing into a very good likeness of herself. "Don't do that!"

"Do what?"

"You know what," Nonie snapped. "You're copying *my* features."

"Maybe Mick would like me more if I looked more like you," Claire replied.

"Ah! Now the truth is coming out," Nonie snapped. She then shook her head disbelievingly. "You know as well as I do that when Yan Farman brought you to Arcadia, you agreed to abide by local rules, to become part of a commune. That's the way things work at Fort Saunders—Midway rules."

"True," Claire agreed, "I may have agreed to that, but I always remained loyal to Yan."

"But you soon learned that Yan liked to spread himself around," Nonie replied. "As there were five times as many women to men at the base, he was like a child in a sweet factory."

"I always remained loyal to Yan."

"You remained loyal to Yan, eh! What about Hal Warmers?" Nonie quibbled.

Claire inwardly cringed, but decided to bluff, "What about Hal Warmers?"

"Rumour had it that you and Hal had a thing going," Nonie replied. "What I've heard is that Warmers was smitten with you and used to visit you whenever he came to Cittavecchia."

Still bluffing, Claire snapped, "Like I said. I always remained loyal to Yan."

"Rumour also has it that your beloved Yan was only too pleased to encourage you to sleep with Hal Warmers," Nonie countered. "As Hal had useful black-market connections, Yan wanted to keep him sweet."

Still bluffing, Claire gave Nonie a savage look, "How many times. I always remained loyal to Yan."

"Okay," Nonie replied. "If you say so. You always were slightly out of step with everyone else. Then again, I suppose it was easy for me, on my home world, most people live in communes.

~*~

Dawn was just breaking when the air-car left the tower. Noting that Bryn Rosslyn and Chou Lan had their backs to him, Ollie began working on the wedge holding his cage door shut. He pushed hard until the door flew open. He launched himself into space and set off in pursuit of the air-car. He vaguely heard the two humans calling after him but ignored them. If his mistress was going to Awis then so was he.

CHAPTER TWENTY

Awis Oasis

Pushley pursues Mick

When Pushley attempted to mind link, Warmers immediately rebuffed it. He noted that the other man was wearing a hat.

Pushley cursed under his breath because it was evident that Warmers now had an air-tight defence. Despite the lack of mind-probing, Pushley read the other man's expression; Warmers was only going along with his plan because he had no choice. Given half a chance, there could be no doubting Warmers would have him kidnapped and force him to return his money. The hostile expression also confirmed, he'd done the right thing moving out of the hotel.

"Yes," Pushley said. "What is it?"

"Let's call it a courtesy call," Warmers growled. "I thought I'd let you know; Tarleton has arrived."

Pushley was on his feet in an instant, "Where is he? Are you going to grab him?"

"Whoa!" Warmers snapped. "We have to tread carefully and bide our time."

When Pushley's expression hardened, Warmers added, "He's not on his own. He's with a small group of people. He has three women and another man with him."

"Show me."

The bubble image immediately filled with a photograph taken at the main gate. Pushley's eyes locked onto Mick Tarmy and Nonie Tomio. He transferred his gaze to a pale-skinned woman with copper coloured hair and amber eyes; it was apparent that Claire Hyndman had come to Awis disguised as her false self. While he was still staring at her, Warmers said, "Which one's the monarch?"

Despite the fact that he had extracted a great deal of money out of Warmers during their last tête à tête in the bar and had a Damoclean sword hanging over him in the form of Oryx, Pushley still didn't trust Warmers and had no desire to provide the other man with too much information. Thinking fast, Pushley implied Nonie Tomio was the monarch.

Returning to the attack, Pushley then said, "So, when are you going to grab him and shake him until he gives me my bag back?"

"For the time being we're just keeping them under observation," Warmers replied.

When an impatient look formed on Pushley's face, Warmers said, "We can't just go charging around like a mad bull. Awis Oasis has security cameras all over the place. Although Awis's official police force is minimal, the markets, shops, bars, hotels, and rich householders in the surrounding areas all employ private security guards to protect them. If we jump the Tarleton group at the wrong time, a fight is going to break out. It stands to reason either the police or private security could intervene. As most of them are armed, it's not a good prospect."

"So, you're just going to watch him!"

"For the time being, yes," Warmers replied.

After Warmers had cut out, Pushley gave a curt instruction to his percom. A few seconds later, Yalt's image appeared in the power bubble. Without preamble, Pushley said, "I need to see you immediately."

Although he'd expected Yalt to make excuses and suggest he was already working, the other man just nodded, "I will come to the house ten minutes, padrone but I will go around the back."

Being impatient, Pushley immediately went downstairs

and walked into the back yard. He immediately felt uncomfortable. Although he knew he couldn't be seen by the street cameras, he knew that someone, or something, was watching him.

~*~

As usual, Yalt arrived with a Prussian respect for time and found Pushley waiting in the yard. After giving Pushley a slight bow of respect, Yalt said, "What can I do for you, padrone."

Speaking to his percom, Pushley recalled the images Warmers had sent him and then said, "These people have just arrived in Awis. I need you to find them, follow them and keep me informed as to what they are doing."

Yalt eyed him, thoughtfully, "For how long, padrone?"

"Until I tell you to stop," Pushley replied and then produced a higher value money card than normal; Yalt took it and swiftly disappeared.

~*~

Nonie's mind suddenly filled with images of Ed Pushley and another man. With more mind images flooding in, she guessed at the truth. Although she couldn't see Ollie, it was obvious that he'd escaped and had managed to follow her to Awis Oasis. It was also obvious that Ollie had picked up Ed Pushley's heat signature and was carrying out her last order; following Pushley and letting her know what he was doing.

A moment later, she saw Pushley create a power bubble image and show it to the other man. When Ollie obligingly used his eagle-eye vision to magnify the bubble images, she recognised Mick and herself and realised the truth; Pushley was still pursuing Mick. Worse, it was also obvious he'd engaged a local enquiry agent to track them down.

A moment later, Ollie sent her more images, one that showed their group with the enquiry agent not far behind

Nonie immediately told Mick Tarmy what she'd just discovered. Overhearing the conversation, Red Moxstroma suddenly changed direction.

"Where are we going," Tarmy demanded.

Out of the corner of his mouth, Moxstroma whispered, "Keep your voice down. I was going to take you straight to Targon Yatboon's place, but if we are being followed, I need to shake off our tail first. If we're not careful, Yatboon could get into serious trouble and then you'll never get your IDs."

Moxstroma added, "I'm heading for the market. We might lose him in the crowds, but we need to stick together in case he tries something on."

After telling the others to keep together, Tarmy moved close to Claire and said, "I might need you to do one of your face changes soon."

Claire gave him a sharp look, "So, I'm coming in useful now, am I?"

"I never said you weren't."

"Why d'you need me to change."

"Red says we're being followed," Tarmy replied. "If you change your appearance whoever is following us won't recognise you, and you might be able to find out who it is without them knowing we've rumbled them."

Dropping her icy demeanour, Claire became practical, "I could make myself look like one of the locals. But I'd need some ethnic clothes, local clothes. And then I'll need somewhere to change. I can't change my clothes or my face in public; it would attract too much attention, wouldn't it?"

After the group had formed a huddle around one stall, so that their tail couldn't see what they were doing, Tarmy paid for some new clothes, and they all set off for a local bar. On the way, Tarmy whispered, "Make sure you take your gun with you."

"I never go anywhere without it," Claire replied.

"Even so, be careful," Tarmy said, "Don't take any unnecessary risks."

"You almost sound concerned."

"I am," Tarmy replied. "I wouldn't send you off on your own if there was another way."

"You don't need to worry about me," Claire replied. "If Pushley is right and I *am* one of those weird monarch things, according to Alex I am far stronger than a normal woman."

"Since when has Alex been an expert on monarchs?"

"Since I asked him to hack into local computer systems and find out everything he could find out about monarchs," she replied.

"And what else did he find out?"

"That's for me to know and for you to worry about," Claire replied.

~*~

Once they'd arrived at a suitable bar, Claire immediately headed for the washroom with the bags of clothes they'd bought, changed and then left by the rear door carrying her outworlder clothes in the same bag that she'd obtained from the market stall.

Outside, she made her way down a series of alleyways and emerged in the main market square. Her ears were assailed by the cries of the local market traders. As she had a basic understanding of the Arcadian language, some of the calls made sense but most didn't because it was obvious that Awis had its own heavy regional accent.

Wishing to avoid having to talk to anyone and betray herself, she dropped her eyes to the floor and only glanced up occasionally. After working herself through the market, she found a safe place and then glanced back at the bar she'd recently left.

Within seconds, her worst fear became a reality when one of the street traders came over waving something in his hand, "Si acquista, si acquista."

Waving him away with a firm, "No," she walked away. A

moment later, her eyes latched onto a face she recognised, Hal Warmers.

Even though she was in disguise, she turned quickly and took shelter in a recessed doorway and muttered, "Go away, Hal."

After allowing a minute or two to elapse, she glanced out again, but Hal Warmers hadn't moved. He was still there, watching the bar where the others were hiding.

As she ducked back into the recess, she was suddenly gripped by a sense of shame because she realised that all the lies she'd told were highly likely to be exposed.

In an attempt to make the shame evaporate, she shook her head and mumbled excuses to herself, "You had to do it. You had no choice."

But despite the self-denials, the memories kept flooding back, and she recalled telling Nonie she'd never been with Hal Warmers.

It had been a blatant lie because the real Claire Hyndman certainly had. Nonie had been right. When her partner, Yan Farman had still been alive, Hal Warmers always paid her a visit when he came to Fort Saunders. More importantly, Yan had approved of the liaison. As Hal Warmers had good connections in the local black market and regularly bought artefacts from Yan, it was in Yan's interest to make sure she kept Hal sweet.

She started mumbling excuses again, "You had to do it. You had no choice."

She recalled the fateful day she'd flown out with mercenary troops in the hope of avenging Yan's death. But instead of taking revenge on the Great Ones, the incursion had turned into a total rout.

Not only had they flown into a well-prepared trap, within a matter of minutes; the mercenary troops had been overwhelmed by the Great Ones' animal army.

Her thoughts turned to more recent events, to Samantha, the humanoid deputy director of Minton Mining Company Security.

When Zia Warmers had been captured, Samantha had swiftly realised Zia could face change. As Claire Hyndman had been dying and Samantha had been extracting money from her father for pointless medical treatments, she forced Zia to take on Claire Hyndman's identity and the other woman had been resurrected from the dead. Worse, by a bizarre twist of fate, both her former lives were entangled with Hal Warmers.

Shaking her head again, she repeated her mantra, "You had to do it. You had no choice."

But once again, bad thoughts kept on breaking through, and she was reminded of the lies she'd told Mick Tarmy.

Mick had always suspected a link between Zia Warmers and her, but she'd never admitted to it. She'd even briefed Alex and made sure he'd backed up her story. But without a doubt, she had once been Zia Warmers, Hal Warmers' terrorist partner.

~*~

Yalt spoke to his percom. A few seconds later, Pushley's face appeared on the viewscreen, and Pushley snapped, "Yes. What is it?"

"I am doing as you asked," Yalt responded. "I think I have found the people you wanted me to follow. I think they are sitting in a bar."

"You think!"

"I can't enter the bar," Yalt protested. "Ab are not allowed in."

"Well, find out if they're still in there," Pushley snapped. He then added, "Anything else?"

"Yes, padrone," Yalt replied. "There is something else. They are being watched."

"What d'you mean being watched?" Pushley snapped.

"A woman and two men watching them," Yalt replied. He took some photographs and sent them to Pushley.

Pushley immediately recognised Hal Warmers and said,

"The guy wearing the leather jacket is on our side. I also recognise the other man; that's Connell. So, keep back; they are
on our side, and I don't want you cramping their style. Understood?"

When Yalt had confirmed he would just watch, Pushley
said, "Who's the woman?"

"I don't know," Yalt admitted. He said, "One of your men has
just gone into an alley with the woman. Do you want me to follow them?"

"I just told you not to cramp their style," Pushley snapped.
"Stay where you are and watch."

~*~

While her mind was still churning, Hal Warmers suddenly
loomed up in the doorway turned and locked eyes with her.
Although she'd changed her features, the look on Warmers'
face told her that he'd seen through her disguise. Calling out
to Connell, Warmers said, "Stay here and keep watch. If they
leave, contact me and follow them."

Warmers then came face to face with Claire, "I've seen you
before."

Dropping her eyes, Claire pulled back shaking her head, "I
am sorry. You are mistaken."

She turned and moved back towards one of the link alleys. But instead of letting her escape, Warmers followed
her, dragged her towards another recessed doorway and then
slammed her into it, face first. He pulled out a small stun
gun and rammed it against her spine, "One move and I'll blast
you."

He reached down and rustled the bag she was holding,
"What's in the bag?"

"Clothes," Claire replied.

Warmers immediately pushed his free hand into the bag
and inspected them. "Very clever, abandon your *outworlder*
clothes for local ones and then change your appearance."

"I don't know what you're talking about," Claire hit back.

In response, Warmers jabbed her spine with the gun again and said, "Show me your hands."

As Claire had no desire to be stunned and enter the limbo world where time seemed to stand still, she raised one of her hands for him to inspect. Warmers immediately let out a whoop of delight, "I thought so. Pushley was lying. You're the monarch."

Finding her voice, Claire said, "What d'you mean? The monarch?"

Warmers said, "The middle three fingers on your hands are virtually the same length. Strange looking hands and feet are one of the side effects of the monarch conversion process."

"I am not one of these monarchs, whatever they are," Claire protested.

"Well," Warmers countered, "I'm afraid you are. Ed Pushley told me."

Thinking fast, she said, "Who's Ed Pushley?"

"You can't bluff a bluffer." Warmers added, "Ed told me all about you, and he also said that Tarleton had a bag."

When Claire remained silent, Warmers added, "Ed hasn't forgotten you. He even said I could have you if I went along with his plan. Not that I need to now because I've caught you already, haven't I? So, I can forget Ed Pushley and make my own plans."

Jamming his gun against her spine again, Warmers said, "Pushley gave me a cock and bull story and said that his bag contained worthless artefacts, but my guess is they must be valuable. So, where's the bag?"

"I don't know what you are talking about," Claire replied.

Warmers responded by firing his stun gun at one of her arms. It immediately went dead and the bag she was holding dropped to the ground. Warmers kicked it deeper into the recess, "Shouldn't worry about your outworlder clothes; where you're going, you won't need them."

He then moved the gun as if he intended to shoot her other

arm, but he didn't. Instead, he aimed the gun at one of the fingers on the other arm. As part of her other hand went numb, Warmers said, "In case you haven't realised it, these shots are warnings. If you don't co-operate, I will slowly disable your body, bit at a time."

He then said, "So what are Tarleton's plans?"

"Tarleton?"

"Don't play stupid with me," Warmers snapped. He then added, "Maybe it's time to try something different."

When Claire remained silent, he grabbed hold of her again and began to frog-march her further down the alley. Eventually, he opened a primitive plastimetal gate and dragged her into a small rear yard. In one corner there was a large earthenware sink raised on bricks serving as a water feature. Pointing to it, Warmers said, "D'you know the best way to get someone to talk?"

Without waiting for her answer, he tripped her up, so she went down on her knees and thrust her face into the water. Although she struggled, she couldn't pull her face out. After holding her under for nearly twenty seconds, Warmers pulled her out and said, "They reckon waterboarding is the best way to get people to talk."

He then said, "So what are Tarleton's plans?"

Claire gasped, "Who is Tarleton?"

"I told you not to play stupid with me," Warmers snapped.

"I don't know who you mean."

Not receiving the answer he wanted, Warmers thrust her head below the water again and this time held her under for thirty seconds. Dragging her out, he repeated his question, "So, what are Tarleton's plans?"

Knowing she'd go under for even longer if she didn't answer, Claire gave in, "He's come here to see a guy who can make false IDs."

"Now that's better," Warmers cooed. "Does this guy have a name?"

"I don't know his name. All I know is there's a guy who

makes them," Claire gasped.

"Address?"

"I don't know his address," Claire replied. "I was just follow-ing everyone else."

"But you weren't were you," Warmers snapped. "You were outside."

"I was told to keep watch."

Warmers was tempted to push her head below the water again but sensing he'd extracted as much information as he could; he dragged her back to her feet and frogmarched her out through the gate. Eventually, they came to a small car park, and Warmers issued a verbal command to one of the air-cars parked there. Its security lights immediately flashed once, and the boot sprang open. Gesturing with his gun, Warmers pointed to the open boot and said, "Get in."

Realising Warmers intended to lock her in while he went after Mick Tarmy; she tentatively moved towards the car but made no attempt to climb into the boot.

"I said get in," Warmers snapped, and moved closer. Claire reacted by swiftly swinging one of her legs, hitting him squarely in the lower abdomen. As he doubled up, she was tempted to kick him again, but instead, she managed to ex-tract her own stun gun. Glancing around to make sure there were no witnesses, she shot him.

Knowing she couldn't leave him lying out in the open, she grabbed hold of his leather jacket with her semi-stunned hand, raised him up and tossed him into the boot. As she did so, she muttered, "Looks like Alex was right; I'm stronger than a normal woman."

She picked up Warmers stun gun, slipped it into a pocket and swiftly went through Warmers pockets removing any-thing of value.

Once she'd finished, she slammed the boot. She walked back to collect the bag with her outworlder clothes in it, returned to the car and then climbed into the back. She changed her clothes and then began to metamorphose again.

Three minutes later her features had changed again but she'd deliberately abandoned any of her previous looks; she now had dark hair, and her eyes had epicanthic folds. After repacking the bag with her ethnic clothes, she climbed out used the control fob she'd taken off Warmers, re-armed the air-car's security system and set off back to the bar.

While she was still walking, she passed Connell, the man who'd been helping Ed Warmers stake out the bar and it was apparent the other man had deserted his post to search for his missing boss. He confirmed her thoughts when he stopped and accosted her, "Hey, you haven't seen this guy have you?"

He activated his percom and displayed Hal Warmers' likeness.

Claire was tempted to say that she hadn't seen Hal but decided it would be more sensible to send Connell on a wild goose chase and said, "Yes, he went that way, he was with an Ab woman."

Speaking to his percom again, Connell displayed an image of Claire as she had been during her previous metamorphosis. After glancing at the image, Claire sniggered.

"What's so funny?"

Claire's mind played with mischief, "That woman has a reputation, she's well known around here."

When Connell frowned, Claire added, "Let's just say they've probably gone off to discuss business."

After swearing loudly, Connell engaged his percom again. A few seconds later, Ed Pushley's face appeared in a power bubble and said, "What is it, Connell?"

"It looks like Hal has gone AWOL," Connell replied.

"AWOL?"

After half turning in the hope that Claire wouldn't hear what he was saying, Connell lowered his voice, "It looks as if he's gone off with a local prostitute

"You're joking!"

"I wish I was," Connell returned, "That son of a bitch has never been able to keep his dick in his trousers."

There was a long pause while Pushley weighed up the situation. As he knew that Yalt was on station, he said, "Find him!"

Connell turned to Claire, "Which way did he go?"

Realising the other man would probably look in the air-car, Claire said, "I'll show you."

She then began walking back towards the small car park. Connell immediately unlocked the air-car and then glanced inside. He did what Claire had feared the most; he went around to the boot. As the lid opened, Claire pulled her stun gun and shot him, and unceremoniously dumped Connell on top of Hal Warmers.

CHAPTER TWENTY-ONE

Awis Oasis

The net closes on Tarmy

Wren's percom buzzed. When he answered, Alton Mygael said, "I've just received some news—Tarmy entered Awis about an hour and a half ago,"

"An hour and a half," Allus Wren objected. "You said we'd know the moment he arrived."

"The message was slow in coming through," Mygael admitted. "But there shouldn't be a problem because the street cameras indicate they were last seen in the main market; I want you to get out there and find them. Once you've found them, report back."

Wren was tempted to ask how Mygael had gained access to the street cameras but let it go. Instead, he said, "And when we find them; then what?"

"We try to talk them in," Mygael said, "I want to get them back here, to our safe house."

"Them?"

"Tarmy didn't come alone. He's come here mob-handed. There's another man and three women with him." To prove the point, Mygael activated his percom and showed them a power bubble image of the group.

"What if they don't want to go to the safe house," Tam Philips interjected. "Do we strong-arm 'em?"

"No. Definitely not. A little more subtlety is required," Mygael replied. "If I was Tarmy, and I was told that Samantha had sent people out here to kill him, I think I'd accept our assistance."

A disbelieving smile formed on Wren's face, "But Samantha hasn't sent anyone as far as we know. Has she?"

Mygael clicked his percom again. After displaying power bubble images of Stert Oryx, Slon Syn and Lane Syn, Mygael said, "I've had a few whispers on the grapevine; the reports indicate these guys are scheduled to be teleported to Awis in four hours. D'you recognised 'em?"

"Never seen them in my life before," Wren replied, quite truthfully.

"Well, let me introduce you to them," Mygael replied. After providing the names, he added, "They're Midwains. To the victors go the spoils. Section Twenty of the Treaty of Voltha dealt with war criminals. It gives the Midwain authorities the power to appoint vigilantes to hunt down known war criminals. Stert Oryx, Slon Syn and Lane Syn have a remit to bring in war criminals anywhere in the Salus System. Awis didn't want to make enemies of the Midwains, so they agreed to Section Twenty. So, Stert Oryx and his gang can exercise their powers here in Awis".

"What's that got to do with Samantha?"

Mygael shrugged, "They could just be acting on their own initiative, but if she suspects that Tarmy is alive, the easiest way of getting rid of him would be to tell these guys where he was," Mygael said. "As Oryx and his men have a reputation for shooting first and asking questions afterwards, I'd say Tarmy doesn't have much of a chance."

Glancing at the power bubble again, Wren noted the long coats Stert Oryx's gang were wearing. As they were voluminous, Wren presumed they' were designed to hide weapons. Without a doubt, Oryx's people would come in armed with pulse rifles.

"I need you to get to Tarmy, and his group, before Stert Oryx does," Mygael said, "And then bring them back here; to our safe house."

"You seem to be forgetting something," Wren replied

"And what's that?"

Nodding at Philips, Wren said, "The only time we met Tarmy was when we were ordered to collect him from his apartment. We dragged him out by the scruff of his neck. Why should Tarmy believe we're on his side now?"

"Because once he knows we want to oust Samantha and his testimony would help to unseat her, I believe he will co-operate," Mygael replied.

"Okay," Wren said. "Always supposing you manage to oust her, what's in it for us?"

"For starters," Mygael said, "I'm paying your wages until we return to Arden. I will also make sure you are rewarded for your loyalty."

"Going back to Arden?"

"Yes," Mygael said, "I have spoken to several board members that I trust. Once Samantha's been removed, I am to take up the reins again. Some board members never wanted Samantha to become my deputy. The ones who placed Samantha in a position of power will be forced to resign if Tarmy and Hyndman can be persuaded to give us their testimony."

When Wren still looked sceptical, Mygael added, "I think it's time you went out and found Tarmy, don't you?"

"It's not a big town," Wren said. "But it's like a rabbit warren. Where exactly do we start?"

In response, Mygael sent him an image of a business card with an address in Awis and said, "If I were Tarmy, I would be trying to obtain new IDs. That would be a very good place to start."

Wren glanced at the card image, "Targon Yatboon." He quibbled, "The card says he makes keys and re-soles shoes."

"He's hardly likely to advertise that he also does fake IDs as well is he?" Mygael reasoned.

As Wren and Philips left Alton Mygael's, Wren whispered, "Go and find Mih Valanson."

As Valanson was very much a backroom boy and was never

involved in operations, Tam Philips showed surprise. Answering his unspoken question, Wren said, "I need to talk to him."

"What about?"

"You heard Mygael," Wren replied. "The silly old fool thinks that he's done a deal with some of the board members. My guess is they'll do the dirty on him. As soon as he arrives back in Arden, he'll be arrested."

"Agreed," Philips replied. "But where does Valanson fit in?"

"You'll see."

~*~

Mih Valanson looked nervous, "Why am I coming with you?"

As the air-car took off and headed out across Central Lake, Wren said, "I thought you might like to go shopping."

"Shopping? For what?"

"Unless I'm mistaken," Wren replied. "You left all your electronic equipment behind on Arden."

When Valanson nodded, Wren passed him some high-value money cards, "I need you to get yourself some new tools, gizmos, etc. and some spare parts."

Valanson frowned, "It might help if you told me what you wanted me to make."

In response, Wren said, "If I'm not mistaken, you were behind the stunt in the teleport, the yo-yo scenario, the boomerang device. The one that Claire Hyndman played when Samantha captured her father."

"Ah!" Valanson replied. "Yes." He admitted, "Samantha forced me to do that. I have to be honest; I don't like messing around with teleport systems; things can go wrong."

"Let's be positive, eh!"

~*~

The last thing Ed Pushley expected was a call from Stert Oryx. Neither had he anticipated that Oryx would say, "We'll be with you shortly."

"With me?"

"We'll be teleporting to Awis shortly," Oryx amplified.

"I wasn't expecting you yet; they said five days."

"Let's just say I pulled a few strings," Oryx said. He added, "Has Tarleton arrived yet?"

Realising that Oryx was just as impatient for the fray as he had been when they'd first met, Pushley was deliberately evasive, "I will brief you when you get here."

"Why can't you brief me now?"

"Because this is an open line," Pushley retorted. He added, "How did you get this number?"

Oryx repaid evasion with evasion, "That would be telling."

He added, "If you've misled me, and Tarleton doesn't turn up in Awis Oasis, you'll be in trouble."

To head off any further threats, Pushley said, "I will meet you at the teleport centre. I'll brief you there."

"It better be good news," Oryx replied.

~*~

Claire crossed the square and went back into the bar, but she took the precaution of returning by a circuitous route and entered the bar by the rear door. She dived into the toilets and shrugged off her oriental appearance. Once her cooper hair and amber eyes were restored, she emerged, approached Mick Tarmy, and said, "I don't think we're being watched now; it would be a good time to go and see Targon Yatboon."

Noting her limp arm and dishevelled appearance, Tarmy frowned, "What have you been up to?"

As Claire had no desire to discuss Hal Warmers and re-activate Tarmy's questioning of her past, she just shrugged, "Let's just say I've removed a couple of serious obstructions."

She nodded towards the back door, "I don't think we're being watched, but just in case, I think we should leave that way."

Tarmy nodded to the others, settled the bar bill, and followed Claire towards the rear door. Once outside, Red Moxstroma glanced around, checking Claire's assertions that no one was watching anymore and set off using the narrow alleyways that ran through the town.

~*~

Walking close to the front of the bar, Yalt glanced in. Catching a glimpse of him, the bartender shook his fist to warn him off, but Yalt just stood his ground and ran his eyes around the interior. Noting a movement at the back of the bar, Yalt realised his pigeons were about to fly and set off in pursuit. After moving quietly around the narrow alleys for a while, he began picking up on the sound of footfalls up ahead. He immediately speeded up his pursuit but made sure he didn't get too close to be seen.

~*~

After they'd been dodging and diving for some time, Tarmy began having doubts, "I hope you know where you're going, Red."

"I know exactly where I'm going," Moxstroma replied. "I lived in Awis for three years, and in case you're wondering why I'm using the alleys, it's to avoid the cameras; the main squares have cameras everywhere."

Satisfied that Moxstroma knew what he was doing, Tarmy carried on following. Ten minutes later, they entered a slightly wider paved passage. Tarmy instinctively looked around for cameras, but after running his eyes over the most likely locations, he realised they had entered a camera-free zone. Then he realised why.

As most of the surrounding houses were boarded up and uninhabited, why waste money on surveillance? The only exception appeared to be a run-down bar with two old men sitting outside nursing small glasses of beer. One of the men cast a swift glance in their direction and then surreptitiously pulled out a percom.

Tarmy's police nose told him that the old men weren't just whiling away the hours enjoying light refreshment; without a doubt, someone, probably, Targon Yatboon, had posted them there to act as lookouts.

Casting his eyes up and down the road, Red Moxstroma recognised a stoutly built stone cottage slightly set back from the main passageway and said, "You guys stay here."

Walking toward the building, Moxstroma began having doubts. Not only were all the windows heavily shuttered, there were no obvious signs of life coming from the house. As indecision was oozing from every one of Moxstroma's pores, Tarmy ignored the instruction to stay back. Once he was alongside, he said, "Didn't you say you'd managed to make contact and this guy knew you were coming?"

"I did, and he remembered me," Moxstroma confirmed.

"So, what are you waiting for?"

Despite his misgivings, Moxstroma moved forwards and rang the bell on the armoured plastimetal front door.

A few seconds later, a small hatch opened, and a pair of eyes appeared. Red Moxstroma said, "Hi Targon, we spoke. D'you remember me?"

When the eyes showed no signs of recognition, Moxstroma added, "I called a few hours back; you did some work for a friend of mine a few years ago."

He nodded towards Tarmy's group, "These are the people I told you about; they are my friends and need your help too."

The eyes immediately flitted towards Tarmy's group, "What do they want?"

Moxstroma played cagey, "As I said, you helped my friend. These people need help too."

The eyes flitted back to the group again, weighing them up. "Okay, bring them around the back; and then take the basement steps."

"Thanks," Moxstroma replied and waved the others to him. He led the way around the back and found a well-worn set of stone steps and remembered going down them before. At the bottom, he waited for the others to join him and then entered the basement room.

The room was much as Moxstroma remembered it; there was a large damp stain on one of the walls, and exotic looking Arcadian fungi were busily colonising another area. He transferred his attention to the security arrangements.

On both sides of the room, there were bright yellow housings. Although he couldn't read the signs directly underneath each blister because they were in Arcadian text, he guessed what they were. Without a doubt, they were fixed stun guns. In the event of anyone cutting up rough, all that Targon Yatboon had to do was push a button, and they'd all be rendered incapable of causing trouble.

While he was still glancing around, there was a slight clatter as a heavy roller shutter began retracting, and Moxstroma found himself facing a salvaged armoured screen, the sort traditional banks used to separate tellers from customers.

Directly behind the screen, there was a man, but as Moxstroma didn't recognise him, he made the obvious assumption; this time, Targon Yatboon was hiding his true face with a distortion collar.

Once Moxstroma had walked towards him, Yatboon said, "I presume that none of these people or yourself are working for any police department or any government agency, planetary or interplanetary."

Realising the question was designed to prevent entrapment, Moxstroma said, "No. We have no connection with police or anyone else like that. We just want your help."

Glancing around the group again, Yatboon said, "Do they all need my help or just some of them."

Tarmy immediately pointed to himself, Claire, and Nonie. Without a moment's hesitation, Yatboon quoted a price.

Tarmy blanched.

Sensing sales resistance, Yatboon said, "It is a fair price, considering."

"Considering what?"

Yatboon glanced at Claire and pulled a slight face, "It's a fair price considering one subject has a non-standard genome."

Tarmy was tempted to ask how Yatboon knew that Claire was a monarch, but he didn't pursue the issue because he guessed that Yatboon's cellar was probably loaded with special detectors.

Sensing Claire's discomfiture, Tarmy backed off, "Okay, we have a deal. How long will it take?"

"Two hours maximum," Yatboon replied confidently. He glanced at Claire again and handed her a photograph, "Might I make a suggestion? Make yourself look like that."

When Claire visibly bridled, Yatboon said, "Your present features are very striking. When someone goes through security, a more mundane appearance is usually overlooked. A highly attractive woman is always noticed."

He flipped a switch, and a deposit box in the screen clanked open. Yatboon smiled, "I have one simple rule. Money upfront."

Selecting some of the high-value money cards from his stash, Tarmy dropped them into the deposit box. Yatboon immediately retrieved the cards, checked the value, and then flipped a switch. Behind them, a shutter dropped blocking off escape.

Pandemonium broke out in the waiting area, "What's going on?"

"There is nothing to fear," Yatboon called out. "It's just a precaution to make sure we remain secure. I don't want anyone barging in while I'm working and I'm sure you don't either."

A moment later, an airlock door sprang open, and Yatboon pointed at Tarmy, "You first."

Once Tarmy had moved through the airlock, he found himself in an area similar to the waiting area. As with the waiting area, Yatboon was protected by another security screen. Despite the fortification that Yatboon had placed between him and Tarmy, there was a distinct smell of unwashed body percolating through the grills. Doing his best not to pull a face, Tarmy tried to disguise his distaste by running his eyes over the screen again.

Noting Tarmy's observations, Yatboon said, "The police have never raided my building, but I still believe in taking sensible precautions."

He waved towards a chair, "Take a pew. What I am about to do may seem slightly alarming, but there is nothing to worry about."

Once Tarmy was seated, a machine detached itself from the wall and began to scan him. A moment later, a series of bubble images appeared. They were all male, and all looked vaguely like Tarmy. Yatboon said, "All these people have Midwain citizenship, Or to be more exact, they *had* Midwain citizenship; any preferences?"

Tarmy frowned, "Not particularly, but how do I make sure the ID is safe."

"That's my job," Yatboon replied. "To make sure they're safe. And they are. As I just implied, all these people are deceased."

"How the hell did you find so many people?"

Yatboon smiled, "As large numbers of people beat a trail to my door every year, I am prepared. Besides, record photographs are taken as people arrive in Awis. As some of them might be prospective customers; I check them out, so, again, I am prepared."

He then said, "What's your first name?"

"Michael," Tarmy replied, "But most people call me Mick."

Yatboon began inspecting his collection of possible subjects. He locked onto an image of a Michael Tregorran, "This man died in a car accident two years ago and has no dependents or known living relatives. It's a safe replacement ID."

When Tarmy nodded, Yatboon instructed a wall camera to take a series of photographs.

Eventually, Yatboon said, "That's it. You'll get your documents as you leave." He added, "Send in the woman."

Tarmy was tempted to ask which woman but checked himself. As Yatboon had referred to Claire as having a non-standard genome, he obviously didn't regard her as being female.

CHAPTER TWENTY-TWO

Awis Oasis

Oryx arrives

G lancing at his watch, Pushley said, "How much longer?"

"Shouldn't be long now," The duty teleport technician replied, running his eyes over a display screen.

Despite the reassurance, Pushley detected a note of worry and wished Yalt was there to advise him, "Anything wrong?"

"These people initially teleported from Midway," the technician replied. "They will have passed through at least twenty relay stations on the way to arrive here on Arcadia."

"So?"

" Those who have undergone lengthy teleports are generally advised to allow at least a five-day recovery period before teleporting again," the technician replied.

"Why?"

The duty technician shrugged, "I just operate this machine, I don't know how it works, what I have told you is standard advice."

When Pushley frowned, the other man said, "Okay - I'll tell you what I've heard. During the last war, the military teleported human troops into battle zones. They didn't bother very much about the effects it had on them. As far as the high command was concerned, they were just grunts, expendable stubble hoppers. As a result, some of the troops suffered badly, because they were not given time to recover between teleport events."

Although he'd heard Zardus at Arcresten warning Oryx, the danger now seemed far more real, "Suffered badly?"

"The worst cases suffered from SHC," The technician replied.

"SHC?"

"Spontaneous human combustion," the technician elaborated. "It usually occurs if the victim suffers a trauma while their bodies are still unstable."

The technician added, "In bad cases, people standing next to an unstable can also be consumed."

While Pushley was still thinking about what the technician had told him, three shimmering images appeared in the teleport. When the technician immediately let out an audible sigh of relief, Pushley realized just how dangerous the teleport procedure had been.

Eventually, Stert Oryx and his two companions staggered out of the teleport bay and were ushered into a room to rest. Oryx immediately gave Pushley a hard look, "Well, are you going to tell me now? Has Tarleton arrived?"

"Yes," Pushley replied. "And I have him under observation."

"Where is he?"

"I'll tell you that when you confirm my bag will be returned before you kill him," Pushley replied.

Ignoring the implied shoot to kill policy, Oryx said, "Why is your bag so important?"

After he'd explained, Oryx nodded, "We'll take him alive and find this bag of yours. Now, where is he?"

"What guarantees have I got that you won't?"

Oryx half smiled, "I've said that I wouldn't kill him until he tells you where your bag is. D'you expect me to put it in writing?"

Pushley considered what Oryx had said. Reassured, he spoke to his percom and created a power bubble with Connell's and Yalt's images inside it. He deliberately didn't include Hal Warmers image in case it sent alarm bells ringing. "Like I said, I have Tarleton under observation. These guys are helping me. I would appreciate it if you didn't kill them."

Oryx immediately captured the images and asked, "So where is he?"

In response, Pushley handed over a scrap of plastimetal paper with Targon Yatboon's address on it.

Oryx hauled himself to his feet and glanced at Slon and Lane Syn, "Time to go boys. I've waited a long time to bring Tarleton in."

"But you haven't recovered from the teleport," Pushley objected. "It could be dangerous if you don't wait."

"I'm not risking him escaping again," Oryx growled and then staggered towards the exit with Slon and Lane Syn swaying behind him like drunks.

~*~

Emerging from a side alley, Tam Philips began glancing around searching for the ubiquitous CCTV cameras that appeared to be dotted around most major public thoroughfares in Awis. After running his eyes over every likely place, he eventually concluded that this passageway was devoid of cameras.

Once he'd passed the information back to the other two, they emerged from hiding and also began looking around. Wren clicked his tongue disapprovingly. Several buildings in the block had their windows boarded up; the rest looked as if they hadn't had a lick of paint for at least twenty years, "I'm not surprised there are no cameras, the whole place looks like a slum. No self-respecting burglar would be seen dead around here."

"That's probably why Targon Yatboon operates from here," Philips reasoned. "Housing is cheap, and not many people come here unless it's absolutely necessary."

As they started walking down the narrow road, Philips began glancing at house numbers. Although most of the houses were completely unmarked, Philips picked up on the sequence. Eventually, he pointed, "That's the building we want."

Wren's tongue clicked disapprovingly once again because the building in question was heavily shuttered. "We could have been sent on a wild goose chase. It looks derelict too."

Noting two old men sitting at a small table outside a nearby bar, Wren walked over to them. Pointing to the shuttered house, he said, "D'you know if there is anyone in."

Eying Wren suspiciously, one man said, "That depends on who wants to know."

Thinking fast, Wren invented a plausible scenario, "There was a group of us, but we were split up in the market. We were going to go to that house, but it seems locked up. We are only trying to find our friends. Did you see them?"

The second man at the table opened his mouth but closed it without uttering a word because the first man kicked him under the table. Pretending there had been no shin bashing, the first man said, "Sorry we can't help you. We've not seen a soul all day. There are not many people living around here anymore."

Moving away, Wren whispered to Philips, "That guy was lying through his teeth, Tarmy's group are probably inside; time to give it a closer look."

Once they were by the front door, Wren said, "Let's assume that someone is in and give them a knock."

Philips hammered on the door and waited. Eventually, he shrugged.

"Try again," Wren instructed.

Philips immediately went back to hammering. "If there's anyone in there they must be deaf."

Running his eyes over the house, Wren noted camouflaged gun emplacements in the eaves. As he suspected that the occupants would be listening in, he said in an overloud voice, "They're obviously not in there. Let's go."

He started to walk away.

"So, is that it?" Philips demanded.

"Keep your voice down," Wren cautioned. "There could be external microphones."

~*~

As Tarmy slid out of the seat and moved towards the airlock, an alarm on Yatboon's percom went off. Yatboon immediately filled the power bubbles with external shots. When Allus Wren's face filled out one of the bubbles, Tarmy said, "Shit!"

"I gather you know this man," Yatboon observed.

"Yeah."

"Am I right in assuming he's not a friend?"

"Correct," Tarmy replied.

"Well, he's outside. But don't worry," Yatboon said, "If he causes trouble, I will deal with him."

A moment later, one of the power bubbles filled with the image of a gun housing similar to the ones in the entrance lobby, except it was camouflaged to blend in with the building's stonework. "We have emplacements all around the house. If they attempt to break in, I'll stun them."

"What happens if they don't break in but just jump us when we leave?"

Yatboon pointed to the personnel door in the wall behind Tarmy. "That door leads to an old mill. There's no water in it now. If needs be, you can use the old tunnel to evade them."

Then, seeming unfazed by Wren's sudden appearance outside, Yatboon repeated, "Send in the woman."

~*~

Once he was out of listening distance, Wren gestured to Mih Valanson. Once Valanson had joined them, Wren slipped a small stun gun into his hand and said, "Make yourself useful, we're going around the back. Keep an eye on what's going on around here, any problems warn us."

Wren led Philips around the house until they reached the

back. Glancing at the shuttered opening at the bottom of the steps, Wren guessed that the building had a basement area. Walking over to the rear yard wall, he noted a pictogram which indicated only too clearly that there was a long drop on the other side. Glancing over, he realised there was a dried-up meandering river bed far below. The gardens of the adjacent houses followed the sharp curve of the defunct watercourse.

Leaning a little further, he saw the end of an arched tunnel running beneath the building and the remains of an old water wheel.

Wren came to the obvious conclusion; before the outworlders had invaded Awis Oasis, the building had once been an Ab watermill. As the invaders did not need such primitive technology, they had closed it down and diverted the water elsewhere.

Leaning over further still he noted that the arch now had a plastimetal gate and fence set into it. More importantly, it had another camouflaged gun emplacement protecting it.

Dropping back onto firm ground, Wren nodded to Philips indicating it was time to leave.

While they were still walking away, there was the sound of running feet close by, and Valanson appeared. After thrusting a stun gun at Wren as if he was terrified of it, he gasped, "I've just shot someone."

"Someone? Who?"

"I don't know," Valanson replied, contrition etched into every wrinkle on his forehead.

"Where's the body?"

Leading to them to the body, Valanson started another lament, "I didn't mean to do it. The gun just went off in my hand. Honest."

Glancing at the gun settings, Wren shrugged, "Don't worry, you've only stunned him, but we can't leave him here."

He gave Philips a nod, "Help me move the body over there."

After dumping the body in the middle of a small group of ornamental trees, where no one could see it, Wren began frisking and found an ID card indicating the fallen man's name was Yalt. Pushing the ID card back into Yalt's pocket, Wren began frisking again. Eventually, he found Yalt's percom. He leapt as it suddenly began vibrating in his hand. Realising a message had just come through, Wren opened it. There was an image of three hard-faced men. Wren immediately recognised Stert Oryx and Slon and Lane Syn from the photographs he'd seen. The message underneath read:

'Yalt. Now you've located Tarleton and his cronies, your task is complete. Don't hang around. Arrest team on their way; these guys shoot first and ask questions later. Leave the area immediately and return to the house so I can pay you - Ed Pushley.'

Wren's mind began to race.

Realising they were probably outgunned, he said, "Come on, it's time to make ourselves scarce." He slipped Yalt's percom into his top pocket.

"What about him?"

"He's not going anywhere," Wren replied unsympathetically and moved off, instinctively dropping down into a crouching run he led the way towards a high brick wall. Once behind it, he moved towards a section that was part dwarf wall and part metal fencing. He slid down and directed the others to follow suit. He passed the spare stun gun back to Valanson. But he didn't release it until he'd said, "Don't fire it unless I say so, got it?"

When Valanson nodded, Wren released his grip on the stun gun.

Philips said, "D'you mind telling me what's going on?"

In response, Wren passed him Yalt's percom. After viewing the images, Philips said, "So, the bad guys have arrived."

"Looks that way."

"Who's this Pushley guy?"

Wren shrugged, "No doubt, we'll find out in due course."

"So, what are we going to do?"

"Firstly," Wren replied. "Forward that message to Mygael."

"Then what?"

"We wait and watch," Wren replied.

"You seem very casual about this," Philips complained.

"Did you look at that building and its surroundings?" Wren asked.

"No. Why?"

"In case you haven't noticed there are very few tall walls near to that building. If there ever were any, they've been removed so that an assailant is denied cover," Wren replied. Then added, "There are at least ten directional gun pods on the outer walls. If this arrest team decide to break into that building, whoever is inside could very well activate the building's defence system and blast the hell out of 'em."

"Surely that's illegal," Philips replied.

Wren shrugged, "This is Awis Oasis, they make their own laws. I'm sure all the wealthy people who live in these parts all have similar defence systems. One thing's for certain; it would be madness to attempt to break into that building unless you were wearing an anti-stun suit."

CHAPTER TWENTY-THREE

Awis Oasis
Oryx moves in

"**M**ore strangers have turned up," one of elderly bar flies reported.

After taking the message and hanging up, Targon Yatboon glanced at Claire, "You people seem very popular."

"Is that so?"

"There were three men outside before," Yatboon replied. "They seemed to have gone away, but now another three have just arrived.

After displaying power bubble images of Stert Oryx, Slon Syn and Lane Syn, Yatboon said, "D'you recognise these people?"

"Never seen them in my life before," Claire replied, quite truthfully. "But I've heard of them; I believe they're bounty hunters."

"Correct," Yatboon replied. "Let me tell you a little more about them. They're Midwains. and they have the power to arrest or kill wanted war criminals. As they're hanging around outside, I can only presume they've come for you and your friends."

Claire's heart sank; was Targon Yatboon going to hand Mick Tarmy over to them? Noting the look on her face, Yatboon said, "Don't worry these people are no friends of mine. I have no intention of letting them enter my building even if they're holding search warrants."

When Claire showed surprise, Yatboon explained, "During the last war, the merchant space transporter I was travelling on was attacked by a Midwain blockade enforcer. Most of the passengers and crew were killed; I was lucky, I suppose, I survived and was captured. As I was deemed a hostile, I was interned on one of the outer asteroid colonies. It was hell; I was lucky to survive."

When Claire showed surprise, Yatboon added, "That was where I learned this trade. Every so often, some of the prisoners would escape using my forged documents."

He added, "Believe me, I'm no lover of Midwains."

After staring at the power bubble images, Claire said, "Why are they here?"

"I've just told you. No doubt they have come to arrest some of your people," Yatboon replied. "But even if I were foolish enough to open the doors and let them in, I have no doubt I'd regret it."

"Why?"

"One look at my tools would be enough for them to realise I'm a forger," Yatboon said, "Without a shadow of a doubt they would set about wrecking all of my equipment."

"Why?"

"For obvious reasons. I provide my customers with false IDs," Yatboon replied. "Having a good quality false ID means that people like Stert Oryx are unlikely to find you."

"If it's that risky, why do you provide people with false IDs?"

Yatboon shrugged, "Because it's the only profession I know, it's well paid, and I'm good at what I do."

"Why are you helping us?"

Yatboon gave her another shrug, "I have never attempted to be judge and jury. In my trade, you don't ask too many questions."

Noting the expression on Yatboon's face, Claire said, "But it's obvious that I'm asking too many questions."

Yatboon went silent for a while and then said, "Okay, you wanted to know why I am helping you. I will answer your question. My clients split into three main categories."

"Some people come to me are probably guilty of criminal offences, but as many of them have had been tried and found guilty by social media long before they have a chance to defend themselves in court, I give them the benefit of the doubt. I have no way of working out the difference between fake news and the real truth."

"The second type is innocent, but the law has presumed them to be guilty because they can't prove that they are innocent. Does that answer your question?"

"That's two types," Claire replied. "You said there were three."

"Ah! Yes," Yatboon said. "There is a third type. People like you. You have been mistreated by society, but that maltreatment is not recognised. Now, does that answer your question?"

"You seem to know a great deal about people like me. How many people like me have you helped?" Claire asked.

Yatboon clammed up, "I'm sorry. I never discuss one client with another; I hope you understand."

When Claire nodded, Yatboon immediately went back to his controls, and a few seconds later, two power bubble images appeared. One image was identical to the one Yatboon had told her to adopt; the other was virtually identical to her copper-haired identity. While she was still looking at the images, Yatboon said, "In your case, it would be sensible for you to have two IDs."

When a slight frown formed on her face, Yatboon added, "Don't worry, the extra cost is included in the payment made by your colleague."

Yatboon clicked a few switches and then said, "Your replacement documents will be completed shortly."

He'd barely finished when an alarm went off. Glancing at the power bubble images of the exterior, Yatboon became slightly agitated because his elderly lookouts had notified him that Oryx and his men were headed in their direction.

"What's the matter?"

"I fear that they are going to interrogate my people and force them to provide them with information," Yatboon said. With concern etched on his face, Yatboon activated the airlock between the reception area and the interview area and said, "Please ask your friends to join you."

Once Claire had done as instructed, and the others had squeezed into the interview area, Yatboon lowered the shutter protecting the front screen and then said, "Your documents will arrive shortly."

As another protective shutter dropped down to seal off the airlock, Tarmy said, "Just what's going on?"

"I'm afraid we may be under attack very shortly," Yatboon replied.

~*~

"That's the building," Slon Syn said.

"Looks locked down."

"There's one way to find out," Lane Syn replied.

Still wobbling slightly from his last teleport, he walked up to the front door and knocked. Getting no answer, he knocked again. He was about to walk back again when he caught a glimpse of a camouflaged gun emplacement. Swivelling his eyes, he noted three more dotted around the roofline.

Walking back to where Oryx was standing, Lane explained the situation. As Oryx was generally gung-ho, Lane expected his boss to escalate the situation by taking out all the gun emplacements surrounding the building.

Instead, Oryx walked over to two men sitting at an open bar table. After tossing a money card in front of them, Oryx asked if his group could join them. One of the men grabbed the card and nodded.

Oryx slid down, gestured for Slon and Lane to join him and then ordered a round of drinks. As custom had been slow all day, the bartender reacted immediately. Once the two men had taken a good swig of the surprise round, Oryx reached in his pocket and then tabled a highly ornate badge of office.

Once the two old men had had a chance to study it, Oryx explained his powers and said, "I believe there are several wanted war criminals in that building, so I'm looking for your help. There would also be a substantial reward for anyone who helps me catch them."

Realising there was an offer on the table, one that far out-matched the pittance that Targon Yatboon was paying; both men immediately became turncoats. "How can we help you?"

"The whole place is heavily fortified," Oryx observed. "Is there a back way in?"

There was a long pause, and one of the men said, "That place used to be an old mill. There's a tunnel running underneath it."

The other old man added, "As a child, I remember playing in the tunnel; there are access doors leading off the tunnel."

Oryx realised he'd just hit pay dirt, "And where does the tunnel come out?"

"It connects to the dried-up river bed," one of the men re-plied. "There are steps down further up the road."

Oryx nodded at Lane, "You stay here with this gentleman and make sure no one can escape from the front."

He nodded at Slon, "We'll go down the steps." He smiled at the other old man, "Would you mind showing us where these steps are?"

~*~

Valanson looked nervous, "They're coming our way."

Philips placed a hand on Valanson's head and pushed. He whispered, "Rule number one, keep your head down. If you stick your head above the parapet, you're likely to get it shot off."

Once the old man had reached the steps, he stopped and began gesticulating. Although he was about fifteen metres away, his voice carried, "The tunnel entrance is at the bottom, thirty metres to your left."

"Thank you," Oryx replied.

"If you catch them, we will get the reward, won't we?"

Oryx smiled, "Don't worry, I'll make sure you get what's coming to you."

Wren immediately thought about the tunnel he'd seen and realised that the two bounty hunters were looking for a back way into the house or to surprise Tarmy if he tried to escape via the tunnel. He also realised that the two old men had sold out to the bounty hunters.

Watching Oryx and Slon pick their way down the old steps, Wren was tempted to fire his stun gun at them, but he rejected the idea. Standard stun guns only had an effective range of eight metres; not only were the bounty hunters way out of his effective range, as they were openly carrying pulse rifles, if he fired, retaliation would be swift and brutal.

After thinking about the situation, Wren leaned over to Philips and said, "The photograph showed three of them, chances are they've left the other man guarding the front door."

"D'you want me to jump him?"

"Think you could?"

When Philips nodded, Wren handed a spare percom to Valanson. He said to Philips, "If you get into trouble, try to message either Mih or me."

"Don't worry," Philips replied. "I'll sort him out."

Wren came back with, "When you do, get the old guys to warn Tarmy that the front door and tunnel entrance is being watched. In my opinion, Tarmy's best bet is to stay put until we can deal with the bounty hunters."

"Leave it to me."

~*~

As Philips moved off, the percom in Wren's top pocket began to vibrate. Inspecting it, he found Ed Pushley calling.

Letting it ring, Wren waited until a rather petulant voice said, "Yalt? Where are you? If you don't get back here pronto, you won't get paid."

As Wren had no desire to alert Pushley to the current situation, he slipped the percom into his pocket and whispered to Valanson, "You stay here." He pointed at the two bounty hunters, "I'm going to follow them."

When Valanson looked alarmed, Wren said, "All you have to remember is only to shoot if absolutely necessary."

He moved off; a few seconds later, Valanson saw Wren cautiously following the two bounty hunters down the long winding staircase.

A minute later, he saw Philips emerge from a side passage and start walking towards the bar. Lane Syn immediately half glanced in Philips' direction and then reached for his rifle. Fearful that Philips was walking into a trap, Valanson checked his stun gun, emerged from hiding and began walking towards the table from the other direction.

CHAPTER TWENTY-FOUR

Awis Oasis
Fireball

Emerging from a side alley, Philips glanced around looking towards Lane Syn and the two old men sitting at the open-air bar table. They were all staring at the heavily shuttered building as if waiting for something to happen, Philips took a cap out of his pocket and pulled it down to partially cover his face, and then began slowly walking towards the group gathered around the table. He was barely twelve metres from the table before one of the old men glanced in his direction.

Dipping his eyes low, Philips stepped sideways as if intending to walk across to the other side of the narrow road. He'd barely made the manoeuvre when Lane Syn suddenly glanced in his direction.

Although Philips could have been an ordinary passer-by, Lane's instincts cut in. Sensing that Philips was an adversary, he swung his pulse rifle in his direction. Self-preservation immediately cut in, and Philips threw himself sideways into a recessed doorway. He'd barely moved before Lane fired in his direction.

As the pulse shot slammed into the stone architrave surrounding the door, the two old men began shouting out in alarm. Their shouts immediately attracted the bartender who stepped out into the street.

Lane levelled his pulse rifle again, "Come out with your hands up."

As Philips knew his stun gun was still well out of range, he did as instructed and came out hands raised, "Are you mad? What are you shooting at me for?"

Instead of apologising, Lane said, "Empty your pockets and drop everything onto the pavement, very slowly."

Knowing there was nothing else he could do; Philips carefully began dropping the contents of his pockets onto the ground. He was just on the point of dropping his stun gun onto the ground when he noticed Valanson approaching from the other direction, stun gun in hand.

Noting the look of surprise on Philips' face, Lane took a few steps back and then swung his gun in Valanson's direction. Knowing that Lane would take Valanson's gun as an open invitation to fire first, Philips raced forwards pulling his stun gun as he moved. Lane reacted immediately and swung his rifle back, but Philips fired first.

Lane's body immediately erupted into a fireball. As Philips threw himself sideways out of danger, the fireball engulfed the two old men and the bartender, and they went up like tinder too.

Realising he was still in danger Philips turned and ran as fast as his legs would carry him and only glanced back when he was a good thirty metres away. Valanson had also retreated; staring in horror at the remains of the four men that had been clustered around the small table.

As the fireball had been so intense, Philips was surprised that the bar itself remained intact. The only thing that seemed to have suffered was the curved canopy that had once covered the entrance to the bar; it was burnt and charred.

Once the heat had died down, Philips walked past the scene of the conflagration and noted the only things left of the four men appeared to be the smoking remains of their shoes and the bounty hunters' pulse rifle. As Philips felt distinctly under-armed, he took a chance and grabbed the pulse rifle as he was passing.

Joining Valanson, he said, "Thanks."

Valanson frowned, "For what?"

"You distracted him at just the right moment," Philips replied. "You also probably saved my life."

"Did I?"

Philips smiled, "I'd been planning to get in close before I stunned the bounty hunter. If I had, I'd have gone up with all the rest. Burnt to a cinder."

"But what happened?" Valanson said, "Why did that guy burst into flames?"

"No idea," Philips admitted. "He must have had some sort of inflammable charge on him, that's all I can think."

As they carried on walking, Philips began glancing around expecting to see people hanging out of windows, staring at the devastation. But not a curtain twitched. He remembered one of the tasks that Wren had given him. If the two old men had survived, he was supposed to tell Tarmy to sit tight and not attempt to escape via the tunnel.

Philips swore and checked his step. He headed towards the back of Targon Yatboon's house, making sure he was out of range of the gun emplacements. Once by the rear wall, he looked over. He immediately saw Stert Oryx and Slon Syn crouched not far from the tunnel entrance, pulse rifles levelled. It was obvious they were expecting to take Mick Tarmy if he attempted to escape via the tunnel.

He spotted Allus Wren creeping closer to them. Realising Wren was trying to get close enough to fire his stun gun; he realised he was in danger. What if the other two men exploded into fireballs too?

Fearing for Wrens' safety, he engaged his percom and sent him a message, "Get the hell out of there. You're in danger. They've got some sort of charge on 'em. I'm on the wall; I've got them covered."

A moment later, Wren glanced up at Philips and began working his way back towards the steps.

Philips activated the pulse rifle and trained its laser sights on Slon Syn. It was then that his level two brainwashing cut in. It was one thing to fire in self-defence; killing in cold blood was entirely another.

While he was still dithering, Slon Syn heard a noise and suddenly stood up and began firing at Wren. A moment later, Stert Oyrx swung around as well. Diving for cover, Wren gave Philips a pleading look.

Wren's visual plea immediately overrode Philips' mind washing, and he began pumping shots at Slon Syn and Stert Oryx.

~*~

As he hadn't heard from Yalt, Oryx, Connell or Warmers, Ed Pushley knew his plan had unravelled somewhere along the line. Realising he'd have to get involved, he went downstairs, left the safe house and began walking to Targon Yatboon's house using his percom to guide him.

Within a matter of minutes, he sensed he was being followed. He then picked up on a memory image and realised that Ollie, Nonie Tomio's pet pterodactyl had somehow located him.

After mind-blasting Ollie, Pushley was pleased by the result; if Ollie was still following him, he could no longer detect it.

Consulting his percom, Pushley set off in the direction of Targon Yatboon's house again. Twenty minutes later, he walked out onto the narrow road leading to Yatboon's house. Within a matter of seconds, his nose was assailed by the smell of burnt flesh and plastic. He saw the burnt canopy over the bar doorway. A moment later, he saw four sets of charred shoes.

Although he hadn't seen the conflagration, Pushley was immediately reminded of what the teleport technician had told him. "Some of them suffered from spontaneous human combustion. It usually occurs if the victim suffers a trauma while their bodies are still unstable."

He inspected the charred footwear again and noted that one set appeared to be of military issue. He was reminded of the second comment that the teleport technician had made, "In bad cases, people standing next to someone unstable can also be consumed."

While Pushley was still staring at the charred shoes, he heard shouting and the sound of gunfire echoing around the area. He could hear Oryx's and Slon Syn's raised voices and sensed that bounty hunters were in trouble.

As the noise increased, Pushley crept down a narrow alley between two boarded-up houses and only stopped when he reached a tumbledown garden wall. Down below, there were three men. One was pinned down and unable to escape, and the other two men were advancing on him rifles blasting.

Stepping a little closer, Pushley heard Oryx's voice again and realised the two riflemen were Oryx and Slon Syn. Just as it looked as if the trapped man was doomed, someone began firing down into the valley.

Oryx and Slon immediately returned fire. Taking advantage of the sudden turn of events, the trapped man broke cover and began running towards a set of steps leading out of the dried-up watercourse.

Realising the man was escaping, Slon swung his rifle toward the running man, but just before he could shoot, the high-level rifleman began firing again, and Slon Syn ignited like a Roman candle. The flash from Slon seemed to create some sort of chain reaction; a moment later, Oryx also burst into flames.

As both men began wildly dancing inside their separate fireballs, Pushley realised he was watching a game-changing event and began re-assessing the situation. With Oryx and his men burnt to ashes, he realised he was highly unlikely to see either the reward money or the money-bag again.

After back-tracking, Pushley set off the way he'd come in. While he was trudging his way back to the safehouse, he decided the time had come to throw in the towel and leave Arcadia. After all, he was no longer a pauper; as he'd more or less emptied Hal Warmer's bank account, he did at least have some money behind him. He reached in his pocket and pulled out the teleport tickets. Yes, it was definitely time to leave.

It was at that point a figure came hobbling out of a doorway. Fearing the worst, Pushley pulled his gun. But before he could fire a plaintive voice said, "No padrone—don't shoot me, please."

"Yalt? What's happened to you?"

"I have been shot," Yalt replied.

Although Pushley rarely performed random acts of kindness, he put his arm around the other man and began helping him down the narrow alley. "So, who shot you?"

Yalt shook his head, "There were three of them. One of them shot me; I can't remember which. My mind is scrambled, padrone."

"Come on," Pushley said, "I'll take you back to the house," and took hold of one of Yalt's arms. As he did so, he became aware that he was getting very little mental feed-back from his Ab associate. Realising why he grabbed Yalt's hat. He glanced inside at the crystals stitched to the headband. While he was looking, Yalt did his best to grab his hat back, but Pushley kept it out of arm's reach. A fraction of a second later, Pushley's mind was filled with Yalt's secret fears. Although he was highly offended by some of Yalt's thoughts, Pushley brushed them aside and then sent a mind slug into the Ab's mind. Once he'd subdued the other man's critical faculties, Pushley said, "Why do you fear me Yalt?"

"You are a spettro," Yalt replied. "A spettro killed my father."

"There are good spettri and bad spettri," Pushley countered. "And I am a good spettro, and I will look after you if you let me."

"A good spettro," Yalt repeated, "A good spettro."

"Yes," Pushley replied. "I don't work for the Great Ones. Like you, I fear the Great Ones."

A few seconds later, Pushley realised his declaration had

born fruit because Yalt's mind stopped issuing negative vibes.

CHAPTER TWENTY-FIVE

Awis Oasis

On the loose

"**C**ome on," Hal Warmers snapped and began kicking at the boot of the car with as much force as he could muster.

But instead of joining in with the kicking, Connell began working his way along the back seat until he located a handle and tugged hard. Two seconds later, there was a distinct click, and one of the seats dropped forward. He felt for the handle of the double seat and repeated the exercise.

As the double seat slumped forward and light began streaming in, Warmers finally stopped kicking, and a look of surprise formed on his face, "How the hell did you do that?"

"I studied magic when I was a kid," Connell replied sarcastically and then began squirming out. Once Warmers was out too, Connell said, "Now what?"

"First job is to find Ed Pushley and get him to unfreeze my bank accounts," Warmers replied. After grabbing his protective hat and jamming it firmly on his head, he cracked his knuckles threateningly, "Then the fun starts."

When Connell didn't respond, Warmers added, "Once we're finished beating Pushley into a quivering wreck, we'll then find that female monarch who locked us in the boot and make her wish she'd never crossed me."

Ignoring the threat to Claire Hyndman, Connell said, "You'll have a hard job finding Pushley if he doesn't want to be found."

"I won't have any difficulty finding him," Warmers replied.

"We know he's staying in a local hotel."

Connell half-smiled at Warmer's naivety, "As he's just ripped you off for thousands, he's going to go to ground. He's probably checked out of the hotel by now."

"No matter," Warmers replied. "He planned to teleport out of here in a couple of days; teleport out with my money no doubt."

"What about these bounty hunters?"

Warmers let out a cynical laugh, "I've had a chance to think. It was all a scam. All the talk about bags and bounty hunters was just a cover story. He just wanted access to my bank accounts."

Warmers added, "In any case, Pushley isn't Pushley."

"Not Pushley?"

As Connell had never met a spettro and had no experience of their mental powers, Warmers just said, "Take my word for it; he's an imposter."

~*~

After helping Yalt stagger back to the house, Pushley felt totally exhausted by the exertions. Once inside, he dumped Yalt on a settee and slumped down in a chair and began to think about the things he'd recently witnessed. As Oryx and his men were dead, his plans were in tatters.

A fraction of a second later, he was reminded of Stert Oryx's last moments; he'd burst into flames for no apparent reason. While he was still thinking, Wren's face floated into his mind; he saw Tarleton and Hyndman close by.

As the mental imagery continued to develop, Pushley suddenly realised why Wren had killed Oryx's people. It was evident that Wren and his men had been engaged to protect Tarleton. Needing to confirm his hunch, Pushley began to trawl the ether, doing his best to latch onto Wren's thought transmissions. Two minutes later, his efforts were rewarded and Pushley mind linked with Wren. After gently probing the other man's mind, Pushley realised he was right; Wren had been engaged by Alton Mygael, the Director of Minton Mining Company Security.

While he was still probing Wren's mind, looking for information, he saw a large house near to a lake. Hauling himself to his feet, Pushley moved into the kitchen and closed the door behind him to make sure Yalt couldn't see what he was doing. He then began searching through the drawers of a tall dresser.

Finding a local atlas, he began studying the shores of Central Lake. A few seconds later, his eyes alighted upon a bubble image which looked identical to images extract from Wren's mind.

The despondency he'd been feeling was swept away and replaced by anger; his anger sparked the urge for revenge once more. Extracting the emergency percom from his wallet, he dialled. The gender-neutral CGI image appeared within seconds. This time it said, "Hello agent Q449. What can I do for you this time?"

"I need to speak to Brigadier Wolff again," Pushley replied.

"I'm tracking your location, Ed."

A few seconds later, the CGI said, "You are at Awis Oasis?"

"Correct," Pushley confirmed and began to think about the mental incursions he'd made into Wren's mind. Although Wren's thoughts implied that Tarleton had not been taken to the big house yet, it was apparent that was where he was going.

A moment later, the Rottweiler's face appeared in the power bubble, but he did not exhibit the hostility he'd shown during their first encounter. His face looked remorseful, "I'm sorry to hear about Stert Oryx and his team, Ed."

"You know?"

"Oryx and his people had subcutaneous body monitors fitted," Rottweiler replied. "The news of their deaths was hyperlinked to us within minutes of their demise. The monitors suggest that Oryx's group were attacked with Therman rifles."

"They were attacked with standard pulse rifles," Pushley

contradicted. He explained that Oryx had ignored teleport advice and had flamed as a consequence.

"That may be the case," Rottweiler conceded. "But if we allow reports to emerge that Oryx died following a teleport accident, it will cause a great deal of unnecessary worry to teleport travellers throughout the Salus System. Our section could also be subject to criticism for allowing Oryx to ride roughshod over standard procedures."

"So, what *are* you going to do?"

Instead of answering the question, Rottweiler said, "Oryx knew that Tarleton was dangerous; we also advised him that he needed more deputies to assist with the arrest, but he ignored our advice."

Sensing that Rottweiler was more concerned with protecting his department from political fallout than pursuing Tarleton, Pushley said, "Can you put me through to Brigadier Wolff, so that I can discuss Oryx's replacement? I know where Tarleton is. He's in a large house at the top of Central Lake."

"If you know where he is," Rottweiler observed, "you could try to arrest him yourself."

"So, I'm going to have to arrest Tarleton on my own," Pushley snapped.

"I was being facetious", Rottweiler replied. "If three of our people can't bring him in, then what chance do you have?"

Annoyed by the response, Pushley was tempted to divulge his inner secret. But he bit his tongue because he knew that if he claimed that he had special mental powers, Rottweiler would probably think he was mad.

Getting no response, Rottweiler terminated the conversation with, "I'm sorry we can't assist you further, Ed."

As Rottweiler's face disappeared from the power bubble, Pushley swore out loud.

~*~

Pushley woke in a sweat and realised he must have fallen

into a day sleep. It was easy to do that on Arcadia when the day/night cycle was three standard days in length. He was conscious that Yalt was close by, "What is the matter padrone? You were calling out."

"I just had a bad dream," Pushley replied, but even as he spoke, he knew he was lying to himself. Without a shadow of a doubt, he'd picked up on Hal Warmers' hostile thoughts. His dream world had turned them into a nightmare.

He'd also picked up on something more subtle; he could sense that Ollie wasn't far away. If Ollie located his exact position, Claire Hyndman would undoubtedly be told where he was too. From being the hunter, he was now the hunted.

Or was he?

He thought about the big house at the top end of Central Lake. If he could ambush Tarleton at the house by the lake, recover the bag and then get to the teleport centre without Warmers intercepting him, he'd be home and dry. He'd have the money he needed to start a new life.

Eventually, Pushley glanced at Yalt and came clean, "There are some bad men after me. I have things that I need to do but when my business is done, can you get me into the teleport centre without being seen?"

Yalt nodded but seemed disappointed, "You are leaving padrone?"

Sensing Yalt was worried his newly found source of wealth was about to come to an end, Pushley said, "If you can get me inside the teleport centre when the time comes without the bad men seeing me I will make sure you receive a very big tip."

Pushley felt Yalt's mind go into overdrive, a very big tip. How large was a very big tip?

But even though Pushley did not attempt to specify exactly how much he'd receive, Yalt's demeanour underwent an immediate transformation. "I know a tunnel, padrone."

"A tunnel?"

"There are many tunnels and underground chambers in Awis," Yalt replied. He added, "My people built them so they could escape in time of war."

Pushley's mind then filled with Yalt's thoughts. Even before the outworlders came to Awis, the oasis had been invaded many times. Sometimes the tunnels were used as escape routes, but they were mainly used as shelters. When an enemy arrived too powerful for the locals to repel, they became troglodytes until they worked up the courage to emerge from hiding and attack their unwanted guests.

Thinking about his teleport booking, Pushley knew it would be at least two Arcadian days before he could visit the teleport centre: six standard days.

He thought laterally. "Once I have completed my business, why don't I hide inside the teleport centre and come out when it is time to leave?"

Yalt rolled his eyes. "No one stays inside the teleport building for safety reasons, padrone. Too many bad rays."

Pushley's thoughts turned to Oryx and his men. They'd ignored the safety procedures and had paid the price. Their bodies had become unstable, and they'd burst into flames.

"Once you have done your business deals, you will have to say here until it's time to teleport," Yalt said.

"How many people know I am staying here?"

"Just me," Yalt said.

Pushley immediately added another. As Ollie knew his approximate location, logic dictated that Nonie Tomio would probably work out where he was before too long. Thinking hard, Pushley said, "I need you to do some shopping for me, Yalt."

Once Pushley had given him a money card, he said, "I want you to go to the market and buy me some clothes, ones that will make me blend in."

He ran a hand over his greying hair, "And get me some brown hair dye. They do sell that around here don't they?"

"You said I could also have a new percom, padrone."

"So, I did," Pushley agreed, swapping the money card Yalt was holding for a larger denomination one.

Yalt was about to leave when Pushley added, "There is also something else I want."

He then pointed to the beads stitched into Yalt's confiscated hat. "I need some of these."

Yalt frowned, "You are a spettro, padrone, why do you want these beads?"

"Protection," Pushley replied. "Once I have stitched them into my hat, I'm hoping an annoying pterodactyl won't be able to read my mind."

~*~

Once Yalt had returned, Pushley grabbed the new clothes and then went upstairs to try them on. He then glanced at his reflection in a long mirror. While he was still staring at his reflection, there was a slight tap on the door, and a timid voice said, "Are the clothes to your liking, padrone?"

After turning to the left and then to the right, Pushley was undecided. Yalt had bought him a long male Kaftan, a pair of matching trousers and a tarboosh hat similar to the type most of the local Ab population seemed to wear. Although Yalt had done as instructed, Pushley felt ill at ease; in his eyes, he looked effeminate dressed as he was.

"Are the clothes to your liking, padrone?" Yalt repeated and poked his head around the door.

Instead of voicing his inner fears, Pushley nodded, "The clothes are fine, did you get me the hair dye?"

Once Yalt had produced it, Pushley stripped off his new clothes in case he stained them and then began applying the liquid; he waited the allotted time before washing it out.

Reasonably satisfied with the result, he slumped down in a chair and then began stitching the beads into the tarboosh hat.

Once he'd finished, he said, "As I told you, before I teleport out of here, I have a job to do. I will need some transport. Anywhere around here that does hire cars?"

Yalt shook his head, "Awis does not have anywhere that hires cars, padrone." He then had a flash of inspiration. "My cousin has a ground van; I am sure he will let me borrow it."

Pushley was affronted, "A ground van!"

"We still used wheeled transport in Awis," Yalt replied. "Our people can't afford air-cars and air-vans."

Pushley gave Yalt a sharp look but kept his tongue in check, "I suppose I shouldn't look a gift horse in the mouth. Okay, ask your cousin if you can borrow it."

~*~

Targon Yatboon looked horrified, "Raise the shutters?"

Tarmy was tempted to suggest that the building could do with some ventilation to remove some of Yatboon's body odour, but he deliberately bit his tongue. "I'm only talking about the ones upstairs."

"Why do you want to open them?"

"We heard a lot of firing and your camera down at the tunnel entrance picked up some flashes," Tarmy replied. "You don't honestly expect us to leave without checking what's going on first?"

Pointing to a set of well-worn stairs, Yatboon said, "I will open one shutter for you."

As Tarmy mounted the stairs, the lights were triggered into action. Once at the top, Tarmy realised that the upper floor was nothing more than a studio apartment. Picking up on the smell of Yatboon's body odour again, he glanced around at the piles of discarded clothes and unwashed dishes. It was obvious why Yatboon lived a bachelor life; clever though he was, he was basically a slob.

Hearing a slight whirring noise, Tarmy moved towards the shutter that Yatboon had opened but deliberately kept himself concealed. Once he was close to the opening, he realised that the old timber frames that had once filled the opening had long since rotted away.

After glancing to the right, Tarmy ducked, and glanced to the left and caught a glimpse of Allus Wren.

Wren saw him at the same instance and raised his hands as if he'd decided to surrender, "No need to worry, Mick. I bear you no ill. This time I'm on your side."

"Is that so?"

"If it hadn't been for us," Wren countered, "The bounty hunters would probably have killed you by now."

"What d'you mean by that?"

"You must have heard the shooting," Wren called back. He added, "Oryx and his gang are dead."

"You killed them!"

"Not intentionally," Wren replied.

"What's that meant to mean?"

"They just burst into flames," Wren called back. He created a bubble image and directed it toward Tarmy's open window and ran a short sequence. It was then that Tarmy caught a glimpse of Stert Oryx's last stand. As Wren had described, Oryx and his associate went up in flames for no apparent reason.

Stunned, Tarmy called out, "What sort of weapons were you using against them?"

"Just a standard pulse rifle," Wren called back. "We didn't use grenades if that's what you're thinking."

While Tarmy was still looking out, the window shutter began to drop. Guessing that Yatboon was getting nervous having the shutter open, Tarmy shouted down, "I haven't finished yet."

The shutter stopped and then went back up. While it was still clanking, Claire Hyndman appeared at the top of the stairs and confirmed Tarmy's thoughts, "Yatboon is getting the willies having the shutter open; he thinks people are going to break in."

"I need it open; I'm still talking."

"Who to?"

"The Black-clad officer who jumped me in my flat a few

months back," Tarmy replied.

Before he could stop her, Claire walked over the window and then glanced down at Wren. Wren smiled up at her, "Nice to see you again, Ms Hyndman."

"What d'you want?"

"We're here to protect you," Wren replied.

"From what?"

After going over it as he'd done with Tarmy, Wren was tempted to replay Stert Oryx's demise but decided against it. As he was now portraying himself as a man of peace, showing Oryx's sudden fiery end to Claire Hyndman might undermine the message. Instead, he said, "As I explained to Mick, if it hadn't been for us the bounty hunters would have shot their way into the building and taken you."

"You still haven't said what you want."

"Just to talk," Wren replied

Tarmy moved closer to the window and then said, "Okay, talk."

Although he'd been hoping for a face to face, Wren walked a little closer and said, "A lot has changed over the last few weeks."

He quickly explained how they'd escaped from Arden using the same route as Ord Morley, Vlad Pen and Ben Lieges. He added, "Mr Mygael would like to see you."

Tarmy frowned, "Mygael. Who's he?"

"The director," Wren explained. When Tarmy's frown increased, Wren said, "As I recall it, you nicknamed him Oddface because he always wore an electronic mask."

When Tarmy didn't respond, Wren said, "The director is here at Awis."

"Why?"

"Because a lot has changed over the last few weeks," Wren responded. "Like I said, the director is here at Awis."

"Why should I want to speak to Oddface?"

"Because you now have a common enemy; Samantha," Wren replied. "One thing's for certain, if Samantha finds out you're still alive she'll have you killed for sure. She'll engage a contract killer and have you rubbed out."

It was at that point, Hen Jameson; Arden's chief of civil police suddenly walked into view and said, "Hello, Mick. Could we talk inside; I'm sure Allus is getting a little hoarse shouting from down here."

Tarmy stared down at his old boss, disbelievingly, "What are you doing here, sir?"

"Can we talk about it inside?" Jameson repeated.

While Tarmy was still thinking about the request, there was a sudden flutter, and then Ollie flew in through the opening. Being hungry, the pterodactyl scuttled the length of the room, hopped up onto a draining board and began eating some leftover food that Yatboon had left lying around.

Glancing down again, Tarmy called out, "I'll see if I can let you in."

~*~

Convincing Yatboon to leave the safety of his cubicle had been hard work. But once he'd succeeded in gaining entry, Tarmy began regretting it. Yatboon's cubicle stank of sweat and half-eaten food, but Tarmy realised it was the lesser of two evils. At least sitting inside the cubical meant he had an armoured screen between Wren and himself.

Following Yatboon's instructions, Tarmy flipped a switch, and the outer door shutter rose. Once it had fully retracted, Wren and Jameson walked in and slid down onto stools on the other side.

Tarmy instinctively glanced at his old boss, "What's going on?"

Jameson waved a hand in Wren's direction, "If you give this man a chance to explain, you'd understand exactly what was going on."

Tarmy glanced at Wren, "Okay. I'm listening."

CHAPTER TWENTY-SIX

Alton Mygael's house

Tarmy takes a chance

Mygael's house was in the region of six kilometres from Awis, not far from the top end of the central lake. As Wren's air-car swept over the lake, the windscreen began developing white patches. Noting his interest, Allus Wren said, "The splodges are insects; they breed in the lake, millions of 'em. Most people keep away from the lakeside; even the Ab keep away. If you go down there, you'll be bitten all over in a matter of seconds."

Skimming over a high outer security wall, Wren landed on a courtyard alongside a large, three-storey stone-built house.

As they climbed out, an armed security guard appeared on the balcony of a watchtower and called down. Wren immediately responded, identifying himself and the others then provided the day's password.

Once the guard had given him the all-clear and retreated back into his cabin at the top of the watchtower, Wren led the whole party towards a two-storey building which looked as if it had once been a stable block capable of housing at least two dozen horses. Taking them up a set of stairs, Wren opened a door giving them access to a long central corridor.

Pointing to doors either side of the corridor, Wren said, "This is our guest annex," and began walking down the corridor throwing open doors as he passed, "We have five guest rooms in this building; as we don't have any other guests at the moment you can take your pick."

He opened a door which was halfway down the corridor and waved a hand around an area designed as a common room. It had a small bar in one corner and tea point at one end.

"I understand that Alton Mygael and his partner Klaien have extended an invitation for you to join them for dinner." He then qualified the invitation; he pointed at a traditional Arcadian wall clock, one divided into four major segments: Red, Green, Blue, and Amber. It subdivided Arcadia's thirty-six, day/night cycle.

"You'll be called around Amber 8."

Converting the time to standard, Tarmy said, "That's a long time to wait." He glanced around at the others. "I could do with something to eat before then."

Wren pointed at an autodis in the tea point area, "There is a menu on the wall, feel free to help yourselves."

Once he'd reached the end of the corridor, Wren walked into the last room and gestured for them to follow. He opened a large walk-in wardrobe. Inside there were racks and racks of clothing, male to the left, female to the right.

Glancing back, Wren ran his eyes over Red Moxstroma who was dressed in a ripped T-shirt, scraggy washed out jeans and fake leather jerkin he'd been given when he'd joined the convoy. "Mr Mygael has provided a selection of clothing for you to choose from. There are similar cupboards in all the rooms. You can mix and match as you wish."

Glancing at Moxstroma again, Wren sniffed, "There are induction showers in all the rooms. Although Awis is an oasis, we don't waste water in these parts. As some of you smell a little ripe, might I suggests you all take advantage of the facilities before changing into your new clothes. Klaien Mygael has a strong dislike for lack of personal hygiene."

Lecture over, he turned on his heel and walked out of the bedroom. "I'll leave you to sort yourselves out and get settled. By the way, I will come back and collect you when it's time for dinner. In the meantime, please remain indoors; we don't want the guards shooting any of you, now do we?"

Claire bridled, "So, we're prisoners now are we?"

"Not at all," Wren replied. "As I explained, you are here so we can protect you. We are not trying to make you prisoners."

Sensing Claire was in a combative mood, Wren changed tack, "Why don't I take you back to the common room and fix you something to eat and drink."

Once back in the common room, Wren swiftly programmed the autodis with their orders and left before Claire could bend his ear again.

Once the machine had fulfilled their orders, they sat at the table and began to eat. But feeding her face didn't stop Claire from griping, "If I'd known they were going to imprison us here, I wouldn't have come."

Wanting to calm matters down, Tarmy said, "Let's not do anything rash. At least if we're here, it's unlikely Samantha will attack us."

Claire wasn't convinced. "If Alex were here I'd agree. With a TK5 around, you can take on most comers, but I don't think Samantha's going to be deterred by a few dozy looking tower guards who've probably never fired a gun in anger?"

Although Tarmy agreed with her assessment, he continued to calm the conversation down, "Why don't we get settled in and then think about our future plans later."

Taking Tarmy's lead, after dumping her plate in a dishwasher, Lascaux Kurgan walked out of the common room and began nosing around the bedrooms. After prowling around for several minutes, she let out a whistle, "Have you seen this place?"

While she still weighed up the room, Moxstroma walked out and poked his head into another room, but before he could really look around, Lascaux shouted out in a loud voice, "This one Red. Not that one."

She briefly emerged and grabbed hold of one of Red Moxstroma's arms and dragged him away with the efficiency of a trapdoor spider. Kicking the door shut behind her, she grabbed hold of Moxstroma, but within a second she turned up her nose. "Yuck! Wren was right. You *do* pong."

"I'll have a shower then," Moxstroma replied and began tentatively removing the jacket he was wearing.

After placing a do not disturb sign on the handle and locking the outer door, Lascaux began to remove her own clothes, "I'll come in with you."

Partway through her strip, she opened the door to the shower room and then stepped back in amazement, "What the hell's that?"

Instead of replying, Moxstroma read a small sign and then depressed a button. The induction shower immediately sprang into action, and a tall power cylinder formed and began to rotate. After reading the sign again, Moxstroma removed the rest of his clothes, kicked them into one corner of the room and stepped into the shower. The rotating waves immediately checked his body out. A few seconds later, the power cylinder changed colour, and the shower went to work on Moxstroma's body; he realised the machine had decided to remove the body hair on his chest and back. Glancing down, he also realised the machine was giving him a Brazilian.

Running her eyes over Moxstroma's depilated body, Lascaux said, "How come it hasn't scalped you?"

"I think its programme knows what hair to remove and what to leave," Moxstroma replied and then waved her towards him.

Realising there was nothing to fear, Lascaux stepped in too. Expanding to accommodate her, the machine set to work on her. Once it had removed what it deemed to be unwanted hair, the machine briefly sprayed them both with a unisex perfumed cleanser and then began removing dirt and dead skin. Ten minutes later, the shower pinged and came to a halt.

Stepping out, Moxstroma walked over to the wardrobe and glanced around inside, but before he could start making a selection of new clothing, Lascaux took hold of one of his arms and said, "You can select some clothes later."

She pulled him onto the bed.

~*~

As Lascaux's door slammed shut, Nonie began glancing through other doors. After stopping outside the biggest and best-equipped suite, she nodded and then glanced at Claire, "This one is definitely ours."

Instead of pausing, Tarmy glanced in the next room. As he did so, Nonie called out, "So, what's your problem, Mick? Have you gone off us? Planning to have a room of your own?"

Before he could answer, Nonie repeated Lascaux's move and pulled him across the threshold. As he entered, Tarmy began glancing around the room, taking in all the plush finishes. He began opening internal doors and discovered that the suite had two full bathrooms, "Mygael doesn't believe in stinting himself, does he?"

"He's obviously been planning his escape route for some time," Claire cut in. "No doubt he's also been salting money away too. Mind you, if you had a deputy like Samantha, you'd want out."

It was at that point Tarmy heard a fluttering sound and Ollie appeared at an open window. Taking in his surroundings, the pterodactyl briefly paused on the window ledge before taking off again and landing on the main emperor sized bed.

As he settled down, Claire's reaction was immediate, "I do hope he's not going to poop on everything, Mygael's not going to be too happy if we wreck the joint. I once knew a woman who kept a huge grey parrot and let it fly around the house; every flat surface was covered in guano."

"He's house trained" Nonie replied. "When he wants to go, he goes out."

Claire still tutted, "It's not very hygienic having him on the bed, though."

"He always sleeps on my bed," Nonie replied defensively.

After glancing at the animal, Claire pointed at single bed in one corner of the room, "If you want that mangy creature on your bed. I'm going over there. When you talked me into this commune idea, I didn't imagine I'd be bedding down with pterodactyls."

Nonie reacted to the comment by moving over to Ollie and stroking him affectionately, "He doesn't cause any trouble."

"He's also very loyal," Nonie expanded. "Don't forget he helped us with Ed Pushley even though Pushley mind-blasted him several times."

Realising Nonie was trying to change the subject; Claire moved in, adopted an authoritative voice, and snapped, "Off."

Picking up on her hostile tone and thoughts, Ollie immediately half-flapped, half-scuttled across the room and took up refuge on the window sill again. As he landed, Ollie sent Nonie a mental message indicating he was hungry.

Sensing that the sudden request for food wasn't real hunger; a sense of rejection had triggered it, Nonie moved over to the window scooped Ollie up in her arms and said, "I'm taking him to the common room to see if I can find him something to eat."

As she left the room slamming the door behind her, Claire looked embarrassed, "I shouldn't have done that should I?"

"She loves Ollie," Tarmy replied. "I think you should go and make it up."

Claire nodded and then left the room too. As she entered the common room, Ollie scuttled behind Nonie. Pausing in the doorway, Claire said, "I just came to say I'm sorry."

"Don't apologise to me," Nonie replied. Pointing at Ollie, she added, "Apologise to him."

"I'm sorry, Ollie."

"You have to think sorry," Nonie prompted. "Think kind thoughts, and he'll understand."

Claire half smiled, "And how do I do that?"

"Just think you like him."

After she'd thought kind thoughts for a second or two, Ollie came out of hiding. Nonie handed Claire a morsel of food and said, "Put that in the palm of your hand and feed him."

When Claire did as instructed, Ollie swiftly grabbed the food with one dart of his tongue and sent Claire a 'feed me again' message, but she didn't understand. Picking up on the same message, Nonie handed Claire another morsel, and she repeated the same feeding operation several times.

Eventually, Nonie said, "He'll keep on begging, but he's had enough now; if we overfeed him, he'll get too fat to fly."

Changing the subject, Claire came out with, "I've changed my mind; he can sleep on the bed."

"That's not the problem though is it," Nonie replied. "When you walked into that room, it was obvious that you were looking for a reason to throw a strop. Why?"

Instead of answering the question, Claire said, "You know, when Mick asked me to metamorphose and sent me out to find out who was following us."

"Yeah."

"I ran into Hal Warmers," Claire replied. "He immediately realised I was a monarch." She held her hands up. "Apparently, being converted alters the length of a monarch's fingers."

Ignoring what Claire had just said, Nonie asked, "What happened? Did he hurt you?"

Shrugging off the waterboarding she'd received at his hands, Claire shook her head and said, "Not really; I think he wanted to take me prisoner and use me as some sort of sex slave! But I stunned him and stuffed him in the boot of his car along with his mate. They've probably escaped by now, but it felt good at the time."

"What's Hal Warmers doing around here?"

"No idea."

Realising she'd been side-tracked, Nonie repeated herself, "So, come on, why did you deliberately throw a strop?"

Claire shook her head, "I don't know."

"You know what I think?" Nonie replied. "You don't know what you do want."

"I'm still getting my head around being a freak," Claire confessed.

"You're not a freak."

When Claire just let out a long sigh, Nonie said, "If you don't want Mick, don't mess it up for me."

"I do want Mick."

"And so do I," Nonie replied. "So, we work something sensible out."

"Now he knows I'm a freak," Claire said, "he may not want me."

Nonie shook her head. "What's not to want? You go in and out in all the right places. Why shouldn't he want you?"

Nonie added, "I'm going to stay here with Ollie for at least an hour and Mick's sitting in that room on his own. Why don't you be sensible and keep him company? I'm sure you can think of something to keep him occupied."

~*~

Wren was about to go to see Alton Mygael when his percom rang, and Valanson said, "You might like to pop down to my workshop and see the gizmo I've made for you."

"Will it take long?" Wren replied

"I just want to show you my handiwork."

Wren said, "Okay. I'm on my way. I'll be with you in two minutes.

Turning across the courtyard, he walked towards a small stone building with a flat roof. Once he'd entered Valanson's newly created workshop, Wren glanced around. Although none of the equipment was a patch on what he'd possessed at Minton Isolation Facility 1, the stone-built shed had an air of purpose about it.

Realising that Valanson couldn't have purchased all the equipment with the money he'd been given, Wren commented on it.

"I found some of the stuff in the basement of the main house," Valanson replied. "One of the Ab cleaners let me in. I'm used to scrounging."

"So, what have you got for me?"

Valanson immediately handed over a small device that had started life as a thermostatic hand controller. He pointed to the only available button, "You just push that and bingo."

After briefly studying it, Wren slipped the device into one of his pockets. As he did so, Valanson said, "You do realise that if you use it, you'll be taking a major gamble? Look what happened to Oryx and his people."

Wren half smiled, "Hopefully, I won't have to use it."

"You think if Alton Mygael goes back, he'll be walking into a trap don't you?"

"Hopefully, not," Wren replied. "Now I've got to go."

"To see Alton Mygael?"

Wren nodded.

"What about?"

Instead of supplying an answer, Wren just tapped the side of his nose.

~*~

Ed Pushley was not amused. Being trapped in the back of an ancient boneshaker; a ground van that had seen better days, he growled, "How much further?"

"Not far now," Yalt said. As if to confirm what the Ab had just told him; a large house emerged from behind a plantation of Arcadian date palms.

Grabbing a pair of powerful binoculars, Pushley said, "Pull over," and wound down his window.

Yalt objected, "This is not a good place, padrone."

Raising the binoculars, Pushley said, "What's not good about it?"

Two seconds later, a large mosquito bit his face; a second one swiftly joined in. Realising why Yalt had tried to dissuade his from opening the window, Pushley swiftly rewound it and swiftly swatted the two bloodsuckers that had attacked him.

Once the killing was over, Yalt said, "I can drive past the

house. There is a hill on the other side which does not have mosquitoes."

"Okay," Pushley replied. "Drive me up there."

Yalt immediately slammed the ageing ground van into gear and drove along the unmade track that wound its way around the lake. Removing his hat, Pushley allowed his mind to link with the ether. Almost instantaneously, he began picking up the thoughts of the bored men standing in the watchtowers surrounding the big house. While he was still probing, one of the guards let slip the daily password.

Sensing he was making real progress, Pushley probed a little harder and was rewarded with mental images of Wren's air-car landing in the inner courtyard. He also picked up mental images of Tarleton, Hyndman and Tomio climbing out and being taken to the guest quarters.

Once Yalt had brought the van to a halt, Pushley passed a large denomination money card to the other man, "I'm getting out and going to the big house, I want you to drive back to Awis."

"But how will you get back?"

"Don't worry," Pushley replied. "If my plan succeeds, I'll be coming back in an air-car, when I do, I will need you to take me down the tunnels to the teleport. Understood?"

Grabbing the binoculars, Pushley climbed out and waited until the van had disappeared from view. He began walking down the hill towards the house but paused when he reached the edge of the wood and began running his eyes around the main defensive wall that ran around the inner courtyard. Noting there was a heavy, armoured door set into the wall facing him, Pushley began to mind probing the guard in the tower closest to the gate. After extracting basic information regarding the layout of the main house, the guest annex, and any internal patrols, Pushley went on the attack and slipped a mind slug into the guard's brain.

Once he was sure that the man was under his control, Pushley came out of hiding and walked nonchalantly towards the gate. When he arrived, the guard allowed him entrance.

Moving out of sight below a plastimetal fire escape, Pushley began working on the guard controlling the front tower.

Once he was sure that he had the second guard under his control, Pushley emerged from cover, and walked over to the annex but couldn't gain access because the lock was the type that had a push-button key. Thinking that the tower guard he was controlling might have the code, Pushley interrogated him but swiftly realised the man didn't know it.

Sensing he was about to run out of mental power very soon, Pushley abandoned his planned attack and moved back towards the fire escape. As light streamed from one of the doors on a middle landing, it was apparent it had been propped open, so Pushley began to climb.

During his ascent, he smelt food being prepared. Once by the door, he listened. Hearing clattering and urgent voices coming from below, he worked out why. The kitchen staff were busy down below and had opened the upper door to cool them down.

After slipping through the door, Pushley released his control over the second guard and began to check out his surroundings. Although his mind was tired from controlling the tower guards, he started picking up on surrounding thoughts.

It was then that he located Wren again and sensed he was on one of the upper floors. With curiosity egging him on, Pushley climbed up an inner staircase. Once he was on the upper landing, he moved toward the sound of voices coming from a conference room. Once he was standing outside, he began glancing around looking for somewhere to hide in case the conference room door suddenly opened.

Finding a stationery cupboard door open, directly adjoining the conference room, Pushley put his head inside and the internal lighting immediately reacted to his presence. Satisfied with his bolt hole, Pushley crept inside and closed the outer door behind him.

Feeling safely hidden, Pushley began gently probing all the

talkers in the other room and swiftly learned they were Alton and Klaien Mygael, Hen Jameson, Allus Wren and Tam Philips. Pushley was also conscious of another presence with a male voice. After more mind-probing, he realised why he couldn't enter the missing person's mind; he was on hyperlink. Alton Mygael's mind supplied the name and the background of the missing party. The hyper-linking person was Walter Verex. After probing Alton Mygael's mind for a few seconds, Pushley realised that Verex was a senior director at Ingermann-Verex, one of Midway's most powerful manufacturing companies.

While he was listening in, someone, he guessed Jameson said, "If I was Mick Tarmy, I wouldn't volunteer to go back to the Fyfield Valley. He's only just escaped from there by the skin of his teeth."

"If you don't mind me saying, that's a rather negative attitude," Walter Verex replied. "I'm sure Tarmy can be persuaded to return."

"And how would you propose to persuade him?"

"His daughter and his friends are on board Salus Transporter Nine," Verex replied. "The Ardenese authorities claim they are guilty of a criminal conspiracy. They are demanding that all the people who teleported up to Salus Transporter Nine should be returned to Arden for trial."

Jameson said, "I would think it's highly unlikely that they'll be sent back."

"I wouldn't be so sure about that," Verex warned. "If I was allowed to speak to Tarmy, face to face, I could convince him that co-operation would be in the best interest of his friends and daughter."

Alton Mygael's mind immediately went into overdrive. Picking up on the other man's thoughts, Pushley suddenly realised that Tarleton had been telling the truth; he was Mick Tarmy, a police officer who'd been seconded to help Samantha attack the Great Ones.

He also picked up on the irony of Tarmy's situation. His daughter and his friends had already been used as blackmail pawns by Samantha. Now Walter Verex intended to use the same blackmail tactics to force Tarmy into attacking the Zuka plantation in the Fyfield Valley.

The knowledge that Tarmy had been a pawn for all of his life did nothing to lessen Pushley's animosity towards him; Tarmy had been responsible for Irrelevant's demise. As Pushley/Irrelevant were now one and the same, why shouldn't he have his revenge on Tarmy?

"If he does co-operate and destroys the Zuka Plantation," Alton Mygael replied. "You will move against Samantha?"

"You have my absolute guarantee on that," Verex promised. "All of our droids, the R9054 humanoid included, are fitted with deactivation devices. To prevent tampering, the deactivation process can only be instigated by ourselves."

He then added, "So, when can I speak to Tarmy?"

"If you are prepared to remain on hyperlink for a few minutes, I will send for him," Alton Mygael offered.

"Of course," Verex replied. "This is important; I want prompt action, the Zuka processing plant and the surrounding plantation have to be destroyed."

Pushley's mind began to race. Without a doubt, his luck had changed. They'd sent for Tarmy. Drawing his stun gun, Pushley began savouring the smell of success.

Once Tarmy was in the conference room, he'd pounce. He mentally modified his plan. As Walter Verex was still connected on hyperlink, he couldn't attack too soon. If he did, Verex would be able to report the attack. He'd have to wait until Verex went offline to take Tarmy.

Almost as soon as his mental plan jelled in his mind, Pushley modified it. As he'd created a mental image of the layout of the conference room, he knew that Philips was acting inner guard and standing directly behind the conference room door. Wren was seated in one corner, facing the door: a gunfighter's position. If he attempted to force his way into the room, Philips' bulk would slow him down. Such an interruption would allow Wren to pull his gun and fire.

As his mental plan continued to develop, Pushley ran his free hand over the dividing partition between the storeroom and the conference room. He smiled. If he fired through the thin partition and sprayed the whole conference room with stun fire, the occupants of the conference room would fall like ninepins.

While he was still thinking about his attack plan, Philips left the conference room to collect Tarmy.

~*~

There was a loud knocking on the door, and Tam Philips called out, "You in there, Mick?"

When Tarmy didn't answer, Philips knocked again.

Sensing Tarmy might open the door, out of modesty, Claire Hyndman slid out of bed, made a grab for her clothes, shot across the room, and then locked herself in one of the bathrooms.

Rolling off the bed, Tarmy called out, "What is it? Dinner isn't until Amber 8, and that's hours way?"

"How about you open the door and I'll tell you."

When Tarmy opened the door a fraction, Philips glanced in. Noting the dishevelled bedclothes, he gave him a wink, "You should have put a do not disturb sign out."

Instead of commenting, Tarmy just said, "What do you want, Tam?"

"The boss needs to see you urgently, Mick."

"Can't it wait until after dinner?"

Philips shook his head, "This is urgent. Get dressed. We have someone on hyperlink wanting to talk to you."

"On hyperlink!"

"Come on," Philips chivvied.

Moving back into the room, Tarmy threw on his clothes. Before he pulled the door shut, he called out, "Sorry, Claire. Have to go."

CHAPTER TWENTY-SEVEN

Alton Mygael's Lake House
Plans are hatched

ushley heard approaching footsteps, and the conference room door opened and slammed shut. Not wanting to miss anything he placed one ear against the partition and tried to mind-lock with Tarmy. When the attempt was rebuffed, he guessed that Tarmy was wearing his protective hat. Annoyed, he mind-locked with Alton Mygael instead.

Being an impatient man, Walter Verex cut the pleasantries to the minimum. "I want to show you something, Mick."

The room next door filled with the sound of groaning. With the groaning still sounding around the room, Verex said, "This is my grandson. He's dying."

~*~

"I'm sorry to hear that," Tarmy replied.

"The reason he's dying is that he became a junkie," Verex revealed. "He became hooked on Zuka a few years back. Now it's totally destroyed his mind and body."

Tarmy once again offered his commiserations.

Verex added, "Over the last few years large quantities of Zuka extract have been flooding the Salus System."

The comment reminded Tarmy of the huge plantation and the processing plant he'd seen near to the Fyfield Valley. As if reading his thoughts, Verex cut away from his grandson's image and displayed an aerial view of the Zuka terraces surrounding the plant.

Verex then said, "I believe this is where most of the Zuka extract is produced."

Tarmy was about to ask why Verex was telling him about the area when Amanda's image appeared on the screen. When a look of surprise formed on Tarmy's face, Verex said, "I'm pleased to tell you that your daughter is very well. As you probably know, she's on board the Salus Transporter Nine. Would you like to talk to her?"

"Talk to her!"

"I've organised a hyperlink," Verex replied. "Well, do you want to talk to her?"

"Of course."

A moment later Amanda's face appeared on screen, and she said, "Hi Dad, we've only got a two-minute hyperlink. How are you? And where are you?"

He immediately dodged the issue of his location, fearing the transmission was being monitored, "I'd rather not say where I am."

He skipped over the bad things that had happened to him over the last few weeks, and said, "Physically, I'm great. I was given life extension drugs, and I'm now fully recovered from my injuries."

He then said, "So, how is life for you in deep space?"

Amanda's face clouded slightly, "The Ardenese authorities are trying to get us back to stand trial."

Before Tarmy could ask for more information, the hyperlink was cut, and Walter Verex's image reappeared. Without preamble Verex said, "Times up I'm afraid. So, here's the deal. You destroy the Zuka plant and torch the plantation, and I promise to intercede on your daughter and friends' behalf and stop the extradition to Arden."

"That's blackmail," Tarmy snapped.

"No, it's not blackmail," Verex replied. "It's the way business works."

When Tarmy still glared at him, Verex said, "We obviously misunderstand one another. At the moment, I have no interest in helping your daughter or your friends. However, my basic business ethics would make me feel obliged to do you a favour if you did me a favour."

"What guarantees have I got that you'll help them if I attack the plantation?"

"I'm the director of one of the most powerful and influential manufacturers on Midway," Verex replied. "I can pull a lot of strings, and I will; if you destroy the Zuka processing plant and its environs."

"And how do I destroy the Zuka plant."

"Don't be tiresome, Tarmy," Verex growled. "I am aware that you have a TK5 at your disposal. You can cause a lot of damage with a TK5."

Verex added, "There is also one more task that I require from you."

Once a man's face appeared in the power bubble, Verex said, "We believe that his man is being held prisoner at the plant. If he's still alive we want him brought back."

"Who is he?"

"His name is Anto Jaks," Verex replied. "He was kidnapped a year ago. He works for our mini-fuser power division."

Verex filled the power bubble with images of the Zuka plantation again. A red circle formed around one of the shapes on the ground, "Without a shadow of a doubt, this building houses a group of micro-fusers."

A second red ring formed around a smaller structure. "We believe this is where Jaks is living. We believe he was kidnapped to help build the fuser installation. Before that, the Zuka processing plant was powered by a wood-burning power station. We need the fuser installation destroying too."

"Won't that spread radiation everywhere?"

"No," Verex replied. "It's a fuser, not a reactor; there will be no radiation released."

A moment later, Amanda Tarmy's face re-appeared in the

power bubble, and Verex said, "So, there's the deal Tarmy. You do me a favour, and I'll make sure your daughter and your friends aren't returned to Arden."

Before Tarmy could vent his spleen, Verex cut the hyper-link, and the power bubble evaporated.

Wren immediately stood up and walked over to Tarmy and nodded towards the door, "Philips and I are coming with you to make sure you do a good job."

When Tarmy said, "And when exactly do you plan to carry out this attack?"

Wren came back with, "No time like the present. If we delay, you will want to discuss everything with your friends. More importantly, I have no doubt your friends will try to talk you out of the operation. Besides, we want the Zuka planta-tion destroyed as soon as possible."

"What's in this for you?"

"If you carry out the attack correctly," Alton Mygael cut in, "Walter Verex will disable Samantha. She will cease to func-tion, and I will be able to claim back my position. It will also benefit the whole Salus System. If you destroy the processing plant and the surrounding area, the Great Ones lose their main money spinner. If you destroy that facility, you will set them back decades."

Tarmy shot a hostile glance at Klaien Mygael, "I'm surprised you are going along with this."

"Why are you surprised," Klaien replied. "Is it because I'm a woman? Unfortunately, needs must when the devil drives."

~*~

Sensing the time was right Pushley set his stun gun to medium stun and viewed the conference room though Alton Mygael's eyes. After making mental adjustments, he aimed at Wren because he viewed the other man as the chief threat. He pulled the trigger. Instead of getting the reaction he'd antici-pated, the stun gun bucked in his hand, and there was a loud bang. He felt the rays coming back at him.

While Pushley was still staggering around from the back blast, alarms started going off, and the cupboard door was yanked open. Tarmy, the man he hated, was crouched in the opening with his stun gun trained on him. Undeterred, Pushley swung his stun gun in Tarmy's direction, but before he could fire, Tarmy took him down.

After moving into the store cupboard with his gun still trained on the downed man, Tarmy flipped the body face up with one foot and said, "It's Ed Pushley."

Wren said, "You know him?"

Tarmy nodded, "I'm fairly sure he's a spettro."

Hearing Tarmy's comment Alton Mygael emerged from the conference room and said, "He can't be a spettro. Spettri die if they leave the Fyfield Valley or the Altos Plateaux area."

"Let's say, he's the exception that proves the rule," Tarmy replied.

Wren said, "He's obviously been listening in ..."

Realising that Wren thought their plans had been blown out of the water, Tarmy said, "I don't think we need to worry about him passing on what he heard. He's a loose cannon. He was after me; I think he intended to fire through the partition at us."

Glancing at the blast mark on the cupboard wall, Tarmy added, "But he obviously miscalculated."

Alton Mygael immediately supplied the answer, "When we bought this place we had extensive security measures installed. Most of the internal partitions are lined with special anti-stun paper. The outer walls also have security cameras and gun turrets installed."

"Well, they weren't that effective were they," Tarmy growled. Pointing at Pushley, he added, "You need to check the whole place, he could have accomplices roaming around for all we know."

"I'll have everywhere checked out," Wren replied. He glanced at Tarmy, "Don't disappear. We'll head out as soon as we've got Pushley firmly under lock and key, and we know no more intruders are prowling around."

"You'll need more than a lock and key," Tarmy replied. "He's a spettro. He'll start twisting your peoples' minds. That's probably how he beat your security."

"Hang on," Alton Mygael said. After rattling around in the conference room for some time he reappeared, stepped into the store, clamped a helmet around Pushley's head and locked it in place with a heavy-duty chin strap, "You seem to forget Mick, I've been dealing with spettri for a lot longer than you have. I took the precaution of having a few of these isolators sent out a few months back."

~*~

Once he'd returned, Yalt parked up. As he started walking he became conscious of heavy footsteps behind him. Glancing back over his shoulder, he recognised one of the bad men that Pushley feared.

As Connell had a very determined look on his face, Yalt sensed the truth; the bad men had found out he was working for Ed Pushley and wanted to question him.

Fearing confrontation, Yalt began walking faster. The footsteps behind him immediately speeded up too.

Panic took over, and Yalt broke into a run. Connell began running too. A moment later Yalt ran headlong into Hal Warmers.

Swinging Yalt around, so he was facing a wall, Warmers rammed one of Yalt's arms up his back and said, "We've been asking around, and a little bird told us you've been helping Ed Pushley.

Yalt's eyes rolled; his worst fears were true. They knew!

"So where is Pushley?"

As Yalt had no pretensions of being a hero, he said, "He's at the big house at the top of Central Lake."

Warmers let out a distinct tut, "You've spoilt it now, Yalt. I was hoping to be able to beat the truth out of you."

As Connell finally arrived, Warmers pushed Yalt towards the other man and said, "He reckons Pushley has gone to a big house at the top of Central Lake and he's going to show us which one aren't you, Yalt?"

Fearing the consequences if he refused, Yalt nodded, "I will show you, padrone."

"Good," Warmers said. "But if I discover you are lying there will be real trouble."

He added, "We need to get back to the air-car."

With Warmers leading, Connell began frogmarching Yalt down a string of back alleys. Eventually, they arrived back in the car park. After slamming the rear seats back into position, Connell pushed Yalt into the air-car and climbed in beside him.

Warmers said, "Top end of Central Lake."

Yalt nodded, "There is a big house."

Warmers relayed the directions to the air-car's computer. Although they were vague, the machine responded, and the air-car set off. Partway there, Yalt decided a display of co-operation might be a good ploy and pointed at Alton Mygael's house. He said, "There it is, there is a place to park on the hill behind the house."

Warmers was in the process of passing on the instructions when Alton Mygael's house suddenly became a blaze of floodlights, and the exterior alarm lights began pulsing. Even though the air-car's windows were firmly shut, it was possible to hear the wail of sirens.

As the air-car drew closer, Warmers saw an outer door open, and four large dogs bounded out with armed guards following.

Warmers immediately gave Yalt a hostile look, "What's going on?"

The Ab gave Warmers a worried look, "How would I know? When I left, Mr Pushley was going to go to the house."

"To do what?"

"I think he was going to break in," Yalt admitted.

Connell let out a slight chuckle, "Looks like he got caught."

Warmers rounded on him, "This is no laughing matter. In case you've forgotten Pushley has had most of my bank accounts frozen."

Connell latched onto the word *most*. Despite his claims of poverty, Connell suspected that Warmers had money squirrelled away somewhere.

Without receiving firm instructions, the air-car began hovering. Sensing its proximity, the defence system on Alton Mygael's house triggered a searchlight which locked onto the stationary vehicle.

Warmers snapped, "Get us out of here. Take us back to Awis."

Realising things hadn't gone well, Yalt said, "You won't hurt me, will you?"

Warmers went quiet for a while and gave Yalt a small card and several large denomination money cards, "I'll do a deal with you, Yalt. I won't hurt you if you let me know as soon as Pushley contacts you again or tries to use the teleport. If you don't cough up the information immediately, and I find out, I'll come around and break every bone in your body. Understood?"

Yalt nodded, "Yes, padrone."

"Glad we understand one another," Warmers replied.

CHAPTER TWENTY-EIGHT

The Fyfield Plantation
The raid

As the survivor tower appeared on the horizon, Wren said, "So, this is where you've been hiding your droid."

"Droids," Tarmy corrected. He'd barely spoken the word before two of the A10s emerged from the top of the tower and moved in on an intercept course. As the A10's moved in and boxed his air-car, Tarmy added, "As well as Alex, the TK5, there are also four A10's."

Wren frowned, "You never said you had A10s as well."

"You never asked," Tarmy replied nonchalantly.

"You just thought you'd keep it up your sleeve."

"If I told you everything I know, you'd be as wise as I am," Tarmy replied. "I've learned that trusting people can be a very dangerous fault."

"Life can be very difficult if you really don't trust anyone," Wren observed. He glanced out at the A10's. "So, what's the story? Where did they come from?"

"Let's just call them spoils of war."

"You do realise that Arcadia has been declared a droid free planet," Wren said.

Tarmy grinned, "It's a rule that doesn't appear to be enforced very vigorously."

Wren shot him a hard look, "Even so, I'd watch your step. If you parade these droids around too much, enforcement officers might come after you. If they are equipped with modern weapons, you might end up with a bloody nose."

"I'll bear that in mind," Tarmy replied. "When we do find somewhere to hang our hats, we'll keep them hidden unless we need to use them."

Wren went quiet for a while and then said, "Presumably the A10s are useful; otherwise you wouldn't have kept them—would you?"

"The A10s don't have the punch that Alex does, but they're interesting machines. They also make up for the TK5's only design flaw."

"Which is?"

"The TK5 is it doesn't have any secondary armament; with only a phaser, Alex has to avoid firing if he is likely to cause injury to his own side. In contrast, the A10's are equipped with long-distance stun guns and various crowd dispersal devices. They can take down individuals at five hundred metres without killing them. Which can be a very useful attribute in some cases."

"A very useful attribute in some cases," Wren echoed. "What cases have you got in mind?"

Tarmy shrugged, "As I said before, I've learned that trusting people can be a very dangerous fault."

After a long silence, Wren said, "Why is it I get the impression you're sending me a message?"

"If I am, I hope you've received it loud and clear," Tarmy responded.

"The question is, why are you sending me the message?"

"It had occurred to me that Alton Mygael might have instructed you to force me to hand over Alex once the mission was complete," Tarmy replied. "If you try that one, the A10s will deal with you."

He added, "One other point if Alton Mygael tries to keep the others hostage, I am willing to take the risk and send my droids into the Awis Mannheim. If Alex is right, droids can survive inside the Mannheim as long as they don't remain for more than two hours - If Alton Mygael tries to keep my friends as hostages, I'll use my droids against him. Understood?"

"I can assure you he's given me no instruction to force you into parting with Alex," Wren replied. "In any case, Alton Mygael knows enough about military droids to realise they form a bond with their controller. If we attempted to take Alex, it's highly unlikely he'd obey our orders unless we knew how to reprogram him. Which we don't."

When Tarmy remained silent, Wren added, "As far as I am concerned, once you've destroyed the Fyfield Plantation and rescued Anto Jaks, you're free to go wherever you want to go and so are the rest of your friends."

"I'm glad we understand one another," Tarmy replied. "But it might be prudent to let Alton Mygael know the situation. I don't want any misunderstandings at a later date."

Wren nodded, "I'll make sure Alton Mygael gets your message loud and clear, and I'll make sure he heeds it."

"I also expect him to make sure that Walter Verex keeps his promises regarding my daughter and my friends," Tarmy growled.

"I'm sure Verex is on the level," Wren replied. "He genuinely wants to destroy the Fyfield Plantation. He wants to make sure that other people aren't affected like his grandson. Believe me; it has become a personal vendetta; if you destroy the Fyfield Plantation, then Verex will play ball."

"Glad to hear it," Tarmy said. "One more message for Alton Mygael; once we've destroyed the plantation and hopefully brought Anto Jaks back alive, Claire, Nonie and everyone else will be flown out to the tower. I expect them to be here when we return, understood?"

Wren nodded and said, "Understood." He put a call into Alton Mygael. After listening to the conversation, Tarmy realised that Mygael had agreed to everything he wanted.

Once his air-car was hovering alongside the tower, Chou Lan appeared at an opening and gave Tarmy a wave.

After manoeuvring, Tarmy landed the machine and said, "You two stay in the air-car until I've talked things over with my people."

As Tarmy climbed out, both Chou Lan and Bryn Rosslyn came over and gave him a combined hug, "You're back."

Chou then glanced into the air-car and saw Wren and Philips, "Who are they? Where are the others?"

"Don't worry, I promise you they're all safe," He said, "Where's Alex?"

Immediately, he felt Alex's invisible presence directly above him. Glancing at Chou and Bryn, Tarmy said, "We need to talk in private, including you Alex," and walked towards the opening in the cross wall.

Once they were all hidden behind the cross wall, Tarmy swiftly explained how he'd managed to organise his daughter's escape from Arden, what had happened while he'd been away and how her escape now looked in danger.

When he'd finished, Chou Lan said, "It's madness to go back."

"As I just explained," Tarmy said. "My daughter and my friends could be in serious trouble if I don't."

"Blackmail is a nasty crime. The victim just keeps on paying," Chou lectured. "You've got a case in point. You've been blackmailed once. Now you're being blackmailed again."

The comment brought a wry smile to Tarmy's lips; an ex-police officer, he was only too well aware that blackmailers kept turning the screw if they thought they could. Despite the knowledge, he said, "This will be the last time it will happen."

"So, you're determined to go back?" Rosslyn said.

"I don't want to go back," Tarmy replied. "I have to go back."

"Then I'm going with you," Rosslyn said. "I know that place. I know the best places to attack."

When Tarmy hesitated, Rosslyn said, "Anto Jaks isn't the only person held prisoner up there. There are more people."

"How many?"

Rosslyn shrugged, "Three or four. I only saw them occasionally. I do not doubt that some may have died; we weren't given much food. But you can't leave any survivors behind; if you do, the Great Ones will have them fed to the wolf larvae as a reprisal."

The comment immediately made Tarmy shiver inside because he'd come to realise that the Great Ones really did still use this form of capital punishment. Glancing back at the air-car, Tarmy began working out if it could accommodate ten people. Did he need to take a second air-car? Satisfied he didn't; he nodded at Rosslyn, "Okay."

When Rosslyn visibly paled, Tarmy said, "Are you sure you're up to it?"

"Of course, I am," the other man replied. "I'll help you."

He then half-turned ready to walk toward the air-car, but Chou checked him by giving him a swift hug. While she had hold of him, she whispered, "I'm proud of you, but you need your head examined, for taking the risk."

She then became practical. Glancing at Tarmy, she said, "I studied the hat you gave me and realised how it works." She then glanced at Bryn Rosslyn. "I have made some more hats."

She immediately ran off, opened the boot of the second air-car and ran back. After giving Rosslyn a hat, she glanced at Wren and Philips.

Tarmy said, "I've given them hats. Have you made any more? A few spares would be useful to give to the people we're hopefully going to rescue."

Once Chou returned with the additional hats, Tarmy nodded towards Rosslyn, "Time to go."

Both men walked away and climbed into the air-car. Wren immediately bent Tarmy's his ear, "What's this guy here for?"

"He knows the Fyfield Plantation and the processing plant like the back of his hand," Tarmy replied. "If we're going to put the processing plant out of production, we want to cause as much damage as possible so that they can't carry out a few swift repairs and get it going again." He told Alex to lead them back to the Fyfield Plantation.

As they moved off, Tarmy handed Rosslyn a sketching tablet and told him to draw an approximate plan of the production plant and the surrounding plantation. Once he'd finished, Tarmy told him to mark, in red, the location of all the major parts of the processing plant inside the main building, the site of the fuser plant and the prison huts holding Anto Jaks and the other prisoners. Once Rosslyn had finished, Tarmy ran his eye over it, "How accurate is this?"

"It's a sketch," Rosslyn replied defensively. "But it's reasonably accurate. As I had to walk around the processing plant, growing beds and the terraces, two or three times a week, I saw a great deal."

"What about the fuser?"

"The fuser building is there," Rosslyn said, pointing at his sketch. "The supply pipes are as I've sketched them. I don't know why but they're shaped like a crown. There are eight mini-fusers in the same building; each one has its own feed."

Glancing at the sketch again, Tarmy noted that the pipes were exactly as Rosslyn had described them. Above the flat roof, the supply pipes had been shaped into a distinctive dome and highly unlikely to be missed. Tarmy put his own notes onto the sketch and then sent the information to Alex.

Half an hour later, the Altos and Razorback mountain ranges loomed up in the distance, and the Great Rock Desert began giving way to scrub grass and clumps of multi-trunked Arcadian cacti which appeared to be surviving on the annual snowmelt coming off the mountains.

Once they'd crossed the Altos, Alex dropped down and began weaving his way through the tops of the forest giants growing in the valleys below. Within a matter of seconds, Tarmy was reminded that the Fyfield Valley was a rain forest because fog banks began forming and visibility decreased. Another ten kilometres in, Alex joined one of the tributaries of the Fyfield River. Almost immediately, an alert appeared on the dashboard display, and the four A10's moved in close to form a box around Tarmy's air-car.

Wren shot a worried glance at Tarmy, "What's happening?"

Before Tarmy could answer, there was a muffled explosion

as Alex took out an incoming hand-launched missile.

As two more missiles were destroyed before they could damage the air-car, Tarmy said, "You didn't think the Great Ones would just roll over and let us attack their plantation without a fight, did you?"

"They must have known we were going to attack them," Wren said.

"Of course, they did," Tarmy replied. "They can read our minds."

He answered Wren's unspoken question, "Even with hats on; we can't prevent some stray thoughts from reaching them. My guess is they had teams of listeners checking out the major players. For all we know, they could have been checking out Alton Mygael."

As two more anti-aircraft devices exploded, Wren said, "I didn't expect them to have missiles."

"They've made enough money from drugs sales," Tarmy reasoned. "They can afford to buy in black-market military hardware. They don't mind paying over the odds if it gets them what they want."

As if to confirm what he'd just said there were two more explosions close by. A few seconds later two of the A10s peeled away and began blasting the surrounding forests with stun fire. Their efforts were immediately rewarded because two Longjaws fell out of a high-level launching platform suspended across a small gorge and landed face down in the water.

With Alex urging them on, the A10s kept up the bombardment and millipedes began dropping out of the trees in their hundreds. But instead of pulling back to avoid the stun fire, more millipedes began squirming out onto overhanging branches and firing venom at the passing air-car.

Inevitably some of the venom splattered onto the air-car's windshield. Reacting to danger, Tarmy said, "When we arrive at the plantation, no one opens any doors unless I say so. Whatever you do, don't touch that stuff; it's lethal; if any quantity of it gets on to your skin, it will kill you in seconds. If you only get a tiny amount on your skin, the best you can hope for is a slow lingering death."

Eventually, the air-car burst out of the side valley and began flying over the Fyfield River. As always, the river was shrouded in this fog.

Lacking Alex's radar, the A10's moved away from the banks and grouped up around the air-car. Despite the fog, Tarmy occasionally caught a glimpse of some of the landmarks he's passed when they'd made their escape from the Fyfield Valley.

Ten minutes later, the dash screen lit up as Alex warned them the processing plant was less than five kilometres away. The screen warned them that there were incoming air-cars. A moment later pulse fire began flashing past the air-car, and an enemy air-car shot out of the mist. One of the A10s immediately returned fire, knocking out the vehicle's computer and paralysed the enemy pilot.

Lacking control, the air-car plunged into the river and disappeared. Undeterred, two more enemy air-cars came at them out of the fog, and a lucky pulse shot punched a hole in the windscreen. Fearing some of the venom splashes might find their way in, Tarmy immediately opened the dash drawer and began frantically searching for something to plug the hole. Finding a can of plastimetal foam filler, he placed it against the hole and depressed the nozzle. Although most of the filler was immediately blown away by the slipstream, some of it stuck. After a five-second burst, the hole was plugged.

He'd barely finished before another enemy air-car, came at them but this time two of the A10s opened fire in unison, and the machine spiralled away.

A fraction of a second later, the processing plant loomed up, and Alex set about strafing the sides to expose the machines inside; he began blasting at the individual elements of the processing plant. Within seconds, the whole area surrounding the plant began swarming with millipedes and armed Longjaws.

As pulse shots began flashing past the air-car again, the

A10s moved in and mowed the opposition down like a scythe through grass. Alex went for the main target, the fusers that powered the plant.

A few blasts later, all the processing plants lights went out. Alex set about blasting away at the terraced walls of the paddy fields closest to the processing plant, and the water began to cascade down, sweeping away the millipedes, and flooding the ground floor areas of the plant with dirty water.

With the opposition mostly subdued, Tarmy turned the air-car's headlight to full beam and took the air-car down following Rosslyn's instructions. A moment later, a running figure cut through the beams but instead of stopping the fleeing man began dodging and diving. The headlights began to pick out other fleeing figures.

Realising that the running men didn't realise that they were there to rescue them, Tarmy called in an A10. The machine immediately bracketed the area with stun fire and brought the fugitives down.

Rosslyn immediately let out a howl of horror, but Tarmy cut him off. "They've only been stunned. We haven't time to chase them; even though we have droids to protect us, we can't hang around here for too long." He pointed to the plugged-up hole in the windscreen. "We're not pushing our luck."

As if to confirm his fears, more pulse fire began flashing through the air as the Great Ones' forces recovered from the initial assault and began fighting back. Swinging the air-car around so that he was shielding the downed men, Tarmy shouted, "Come on, let's get them into the air-car."

Wren and Philips immediately climbed out and began dragging the bodies back, and unceremoniously tossed them into the air-car. They dived back in and slammed the doors. They'd barely closed the doors before there was a heavy thump on the side of the air-car. A cacophony of sound swiftly followed the first thump, as more and more giant Arcadian millipedes arrived and hurled themselves onto the air-car.

As Tarmy had experienced a similar event in the past, he knew exactly what was happening. The millipedes were weighing down the air-car and hoping to prevent its escape. Tarmy pulled back and began firing at it through the roof of the air-car, but it had little effect.

Re-programming the stun-gun from minimum to maximum, Tarmy fired again, but it still appeared to have little effect on the squirming mass directly overhead.

He caught a glimpse of the colouration on the millipedes and realised why his gun wasn't affecting them; they were king millipedes.

In a last-ditch attempt to dislodge them, Tarmy instructed the air-car to take off. The machine immediately began to shake as it struggled with the combined weight of its human cargo and the mass of king millipedes on the roof. As it finally lifted off, Tarmy began firing again and instructed the air-car to swing from side to side. He was instantly rewarded; some of the millipedes that were clinging to the sides of the air-car dropped off.

As the side screens cleared slightly, he caught a glimpse of an A10 using its stun arrays to pick off more millipedes. More importantly, Tarmy could sense the air-car's engines gaining strength with each millipede that dropped off. Tarmy instructed the air-car to rock from side to side. As it did so, a mass of wriggling bodies suddenly fell off, and the air-car surged ahead. Wren suddenly shouted out, "Have we picked up Anto Jaks?"

In response, Rosslyn shone a torch on the four men's faces. A second or so later, he pronounced, "This is Anto Jaks."

Tarmy immediately instructed the air-car to set off back to the tower via a different route. Noting the instructions, Wren queried them.

"A wise man never overflies where he's already been," Tarmy replied. "A rifleman might miss you the first time, but once he's alerted to your presence, he'll be ready for you. Make no mistake about it there are shed-loads of spettri down there wanting to claim our scalps."

The words had barely left Tarmy's lips before he felt something cold jar his temple. The man behind the gun gave Tarmy a yellow-toothed smile, "Cancel the last order you gave the air-car and tell it to turn around."

Knowing that going back would be a death sentence, Tarmy said, "If you kill me, it will be a quicker death than being fed to the wolf larvae."

Yellow Tooth immediately pulled the gun off Tarmy and placed it against Rosslyn's head. "Turn back, or I'll kill him, and then I'll shoot everyone in the air-car."

When Tarmy hesitated, Yellow Tooth hit Rosslyn with the gun and screamed, "Turn back now!"

As Tarmy did as instructed, Wren gave him a worried look. In answer to the unspoken question, Tarmy said, "It looks like we picked up a spettro by mistake. Spettri are resistant to stun fire, that's why he's recovered so quickly. No doubt he was living with the captives and passing information back to the Great Ones."

Yellow Tooth smiled, but there was no humour in it. "

You are very perceptive, Mr Tarleton. My masters will enjoy being reunited with you, now tell the air-car to descend."

Although Tarmy gave the instruction, the air-car didn't move. All they all heard was a slight bump from underneath, and the air-car began to rise. Although he didn't comment, Tarmy guessed that Alex had seen what was happening and had ordered one of the A10s to fly underneath the air-car and stop it descending. A few seconds later the air-car returned to its original course.

"What's going on?" Yellow Tooth demanded. "I'll kill this man if this machine doesn't turn around and descend."

Tarmy attempted to change course, but the air-car didn't respond. Guessing that Alex had taken control of the air-car, Tarmy glanced at Yellow Tooth and said, "Sorry. I can't make it respond."

A look of real fear crossed Rosslyn's face, but just before

Yellow Tooth could fire, one of the A10's moved in close and fired a stun shot through one of the windows at point-blank range. A fraction of a second later, the passenger door behind Yellow Tooth opened and one of the A10's mechanical arms pulled the spettro out. The A10 went into a steep dive before dumping Yellow Tooth on the ground.

The door sprang back into place, and the air-car began increasing speed and moved away on a new course. Letting out a sigh of relief, Tarmy glanced back and was pleased to note that the production plant was well ablaze. Wren also glanced back and started recording the damage. Noting Tarmy watching, Wren said, "Walter Verex is the sort of guy who will demand proof that we really have damaged the plant."

"Now we've done our bit," Tarmy replied. "I hope that Alton Mygael is going to honour his pledges."

"He will," Wren promised and tapped send on his percom. "Once he sees these images, he'll send your people out to the tower as promised."

"He'd better."

"He will," Wren promised and glanced out at the thick forest down below. He glanced through the pulse damaged windscreen towards the Altos and Razorback mountains on the horizon. "So, where will you go now?"

Tarmy shot Rosslyn a warning glance before saying, "Somewhere where we can't be found."

He added, "What about you? Do you really believe that Alton Mygael can oust Samantha and regain control?"

Wren shrugged, "Only time will tell." He felt in his pocket for the device that Mih Valanson had given him and hoped he'd never have to use it.

As the air-car continued to close with the Altos Mountains, rain began hammering at the vehicle. The deluge was so heavy, Tarmy was forced to turn the windscreen wipers onto full power. He was pleased to note the black millipede venom was washing away.

After being pummelled for nearly forty minutes, the rain

stopped and turned into sleet as the air-car finally crested the mountains. Ten minutes later, the scene below turned back into scrub grass and cacti again; the cacti then gave way to the true desert terrain.

Shortly afterwards, the tower came back into sight. Being cautious, Tarmy sent one of the A10s ahead to ensure there were no lurking surprises.

Once back at the tower, the machine sent back images that dispelled most of Tarmy's fears. Claire, Nonie and Red Mox-stroma were clearly on view and Alton and Klaien Mygael were standing in the background.

After instructing Alex and the four A10's to deploy around the tower, Tarmy took the air-car in and landed. Claire and Nonie moved in and threw their arms around him. Although they both seemed pleased to see him, Nonie said, "Don't ever do that again."

"Do what?"

"Fly off without telling us where you are going," Nonie scolded.

Wren cut in, "He didn't have a lot of choice in the matter." He then pointed to the three stunned escapees in the back of the air-car. "Anto Jaks is coming with us, what about the other two?"

Rosslyn cut in, "I know them; they'll come with us."

Once Wren and Philips had pulled Jaks out of the air-car and carried him over to Alton Mygael's air-car, Tarmy said, "Have you heard from Walter Verex?"

The other man nodded and then created a hyperlink power bubble, Amanda Tarmy's image immediately appeared inside it with Ord Morley, Vlad Pen and Ben Lieges clustered around her. "They are granting us asylum, Dad."

While Tarmy was still talking, Wren nodded to Rosslyn, took him to one side and said, "Where are you going when you leave here?"

Glancing over at Tarmy, Rosslyn said, "He may not want me to tell you."

"I'm sure he doesn't," Wren returned. "But if you allow him to cut you off, it could rebound on you."

Rosslyn said, "In what way?"

"If you isolate yourselves," Wren replied. "If you lose all contact with friends, you could be in serious trouble if we can't tell you what's going on."

After thinking long and hard, Rosslyn gave Wren an address. He said, "I hope I'm not going to regret telling you."

"You won't," Wren replied.

As Wren moved away, Klaien Mygael intercepted him and gestured for him to move away from the others. Once well out of earshot, Klaien said, "Alton intends to return to Arden."

When Wren remained silent, she added, "I think he's making a big mistake."

"In what way?"

"Walter Verex has agreed to deactivate Samantha," Klaien replied. "But I'm not sure he can."

Wren said, "Why not?"

"Samantha is an Ingermann-Verex R9054 humanoid, one of the most intelligent droids ever made," Klaien replied. "Don't you think she's already realised that someone will try to deactivate her? Don't you think she's already worked out a way of avoiding deactivation?"

"That had occurred to me," Wren admitted. "But what can I do about it?"

"I have a plan," Klaien replied. "I need a favour. Can we talk privately about it later?" She nodded towards Tarmy. "Can we talk once we've seen them off and we're back at the house?"

"Sure."

Suspecting what the favour might be, Wren slipped his hand in his pocket and gently caressed the device that Mih Valanson had given him, "Of course we can talk privately."

"Did Tarmy say where they were going?"

Although Rosslyn had provided him with the information, Wren shook his head, "'Fraid not. But I'm not surprised. The way he's been treated over the last few months, he's not very trusting anymore."

Wanting to change the subject, Wren gestured towards Tarmy's group, "Shall we see them off?"

Ten minutes later, and with farewells completed, Tarmy's two air-cars left the tower and set off across the desert with the four A10s clustered around them. Although invisible to the naked eye, Wren knew that Alex was there as well, leading them to safety.

CHAPTER TWENTY-NINE

The Teleport Centre

Wren's gamble

A hyperlinked bubble image appeared, and without preamble, Walter Verex said, "You might like to see this."

Samantha's image appeared in the bubble. The display panel near to the top of her conical body enlarged, but instead of a haughty face, the panel was just showing the word, "Retired."

A moment later, a Black-clad officer appeared and made an urgent request for assistance. After allowing the plea to continue for nearly a minute, Verex's image returned and said, "I promised to deactivate Samantha, and it's been done. "

~*~

Yalt recognised Mih Valanson the moment he walked into the teleport centre; he was the man who shot him. Catching a glimpse of Yalt, Valanson looked surprised, confirming Yalt's thoughts. But instead of confronting one another, they both remained silent. It was as if they'd come to an unspoken understanding; it was water under the bridge.

Alton Mygael glanced at Klaien and said, "Once we arrive, and I know everything is under control, I will contact you and everyone will be able to teleport too."

"I don't want you to go back," Klaien replied. "It's a trap."

"That's not going to happen," Alton Mygael replied. "I have spoken to several Board members who have confirmed that

Samantha really is defunct. They have also confirmed that I have their support and that I won't be arrested. I have to go back."

He glanced at Wren and Philips. When they immediately came to attention, Alton Mygael said, "See, us Zadernaster boys stick together."

He began walking towards the teleport bay. Klaien immediately looked at Wren and said, "Do it!"

Wren slipped his stun gun out of its holster and shot Alton Mygael. Yalt tried to run off, but Valanson grabbed hold of him and restrained him. Philips moved in to assist and made sure he couldn't escape. Giving them both a wide-eyed look, Yalt said, "What is going on?"

Klaien walked over and said, "My partner wouldn't listen to reason."

Wren joined them, "We think he was teleporting into a well-laid trap. So, we stopped him going."

When Yalt just stared at him open-mouthed, Wren spoke to Valanson. The other man handed him two cards, and Wren put them into his shirt pocket. He nodded at Yalt, "Come on then, time for you to teleport me to Arden."

Yalt objected, "Three of you are supposed to teleport."

Wren patted his pocket and then glanced at Valanson. "I've been told these two cards will make the teleport indicate its transporting three people; namely, Alton Mygael, Tam Philips and myself but I'm the only one going."

"Have you got your return ticket; in case you need it?" Klaien asked. Wren felt in his pocket for the device that Mih Valanson had manufactured for just this sort of eventuality.

After nodding, Wren stepped onto the teleport platform. As anticipated, the teleport confirmed it was transporting three people. Philips gave Yalt a nudge, "Do it."

Reluctantly, Yalt pressed a button. A moment later, Wren's body turned transparent and then disappeared from view.

Printed in Great Britain
by Amazon